a novel by

DEBRA WHITING ALEXANDER

LUMINARE PRESS

WWW.LUMINAREPRESS.COM

"The House Remembers You" and "My Moon Necklace" by Diana Griggs from *The House Remembers You*. Copyright 2014 by Diana Griggs. Reprinted with permission.

Excerpt from the poem, "Joy" was written by Carl Sandburg (1878-1967).

Nursery rhymes used throughout this story came from *THE BIG BOOK OF MOTHER GOOSE*, Grosset & Dunlap Publisher, NY (1973 Printing).

Printed in the United States of America

Cover Design: Claire Flint Last

Luminare Press
438 Charnelton St., Suite 101
Eugene, OR 97401
www.luminarepress.com

LCCN: 2017958401
ISBN: 978-1-944733-43-8

PRAISE FOR *ZETTY*

Rilke, the 19th Century poet, once wrote of longing for the landscape of his mother's face. *Zetty* brings us that longing and the joyous quenching as we journey with a young girl whose mother was stolen from her by mental illness. But Zetty learns that mothers can be stolen in many ways. In the midst of sorrow, Debra Whiting Alexander gives us laughter, singular characters, fresh images, wild friendships, wisdom and most of all, love. *Zetty* is a master piece of heartache and joy, the very stuff of life. Read with tissue at hand.

—JANE KIRKPATRICK
New York Times bestselling author of more than twenty-five books and award winning author of *All She Left Behind*

The funny and poignant journey of Zetty, a young girl aching for her mother, who circumstances have ripped away from her. Propelled into adulthood with an independent spirit and a fierce determination, she tries to unravel the mystery of what happened to the mother and family she lost. Alexander keeps the reader invested in Zetty's story with humor and pathos—a real page-turner and a heartwarming story of a daughter's love."

—JANICE CARR
Television Production Supervisor, "Santa Clarita Diet"

This is a brave story—plumbing the existential life of the schizophrenic and the reality of those who love them. Alexander writes with the prowess of heart.

—DANUTA PFEIFFER
Eric Hoffer Finalist and award-winning author for
Chiseled, A Memoir of Identity, Duplicity and Divine Wine

I can't remember when I was so pleasantly surprised by a novel...*Zetty* unfolded like one of those Olympic gymnastics routines where some unknown is suddenly hitting every move and the crowd realizes they're amidst something special. Frankly, I loved everything about this book: the story, the inspiration and the writing itself...I can't sing the praises of *Zetty* loudly enough...a story that's stayed with me long after I closed the back cover. Bravo, *Zetty*. Bravo, Alexander.

—BOB WELCH
Award-winning journalist for *The Register-Guard*
and award-winning author of more than 20 books
including, *American Nightingale* and *Pebble in the Water*

2018 WILLA LITERARY AWARD WINNER
IN CONTEMPORARY FICTION

WINNER FOR WOMEN'S FICTION
2018 NATIONAL INDIE EXCELLENCE AWARDS

FINALIST FOR REGIONAL/WEST FICTION
2018 NATIONAL INDIE EXCELLENCE AWARDS

In memory of Cori

For our grandmother,
Adelaide Gehl Peterson

PART ONE

1963–1964

The House Remembers You

...cowboy boots on the tile floor
your shadow stretched across the arroyo
where morning glories hang
white with winter.
Nights of deep darkness
that's when I see you clearly
your perfume
slides under the door.

—Diana Griggs

MARJORIE SAT IN FRONT OF THE CLOCK RADIO AND TWISTED the knob, yellowed like an old tooth. When the dial landed in just the right spot, static vanished. The London Symphony moved everything aside and softened the air. She turned the volume up, closed her eyes, and crossed both arms against her chest. She knew there was no better way to clear the chattering of her mind than deep listening. It was a normal enough thing to do, she thought. It was a way to obstruct the voices. A way to hide them from everyone. Especially Zetty. But what was so mysterious, even to her, was how the line between sanity and insanity kept growing blurrier. More than anything, Marjorie feared she was destined for an even worse fate. A fate even mother-love couldn't conquer.

INDENTATIONS OF THE HEART

MY DOG WAS THE FIRST TO NOTICE.

I caught him watching Mother when she was just starting to come undone, like a loose stitch unraveling itself from the edge of a worn and tattered blanket. Tuffy, whose almond eyes missed nothing, kept a careful watch over her. He used to sit next to her in the rocking chair, nudge his nose under her hand, and rest his head in her lap. It was as if he could sense something fragile inside Mother that Father and I didn't.

For a long time, the signs were there—the vacant hole in Mother's eyes that spiraled down into another galaxy, and the tinny echo of her giggle that clanged in my ears. I should have felt the shell surrounding her trunk when I swung both arms around her hips, climbed on top of her feet and held on tight—afraid she might evaporate if I didn't cling to her like a barnacle. And sometimes I imagined that if I let go too soon she might be swept out to sea by a sneaker wave, or swallowed up by the sky.

I was only a child when she left, but still. The signs were there that something was wrong. The only reason Father didn't see anything was because he wore blinders the size of elephant ears.

Tuffy was watching when the very last thread holding Mother together slipped away for good.

I've heard that life-changing experiences put permanent dents in the heart; they make their mark and are remembered. And with every impression made, the heart bends and stretches—sometimes completely changing form. My own heart seems living proof of it. Even after thirty-nine years, which seems impossible, the memory of what happened when I was only nine remains remarkably vivid. It rearranged everything inside me.

That year, my aunt, uncle, and three cousins spent Thanksgiving with us. They were eager to leave Idaho for the warmth of California and drove to our home in Windansea—where every day was a beach day. Of all the cousins, Max was the oldest, and the one who annoyed me most. He didn't seem to know where he stopped and other people began.

Max always had his hands in someone's face, or in my case, worse. That morning he gripped me around the neck and started squeezing while I watched Mighty Mouse on the tube. My uncle peeled him off my back and loosened his grip just in time. Max went for a cat next—tried to wring its neck behind the two giant palm trees in our backyard. For that, he did time in the corner on a wooden stool and mutilated the wall he was facing with Mother's favorite blue fountain pen. He scratched nasty pictures and foul words all over the aqua, flowered wallpaper with every drop of ink it had. It was the kind of thing he would do.

I saw Mother raise her eyebrows, her chin resting on two fingers when she asked, "Where in the world did he learn that?"

"Learn what, Mother?"

She shook her head in disgust, "Never you mind, Zetty."

I knew whatever "art" Max left bleeding on the walls, it had to be bad. Father kept us out of eyeshot. "All you kids, out right now," he said in a voice that made you listen, or else.

Uncle Ben tore out the portion of the wallpaper Max destroyed, and we never did find out what smut he created. Later, we moved Father's bulky, beige, vibrating recliner with a saggy rump, and positioned it kitty-corner to hide the damage.

Aunt Julie and Uncle Ben lit into Max over that incident, but no matter what he did, or how many things he ruined over the years, Mother never stopped being kind to him. She told me once, "There's good in him somewhere, Zetty. Just remember, no one's perfect."

There was a wildness about Max that I didn't trust, but I did my best to play with him like I would with any other kid. I tolerated his taunting and bullying the way I knew Mother wanted me to. Even so, the truth is, each time Max came to visit, I spent time in front of a mirror before he arrived. I balled up my right fist, flexed my arm muscle, and practiced an undercut swing from the hip that, someday, I hoped, would carry my revenge to the underbelly of his jaw and shut his trap for good.

It didn't take long to figure out Max was beyond mean. After I showed my best friend, Gabriella Taylor, the wall damage, and told her about his murderous ways and wicked attempt on my life, we started referring to all cruel and malicious people as "Max mean." It said it all.

The Vanishing Act

PANDEMONIUM BROKE OUT IN OUR KITCHEN EVERY Thanksgiving. That afternoon sausage and onions snapped in a pan over the stove and a crispy, golden brown turkey, the size of an atomic bomb, lay in the oven sizzling in its juices. I took a long, slow, deep breath hoping the aroma would be enough to quiet my growling stomach.

Aunt Julie pulled up a chair next to me at the dinette. She reached for the extra nutcracker and in her usual cornball way, said, "Let's get crackin'. Any more Broadway shows planned?" She had already split two by the time she asked.

Mother spun around from the stove, "As a matter of fact, yes! We have a play in the works about a famous rootin' tootin' cowgirl, don't we Zetty?" Tuffy plopped down on top of her feet and rested his head on the corner of the throw rug she was standing on.

"Yup. I get to be the rootin' tootin' cowgirl's daughter." I swung my hips around and did an exaggerated leg lift to show off my red leather, carved cowgirl boot. "What do you think, Aunt Julie?"

"I absolutely love them!" she gushed.

"Mother bought them for me. I'm breaking them in for our show. We're famous cowgirls, Mother and me. We lived a hundred years ago in a town that was infected with stinking, evil-eyed outlaws. Right, Mother?"

"Right!"

I set my nutcracker down and continued to recite Mother's description of our play. "The famous cowgirl is played by Mrs. Marjorie McGee, and her daughter is played by me, of course, Zetty Pearl McGee. We ride furiously into town, practically fly off our horses, and stomp fearlessly through the saloon doors Father made for us. Just like on *Gunsmoke*."

Mother's gray-and-black-speckled phonograph, the size of a suitcase, sat on top of her glossy, black baby grand piano. We used to blast the dance numbers through the window facing the patio—our Broadway stage. My favorite part in rehearsals was barreling through the saloon doors in time with the music. First, I laid one hand on my right hip, and the other on my holster. Then I imagined Max sitting on a stool at the bar when I barged in, just to be sure my best tough-guy face came across as authentic.

Father made the saloon doors in between working at his job as an aeronautical engineer, and building his own airplane in our garage. His home-built CP-328 Piel Super Emeraude went on to fly around the world thirteen times after it was finished. Father was featured in the newspaper and became a celebrity when the six o'clock news filmed the christening flight. But it was the two rustic, brown wood saloon doors he made for our stage that impressed me most. Every time I sashayed through them, my acting ability improved 100%.

"It sounds wonderful, Zetty." Aunt Julie shook shells off her apron into a trashcan and sat back down. "I loved the one you did last summer. Seriously, honey, you were amazing, and the stage was fabulous!"

I smiled and rolled two whole walnuts against my cheeks to cool them down. Whenever Aunt Julie complimented me they turned hot like potatoes; I believed her compliments more than the average person's because she was a casting director in high school.

Father and Mother lifted the two-ton turkey out of the oven and cautiously rested the black speckled roasting pan on top of four potholders. I noticed Mother's eyes were still red and swollen from crying about the president being shot and killed driving in his convertible. It happened a few days earlier, and she was still carrying a wad of tissue in her apron pocket, wiping her eyes whenever the grownups started talking about it.

The kitchen cupboard squeaked open. "The play last summer took months to plan," Mother said, stacking plates in the crook of her arm. "But we set up the patio in one weekend." Tuffy jumped up and followed as she leaned into the swinging door with her shoulder, and passed through to the dining room, both arms hugging a tower of plates. I heard her giggle in a giddy way, but wasn't sure why. It was the same offbeat little twitter I heard when I found her lying on the living room carpet once singing lullabies with my stuffed rabbit, Herbert. I always thought she was singing to me. Now I'm not so sure.

Right then, Max burst through the back door and slammed a yellow tennis ball against the refrigerator. It ricocheted past us and just missed the canned yam casserole. Aunt Julie flinched and looked exasperated. "Max, please, not in the house! Take Tuffy outside to chase that ball."

"I tried! He's too stupid to go with me. Dumb, stupid dog."

The hackles on my neck rose. Nobody was allowed to talk about my Tuffy that way, and just as soon as I thought it, a surge of strength shot into my hands. A loud snap sent a fractured shell flying. I hoped it would stab him.

"Then go read a book in the den with your brother and sister," Aunt Julie ordered.

Benny was the middle child. He always carried a book, and hung on to it like a baby with his blanky. It went everywhere with him. Even to the dinner table, which I thought was a bit much.

Aunt Julie turned to me. "Are Benny and Queenie in the den?"

I nodded emphatically, *yes*.

"Okay, Max. Outside, to the den, or we'll put you to work," she threatened.

Out he went.

I gave a good-boy nod to Tuffy, thinking what a smart dog he was for staying in the protective shadow of Mother and avoiding the likes of Max.

Aunt Julie's head turned to the side to glimpse at me when she said, "You have a special mom, don't you?"

It seemed like an odd question coming from a relative who had known her longer than me. "Sure," I told her, "she's the best actress I've ever seen. Including Doris Day."

"And she's beautiful too, isn't she?"

"That she is," Father interjected when he slipped past us to find the big carving knife.

"My friend, Sue Willy, tells me all the time how pretty she is." Aunt Julie looked up from her handful of nuts and sat perfectly still as I continued, "I told Sue Willy, 'I know, because she was a real live beauty queen.' Aunt Julie, did you know Mother has a white sash with writing in gold that says, 'Windansea Beach Fair Queen – 1960'? They put a crown on her head and everything. I was only six, but I remember."

The truth is, I remembered a lot more than I said. When we came home that night after the fair, I couldn't find Mother. I searched everywhere until Tuffy led me out to the backyard where we found her lying in repose—flat on her back in the dark. She was staring up at the night sky, its broad expanse bowing over our heads.

I stepped alongside her and felt the tickle of grass on my ankles. "What are you doing?" It seemed a peculiar position for anyone to be in unless they were sunbathing.

"Watching," she sighed.

"Watching what?" I looked around but didn't see anything.

"All the stars. And the broken sliver of the moon," she said in a peaceful sort of way.

"What for?"

She pushed herself up, took my hand, and we walked to the chain link fence at the edge of the yard. On a clear day you could take in a patch of blue ocean on the horizon, but standing there at night, it was as if a treasure chest had been opened and the city lights sparkled like jewels for as far as we could take in right to left.

"Here," she said, and bent down to hoist me up. Her hands felt large under my armpits when she lifted. I straddled her left hip, hurriedly wrapped my legs around her waist, naked feet dangling, and circled both arms around her neck. I buried my nose into the silky skin I found concealed beneath her cotton collar, and inhaled a pleasing, clean fragrance. I placed the flat of my hand on top of her head and pressed down on her puffy, bouffant hair-do. When I let go, it bounced back up in perfect form.

"Where's your queen crown?" I tried to tuck a clump of hair behind her ear but it wouldn't budge.

Over the nighttime chatter of crickets, she said in her best actress voice, "Uneasy lies the head that wears the crown."

I wanted to ask more, but the only thing that came out was "Huh?"

She arched her head back and scanned the stars piercing the sky like a diamond-studded pincushion. I tried to do the same, but felt dizzy when I looked up for too long. The open space frightened me. I imagined it swooping down and swallowing me up, or worse, swallowing Mother and taking her away. I tightened my grip around her.

Mother pried my wrists from her neck, let me slide to the ground, and combed three fingers through my hair, the way she did sometimes to help me fall asleep at night. "Everything comes to an end, Zetty. But the sky lives forever."

I climbed on top of her feet and gripped the shiny black belt cinched around her waist.

I remember asking, "Is that where dead people go?"

She hesitated, but then looked sure of herself, "Nothing can touch us up there. All the suffering in the world stays right down here."

Which of course was not what I asked.

An echoing bang bounced against the canyon walls before an explosion of green, pink, and white fireworks lit the bowl of blackness and glittered peacefully across the heavens. I jumped behind Mother and she broke into a silly laugh. But I was serious, nearly begging, when I told her, "I don't want to go there. I want to stay here with you."

I squeezed a walnut extra hard then handed it to Aunt Julie. Her jaw dropped when I told her "1960" was printed on Mother's beauty queen sash. "Three years ago," she sighed, "I remember it like yesterday."

Father bent down, reached to the back of the knife drawer. "Your mother's heart is as beautiful on the inside as she is on the outside. If you grow up to be even half the person she is, Zetty, you'll be amazing." He pulled out the knife he wanted, and headed toward the bird like a hired henchman.

Aunt Julie sounded a little taken aback, "What a lovely thing to say about your wife, Hank." He flashed a two-second grin and then hollered out to Mother asking how much dark versus white meat he should slice. Aunt Julie leaned towards me—love in her voice, "My big brother doesn't always say what's on his mind, but I like it when he does."

"Me too," I smiled, and meant it. That was when Father was still a deep-hearted, cheerful man.

One by one I lined up walnuts in a long row across the table and let Aunt Julie grab and crack while I kept the procession moving. She almost had a small bowl filled when she reached for a handful and sprinkled them on top of the sweet potato casserole. "I wish I could be here to see you sing and dance in those red boots. I'm sure it'll be a smashing success. Raise your ticket price, though. Seventy-five cents, at least."

"I agree," I said through gritted teeth, trying again to wrangle open a stubborn one with all my strength. "Maybe the cowgirl show will make us rich!" Aunt Julie held out her hand, motioned for me to give her the walnut, and in one fell swoop, cracked the thing right open.

Mother rehearsed dance moves at the oddest times. I spotted her in the middle of the street once on my way home from school. I dashed so fast to meet her that my Cinderella lunch pail gave me bruises on one thigh. "Hi Mother!" I yelled, and then realized she was performing for me. A dance, right there in front of everyone. "Mother," I warned, "look out for cars!" I could tell she was aware of them when she swirled closer to the curb each time one passed. Everyone seemed fascinated. The cars decelerated and drivers stared out their windows, gawking. The next day, she was the talk of the neighborhood. "It's what actresses do," I explained to Gabe.

I asked Mother once why she didn't become a stage director like she always wanted. She told me, "Not all dreams come true, honey. I got married instead. Everything happens for a reason."

Even though I didn't hear an ounce of regret in her voice, there was something else that lingered around her words that I didn't quite recognize. Perhaps it was a looming sense of doom.

"Well, you could still do it. Hollywood is only two hours away. You should do it now, Mother."

She laughed, but I was serious.

I used to wonder where she might be if she had taken my advice, and if it would've been enough to change the course of her life.

And mine.

By THE TIME WE SAT TO EAT, THERE WERE BARELY ANY RED marks left on my neck from Max's wart-infested fingers. I worried for a long time I would catch the nasty things and wake up one morning with a colony growing like cauliflower around my neck. It never happened, but Gabe told me, in her expert opinion, that the whole experience was the start of my condition.

"What condition?" I asked her.

"I don't know," she said, "but you worry about dumb stuff and it's weird." I wasn't offended. No one else noticed as much about me as Gabe did and, frankly, I was happy she was willing to pay such close attention to the way my brain worked. After Mother's went sideways, I had reason to worry.

That Thanksgiving, Father carved the biggest turkey in the West. I've not seen another bird of its massive girth since. We had dressing with red apples and sausage in it, sweet potato casserole, and raspberry gelatin molded in a fancy dome with cranberries, pineapple, and walnuts floating on top. Everyone smothered the steaming hot, flaky biscuits with butter and apricot jam. To top it all, Mother made everyone's favorite dish: green beans in a mushroom sauce, topped with crunchy onions right out of a can. And she put her favorite tablecloth on for the occasion. It was butterscotch yellow with bright red, purple, orange, and blue pansies covering all four corners. My favorite candles, orange and gold carved turkeys, stood proudly, flanking the butter dish and salt and pepper shakers.

We went around the table, heads bowed, each giving thanks for what we were grateful for. I was sincere when I prayed, "Thank you for letting us live near the ocean, for making waves to dive under, for Tuffy, who, by the way, thanks you for tennis balls, and for letting me live with my mother and father forever."

Max ruined it all. "You can't live with them forever, because they're old and they're going to get sick and die!"

Uncle Ben gave him a don't-start expression. "Maxwell, that's enough."

I shot Max my dirtiest look yet, but he was already glaring at me with a satisfied smirk on his face. His remark troubled me. He obviously hadn't learned what I had in Sunday school about eternal life. I held my hands down in my lap while my left examined each knuckle on the right as it tightened into a solid fist. *If only I could let it fly now*, I thought.

I remember the details of that meal as if it were the "last supper," which, in a way, it was. Mother was especially hungry, taking seconds of almost everything, racing to eat as much as she could. Maybe she was in a hurry to check on the next batch of biscuits, or whip the cream for pie, or maybe she sensed she should store up as many calories as she could.

Queenie, the youngest, plopped a yellow cherry tomato in her mouth, and with one determined bite, accidentally sprayed everyone across the table. Mother was always first to see the funny side of things; it gave us all permission to be silly. Her laughter could be infectious and, at the same time, soft and delicate like her. Sometimes when she laughed, it was as if the sound had rolled gracefully off a dance floor, and spun gently around the dining table like a familiar waltz.

I remember the happiness in Father's deep blue eyes, too, sparkling like the ocean. He glittered with delight when he watched me dance, or when he sat and observed Mother—as if she were a painting so full of color and emotion that he couldn't find words to describe his appreciation for her. Father was a man of few words, which Gabe said made him "hard to read" sometimes. It was true, I guess, that he was guarded, and didn't communicate a lot. But I always felt underneath his silent, often tough exterior lay a heart the size of Texas. And better to be the strong, silent type, I decided, than like Gabe's dad who was a man of too many words. The kind we weren't allowed to repeat.

But during that meal, even Father, with his Clark Kent-like seriousness, lost composure when a single cherry tomato sprayed his family. While Benny furiously wiped at his book spattered by the explosion, I saw Father turn his attention to the gravy bowl, adjust his black-framed glasses, and give the gravy a quick stir trying, I suppose, to stay in control. But his defenses broke and he joined in with the rest of us when Max, his forehead encrusted with tomato spit, burst out laughing like a wild demon—an outlandish chorus against Mother's angelic chortling.

Everyone gulped for air trying to unwind belly spasms, but another round of hysterics began when Father let out a snort and started choking on his vegetables. Long, skinny French green beans came climbing out his long, imperial nose, one after another into the white cotton hankie Mother ironed for him that morning.

I don't remember a time at the dinner table when every one of us laughed so hard. For one brief moment of pure insanity, even Max looked human again.

That Thanksgiving was the first and last for many things. By the time my plate was clean, a string of nervous, empty giggles filled Mother's throat as if a different woman had taken her place. She stared at the table as she chewed, her mind somewhere else, eyes unoccupied by her surroundings. It bugged me. Someone needed to make it stop.

"Mom! Stop daydreaming," I demanded. "We want more taters!" Her face shuttered open and she turned toward me. *Good*, I thought, *she's paying attention again*. Tuffy leaned into her leg, and lightly whimpered. I thought he was being unusually clingy, but then who could blame him with a boy like Max around.

When all the kids started chanting for seconds, Mother sprang up like normal, and bustled into the kitchen.

Then poof; the mother I knew disappeared.

THE BOYS LOADED UP THEIR KNIVES WITH GLOBS OF BUTTER, and we waited.

Max beat the table like a drum, a fork and spoon in each fist, and led the chant, "Taters, taters, for out-of-staters!" Father was so busy chattering about his airplane with Uncle Ben and Aunt Julie, they didn't seem to notice the noise.

I went to the kitchen to see what was taking so long, but Mother wasn't there.

I found Tuffy at the big picture window in the front room, standing at full attention, looking regal—as only a golden retriever can. He flinched a little when I walked in, but he never, not for one second, took his eyes off what he was watching outside.

Wind and rain are rare in Southern California, but that afternoon under a dark, thick band of clouds, the wind whipped tumbleweeds the size of boulders into a frenzy. A ghostly sound shivered through the cracks of the window-sill like a death rattle. I knew Tuffy must be focused on something serious. So, it surprised me when I saw that it was nothing serious at all.

Mother was outside on the sidewalk, still wearing the yellow and white daisy apron around the copper-colored shift in which she had served dinner. A white mohair sweater was draped over her shoulders and a sheer gold scarf was tied under her chin to protect her teased-up, dark auburn-dyed hair from the threat of the storm.

I assumed Mother ran outdoors to watch the tumble-weeds barrel down the street, swirling and dancing their way past cars, shrubs, and telephone poles. The neighbor-hood came alive when nearby canyons cut their prickly sticker bushes loose, chasing children from one block to the next. Sometimes they rolled after us and we screamed and carried on all the way down to the beach. Then I noticed Mother had kicked off her beige flats and was standing barefoot on the white chalked lines of the hopscotch I had drawn that morning. When I saw her stretch out my favorite purple jump rope and begin jumping, I jolted into action.

"There she is! Mother's outside playing!" I broadcast it like opening day at the horse races, minus the gunshot.

"Come on, Tuffy!" Oddly, he ignored my invitation, choosing instead to stand guard where he was, both eyes on Mother.

All three cousins came stampeding to the front door, but I had already grabbed my favorite button-down royal blue knit cardigan, yanked up my matching knee socks, and was out at high speed, frantic to be first in line.

"I'm next, Mother! —after you finish this song!"

She continued in perfect step, skipping over the rope and singing:

"Here I am, /Little jumping Joan; /When nobody's with me, /I'm always alone."

"Here I am Mother!" in case she hadn't noticed.

She didn't seem to hear me. Mother kept reciting the same rhymes, over and over and kept right on skipping, but she wasn't smiling anymore. Her eyes were cold and flat, as if reading from a tedious, mind-numbing textbook in front of class. She continued, like someone developing a dreadful case of stage fright, not like the mother I knew at all.

"Little Polly Flinders/Sat among the cinders, /Warming her pretty little toes! /Her mother came and caught her, / And whipped her little daughter/For spoiling her nice new clothes."

By then Max was running in circles around us with his fist in the air shouting, "Do 'Sing A Song of Sixpence'! 'Sing A Song of Sixpence!'"

It rolled right off her tongue: "Sing a song of sixpence, /A pocket full of rye; /Four-and-twenty blackbirds/Baked in a pie!"

Since she was in no mood to share, I jumped alongside her, pretending to have my own rope. Max, Queenie, and Benny, joined in at our favorite part. Only Max, of course, screamed it at the top of his lungs, a vein in his neck pulsating, "The maid was in the garden, /Hanging out the clothes; /When down came a blackbird/And snapped off her nose."

Anything with blood and gore got him all worked up.

I tugged on her apron and her sweater dropped to the ground, "My turn, Mother. Please. May I jump now?"

No response. No smile. No nothing.

She started singing again but her words began to falter. "Spring is showery, flowery, bowery;/Summer is hoppy, croppy, poppy;/Autumn is wheezy, sneezy, freezy;/Winter is slippy, drippy, nippy."

"Mother, let me now!" I grabbed for the rope, but missed. At a snail's pace she turned her face toward mine and looked directly at me as if I were a complete stranger. The emerald green eyes that had forever been so full of love no longer revealed any hint of the person behind them. My heart collapsed.

"What's wrong with you?" I kicked a rock from a square on the hopscotch and sent it sailing into the street. And then I kicked another, this time aiming at her feet, but it flew under the rope in perfect time. "Let me play!" And then I yelled like I had never yelled before. "What is your problem? Are you crazy or something?!"

Aunt Julie's strong hands cupped my shoulders and turned me away from Mother.

"All of you—go inside now and play in Zetty's room."

Tears hatched, trickling down my cheeks, over my jaw and down the opening of my shirt collar. My neck was cold and wet and Mother didn't care.

Max spit like a dragon and danced around me like I was tied to a stake. "Bawl baby! Bawl baby! Big fat bawl baby!" The tears ran full force. I lost all control and resigned myself to it. I didn't know then how hard it would be to get that control back again. At least in the way I wanted.

Aunt Julie tried to reassure me. "It's okay, Zetty. Go on inside now. It's okay."

When I came up for air between waves of hurt, I begged for answers. "But what's wrong with her? Why is she like that? What is going on?"

Every round of questioning was met with the same response in Aunt Julie's friendliest voice, "It's okay, honey."

Well, if this was "okay," then I figured Aunt Julie must be crazy, too, but at least she looked normal.

Marjorie

Dear God. I was only going for potatoes.

They were on top of the stove in the yellow Pyrex bowl. Part of a four-piece set Hank and I received for our wedding. It was covered with a blanket of terry cloth towels and a mishmash of tatty pot-holders, keeping them steamy hot. The kids wanted seconds. You see, for a long time I remembered all of this. I thought I'd be okay.

The children were chanting for more of my buttery whipped potatoes. Of course they would. It was a perfect batch, I thought. I told myself that's who I was hearing. The voices were familiar after all; I tried not to be afraid. But when the chatter grew louder, and the voices clearer, words filtered through that weren't childlike.

Look how clumsy you are, someone mocked.

She's never going to be right! another chimed in.

My thoughts started to spin and break apart.

Listen. We aren't going away.

I hugged the bowl against my waist, the heat pressed into my midriff. *Stop!* I screamed inside.

Be quiet, or I'll whack you! the ugly one threatened. *You contaminated the food. You're going to make them sick.*

I released the bowl, jerked my head around, but no one was there.

One of them hissed with disgust, *Women like you need to go to hell.*

No, I told myself, these were not the words of the children around my supper table. The sinister ones were back.

"Not today," I begged out loud, "Not on Thanksgiving. Please!"

I thought the evil beings were gone. I wished for them to die, prayed for them to be taken, and I believed they had. But my mind populated with their words again—far more powerful than anyone could understand. I wanted to shriek, but they forbade me. Took my voice away as if muzzled in a nightmare deep in the night.

They heckled, berated, cursed. Vicious—like rabid animals.

Go ahead! Do it bitch! they dared.

"Stop," I whispered, "don't make me hurt them."

That's when my hand plunged into the burning bowl of spuds. Steam rose from the trash bin where I chucked everything—my palm like lobster-red flesh. But once again, there was no pain.

The voices took control like never before. They were simply too strong. I had no choice, you see, but to run.

I descended into the underworld in my own front yard, and nobody even noticed. I sank into another dimension no one saw, but me. At least that's what I told myself. But not all of me was taken. The evil ones missed a part. It was only a small part, but I kept it in hiding and let it appear only when it was safe.

As soon as a tall oak of a man in a white uniform approached, laughter poured out of me like a fountain. The daftness I felt was unusual, of course. Even I could sense that. But it came from somewhere inside me I couldn't reach. I had no authority over it.

"This is all a mistake," I stopped and giggled. "I'm not a child," I told him. "I only came out to play because it helps me relax. I'm fine now."

"I understand, Ma'am," he said.

Like hell you do, I thought.

I heard him speak gibberish into a hand held radio while his partner wrote notes on a clipboard.

Of course I knew I wasn't fine. I had only hoped to convince them I was. I knew from the start the voices were a problem in me, and no one else. My own words, even simple ones, came out wrong when they ambushed me. But the funny thing was, I could recite nursery rhymes without any trouble at all. And they usually shut the voices right up. So did music. But this time nothing helped; not the rhymes, not the singing, not even playing with Zetty. The voices began to intrude again.

You're a monster! one taunted.

She's a lunatic! several sneered.

I found a way to my own words and used them. "Don't take me from my home!" I shouted. I heard a wicked snicker, *You don't deserve to be here.*

The air waves were full of static and confusion but through them came a voice I welcomed—a voice I cherished. "Margie," Hank said, "I'm right here. I'm following you to the hospital. I'll be right behind you."

His speech pulled me back. I was in command again. My mind felt clear and stable. "But what about Zetty? No, Hank. Please, don't leave her."

"Zetty is fine, Marge. Julie is here and Scarlett is right across the street. It's all taken care of." He caringly squeezed my arm. "There's nothing to worry about, honey. You'll be fine in no time."

"Yes, I will. I'm better now," I assured him. "Really I am. I'll be home right away."

"Good, sweetheart, good."

"Tell Zetty I've simply gone away on a short holiday so she shouldn't worry," I told him.

He kissed me on the forehead and slid my knees to one side before a heavy door shut the world out.

I heard the clunk of a strong lock and knew there was plenty to worry about. I was, after all, being taken away in a paddy wagon.

I felt the weight of mattress-thick foam enclose me. There wasn't enough air and the odd vinyl smell permeating the atmosphere began to burn through my nose, and down my throat. Nausea and shame clung to my insides. I curled into a ball and gagged, but couldn't rid myself of it.

You'll never see Zetty, again. She hates you now, they scoffed.

"That's not true!" I screamed. But inside I knew; along with my mind, I was also losing my daughter. So much would be left unfinished.

"You can't take a mother away from her baby!" I yelled. "It's not right." I planned to escape when it was safe. I imagined the moment. I would rip myself from their grasp, leap into the canyons and dart through the bushes where they'd never track me. I'd find Zetty waiting on a horse, ready to go. The cowgirl's daughter would save me. I would vault on to the horse's back, grab Zetty's waist, and giddy-up—we'd be gone.

Now be careful what you say, a voice warned. *Stop talking. Don't tell them your foolish plan.*

But I knew it wasn't foolish. My young daughter would be waiting. How could I leave her waiting and not return? The pain of such an abandonment would be too much to bear.

And then a woman's voice pushed through, *She has Hank. It'll be alright. She's safe with her father.*

But the air around me was metallic and acid. It tasted

bad when my lungs inflated. I didn't know if that voice could be trusted, either.

Marjorie, everything will be okay, the woman said. *You can conquer this.*

"Did you say something?" I asked the faces floating around me.

"No, Ma'am," someone answered. Nevertheless I felt more secure, even as a sharp sting poked through my skin and began to burn. An engine rumbled alive and the pull of its force rocked us backward.

"They're listening," I told the white shirts around me. "They don't want you to know, but they're still around."

And then I relaxed into the sway of the roads and basked in a pleasant wave of calm that kept everything at a safe distance. If only, I thought, I could feel this way all the time. Everything would be okay. But the feeling stopped way too soon.

The mollifying drone of the motor went silent and I stepped out to a chilly blast of air. Piercing light penetrated my face, sealing both eyes shut.

"She's okay to walk in," I heard one say to the other. Knuckled hands wrapped my upper arms carrying most of my weight. I toddled slowly through hulking steel doors pushed open by the strong backs of two men. There was no energy left to fight or escape their grasp. I gave up the absurd fantasy of trying. I started giggling, thinking of my ridiculous plan to ride off into the sunset on a horse with Zetty. I couldn't wait to tell her about it. We'd laugh until our stomachs hurt.

I tried to understand the conversations buzzing around me. But I didn't know anymore what words were my own or those of others. Were they inside my mind, or outside of me? I couldn't be sure. And then I stopped caring. I was numb, empty, tired. All I wanted was sleep.

She has Hank. She has Hank. She has Hank, I heard repeatedly. The woman's voice said again, *You can conquer this.*

And then a heavy wave of darkness rolled over me and pushed everything away.

To Dance Again

I HAVE NO MEMORY OF WHAT MY COUSINS AND I DID IN MY room the rest of that evening. I don't recall what happened to the leftover turkey or whether anyone ate Mother's chocolate cream pie with the graham cracker crust. I only remember it was past my bedtime when Uncle Ben, Aunt Julie, and my cousins packed up to begin the long drive home.

Father and I waved goodbye until their station wagon disappeared around the corner and then, gazing at my bare feet hanging over the edge of the curb, I asked him where Mother was.

"We had to get her to the hospital, but she's fine. She'll be just fine." I stared straight down at my big toe, the one with a chip of pink nail polish left on it and knew he was lying.

"How can she be fine if she's in a hospital?" I asked.

"I don't expect it'll be for long; a little something just came over her," he said. "We'll have her back in no time." I remember the warmth of his large hand pressed between my shoulder blades when we turned and walked back into the house. And I'll never forget the sound when we stepped inside the entryway: earsplitting silence. It was the loneliest sound I ever heard. It hummed in the air all night long.

Father twisted the lock on the front door, unbuttoned the stiff collar on his starched gray shirt, and then flipped off the yard lights. He glanced back at me as he headed down the hallway and said, "Good night," as if nothing unusual had happened at all.

I wanted to know why Mother wasn't there to give me a hug and kiss goodnight, tuck my blankets in tight around me, and read with me. We were only on page forty-four of *Hitty: Her First Hundred Years*, by Rachel Field. I couldn't bear to go to the next chapter without her.

And she wasn't there to pray with me, either—to a God who she said "promised never to leave us." What God in his right mind would have let this happen if he was with us? Like Santa Claus, I woke up that evening and discovered the lie. There was no longer anything to believe in, and even worse, I realized, Max was right—I couldn't count on being with my parents forever. Not here, not in heaven.

I stood still, unable to move, petrified at the thought.

"Dad? What does she have?"

"Nothing to worry about, Zetty." He stepped into his room.

"But—"

"See you in the morning," he said clearing his throat a little, and then closed the bedroom door leaving me to figure things out by myself.

Whatever it was she had, I hoped it wasn't catching. My stomach turned queasy at the thought I could be next.

AROUND MIDNIGHT, I CREPT DOWNSTAIRS TO THE KITCHEN, poured some milk into a small saucepan, and turned up the flame on the burner as high as it would go. I dragged the metal chair from the dinette to the cupboards and stepped up on the green vinyl-covered seat cushion to pull down a box of cocoa and a red plastic canister of sugar. Mother always gave me cocoa when I couldn't sleep, and if I remembered right, this was how she made it.

"If you ignore the pan," she taught me, "it will boil faster." So, to speed things up, I paced across the polished wood floor, turned sharply on my right heel and twirled at the end of each lap, performing the move like a fancy dance step. And then like the sting of an angry hornet straight to the heart, I remembered Mother wasn't there to admire it. She wasn't there to dance with me the way we practiced for our show, either.

Tuffy was our only audience for the first rehearsal. He lay watching on the spongy grass, head resting on his golden paws. Picnic table benches and folding chairs would be organized into theater aisles on show day—the front row, as always, reserved for Father, Gabe, and her mother, Scarlett. Maybe our friend, Sue Willy, if she was around, and Gabe's dad too, if he felt like it. Dennis usually felt like it after a couple beers.

I tied a bandana around Tuffy's neck. Purple stood out best against his glossy bullion-colored fur, which I brushed daily. I wanted him to shine for his moment in the spotlight, a walk-on part. In a particularly exciting scene, he was to retrieve my gun and deliver it to me so I could save Mother from the outlaw hooligans threatening to steal her away. I only had to hide Tuffy's tennis balls for one week and make him fetch my silver-capped pistol to get him used to the idea.

The script called for Tuffy to take a bullet to save me, but because he played dead with such illustrious skill, I found myself so fully immersed in the scene, I couldn't bear it and went mute. My eyes saw he was alive, but my heart kept right on wrenching. Mother understood the problem immediately. A dead Tuffy, even a pretend one, undermined my talent so she re-wrote the script on the spot announcing, "Tuffy lives!" And suddenly all my lines came back.

Mother and I hid a pistol in our right boots for the big shoot-outs. Both cracker-jack shots, we busted whiskey bottles in mid-air, poker cards held by cheaters, and ear-lobes when necessary. Of course, we saved babies, too. We rode in, cleaned up a town full of gun-slinging, drunken varmints, and tamed a corner of the Wild West. Something, as far as I know, never accomplished by a woman and her nine-year-old daughter.

I used to do the "can-can" at the side of the stage to kick out the fidgety, pent-up energy charging through me. The instant I hit the stage, I stepped into another dimension. When the opening number bounced through the air, my heart galloped up my throat and goose bumps danced down my spine. Happiness surged through me like something holy. When the curtains opened, *Zing*! I was shot at once into the world of showbiz.

During rehearsals, the clock ran in circles until the sun sank low in the jet-streaked sky. Shadows of palm trees blanketed the yard and a light mist rolled off the ocean and coiled the hair around my cowgirl hat into frizzy wisps. Time took another day, like a disappearing act. I was immersed in concentrated pleasure; lost wholly in the satisfaction of doing what I loved.

I didn't know at the time just how rare a thing pure, unbridled joy could be. Or how quickly it could be taken. I didn't know then how much more I would have to lose and how hard I would have to fight to be able to find my way back to that joy again.

The pan of milk spat at me and sputtered like it might be hot. I daringly dipped a finger in the pan, but it was only lukewarm. I paced faster and turned on my heel harder. The next time I spun around, I saw Tuffy, blocking the doorway, studying me in the same odd way he had stared at Mother earlier.

"What're you looking at?" I turned off the burner, grabbed the pan, and flung it over to the sink so fast it splashed like a tidal wave across the aqua Formica counter. I slapped the light switch off and shoved my way past Tuffy's searing gaze, kicking him in the side. His ears flattened and he slunk backward, examining me with wounded eyes. I stared right back at him and yelled, "Stupid dog!"

It was Max Mean, and it felt good.

I threw my red leather cowgirl boots to the back of my closet and went to bed. I thought back to our first rehearsal like a perfect dream. But no matter how hard I tried to go back to it and stay there a little longer, it slipped away.

THEY SAY UNEXPECTED MOMENTS ARE THE BEST ONES IN life, but I can tell you it's not true. I never played again at the spot on the sidewalk where Mother skipped herself away into another world. The mere sight of it made my stomach ache.

Everything I knew up to that point vanished, like steam rising up into nothingness. I heard once that faith and hope and love return slowly to those who lose everything. It may come back, they said, like gentle rain filling a river, one drop at a time. I didn't believe it then, but I did learn nothingness doesn't exist in life. Even evaporated steam exists somewhere. It rises slowly, changing, even from the deepest abyss of grief.

I still remember clearly the unspoken rule that rapidly engulfed our home after she disappeared: Don't talk about Mother as if she's really gone, and don't talk about the memory of what happened that day. After Mother left, Father was nearly mute. He seemed able to slip what happened sneakily underground into the far reaches of his psyche—his feelings conveniently disguised and under wraps, out of the watchful eyes of others. It may have been a curse, or a blessing; I only know for me, the memory of losing Mother imprinted itself so clearly, and with such force, that there was never any hope for escape.

For a long time, I tried to get more out of Father. Sometimes I would slip in a question while he was working in the kitchen, or while we were shopping at the Lucky Seven for groceries. When he was tucking a triple-layered roast beef sandwich into a black lunch box the size of a Cadillac, I'd casually say, "Mother must be feeling better by now, huh?" or, "I'm sure they have medicine to make her well, right?" or, "Maybe we should buy extra hamburger because Mother might be home this weekend, do you think?"

Father simply nodded his head to every question. Every now and then I heard an unconvincing grunt of agreement. There were times I wanted to grab him like Max did me and squeeze the living daylights out of him—force him to expel the hefty piece of truth lodged in his throat. Just spit it out already! I screamed at him in my mind.

There was nothing but dead space around the mundane routines we stepped through each day. We slept, showered, bowed our heads to Jesus, fed Tuffy, went to work and school, cleaned, shopped, and took care of all the necessities. And every night Father retreated to the garage to a nearly thirty-foot-long, fully aerobatic fuselage constructed of all wood.

It was always Father's dream to build and fly his own airplane. He called it his labor of love, consuming almost every evening, weekend, and our vacations—his lifeline after

Mother left. He enjoyed a brotherhood of air-minded nuts in the home-builders' circle, who eventually volunteered their talents to help his aircraft take flight. It was his driving ambition, the only thing that remained constant.

Mother's piano was the only viable organ left in the body of our home. She taught me to play, but I only performed when Father was gone, or when he was at the table saw in the garage with ear-plugs firmly implanted. I sensed more sadness might be awakened in him by my playing.

I missed swing dancing, too. Mother used to watch for me at the picture window when I came home for lunch. I'd see her wave and then make a mad dash to the stereo. Just as she pushed the heavy, black front door wide open, the big band music began, blasting right out into the street.

First we'd hear the start-up notes to Glen Miller playing "String of Pearls," our signal to get into position. The sound of trumpets thumping against my chest made my insides shake. I was ready to burst in the second before we started. My heart beat faster than I could count. Mother would take both my hands at once; always just in the nick of time when the song took off like a rocket and away we went, just like in the movies. Step, step, side, step, back, step, side, step, forward step, back step. Then Mother would cry out, "Swing!" and around I went, twirling under her arm, round and round and out and in. Then the big slide: right between her legs and up again.

I never felt so alive as I did dancing with Mother. The thing I wanted most was to do that dance with her again.

"We are born dancers, Zetty!" Mother used to tell me. "You inherited every one of my dancing genes." It felt like a great gift at the time. Later, I could only hope the dancing ones were all I got.

I tried to spend as many hours in the day as possible at

Gabe's house where it was pure madness. Gabe liked being in our home, because I didn't have an annoying brother or parents who yelled at each other. She could count on peace and quiet. For me, the quarrels, bickering, and crazy tension between the Taylors was as soothing as balm. I preferred any kind of noise to living in a museum filled with ancient artifacts belonging to a ghost. All the commotion at Gabe's helped sidetrack my inner unrest; I pretended I belonged there, in a family that stayed together no matter how bad it got.

Unless Tuffy was next to me, I never really felt at home in our house again.

The following December, more than a year since I'd seen Mother, life promised to return to normalcy. I came home from Gabe's, a short walk across the street from their cul-de-sac, and before my feet hit the front porch, Father appeared at the screen door, both hands relaxed on his hips. "Zetty, pull out the Christmas decorations," he said smiling. "She's coming home."

A Blue Christmas

Father's voice sounded alive, undeniably certain, and it gave me a thrill just to hear it. I stepped up on the porch cautiously, afraid I might break the spell of his cheery mood.

"For real, Father?" He held the screen open for me as I walked in.

"For real, Zetty. And honey, she sure does miss you. She can't wait to see you."

"She's all well?"

"Just in time for Christmas!" he said.

I did a quick calculation in my head and realized if we hurried, our cowgirl show could still go on over the holiday break. "So, what she had is gone? Cured, I mean?" I stood in the hall entry trying to sort out Father's words from the dizzy-making thoughts buzzing in my mind.

"It will be, sweetheart. Everyone's praying for her. Not just you and me, but everyone at church, too."

The guilty truth thumped me in the gut. Her coming home wouldn't be because of any of my prayers. I decided it was best not to confess this, knowing Father would be crushed and I'd feel like a louse.

As a surprise, and for atonement, I put together a two-foot-high, shiny, silver metal tree and covered it with all blue lights that twinkled non-stop. I set it up on the wide window ledge in their room above the bed, just for something extra special. She loved blue.

And then Father and I decorated a six-foot-tall tree sprayed with thick white foam for a snowy look—her favorite. We set it up at the picture window in the front room and wrapped all blue lights around that one, too. I used to love Christmas. Even the worst part of it. Father insisted every little silver strand, supposedly icicles, hang evenly apart on every branch.

Every year I argued that icicles melt, and some clump up on branches unevenly, so it naturally wouldn't look the same everywhere.

"One at a time, Zetty," he prompted.

The thing is, I didn't like decorating with Father. If Mother had been with us, we would have been listening to Bing Crosby and Andy Williams singing Christmas carols. She would have served us cocoa with whipped cream on top and caramel-coated popcorn balls. And she would have let me hang the icicles in clumps.

Father and I went through the motions awkwardly with frozen conversations.

"I think it's almost done in the back," I said.

"Good. We're making progress," he replied.

"This sure is a big tree," I added.

"It's a full one this year."

"Can't smell it flocked over like this," I complained.

"No, sure can't. I miss smelling pine."

"Me, too. We're almost out of ornaments."

"We sure are."

Our conversation was as stiff as the starched white collar on his Sunday shirt. It was hard to relax. And you can't have fun when you aren't relaxed. Not really.

We did it, though. We managed because the house

needed to look right for Mother.

And then—Father turned off all the lights in the living room.

He went to the tree and with a flip of the switch all the blue lights illuminated instantly. That blue was really something against the white rubber stuff. Every pink, yellow, aqua, and lavender ornament caught the radiance and sparkled like jewels in a treasure chest. "Wow!" I yelled.

And my heart leapt into my throat because I remembered Mother was really coming home. "When do we pick her up?" I pushed my headband back so I could see Father's face perfectly.

"What do you think about tomorrow after church?" His old voice was back—the happy one.

"Tomorrow?!"

"She'll be ready around two." He collapsed into his recliner.

Tuffy clambered backward from under the coffee table, lumbered across the room and leaned into my side.

"Wow." My stomach was rolling in a ball of motion, like riding the Tilt-A-Whirl at the fair. I bent over, wrapped both arms around Tuffy and hugged him while he covered my face with his lapping tongue.

Father wove his fingers together and relaxed his clasped hands on his chest. "It sure will be good to have her back."

When he said it, I heard more relief in his voice than anything. Like a man who had just been liberated from a world of misery.

I wanted everything to look perfect for her. After Christmas decorations were up, I cleaned my room and positioned our book on my end table, slanting it a little. "Just think, Tuffy. Tomorrow night at this time we'll be done with the next chapter about Hitty. Finally!"

After that, I pulled everything for our cowgirl show out of my closet that had accumulated dust and a pincher bug or two. I organized things in the corner of my room with my red leather boots, and black cowgirl hat at the center of it all. "On with the show," I announced to Tuffy, who changed position to stay close to me. He panted happily when I cooled him off with water from a spray bottle. Even in December, Windansea was humid. Tuffy shook and a flurry of small beads scattered, cooling my arms and legs. As soon as I adjusted the window fan to blow directly at us, Tuffy lunged into bed. When I crawled in next to him, he stood, stepped on my legs, and then collapsed on top of me in a heap.

I talked to him about everything, again. "She can't wait, boy. She misses me; she wants to come home." I almost added, *I sure hope she looks normal.* The thought came and went like a spasm, a simple twinge that didn't grab hold for long, but smarted just the same.

I was wound up aflutter, expecting to lie wide-awake all night. But as soon as my head sank into two feather pillows, and Tuffy nudged his nose under my arm—nestling his head into my shoulder, sleep came fast and hard.

I slept so well I didn't hear the alarm go off the next morning. Father and I were late for church, and it was the first time I didn't hear a lecture about it.

Marjorie

SOMETIMES FRAGMENTS OF MY FORMER SELF DANGLED into consciousness like a pleasant dream. Memories like the shine of my ebony baby grand, the red leather cowgirl boots Zetty wore, the stage play, our dance routines, the book we read together, Hank's embrace, and the sweet spot of Zetty's cheek against mine, for instance. Those were the memories that kept me alive that year. But they only slipped into awareness when it was safe—when the sinister, evil voices weren't there.

It was Hank and Zetty I missed most. From the first night on, I imagined their hands in mine so I could sleep.

I tried so hard to find a way back to them. My visits with Hank were wonderful, but I needed to see Zetty. A grown man would survive. Hank would always know and love me, but Zetty's last memory of me couldn't be what it was. A young girl needed to remember her mother's love and connection; the bond knit together since birth. Not the memory of a mother gone mad. More than anything, I wanted to be home with Zetty.

That morning, I wandered down the narrow hall, yellowed from years of smoke and grime. If only Zetty were here to paint these walls with her art, I thought. They need her inspiration. That's when the loud clomping footsteps began to echo behind me. When they sped up, I turned to look, but saw no one. The walls stretched like canvas and started moving in tight around me. My breathing sped up; I started to panic.

Marjorie, I heard my name clearly, *over here!* I glanced front and behind, left to right, but there was no one. It was the evil, invisible one encircling me—scaring me again.

"Leave me alone!" I screeched, collapsed to my knees and began to cry. Someone reached down to save me. I pulled on the arm, the silky black safe one, who helped me stand.

"Margie, honey. It's Eleanor. Let me help you up." She gently guided me back to my room.

And that's when I saw them, right next to my bed. Their faces eager, bright, relieved to see me. I opened my arms to Zetty first and waited for her to spring into my lap, the way she always did. But her limbs stayed put.

Zetty and Hank were there until my nurse told me they weren't.

"It's your illness again, sweetie," Eleanor explained, "It tricked you into believing it."

In that moment I realized I may never return to my right mind again.

"Your family really is coming today, Marjorie." Eleanor's voice calmed my thoughts. "They'll be here soon. We'll let you know when."

I only hoped I'd be able to discern if they were real or not. I honestly didn't know how I'd know for sure. I went under my mattress and pulled out the supplies that only Eleanor and I could see. I needed to work on my netting.

"What a clever idea, knitting an invisible net for your bed," Eleanor told me.

"Yes," I explained, "It protects me from the evil beings while I sleep. You should tell others here to do the same."

"I need to finish up a few things, and then I'll be back," she said.

I hated it when Eleanor left. The voices orbited around my brain as soon as she hurried out my door.

Listen to us or else, they warned.

Zetty and Hank must die, a voice loomed, *Go with the imposter—the man pretending to be your husband. Let him kill your family today or we'll destroy you.*

I was told I wasn't crazy, or possessed, but in my case I believed they may have been wrong. My own mind would never have agreed to let that one in.

Eleanor came through the door carrying clothes. She laid out a long-sleeved, forest green, belted dress on my bed. "Would you like help getting dressed, Margie?"

"No," I said as carefully as I could. I felt the knife pushing into my spine, *Shut up about us, or we'll hurt her, too.*

Eleanor fluttered the wrinkles out of my beige half-slip, and set it carefully next to my white cotton briefs, and Cross Your Heart Playtex bra. "Your family should be here in about a half hour. Let me know if you need anything." As soon as she left, again the demands continued.

Don't undress or you'll fall apart, a wretched voice threatened.

I knew what I had to do. "Go ahead. Destroy me," I told it.

With one deep breath, I tugged at my neck. The snap came apart and I lifted each arm out of the cavern-sized sleeves. I dropped the limp, stained gown to the ground where it warmed my feet.

I rested my bare bottom on the edge of the mattress and with my invisible needles, knit the air in front of my exposed breasts, and waited.

In Quest of a Queen

THE SERMON DID NOT IMPRESS ME. OF COURSE, I WASN'T really listening; I had learned how to tune the pastor out from the start. I doodled on the program as if taking notes, and then folded it accordion-style and fanned myself. After we sang Christmas carols, I counted the number of panes in the stained glass picture windows, over and over. I had to, because the numbers came out different every single time I did it.

We didn't stay after the service like usual. Instead we hurried through the multitude of adults holding their Styrofoam cups filled with steamy swill on the red brick breezeway outside the parish hall. Children scrambled to silver trays stacked with Oreos and Lorna Doones, loading up with fists full. We snaked through vociferous chit-chat, every few steps hearing platitudes directed at us from the right, "How are ya, Hank? Merry Christmas, Zetty," and then from the left, "Good to see you both!" "Cloudy day today, but it's supposed to be beautiful tomorrow!" Blah, blah, blah. Tired expressions whirred in my ears until I wanted to stick my fingers in them and muffle it all.

It would have been better, in my opinion, if we had skipped church altogether. I thought we had reason enough, but Father had signed up to usher that day, and was against the idea.

We came straight home for lunch, but I didn't eat. Nerves zapped my appetite, ate up the hunger that normally rolled around my stomach before communion was over.

Father wolfed down half a bologna and Velveeta cheese sandwich instead of the usual whole. I detected trembling in both his hands; he nearly broke a glass just pouring milk into it. But I pretended not to notice how flustered he was; I liked it better when he was in complete control of himself.

Father got up from the table and put his suit coat back on, straightened his tie in the hallway mirror, combed his hair back, and used the heel of his hand to push up a little wave in the front. He looked like he was getting ready to go out on the town with Mother for a swanky date, the way they used to. Our three-bedroom, two-bath ranch was beginning to feel like home again.

The garage door was as heavy as the leaden sky brooding overhead; it took all my might to hoist it. The white, wooden, crisscrossed diamonds nailed to the front must have added at least fifty pounds to the thing.

Father's airplane had almost taken over the inside, but he skillfully squeezed the car out like a pro. After it rolled to a stop in the driveway, I wrenched the garage door back down cautiously, scanning the ground's edge for signs of Tuffy. It dropped on his paw once and agonizing shrieks punctured the air, a desperately dreadful wailing I still hear clearly to this day when I remember it. He limped for a week. From then on, whenever he wanted my lap, he performed that same limp like a trained Lassie. It worked on me every time.

"I'm glad we didn't move anything around, Father. She'll be able to find all her stuff just the way it was." I pushed down the lock on my car door not wanting to risk it flying open on the highway. As soon as the thought entered, a reel started playing: I saw myself being sucked out at high speed, chucked to the ground, and smashed to smithereens. I scooted a few more inches away from the door. I lifted the lock and pushed it down again, this time harder, just to be sure.

"I'm certain she'll have no trouble finding anything, honey."

Driving with Father was like flying in an airplane with him. At every corner he announced, "Clear Right," "Clear Left," or "All Clear." Then, like a jetliner on a runway, he sped down the street like a rocket. And yet, I can tell you, Father was a courteous man on the road. He treated all the traffic around him as if they were his Air Force buddies. He gave a general's salute and a nod to anyone who let him merge on the highway, or to others he let merge in front of him. It felt very official going places with Father. He finally throttled the gas pedal, jetted up the on-ramp, and effortlessly merged into the flow of freeway traffic. It was a relief to be moving fast.

"Is this a new hospital we're going to?" I asked.

He squirmed in his seat and rolled down the window, the air whizzing past, batting our ears. "No. It's been around a long time."

"I thought it was near the bay, not this direction."

"She's not at the one where you got your tonsils out."

"Oh—why not? This seems awful far away."

"Just a different hospital. That's all."

He was hedging again, but I was too excited to make a big deal out of it. I wasn't going to let the confusing things Father said spoil the day. Instead, I concentrated on the thoughts darting around my head. I rehearsed what I wanted to tell her, *I've missed you every single day Mother. I can't wait to put on our show. And Hitty is still waiting for us; I refused to read another word until you came home—and please—don't ever leave again. I need you home.*

I glanced at myself through the window and out into the side view mirror and raked four fingers through my thick, wavy, russet-brown hair in a futile attempt to give it style. I wondered if we would recognize each other.

An uneasy image crossed my memory again; the one of Mother when I last saw her. She was embarrassingly familiar, but not the mother I knew. Or wanted. I cringed at the thought I might have to see that one again. For a moment, the weight of guilt made my heart go black, because I didn't want to drive home in the same car with an imposter. I wanted my *real* mother.

But she was fine now, I reminded myself, and she would be herself again. Father said she would. But what if we didn't know what to say? It was ridiculous, I thought, to feel we could ever be strangers. Still, it had been over a year. I was ten now, and my legs were getting hairy.

Father reached for the radio knob, and adjusted it, first to a religious station reciting a prayer so slow, I thought the woman saying it was having trouble remembering her lines: "Holy. Mary. Mother of God. Keep us humble and obedient—" It's all Father could take, so he switched it to something faster moving, "X, E, X, dey etta wah, Ti-juana, May-hee-co" and left it there. I usually sang along with the brass horns that played the station's jingle, but my mind wasn't focused enough.

I leaned my head against the back of the seat and closed my eyes, remembering Scarlett and Mother taking coffee breaks together. Scarlett would surely come by and chit-chat at the kitchen table with her again, just like old times. I always sensed when we left the room, it was anything but "small" talk they exchanged though. It's not hard to detect the change in atmosphere when the air gets thick from secrets hanging around. The air in our kitchen got thick from smoke, too. Scarlett always sucked on a cigarette like a skin diver desperate for the last ounce of air in her tank. Her nostrils pressed in when she inhaled and flared when she blew out clouds of gray charcoal breath.

Scarlett quit smoking a few months before Mother left us, after Gabe drew a graphic picture of her mother's black lungs dripping yellow lumps of pus. She entered it in the annual art show at school and won second place in the "health" category.

That Thanksgiving when Aunt Julie walked across the street to tell Scarlett about Mother, I saw Scarlett take a cigarette from the front pocket of my aunt's red-checkered apron and light up again.

Scarlett went out of her way to do extra nice things for me after that; she baked birthday cakes, took me school shopping, and demonstrated for both Gabe and me how to cinch a pad to our first Kotex belt. She also gave us Nancy Drew books to swap, and bought me the albums from my favorite musicals: *South Pacific*, *Oklahoma!* and *Camelot*.

My mother loved Gabe, too. On her seventh birthday, she gave her a small, sterling silver crescent moon that hung on a delicate chain with her initials and birth date engraved on the back. Gabe wore it almost every day from then on. When Mother was wrapping it, she explained it was a special birthday present, but I shouldn't be jealous. I wasn't. Not ever when it came to Gabe. I was thrilled my mother treated her just as she would my own sister. Gabe insisted I get to wear the moon too, so we passed it back and forth every birthday for the next ten years.

Father got rattled when a shiny green convertible abruptly swerved into our lane; he slammed on the brakes and both of us jerked to full attention. He loosened his tie with two fingers at his throat as he recomposed himself.

We left the freeway off ramp, and a short distance away, pulled into the hospital parking lot. A gasp tripped out in front of my words, "Whoa! This is where she is? It looks like the White House!" Ten majestic white stone pillars, positioned at the top of a long, broad, series of steps, lined the front entrance.

"Well, it's not," Father responded flatly, as if I had said something insulting.

He circled the car around and cautiously moved into an open spot, double-checking the yellow lines on either side of us. I reached to unlock my door, "Sit tight, hon," he said. "Remember? You're too young to go in."

Every week when Father went to visit Mother, I begged to go with him. He wore his best shirt and tie, polished his shoes, and sprinkled cologne into his wide open hands that he patted along his jaw line. Then he would press his razor sharp cheek into mine, with a quick kiss goodbye. I caught friendly whiffs of him on me for the rest of the day. But he always explained hospital rules didn't allow him to bring me. It was a pitiful excuse that I half believed for way too long.

I wanted to ascend those stairs with Father and pass through the pillars like some kind of queen, or Cinderella princess. But I waited behind instead, and kept watch for them. To help pass the time, I picked up an A&W paper napkin off the floor, polished my black and white saddle shoes, and admired how small they made my feet look, even though they were tight as tourniquets. I wore them anyway, hoping she might be in the mood to swing dance again. I wanted to be ready, in case.

My legs wiggled, like a battery-operated toy made to shake non-stop. I paddled my feet in mid-air to try and change the pace. My fingers wanted something to crack, only I never could pop my knuckles the way Gabe did. So I pressed both hands under my thighs and tried to hold something still.

The restlessness in my legs finally quieted under a block of hot sun radiating through the window. The warmth felt calming, almost hypnotic when I leaned my face under it. I waited—eager for Father and Mother to walk out the front entrance and descend the steps like royalty.

Marjorie

THE METAL BAR ON THE DOOR LIFTED. AN ORDERLY POKED his head inside my room, a thin man with the most preposterous looking face. I knew when his chin stretched like pulled taffy to the floor, the mean ones were playing tricks on me again.

"You have a visitor checking in Mrs. McGee. It's your husband," he announced. "Need to get dressed now."

I blinked over and over again, until his chin sprang up and went back into place.

"Mrs. McGee?" he hesitated.

"Yes, I will," I said, reaching for my clothes.

As soon as he left, I laid the delicate lines of knitting on top my pillow, careful not to tangle them or lose a stitch from the needles. In front of the blurry shatterproof shine they called my mirror, I examined the ever-so-faint tan line running above my breasts and the ivory smooth skin of my belly and breasts. I started to comb a lump of hair, streaked with silver now, until I remembered it wasn't Hank who was coming for me. It was only the man who wanted them dead. I tied my hair into a loose bun and pitched the comb across the room, pulled the door open and stepped into the bright light of the hallway, and marched straight toward the imposter.

I only wish I could tell you what happened next. The memory was erased—by the evil ones, no doubt. What I can tell you is my real husband would've responded to my nakedness with untainted pleasure. He would've taken me in his arms, gently cupped my breast, and kissed me with such gentle, burning passion that the pull between us would've been unstoppable—like a magnet to steel. We would've made love the way we always did.

But that's not what happened. That, I would remember.

I only know I would've done anything to save Hank, and Zetty. Anything at all.

And, by the grace of God, somehow I did.

The Weight of Expectation

Between the crack of the window and rear view mirror, I finally spotted him. A man with a quick step who was undeniably, without a doubt, my Father. But something wasn't right.

Mother wasn't with him.

Father veered away from a woman in a white cap and dress, and trailed a different footpath alone, his steps taut and unyielding as he approached the car. Maybe he was coming back to get me. It was a hopeful idea that evaporated almost as fast as it came. Father seemed ill at ease, his eyes centered on the ground. He was bothered by something. Even his hair was disheveled. I forced myself to breathe when my stomach sank downward. I wondered if Mother had this sinking feeling at some point, too.

As soon as Father unlatched his door, disappointment poured in. He folded himself into the driver's seat, remaining steady and composed even though I felt the car flood with heartbreak.

Father put on a facade. He tried to appear as if everything was as it should be. As if everything made sense. As if Mother could be getting a few more things, the woman we used to know and love, and would be out in no time to come home with us.

I tried to pretend everything was fine, but I knew it

wasn't. I didn't know how to do what he did. I wasn't good at it—pretending things were normal when they weren't.

The car filled with an awkward, foreign energy.

"Well?" I asked tenuously.

"Yes, I'm sorry," he said like some official. "There was a misunderstanding." He turned the key and cranked the engine over.

I didn't know what to say. Even if I had, I couldn't. I felt anaesthetized. Like I'd been gassed by whatever he brought into the car with him.

"Next time," he choked a little, "she'll make it home."

"But not for Christmas?" *The decorations,* I thought, *we did them all for her.*

A crack appeared in his tone, "I'm afraid not, Zetty."

And I knew then she was still sick. And I hoped it wasn't my fault. Because I hadn't prayed for her.

And I also knew I never wanted to decorate for Christmas again. I was done dragging out one-hundred-year-old glass ornaments, and thousands of all-blue lights, tangled up in knots with one blown bulb that shorted them all out, and plastic-wrapped candy canes, cracked with age, and tinsel—the ridiculous single-strand icicles—and a cross that had purple blinking lights that drove me insane because they never, ever quit, and rolls of green and blue garland that shed worse than Tuffy, and angels made out of hard foam and glitter flying through the air like fat fairies, and sharp pine cone wreaths that hacked up my fingers just pulling them out of the box, and carved nativity statues, with bright painted faces (so phony!), and red wooden sleighs made into candle holders that were full of melted wax from the sixteenth century, and six-foot-long posters of jolly old Saint Nick. Ho. Ho. Ho. I didn't care if I ever saw any of it again.

Even though they were all things I loved before Mother left.

Father cleared his voice several times before he finally said more. "It's complicated, Zetty. I'm sorry I got your hopes up." His words were cloaked in secrecy again. "There are just some things you can't understand yet."

"That's not true!" my voice cracked, something, no matter how I tried, I never seemed able to control. "You said she was coming home."

"I believed she was," his voice was so serious. "I had faith the good Lord would make it happen."

Well, that was your first mistake, I thought.

I wondered how snow could happen in Windansea but a simple thing like getting Mother home couldn't. Slushy clumps of ice fell through the air once and everyone acted like gold was dropping. It never stuck to the ground, but they canceled the whole day of school anyway. The excitement was too much for everybody. Like a miracle or something.

More than anything I had wanted Mother back. I wanted to fly out of the car, leap into her arms, and hold on for dear life. This wasn't what I wanted. I tried to tell Father that, but the words got caught high in my throat and cut my voice off. The gap continued to expand between us, like a monster sinkhole.

Father drove across the hospital grounds like we had nitroglycerin in the back seat. We crept past acres of mani-cured perfection. We passed a formidable white fountain curling cascades of water, a pond—the colors dark and mossy with lily pads stretched across the surface, and gardens containing dozens of blooming hibiscus bushes, ruby-red like Dorothy's magic slippers.

The scenery proved to be a temporary distraction. Before long, a strange sensation crept up my craw and the next thing I knew I was screaming at Father. "I want to know what's wrong!" I started to cry. "Tell me please. Just tell me what happened."

Still, he said nothing. Not one word. He simply took one deep, shuddered breath and kept driving.

I didn't feel like I mattered at all anymore.

I turned my head toward the window in search of uncontaminated air. My stomach twisted at the thought it could be in me, too. Whatever she had. I didn't lock my car door. I wished it would fly open and the gruesome vision I had on the way there would come true.

And just like that we left the palace with pillars I thought was meant for queens.

CHRISTMAS CAME AND CHRISTMAS WENT—SEVEN MORE times. Mother wasn't there for any of them.

Naturally we quit decorating. Father told everyone it was because we wanted to focus on the real meaning of Christmas: the birth of Jesus. "Oh Yes. Let's," I told him, because I had no intention of wrangling with his pain-in-the-ass icicles ever again.

Gradually, a 'new normal' settled over our lives even though it was fake. Mother's disappearance was anything but normal, but Father kept up the act. His psychological vault of secrets remained locked and my resentment towards him only built with each passing year. It wasn't until I turned seventeen that something shifted. My anger finally went rogue and ripped open the wounds of our relationship.

That's when I decided there was no going back. Only forward.

Part Two

1971–1972

Let a joy keep you.
Reach out your
hands
And take it when it
runs by.

—Carl Sandburg

UNFOLDING SECRETS

IT WAS JUNE, 1971, WHEN A FIVE-DAY HOT SPELL BROKE all previous records going back at least one hundred years. Even the ocean climbed to bathtub temperatures, making it a brewing pot for jellyfish. The lifeguards issued a red-flag alert, warning beach-goers to stay out of the water. That year was etched in memory like none I've lived through since. I was only seventeen, but once again my heart completely altered from the inside out.

We baked in heat. Gabe and I dipped our cotton tie-dyed scarves in iced water, wrapped them around our heads, and then sat bra-less in muslin halter tops directly in front of a high-speed fan, when the phone rang. The Taylor house was buzzing with commotion as usual, which was always music to my ears.

"Zetty! It's your dad." Gabe's mom stretched the gold-coiled cord out as far as she could and held out the receiver when I sauntered into the kitchen. She had a bright yellow pin on her cotton blouse, with words in royal blue that read, "Uppity Women Unite." Scarlett was a women's libber. She predicted that the old revolution, started by suffragettes, was about to catch fire again and become a new women's movement. To help kick things off, she burned some of her bras to protest and further the cause of equal rights. She told her husband, Dennis, she was going to college to become a career woman whether he liked it or not.

Even though we all thought she was way too old, she did it anyway, and at thirty-nine became a therapist for people who needed to pound pillows with rubber bats, scream, and then roll around in a fetal position to make themselves feel better. She called it "inner fetal recovery work," and said it released people's hang-ups when they did it.

I asked Gabe, "Why on earth would anyone want to do that?"

"Because," she explained, "they are under the mistaken belief that it will help them find themselves. And," she added like a know-it-all, "they're desperate."

"You'd think there'd be an easier way."

"You would think," she put in drily.

That was the point when Gabe always rolled her eyes around and bent her mouth crooked to the left.

Dennis said, "Darlin', if you can get people to give you money for that, you're smarter than I think." And Gabe's brother just made a joke of the whole thing by prancing through the house shrieking, "Dear God, where's my rubber bat? I need to pound my pillow!" Then he curled up into a fetal position and rolled around like he was possessed by spooks.

That was the first time I heard such robust laughter come out of Dennis when he didn't have a beer in his hand. I admit it was funny, but I didn't laugh on account of not wanting to hurt Scarlett's feelings. She shrugged it off, but still. At least she was trying to help people who had problems.

I've often wondered if torching a few bras and pounding a few pillows in the fetal position might have helped Mother. It seemed to do wonders for Scarlett.

I clumsily took the phone out of her large, red oven mitt. "Thanks Scarlett. Hello?" I walked closer to where the phone was mounted on the wall and tried to stay out of Scarlett's way. The hum of electric air in the background made me speak louder than usual.

"This is your dad, Zetty."

"Oh, I know," I said like a smart-ass.

Shredded beef and onions, seasoned with Mexican spices, snapped on the stove and filled the kitchen with the aroma of home-cooked happiness.

"Honey, you've been over at Gabe's an awful long time. Shouldn't you be coming home?"

"Scarlett and Dennis said—"

"You mean, Mr. and Mrs. Taylor," he corrected.

"Riiiiight. Well, they said I'm welcome to stay for as long as I want. Whenever I want. Including dinner."

Scarlett was chopping tomatoes on the cutting board, grinning in approval.

"That's very nice, and I'm sure you'll thank them, but I'd like you to come home now."

The window over the kitchen sink was cranked wide open and a wasp the size of a small beast flittered against the screen. I flicked it with two fingers, just to piss it off. "Gabe really wants me to stay for dinner. We're having tacos. Real homemade ones. I'll eat fast and come home." I decided to whine in case it worked, "Pleease?"

With every flick I smacked against the screen, the wasp grew bolder, spoiling for a fight. Then it went ballistic, slammed itself against the screen in a frenzy, just to piss me off, so I flicked even harder. I clamped the window shut and trapped him, pleased with my ingenuity and satisfied he would die a long, slow death. Another Max Mean moment, I realized, but I felt justified. They sting people just because they can.

"I just wanted to share some good news, that's all," Father said.

The wasp wormed its way through a crack, like a snake, and came flying at me. I screeched, dropped the phone receiver. "Kill it! He's in!"

Scarlett pitched her oven mitt at it, grabbed a dish towel and started swatting; she missed with every swing, so I screamed more. When it dive-bombed into my head two times, Scarlett started screaming, and then we both ran around screaming together having no idea how to make it stop.

Gabe lumbered in like a cop surveying the scene. Her waist-length hair, the color of roasted coffee, fell shimmering in a straight line—her olive complexion and brown eyes popped against the rose painted wall behind her. I wouldn't have been the least bit surprised if she had pulled a pencil from behind her ear and flipped open a notepad to document the situation. She didn't say a word. Just picked up a whole tomato, gave it a little toss from one hand to the other, squinted at the small beast, now flailing against the cupboard door, took aim, and then pitched like she was outing someone trying to steal first base.

Bull's-eye.

The legs crumpled, and the corpse lay soaking up to its antennae in pulverized red slop.

"Thank God!" breathed Scarlett.

Dennis walked in just in time to see the splat against the cupboard, "What the hell is going on in here?"

Scarlett swooped her arms around Gabe. "She saved us. We had a wasp on a rampage."

In a sissy voice, Dennis mocked, "We had a wasp on a rampage." Then he shook his head, and dropped his voice again, "Women!"

"Yes, Dennis," Scarlett piped up. "That is correct. We are women. And that thing was a maniac; you should have seen it! It was out for blood—Zetty's blood! Slammed right into her head over and over again! The thing was possessed. Absolutely deranged."

"Yeah!" I said. "Yay, Gabe."

When the furor died down, I helped Scarlett wipe clean the pine cupboard, Formica counter, and tile floor, then remembered the phone.

I grabbed the receiver dangling just off the floor. "Dad! Gabe just killed a wicked, maniac wasp with a tomato!"

He laughed. "So, I heard! Okay," he said, resigned to the idea. "Stay for dinner and then come on home. My good news can wait."

"Okay." I forgot all about tacos and killer insects and wondered if I'd won something. And then it registered—I had actually heard Father laugh. He never laughed. Not in a long time, anyway.

AFTER GABE AND I DID THE DISHES, I SPRINTED AROUND the curve of the cul-de-sac, across the street, and burst through the front door—all the wind knocked out of me. Father was sitting in the recliner watching the evening news.

"Is it something about Mother—your good news?" I knew better than to expect it, but I always did. He had laughed, after all.

"No honey, but Aunt Julie has invited you to stay with them for a few weeks." He pushed back the recliner with a thud. "Isn't that nice?"

Not really, I thought, but asked, "Why?"

"Well, she thought you might like to have a visit with family. That's all."

I had flown there once years ago on an airliner from

hell. *Never again.* "We have family," I said.

"Hardly. You know your other aunts aren't anything like Julie."

"True." I rolled my eyes. "I basically have an aunt a thousand miles away, no grandparents, and no mother. Seeing Mother would've been the good news, Dad. Not going to Aunt Julie's."

"Zetty," he said sternly, "you should appreciate your Aunt Julie. She's always been there for you."

"We haven't seen her in ages, Dad. And she's not my mother."

"Zetty."

"Look," I interrupted, "I love Aunt Julie. I always have. But when you said you had good news, I just thought maybe—" I sat, pulled off my bandana and wiped my neck with it. "Never mind." I huddled next to Tuffy on the davenport.

"Zetty, the good lord will bring your mother home when he's ready."

I shook my head in disgust. "Unbelievable."

"It's not for us to know when, Zetty."

My mouth gaped open, but I shut it before something freewheeled itself out that would send me straight to perdition. *It's not for us to know.* I wasn't buying it. Of course it was for us to know. Including me!

"I heard you tell Aunt Julie she didn't want to come home." I said it as if I had planned to, which was the surprising thing about it, even to me.

"That was a long time ago," he said, clearly flustered.

"I know more than you think."

"It was wrong to listen in on our conversation."

"I also heard you say there were plans to move her to New York. What about that?"

"That's for her doctors and me to handle, Zetty."

He should've seen the steam jetting from my head, but didn't say a thing about it.

"I haven't asked you anything in a long time, Dad." I took a moment to fill my lungs with newfound strength. "But I'm seventeen now. Come on." I exhaled. "If she's sick she has to have a diagnosis. I want to know."

"No, she doesn't. I won't have your mother given some meaningless label she'd have to carry for life. I won't allow it."

"She's already been gone for life."

Father sank into silence.

"Why did you stop going to see her?" I challenged.

Father pulled a hankie from his front pocket and blew his nose. By the time he had rummaged through both nostrils, I knew he wasn't going to explain that either. He used to come home from seeing her and once in a while he'd say, "Your mother loved the painting you did for her—I hung it up immediately. She's fine and says hello." Now really. How fine can a person be waking up every morning for years in a hospital? If he had been telling the truth he would have said, "Your mother is alive, but still doesn't know up from down." And if he cared, he might have added, "She's sorry for leaving you."

After she left, I used to stand at my easel with a plate full of acrylic paint and imagine the landscapes she might recognize—the places that would help her remember home, and me. I poured myself into every scene Father gave her. I hoped those paintings would help her want to come back.

I took in extra air to reinforce my backbone, "Did she leave, Dad?" I hoped he'd be sick of questions, and finally give in. "You stopped your Sunday visits a long time ago."

Father's face froze and I thought I noticed guilt on it, too. "I've tried to do what's best for her, Zetty," he said weakly.

"Did she go to New York? Is that what happened?"

"She's getting better, Zetty. That's all that matters."

"Getting better?! After *eight* years? What the hell," is all I could say.

"Zetty!"

I fully admit I enjoyed seeing the shock on his face when he heard me curse. It was exactly what I intended. "You still speak to me as if I'm a child," I said. He started to deny it, but I kept going, "You do, Dad. It's ridiculous."

"I know you're not a child, Zetty. But at seventeen, everyone thinks they know everything. You think you've got life all figured out, but you don't. Someday, you'll see what I mean."

"Speak for yourself," I told him.

He wasn't entirely wrong, of course. But he wasn't entirely right, either. I only know that the very essence of who I was at seventeen is still who I am today. I realize everything else grows old and changes, but the soul is ageless.

Father continued to alter into someone I no longer recognized. It didn't help that he wore denial like a pair of thick glasses. It evidently changed his perspective to something he liked better than the truth. His eyes lost their sparkle, his attention turned farther away from me and rested solely on building his airplane. The Great Wall of China finally slammed down between us. He pushed me away and distanced himself so fully, I barely felt related to the man. At seventeen, I realized, I had lost my father, too.

I straightened the throw pillows on the davenport, folded the lap blanket into a perfect square and with both hands on my knees pushed up. "Please tell Aunt Julie thanks, I appreciate the invite, but I have too many plans this summer. It's not a good time, Dad."

THE INFLUX OF HORMONES, MISERY OF CRAMPS, ONGOING
practice in the theatrical arts, and constant stream of Joni
Mitchell songs, fueled my strong-minded goals for independence. Rebellion seemed a power worth possessing, then.
But the sometimes snarky behavior I inflicted on Father
wasn't entirely warranted. I just didn't know it yet.

I heard Father drag a stool across the concrete floor in
the garage. After he snapped on the radio to the twang of
his favorite country station, I slid into the lap of Mother's
piano. The ebony finish, decadent to the touch, was pure
solace to my senses. Especially the fragrance. Like climbing
into the embrace of crisp laundered sheets, or breathing the
air caught between rows of fresh-cut Christmas trees, or the
scent of Mother's arms with a Coppertone tan. Pianos, like
people, have their scent, too.

I relaxed into the keys and lost myself. The outside light
of day dimmed, the sun sank below the horizon, and the
room slowly darkened. I continued to play, my eyes straining to see the black keys. I liked playing in the dark. It made
it easier to hear what I wanted to create. Except for Gabe and
Tuffy, no one knew I played piano by ear and composed my
own music. And if it didn't make me cry, I knew it wasn't
good. When it came to music, I was syrupy sentimental.
The first time Mother played Beethoven's *Moonlight Sonata*,
I collapsed on the sofa behind her and wept.

"Zetty," Mother said with care wrapped around her voice,
"Honey, are you okay?"

"Don't stop. Keep playing," I said, as if my life depended
on it.

She went right back where she left off and kept glancing at me to be sure I wasn't too big of a mess. The pure beauty of it stirred something so deep inside me I couldn't explain it.

"I understand," is all she said to me afterward.

That night I felt the tone solid and strong beneath my hands. I relaxed as each note, full of mourning and beauty, left the yellowed ivory keys, lifting into the evening air, like sweet jasmine floating on a warm breeze.

THE NEXT MORNING, I UNCOVERED A PIECE OF TRUTH— evidence that started to answer some questions. I hated what I discovered, but some things began to make sense. I thought I finally understood why Father pushed me away.

I flipped on the light switch in the den; the smell of burnt dust saturated the air. I cranked the window open and sun poured in through the patterned, cut-out lace panels floating over the window. A kaleidoscope of fractured shapes danced on the opposite wall whenever the breeze sifted through the screen.

Father was donating blood again. He always considered it a privilege. He never complained about jury duty, either. "Always remember to give back, Zetty," he used to say. "It's our civic duty." I admired him for that. But at the time I didn't give him much credit for anything.

I was snooping through drawers filled with family memorabilia just for something to do. I sat cross-legged on the beige carpet leafing through Christmas cards, black and white photos of mother and father, baby pictures of me, postcards of lakes in Minnesota, and old souvenirs from family vacations. I shook the snow globe with Old Faithful inside, sorted the newspaper clippings about Father's time in the Air Force, and read the "Hints from Heloise" columns

Mother read religiously.

I found pages of Blue Chip stamps collected for years. One sheet was stuck to a yellow, tattered envelope addressed in faded typewriter ink to Mr. Harold McGee. The return address, from Windansea Community Hospital, Department of Medicine and Obstetrics. I pulled out a gauzy, coffee-stained piece of typewriter paper. My hands trembled when I unfolded it as if my hands knew before I did that this was forbidden information.

The paper had grown frail at the crease, soft like silk. I tried to hold it steady, but my fingers quivered, making the page jump. Sections were so faded, many words had completely disappeared. I glanced about guardedly, and then read:

May 4, 1949

Dear Mr. McGee,

I am responding to your inquiry regarding the risks of bearing children...wife's medical condition...incurable at this time, worsens with pregnancy...case review... caution you again about the extreme risks. I fully concur with the opinions of the medical team...It remains our conclusion that should Mrs. McGee become pregnant...likelihood of complications...severe illness....genetic transmission...permanent condition. We encourage you to consider another avenue...adoption, to meet your goals for parenthood.

Sincerely,

Dr. Graham Fr...
Medical Director
Windansea...Hospital

I studied each line two more times before my unsteady hands wrestled it back into the envelope. I placed it in the drawer and scooped up everything else sprawled on the carpet around me. I struggled to spring to my feet, but both legs had fallen asleep and no longer felt attached. Needles and pins started racing up my thighs but I still couldn't move.

"Tuffy—come here!"

He sauntered over nonchalantly, as if he had all day. I leaned against him, and lifted myself up on lifeless limbs. Tuffy braced himself dutifully while they tingled back to life.

I reached for the worn leather leash draped over the doorknob and clipped it to his collar. I stared into his eyes, waiting, wanting him to console me. "How ridiculous," I said out loud, and felt silly for expecting it.

My face flushed; I pressed one cheek, then the other, against the cold glass in the front door window. So much separated me, I realized, from the life I used to have.

I pulled the door tight behind me and latched it, performing the routine like a robot.

Tuffy and I headed west, my thoughts twisted around the words I had read.

"Stay with me, Tuffy." My legs stretched as long as they could, and I marched high-speed, until I found myself jogging through the streets and past homes I had seen all my life. I noticed nothing new, or familiar. I simply scurried to escape the truth, to try and outrun the facts.

Which as far as I could understand were this: I was either adopted or I was a terrible mistake. The first was impossible. Aunt Julie was there when I was born. She saw me come out of my mother with her own eyes. Plus, I had seen plenty of photographs of Mother at my age; we looked nearly identical.

The worry it could happen to me next was merited. I had read it right there in the letter: "genetic transmission..."

It was true then; I was doomed.

Tuffy and I reached the cliffs I had been coming to since he was a pup. I sat on my favorite ledge overlooking the ocean. My fear of heights disappeared there. Maybe it was because the ledge had fencing below it. I knew if I were to accidentally trip and fall, or give in to a crazed impulse to leap, I wouldn't get far.

Tuffy sprawled over the top of my feet, head up and alert to the squawking seagulls circling in front of us. The sound of the tide rushing in and out always had a way of changing my thinking; it made everything seem perfectly clear.

"I'm the reason, Tuffy. I am the big fat mistake. No wonder Father acts the way he does. He resents my life, and I don't blame him. I took her away; I'm responsible. Every time he faces me, he remembers who he lost, and why."

Tuffy and I sat for a long time. I honestly believe he knew what I was saying by the way he leaned into me, softly stroked my feet with his warm tongue, and gazed into my eyes whenever I spoke. It was as if he was trying to tell me something.

And then I heard an unfamiliar voice say right out loud, "You're meant to be here." I jerked around, but no one was there. No one was around anywhere. But it was someone's voice, loud and clear. It had to be in my own mixed-up mind making things worse. And yet, a seed of doubt remained.

I leaned down, inhaled the musty bouquet of Tuffy's ears—and when I hugged him, a wide band of love tightened around my chest.

When the sun melted into the sea, orange and yellow shimmered across the water. I watched the ocean drink the last color of light while a squadron of seagulls swept across the horizon like a curtain closing down the stage. I felt a couple of sprinkles hit my face and the top of my left hand.

But it didn't do more than spit a little, and then stop.

I decided to take the long way home. I realized for the first time in my life following a magnificent sunset, over the sea I loved, next to the mender of my soul, I felt sorry to be alive.

Marjorie

I USED TO END LETTERS I WROTE TO ZETTY WITH: *I LOVE you for eternity.* But as far as I know, I never sent any of them.

I was careful to hide what I wrote so the evil ones couldn't inspect my personal feelings. For years, I jammed wads of paper through the coils underneath my mattress or taped them to the bedframe where I knew the protective net would easily reach. Zetty might be a target again if they knew what she still meant to me. I couldn't risk it.

I'm not sure when the jumbled marks that came from my crayons started to make no sense, but when they didn't I simply spoke to her, instead. I had no idea it was so easy. When the room was quiet and the electricity ran over the building just right, I sent her my thoughts. Just like a telegram, I suppose.

Thoughts like, *I planned to always be there for you—I never meant for this.* And, *Here I sit, in and out of some strange world I hardly understand, and yet your memory is constant.* And, I warned, *it's for the best I'm still here right now; it's not safe yet.*

Of course I knew Zetty had grown, but I saw her in my mind as she was at age nine. It was impossible to imagine her any other way. And when I tried, the guilt was unbearable. So many years had escaped me. Years I promised to return and didn't. It was dreadful of me.

The currents were surging overhead just right that afternoon. I couldn't wait to connect with her. *You need to know I love you, Zetty. I still have enough sense left to know that, at least.*

And then, as if I had tapped into a supernatural power-line straight from the Almighty, out came this: "Zetty. You're meant to be here." I scanned the room. I was still alone, but the sound of my words made me think otherwise. They bounced around as if disconnected from myself, but they were coming from me. "Focus on what's right about life, not just what's wrong," I told her. "Beautiful things come when you stand in the light."

I should know, I thought. *I created her.*

And just like that, I went back to the first time she spoke to me.

Coming from Zetty's nursery were the sweetest sounds ever heard on the whole entire planet. Soft, high-pitched squeals and delicate cooing pirouetted in the air above her crib. Outside, train horns and the clickety-clack of iron on tracks sang like a lullaby across the canyons in the distance. Rusty-breasted robins chirped around the window like chimes. Perfect nap time music.

"My little bug," I said when she fully awakened, "a sweeter baby cannot be found." I gathered Zetty in my arms, her eyes staring into mine when I breathed in her pleasurable scent—soft as fragrant rose petals. She reached up, rested both hands on my cheeks, and held my face between her baby palms. Our eyes locked together when she vocalized something meant only for me. That it made no sense was irrelevant. The way it made me feel was all that mattered.

A loud announcement clanged down the grungy hallway outside my room and pinched the memory. "Attention please. Evening medications are now ready. Please proceed to the line for evening medications. Thank you."

I cracked open the window, pushed back the rumpled sheet and blanket on my bed, positioned myself on the edge and knit the air under a narrow shaft of dull light. I listened with all my strength, tried to will the memory back—coax it out of hiding, but the sound of my baby was lost.

I took my place in line for evening medications and looked forward to sleep under the sinking light of sun that cast shadows over my bed. Somewhere out there I knew there was an ocean sunset I had missed and I ached to find my way back to it.

GOING UNDER

THE FRAIL LITTLE LETTER WITH THE CAST IRON MESSAGE
soaked up enough guilt to fill an oil tanker. I considered
destroying it, as if that would undo everything. But I left
it there in the den, clinging to the insides of a threadbare
envelope, buried under the ancient ruins of our family
history. There was simply no way to change what was, so I
submerged the knowledge the best I could. It became the
emotional shipwreck in my life that nobody saw, but it only
sank so far.

My bedroom was in full morning light when I packed
my beach bag and made a run for it past Gabe's house. Not
that she would have minded my going to the beach with
Sue Willy. Gabe wasn't jealous that way. It was just that I
was feeling brave now that I was seventeen, and you had to
be brave to be around Sue Willy. Gabe warned me, "Just be
careful, Zetty. Sue Willy has a dark side."

Don't get me wrong. Gabe liked Sue Willy—a lot. So
did Scarlett. In fact, after we met her in the fourth grade, it
wasn't unusual for Sue Willy to be over at their house for
days. Her mother had a habit of disappearing for weeks at
a time. Sue Willy told everyone the same thing her mother
did: *she had to travel a lot being in rock bands.*

We all knew it wasn't true. Scarlett explained Sue Willy's
mom was following musicians around hoping to marry a

rich one. "Not a bad idea," Gabe offered. I wasn't against the idea, either. And no matter how long Sue Willy's mom was gone, at least she always came back. Unlike mine.

But being alone didn't seem to bother Sue Willy. She told me she didn't go for the "family" life anyway. Said she dug the freedom of not having authority figures telling her what to do. Her mom wasn't part of "the establishment" like other parents, she said, so even when she was home, they were more like friends. Sue Willy could do whatever she wanted; it was a lifestyle I was captivated by.

As usual, what Gabe knew instinctively, I had to learn through experience.

I dreamt about ways to leave home so Father wouldn't have to be constantly reminded of how I had changed his whole world, stolen his marriage, and taken away the love of his life. Maybe, I imagined, Sue Willy was my ticket out. Maybe instead of going to the beach we could leave today for New York. Sue Willy told me thousands of people were going to Woodstock for a psychedelic rock concert to make history. She and her mom were going, so, why not me, too? Maybe we'd all hit the road and never come back. And if Mother was there, maybe I'd see her, too.

But Sue Willy and her mom packed up that morning and left for New York without me. Their car only made it as far as Fresno, but even now, Sue Willy talks about Wood-stock like she was there. She lied about it so many times, she believed it herself.

So I went to the beach alone that day and ignored the number-one rule when swimming in the sea.

DON'T EVER TURN YOUR BACK ON THE OCEAN.

Even peaceful waves turn violent sometimes. That's what they say. The warning was printed on wood signs in at least three spots I passed that morning, but the truth is I stopped reading them a long time ago.

The words zipped through me at lightning speed and pounded in my ears. But, by then it was too late. The current had already trampled over my back and beat all the air out of me. My face grated against the coarse sand and I felt the sting of raw skin. My eyes opened to a slit, but it was like trying to see through the windshield inside the car wash. Everything was smudged.

And then the whole scene went pitch black—as in all-the-life-was-sucked-out-of-me blackness—and I knew I was on the edge of some supernatural realm. Not heaven, mind you. Not God, either. Just the real deal twilight zone.

White jagged lines flashed beneath my eyelids, springing around like a pinball machine. It's true what they say—you really do see stars before you pass out.

And then there was hollowed silence. Nothingness.

I relaxed into it. An acceptance that this was it. *Oh well,* I told myself, *guess this is how I'm going to go.*

No one was waiting for me anyway. Father wouldn't notice my disappearance. Not that much. Gabe had her mother and family. And Tuffy would forget. I read once it takes two weeks for dogs to lose memories of people and routines. Or was it just routines? I convinced myself he would survive.

Well, it was a relief anyway that there was absolutely no one to scream my name hysterically when my body washed up. And even in the best case scenario (say, I lived), there wasn't a mother to swoon and cry over the near tragedy of losing me. No one to wrap me in her arms and say how scared she was and then lecture me with the warning I've heard a million times: *Don't ever turn your back on the ocean, Zetty.*

Now really. How can you be in the ocean and never have your back to it? That was just dumb. And yet, at that very moment, pinned to the ocean floor, I appeared to be living proof there was some truth to it.

With another push of force, I started rolling in somersaults, flailing in a twisted ball of commotion. My head broke through to the surface where I drank in a gallon of air, and then gulped for more.

I was surrounded once again by the clamor of happy children, floating on a sea of noise. They clung to white foam body boards, shiny plastic yellow and blue inner tubes, and some ran to the outstretched arms of mothers.

Beach sounds have always reminded me of big city noise. Instead of honking cabs and screeching brakes and cars whizzing by, you hear the constant roar of unfurling waves, children squealing, and squawking seagulls. Instead of gas fumes, hot dog stands, body odor from herds of passing strangers, or burnt rubber and metal lingering in the subways, you catch whiffs of salty air, golden bulbs of seaweed that pop with a pleasant crunch underfoot, dry sand, crackling bonfires, and sun. I can smell the sun; I don't care what anyone says.

Even though I was nearly dragged unconscious out to sea, not one thing stopped because of me.

Except, perhaps the lifeguard who noticed something was wrong. Like a shot, I sucked in my gut and tried to look normal when I saw his binoculars peering at me.

People told me all the time I looked like Sally Field. They said things like, "You have the same mouth, the way you smile," and "You look exactly alike in the eyes and nose," or "Your apple cheeks look just like hers when you laugh," and

"Even your hair is the same color." I secretly knew it was true, but I didn't want to sound stuck-up so I acted shocked every time anyone pointed out the resemblance. I hoped I had her flair for acting, too.

The lifeguard was studying me. When he lowered his binoculars, I noticed a slight squint to his eyes, a Robert Redford kind of cardiac-stopping gaze that suddenly pressed in on me. And he was ready for action. If I could stop choking on salt water, breathe normal, calm my heart flipping like a fish, and just look casual, I thought I could stop him from trying to save me. Because here's the thing: I had to avoid a rescue scene. It would've been entered into his rescue log as the first seventeen-year-old in a near-death drowning who was saved in knee high waves. Slightly ridiculous.

When I later told Gabe about this whole mess, she asked why I didn't introduce myself and thank "Robert Redford" for being ready to save me. Then when I got to the part where I told her I was in knee-high water, she halted, "Oh. Well. In that case, you did the right thing." Gabe tells the truth. It's what makes her my most stalwart friend.

Sue Willy on the other hand told me, "Are you crazy? You blew it, Zetty. You should have let yourself choke to death so he could give you a 'mouth-to-mouth' smack-a-roo, and then faked a fabulous faint, southern belle style. And then dropped into his arms just the way they do in the movies, but not before you untied the top of your bikini so when you 'came to' he'd have to help you fasten it." That's what she said, because that's the kind of friend Sue Willy was.

I sauntered up the shore to my royal-blue-and-orange-striped beach towel, still spread out evenly over mounds of white sand and plopped down. I sat up and out of habit scanned myself for blood, quickly glancing at my crotch for signs of my period. It was all clear. I lay back and relaxed.

It was warm underneath me but the rest of my body was cool. Drops of saltwater clung to me in tiny puddles; they trickled down and startled me sometimes, like an annoying fly crawling over bare skin when you're trying to sleep. I heard my heart pounding so loud it drowned out the hum of the ocean.

None of the people there that day had any idea just how close they came to seeing my corpse float across their paths.

I decided to walk home and make myself forget the whole thing. I shook out my towel, slipped my Hawaiian floral shift over my head, and stepped into my hot-pink flip-flops. The sand was hard to hike through, as if I was still carrying the weight of the ocean current on my back.

But no matter how hard I tried, the warning, *Don't ever turn your back on the ocean*, kept swimming through my head. It's what I got for thinking I was safe. It's what can happen when you stop feeling afraid, even for a second. I had a mind-bending, head-spinning-off experience but like I said, it wasn't all bad. I found an original, albeit unusual, way to forget all my problems that day. At least for a little while.

Because I never forgot how peaceful it was to go under into nothingness.

Summer Lake

I BECAME REMARKABLY SKILLED AT REENACTING MY drowning experience for the purpose of escape and relaxation. I felt myself sink into the smooth silence where no lights or voices could intrude. I described it as "going under" all by myself with no help at all. I kept it quiet at first, but then it popped out on a camping trip to the shock and horror of everyone around me. Which I told Gabe was ridiculous.

Gabe and I were inseparable the summer before our senior year—three months on a charm bracelet. Sue Willy flitted around, accepting the open invitation to the Taylor home whenever she needed. Scarlett and Dennis knew she was living the life of a wild child and worried about her. She chose to party with her mother, so wasn't around as much as they hoped. I selfishly relished having the time with Gabe and her family by myself. Something Father didn't seem to mind either.

The moonlight swept across Gabe's bedroom through the open window, lighting everything in shades of gray. Sleeping bags and camping gear were piled near the door, ready to load in the Taylors' car before dawn. It was tradition. Every summer, Tuffy and I went with the Taylors to their favorite lake.

"Gabe. We leave in two hours and we're still not asleep."

"I'm aware of that, Zetty." Gabe sat up to adjust her blankets on the bottom of the maple bunk bed. It creaked and shook the frame all the way to the top when she turned to face the wall.

I rolled to the edge, hung down like a bat, and got an upside-down look at her. "Maybe we should just get up and forget it. We can sleep in the car, or when we get there."

"Or, maybe we could actually sleep now."

"But I'm wide awake. You know how I hate it when I'm the only one awake." I said it only whining slightly.

"Then sleep," she ordered. Only right after she said it, she bolted out of bed, caught her big toe on something and hopped like a clod, stumbling across the room. She reached the windowsill one second before falling flat on her face.

"What's going on?" I sprang up and smacked my head on the ceiling, but was pleased to see she was fully awake.

"My mom's car just started."

"But nobody's up yet," I said.

"Someone's backing out of the driveway." Her nose pressed flat against the glass and air gushed out her nostrils.

"Call the police!"

"Shhhh!" Gabe put one finger to her lips and held a hand up like a stop sign.

I hushed my voice and said it again, "We should call the police, Gabe."

With firm conviction she told me, "It's my mother."

After we heard the car rumble down the street, Gabe flicked on the light and startled Tuffy. When he saw me, he tapped his tail against the floor three times and then closed his eyes again. Gabe was wearing red flannel pajama bottoms with reindeer on them and a flannel shirt from a different set. It was light blue with chocolate cookies, two sizes too big. I had on my usual: a red and green flannel nightgown picturing wild horses jumping over cactus plants. Our hair was in sloppy ponytails, clumps of hair escaping the bands. I readjusted my retainer and Gabe pushed up the hot-pink-and-orange-polka-dotted sleep mask like a hair band.

"She snuck out to meet someone." Gabe said it like a known fact and began pacing.

"Who?"

Gabe's eyes narrowed; her pace quickened.

"What are you thinking?" I asked suspiciously, "An affair?" I was only a little thrilled when I asked.

Gabe switched the light off again and lurched back into bed. "My mother's not the type."

That's what they all say, I thought, but tried to offer a plausible excuse instead, "Maybe she went for ice."

"Oh, please," Gabe balked. "We should have stolen my dad's truck keys and followed her."

"We'd be in jail," I said. Neither of us had a driver's license, but that never stopped Gabe.

"Something's going on," she told me. "Trust me."

I did trust Gabe. I trusted her more than anyone.

THE SUN PICKED AT THE LOCK OF NIGHT; IT SEEMED IN AN instant the sky turned from inky blackness to a golden dome. We had only been on the road fifteen minutes, and already Gabe was fast asleep.

I could see Tuffy up ahead riding with Gabe's brother, Tom, and his best friend, Jack. A bumper sticker on the tail of Jack's yellow Volkswagen van said, "Peace, Love, and Surf." Their shaggy, sun-streaked hair blew everywhere. Tom had naturally loose curls that fell across his tanned forehead, the kind you want to rake your fingers through. Tuffy's head hung out the window, ears like flags, flapping in a frenzy, his snout raised high, catching the world on the air—pleased to be one of the boys.

Gabe wouldn't admit it—she never wanted to be seen as the boy-crazy type—but I knew she had a thing for Jack. No matter how hard she tried, I saw her face go soft and luminous every time his name came up. And what she didn't know was I had a thing for her older brother, but I couldn't tell her. If I had, she would have laughed and never, ever, stopped.

The soothing vibrations of the road and the hum of the engine put me into a mild trance. I imagined the ocean current pulling me out every time I closed my eyes—all my senses going under, the way it seemed Mother had. I felt her kiss flicker against my cheek, and then dissolve. Her memory swept away before I could feel her love fully come back.

Occasionally, I tuned in to Dennis and Scarlett, their voices fading in and out. He was listening to AM talk radio and she was staring out the window in a daze. Every now and then, her head tilted and I saw from the reflection in the window that she was writing something in a red spiral notebook. Gabe said her mom had decided to try and get published since she joined a group called The Wayward Women's Writing Circle. She had sent some things out, but didn't have any luck yet. Or no talent. We weren't sure which.

I heard Dennis give the radio a piece of his mind and lay into the peace activists. "Damn right that's the way it should be!" and "Hell yes, give em' the chair! Damn hippies." I think he liked to hear himself rant and rave. He seemed satisfied with himself in a wound-up, overwrought sort of way.

Dennis and Scarlett had managed to stay married twenty-one years so far. Gabe said they were opposite people when it came to a lot of things, but her mom said their bond ran deep and the strength of it pulled them through hard times, past their differences.

I always liked Dennis, even though he had a charm deficiency and went berserk sometimes. It was true he was impatient, and not an easy-going man. Tension rode around him like a hot electrical current. Still, I liked that he was sure of himself, and that you always knew where you stood with him. But Gabe was right. He wasn't the nicest-sounding man especially when he spoke to the people he loved the most, which was the peculiar thing about him.

For example, once Scarlett dropped the lid to a bottle of juice on the kitchen floor. He scolded her first and then lectured her for the next ten minutes about how floors get dirty from dropping sticky things on them. *Duh.* I thought, *What's your point?*

And another time I heard Scarlett disagree with him on politics. He called her "Hitler" and a "communist" when she announced she was marching in an anti-war rally. That was the thing about Dennis; you didn't know if you had seen the nastiest he could get, or if the worst was yet to come. A lot like Hitler, actually.

When we pulled off the dusty, pot-holed road and stopped, Tuffy leapt across Jack's lap, squeezed himself through the half-open window so fast he couldn't stop him. He crashed to the ground, took a roll in the dirt to spring upright again, and galumphed down the beach like a big, happy goofball. Then Tuffy launched into the glassy lake and set off an explosion of ripples across the water. His paws slapped the clear surface, legs kicking up a frothy foam, his head arched high, straining for the chance to bite the lines of water that dissolved, making him crazy. Tuffy's whole body quaked with bliss. I remember standing outside the car, staring with envy. It must be nice, I thought, to find so much joy from something so simple.

And then it started. Dennis was fired up like a missile. I thought he was joking at first when he yelled at Scarlett— "You can't wear those silly shoes here! What the hell were you thinking?" and "Can't you figure out how to open a chair? What's wrong with you?" and "Face the god-damned cooler the other way! Do you hear me? Jesus Christ almighty, Scarlett! Turn it the other way, what's wrong with your ears?"

It was foreign to me, this mean-spirited way of talking to family. Father never spoke a harsh word to anyone, as far as I knew. It took a lot to unhitch him. He didn't believe in being mean for nothing.

Gabe stuffed her pillow through the tent flap and groaned, "Here we go again."

As usual, Scarlett took the brunt of it. She stayed calm mostly and tried to reason with him, but there's no reasoning with men like Dennis. Anyone could see Scarlett was battle-weary from trying.

Gabe was different. Given the chance, she gave it right back to her dad, and when she did, things always got worse. The boys were off on their bikes and Scarlett suggested Gabe and I take a walk.

"Gladly," Gabe said loud enough to be sure Dennis heard. "Anything to get away from this." Her eyes were fixated on his face, even as she turned to leave.

Dennis sprang to his feet, ready for a fight. "Well maybe I need to get the hell away from this too, did you ever think of that?"

I couldn't believe he said such a thing to Gabe in the tone he did, or that he meant it. Anyone who knew Dennis could see the devotion he felt for his family, at least when he was in a good mood. I remember thinking at some point he would regret his meanness, the same way I regretted my own. Because sometimes you never get the chance to take things back. I knew he'd be sorry someday, and I was right.

Gabe snapped back, "Fine! Leave for good!" She spun around taking a shortcut down to the shore, lifting one hiking boot and then the other over bowling ball rocks until she got to the other side of them.

Then Dennis launched into another profanity-laced tirade. I followed Gabe, trotting along the shore in the direction that took her away from her dad the fastest.

"I can see why your mom likes to pound bats. I'd be doing the same, listening to that all the time."

Gabe thrust her hands deep into her pockets, and picked up speed. "He'll apologize, sweeten up, then she'll like him again. Works on me sometimes, too. He tells me, 'Oh, come on puddin.'" Gabe's voice turned sarcastic, imitating him in a sing-song tone, "'it's not that bad, you know I love ya.'"

I was out of breath trying to keep up with her pace. "Well, does he mean it?"

Gabe braked abruptly, plopped down on a fallen tree trunk across the sandy beach. "Sure he does. But he never changes. My mom will change everything else in her life except him." She swiped dust off her sleeve. "Maybe she *should* have an affair." Gabe pulled her right foot out of her boot, tipped the heel upside down, and shook until a small pebble dropped into the sand.

The air felt cold when the sun slid behind the hills. I sat beside her, zipped up my windbreaker, and admired the long streaks of mauve painting the sky, like silky scarves floating over the mountaintops.

"I don't get it," I told her. "Why does he have to be like that?"

She yanked on her boot strings, tightening them as she tied. "Because he looks at everything wrong. He's not a believer."

I cringed, knowing I wasn't either.

"My dad has no faith. I mean look at this, Zetty." Her eyes rolled over the horizon. "This is all the proof we need. But my dad refuses to see who God is."

"No one knows who God is. Not even you."

Gabe's head bucked. "Of course we do, Zetty. And we know he doesn't talk like my dad. We do know that." Gabe gave a ruthless tug to my arm. "Come on!"

I saw Tuffy standing behind the trees, eyes fixated on me. When we started to move, he sprinted out, rambled through the bushes and plowed into my legs, full force. I buckled to the ground, "Good boy, you found us!" He nuzzled my ears, poked his nose around my neck and started lapping in giant, lusty strokes. "Stop!" I begged, but he knew I didn't mean it. I succumbed helplessly, loving every sloppy drop of his attention.

Gabe pulled two marshmallows out of her pocket and gave me one. I ripped it in half and signaled Tuffy to sit, and held it to his mouth. "Here, sweet boy." With tail thumping and quivering lips, he delicately pried it from my fingers. He turned and sprinted ahead until we lost sight of him.

"Gabe, do you love your dad—I mean really love him?"

Her hands sank deep into her pockets, again. "Sure. When he's not being a jerk."

"So does your mom," I said sure of myself. "Even when it gets bad, no matter what, at least she stays." And then out of nowhere I added, "Unlike some mothers we know." I could almost taste bitterness as the words rolled off my tongue. "I needed my mom Gabe, and she never came back. I was only nine." It caught me by surprise, how cross I felt.

"I don't think she could help it, Zetty. Like that letter said, she was at risk for something bad."

"Only because she had me."

"Then why did she get pregnant?"

"I told you, I was a mistake."

"I don't know. Maybe someday you'll know more."

"Oh, I will. A lot more," I said decidedly. "I'm done with this."

"Done with what?" she asked. An uneasy caution dotted her words.

"With the charade my dad puts on," I said resigned. "I'm tired of secrets."

Gabe stopped and faced me. "I don't blame you. And I wanna help."

"Really?" I asked.

"Yes, I'm serious," she said. "Let's find out what he's been hiding."

"I think she's in New York. Like he told Aunt Julie."

"I don't know." Gabe emptied her pockets of jagged rocks and pinecones. "Listen, you found the hospital letter, Zetty. There has to be more. Think about where he hides things, and start snooping."

"Already have."

"Everywhere?"

"Turned the house inside out."

"How about his address book?"

"Nothing. I even went through the garage. And his car. But I just have this feeling." I halted.

"Go on," Gabe said.

"I know you don't agree, but I still can't shake this feeling that my mother's fine. Like she's in New York, but not in a hospital at all. Maybe living in lower Manhattan, auditioning on Broadway, or directing a play. She could be living a new life, and that's why my father won't tell me. I encouraged her to go back into the theatre, Gabe. I suggested it all the time."

Gabe folded her arms, and leaned back.

"If she's found a new life," I continued, "I'd be hurt, but I'd understand. I *would*! Theatre to us was like flying is to my father. I get it. I just want the truth."

"You absolutely deserve to know," Gabe said. "He can't hide this from you forever—not if we have anything to do with it."

Gabe's arm linked mine. Hostility was easier to bear when she carried it with me. And looking back, I can see it was the same for her.

"We'll find a way," Gabe said. And then we walked in silence, locked at the elbow, until the sky went black.

WE HEARD DENNIS AND SCARLETT LAUGHING WHEN WE reached the campsite. They sounded happy again.

"Welcome to my world," Gabe said. She stopped in front of our tent. "Tonight, we find out what my mother's up to."

"What?" But before I could ask more, she strolled past me to the campfire where everyone was sitting. I flashed Gabe a puzzled expression, which she mirrored back and then ignored me, as if to say, *wait and see.*

"Tuffy ate a supper fit for a king, Zetty," Dennis assured me.

"Thanks, Mr. Taylor." I sounded extra polite, hoping it might help him stay nice.

"Mr. Taylor?" he sounded perturbed. "Come on, Zetty, you know me better than that! Just call me Dennis, sweetheart." He chewed into a rack of beef ribs like Tuffy on a leather shoe.

I didn't know it then, but before long I really would get to know Dennis better than that.

Jack squatted on his heels, palms open to the flames, and Tom whittled a branch with his pocket knife for roasting marshmallows. Gabe and I grabbed hot dogs and chips off the picnic table, and Tuffy repeatedly dropped his yellow tennis ball at my feet. He lodged his warm body between my legs; his hint that he wanted to play. I threw his ball a short distance so he didn't have to go too far. Tuffy felt his arthritis after camp days like today, but he still returned with a gallop, dropped the ball at my feet, and flipped my hand up with his soggy nose so I'd keep throwing.

I saw him panting a little too hard. "Time to rest, Tuffy. Come lie down," I directed. He circled around one spot three times and dropped himself to the dirt with a thud. He let out a guttural grunt and exhaled fiercely through his nose, horse-like. He licked his chops approvingly and rested his head on paws coated in sand.

Gabe and I sat in the chairs closest to the boys. I kicked off my right tennis shoe and rested my bare toes on the top of Tuffy's head, his face sprinkled with gray hair around both eyes, like The Lone Ranger's mask. I circled my ankle around massaging his eyes, along his snout, and up through the middle of his brows again. Tuffy's eyes closed, but every so often he lifted his head so I could reach the favorite spot under his chin. It was faint, but we all heard him purring with pleasure. I pulled my foot back to balance the plate on my lap, aware that my doting on Tuffy that way may have looked silly to the boys.

Tom was almost nineteen, a grown man as far as I was concerned. He was loaded with the kind of self-confidence that made my insides swirl the way they did when I rounded the top of a Ferris wheel. Compared to the boys my age, I thought Tom was very mature. I could tell he had lots of experience being older by the way he poured himself a cup of coffee, checked the engine oil in Jack's van, and the strong way he handled the canoe. Even the way he sat on the tree stump whittling away made my stomach flip. Remember, I was seventeen.

It was when Tom raised his right leg and proudly forced out a long, unruly fart around the campfire that I remembered he was human. Dennis raised a beer in his honor and Jack saluted as if Tom had just raised the flag.

Gabe shrugged her shoulders, turned to me, and said, "Like I said, welcome to my world."

Tuffy settled in closer between my ankles and rested his head on top of my feet. Every now and then, he lifted up the bottom edge of my Levi's to find exposed skin to gently lick. Even when it was ninety degrees outside, and my feet were boiling, he did this very same thing. I never moved, because I felt complete with him connected to me that way. I wanted to get a bottle of pop, but I didn't get up because I was too relaxed, and I wanted to enjoy the warmth and love he was doling out.

"I want to share a dream I had," Gabe announced.

"Oh, good, let's hear it," Scarlett said. "Then, we can go around the circle and everyone can share something."

Dennis grumbled in a deep, smoke-charred voice, "Yeah, yeah, yeah. Ring around the rosy, posy. *Oh, goody.*"

Scarlett smirked at him and went on, "Let's share a symbolic image or feeling we've had in a dream and then analyze it."

"Oh—come on—" Tom droned in a not-this-again voice.

Dennis piped in, "Yeah, don't start with the mumbo-jumbo."

Gabe rolled her eyes and began, "I had a dream that was certainly odd. You, Mother, ran off in the middle of the night."

I aimed a horrified look at Gabe. She read me perfectly, but continued anyway, "You were meeting your lover."

I choked on a corn chip, Dennis made a wisecrack about Scarlett meeting some "Romeo," and the boys cackled like a couple of hyenas. Scarlett didn't move. She sat perfectly quiet, her eyes fixated on the fire.

"My turn," I said, desperate to change the subject. "I like to dream that I go under water into nothingness; I pretend I'm drowning, even if I'm not really asleep."

No one responded. When I looked up to see if anyone was listening, I saw five acutely disturbed faces peering at mine.

"What's wrong with that?" I asked, ready to argue if necessary.

"Uhhh— that's definitely twisted," Jack said. His face crinkled like he had just gotten a whiff of something bad, which maybe he had.

"Why do you say it like I have a disease? It's just a dream—sorta." I leaned down and started stroking Tuffy so fast I woke him up. He lifted his head and stared at me, too. As if I had just told them all I was communicating with Martians.

"Sorry, but Jack's right," Tom said, "you must have a death wish or something."

Scarlett got up and passed around graham crackers, a bag of marshmallows and chocolate bars. "We're talking about dreams, people. Move on."

I never thought it was "twisted," but I had to admit, it had a peculiar death wish quality about it. Apparently, I decided, I had just uncovered another abnormal chink in my personality.

Dennis hacked up snot from the back of his throat and slung it off his tongue into the shrubs. Scarlett cringed, Gabe slowly shook her head, and I took a deep breath trying to ignore the vomity feeling that stirred up in me. Then he tipped back his chair, both arms reaching toward heaven. His right hand grasped a shiny gold can of beer that glinted off the firelight, waving it in the air as if to make a toast. "Hallelujuah, Jesus!" he bellowed. "Group therapy is officially over!"

Everyone laughed, including Scarlett.

When Dennis closed his eyes, his hands rested on his chest like a dead man. Every few seconds we watched his feet and arms twitch. His head swayed to the left and then jerked backward. He began to snore. I sat on the dirt next to Tuffy, and gave him my lap as a pillow. "If you could be anything, Scarlett, what would it be?" I asked.

Without a hitch in her voice, she answered, "What else? A world-renowned psychotherapist."

Gabe leaned into my left ear and whispered, "There's a reason they put 'psycho' in front of it." I resisted the urge to laugh, but inhaled and choked again.

"I'm going to be a doctor," Gabe said with no hesitation. She bit into a carefully crafted s'more—nothing oozed out the edges or smeared across her face. Tuffy stayed close to me where he had a real mess to clean up.

I knew exactly what I wanted to be. Because at that age, I was sure I knew. The first time I put *South Pacific* on the record player something inside me split open. Mother agreed with Scarlett. "If it doesn't make you zing," she said, "don't do it. Everyone has to find the thing in life that makes them zing, or they won't be happy." Staging shows for the neighborhood had convinced me they were right, and I accepted that my mission in life was to follow that feeling no matter the cost.

The fire crackled and hundreds of embers shot into the air. Three of them landed on Tuffy, but I smothered them with the arm of my jacket, panicked at the thought of his fur turning into kindling. When I knew he was safe, I told them, "I'm going to be a modern dancer on *The Carol Burnett Show*."

And with that, the boys went wild and Scarlett politely said goodnight.

Tom and Jack didn't stop snorting until Gabe stood directly in front of them. "Shut your trap, Tom! And you too, Jack Parker. You should see Zetty dance! She's so good she was asked to perform at the fair with the Windansea Dance Troupe this year."

All three of us looked at Gabe in amazement. I was dumbfounded, but I liked the way this little fib made me feel. The boys didn't say another word and so I didn't either. Gabe always had my back and I appreciated the lengths she went to cover it.

The fire let out a loud snap, I slapped a mosquito against my arm, someone cleared their throat, and that's all that was said about that.

When Gabe and I crawled into our tent and shimmied into sleeping bags, I turned to face her. "That was a lousy thing to do, telling your mom about that so-called dream of yours. In front of everybody."

"I know, but did you see the way she reacted? I had to watch what she did."

"She did nothing."

"I know. Exactly."

"Well, what does that tell you?"

"Plenty." But Gabe never explained. She flicked off the flashlight, and jabbed me in the leg with one foot. "Hey, by the way, Zetty. You know that drowning thing you say you enjoy doing? Well, that's something you should definitely stop. It's not normal."

I flipped over, and had to think fast. "I can't believe you fell for that." I pushed the actress button and was so convincing, for a moment, I believed it myself. "People can't take a joke."

"Yeah," she said unmoved, "well, you might want to stop it anyway." She turned over, put her retainer in, and went to sleep almost as fast as she said it.

I had the uneasy sense that Gabe noticed something dangerous about my "going under." I tried to pay it no attention but I did wonder if she thought it was a precursor to mother's illness—and that's why everyone was edgy about it. Maybe they worried I'd go under and never come back up. Like Mother. I admit, it had crossed my mind, too. And so did the voice I heard at the ocean cliffs when the only living soul next to me was Tuffy. That, I decided, would never be prattle for a fireside chat.

A blast of air snorted against the dirt on the other side of the tent flap. I saw Tuffy's shadow with ears flexed forward, tail swinging, and knew he wanted in. It took several tries for him to curl up on top of my legs into the exact position he wanted, but by the time he tucked his head into the side of my knee, Gabe's breathing deepened into complete unconsciousness.

I could see the full moon through the netted window. It was lit like a muted sun, with lumpy clouds floating around it, like curdled soup. And I wondered if there was even the slightest chance that Mother had the same view, and in the same moment was watching it, like me. It came to me that night as big and clear as the moon—the realization that I still loved her. Somewhere, I wanted to believe, in the shell of my mother, down the back alleys of her mind, there had to be a woman who still loved me, too.

I stroked Tuffy's back when another question stabbed me like a dagger: will I ever see her again?

I was no longer a believer, but that night I prayed. It was a desperate act on my part, since I no longer trusted this particular form of communication. Still, I prayed in good faith, without faith. Just in case.

First, I prayed that Gabe was right. Maybe Dennis would be a nicer husband and father if he had some jaw-dropping religious experience. Maybe he'd stop pushing his family away, belittling them with snotty remarks, and stop yelling over spilled milk. Gabe said that kind of talk was a recipe for disaster in a family, and she could quote Holy Scriptures to prove it. Even though I wasn't technically a believer anymore, that much I agreed with.

Second, I prayed the same request I tried for years. That Mother would recover from whatever she had and would want to come home, even though I was convinced that one got shot down a long time ago.

The last thought I remember, before sleep scrambled everything up, was about Scarlett. The idea she might be hiding something chewed on me, until it burrowed down into a tedious, raw ache. The last request, in case someone was listening, was about her. At least, I prayed, let Gabe keep *her* mom.

I WONDERED SOMETIMES IF FATHER EVER MISSED ME, EVEN a little, when I went camping with the Taylors. If he did, he never said so. I imagined he cherished his solitude to work non-stop on his airplane when I left, so I never felt bad when Tuffy and I were gone.

I smelled onions and hash browns frying on the camp stove. I saw the crisp slant of the morning sun cut through our tent, and I let it filter through my closed eyelids hoping to slip back into a deeper sleep. In the distance, I heard the lake water lapping against a small dirt bank and Tuffy's jaws snapping clumsily at the waves from passing motorboats. I heard sparklers pop, sizzle, spit and children hollering, "Happy Fourth of July!" One rocket screamed into the air with an unimpressive bang.

Then I felt the dull, but noticeable, ache caused by a jagged rock piercing my left hip. I was lying flat on the ground after my blow-up mattress with the "life-time guarantee" sprang a leak in the night. I announced to Gabe that I'd been impaled. She didn't move.

Dennis was talking to the boys about carrying life jackets in the canoes. "You gotta carry them, one for each of you—and don't forget Gabe. She thinks she can swim, but we all know differently. Make her wear it."

"Yeah," Tom said. "I put in two for her."

Longing to go under into nothingness was almost a habit. But that morning, when I felt myself slowly rise to the surface again, a different sensation spread over me. It was a day, I realized, I wanted to be in. It was okay to wake up and breathe. The trees cast a pleasant smell; the fragrance descended on our tent like mild smelling salts, gently waking all my senses. I was going to fully live my day, in happiness.

It's still hard to believe it held such promise when it began.

I heard our tent flap unzip and Tom started barking

orders. "Get up! Let's go! It's the Fourth of July, what are you gonna do, sleep all day? Get out here or get left behind."

Gabe bolted up. "Excuse me, out of our tent! We aren't decent yet!"

Tom snapped back, "You'll never be decent, so just get out here so we can go." We heard the crack of twigs against the dry earth as he clomped away.

"Zetty," Gabe whispered to me, "I want to go with Jack in his canoe, do you mind?"

"What, and leave me with Tom?" At the very least it was a line worthy of an Oscar nomination.

"I know, and I'm sorry—but will you? Just this once?"

"Oh, alright. Just once," I said, feigning disappointment. I still couldn't risk the truth; she would have found the idea of my crush on Tom absolutely ludicrous. "Tom?" she would have choked. "Are you joking? Have you lost your mind? What could you, or any girl, see in my brother?" To prove her point, she would have spent the rest of the trip describing every dumb thing he had ever done. And so, I had no choice but to keep my mouth shut.

"You talked in your sleep last night," I told her.

"What did I say?"

"You told me to be careful. You didn't want me to drown."

"Good. I hope you listened," she told me.

We hooked our bras, pulled on shorts, and wiped the sleepy seeds from the corners of our eyes. Gabe's comb slipped through her hair like silk, while I wrestled a hairbrush through my mole-brown tangled-up knots—wincing, practically in tears from the pain of it all.

"Somehow we'll figure out where your mom is, Zetty. If she's alive, we're going to find her. Count on it." Gabe licked her eyeliner brush a couple times and twirled it around in the little plastic pot of raven-black paint. Her mouth dropped open as she followed the curve of her lower lid.

"I am, Gabe. Believe me, I am." My head punched through the top of my t-shirt. "We have to worry about your mom, too."

"No need. I'll watch her like a hawk."

She finished dressing, and I applied just the right thickness of eyeliner above and below my lashes. Then we painted our lids with white frosted eye shadow and matching lipstick in two minutes flat. Mr. Taylor called us ghostly creatures, but we paid him no attention. The look was all about "Twiggy," and we knew we had it.

After Gabe and I ate a farm-style breakfast, she jumped into Jack's canoe before any discussion could begin about it. Tom pushed ours off from the shore and hopped in just before the water reached his hips.

I paddled at the front, my eyes cast down studying the water. A parade of rocks and weeds and shadows passed under us, murky in places, and full of slimy things I didn't want to fall into. I had my life jacket under both knees for more cushion, because I fully expected Tom to save me in the unlikely event something should happen, as in tipping over or springing a leak.

This was Tuffy's favorite part of the trip, swimming along like the captain of our ship. Normally, I'd help him climb in and ride along with me until he spotted something to dive in for. Then he'd belly flop wildly through the air after it, return to the canoe, and do it all over again.

But this time was different. Tuffy slapped the water in circles and refused to follow us past the sand bar. "What's wrong, boy? Come here lovey," I sweet-talked. "You gotta help us win!" Tuffy seemed to want to follow, but kept stopping himself. He finally steered back toward shore, biting at the suds he kicked up like a fountain in front of him. If I had listened better, I might have heard the warning he was trying to give. The fact I didn't remains one of the greatest regrets of my life.

Tom shouted, "First canoe to the center island gets out of chores tonight!"

"Deal!" Jack confirmed.

We lined up the tips of our boats, when Gabe, in her pink paisley halter-top, called out, "Go!" I paddled as if someone's life depended on it. It was a helpful idea when I had to do something hard.

We passed Dennis who was sitting in his rowboat, fishing line in one hand, cigarette in the other. A gold "San Diego Padres" ball-cap rested low on his forehead.

When I turned sideways, I heard Tuffy bark his way back to shore, still complaining about something. I tried to stay focused; I wanted to show Tom he wouldn't be sorry I was with him. I gave it all I had and paddled faster, and harder, through water that sliced like creamy caramel and lapped the side of the canoe in a steady motion, caressing like a soft lullaby.

"No chores for us," I said. We beat Jack and Gabe by a landslide. I stopped paddling and turned my face to the sun and noticed for the first time that the sky was brittle blue. If I tapped it with a spoon, I was sure it would ring like expensive glass crystal. But, then I wondered where everyone else was.

Tom turned to look behind us, "Zetty—something's wrong."

Beneath the Sheltering Tree

It's probably nothing, I thought, until I saw a crowd circled around someone on the sand bar. People were in emergency mode; taking action like paramedics surrounding a car crash. Someone needed help.

There was a nervous fluting to Tom's voice, "Did Gabe have her life jacket on? Do you remember?"

"No!" My breathing sped up; it came in hot gasps I couldn't control. "I mean I remember that it wasn't on."

"Are you sure?"

"Yes! Your dad didn't notice when we went by. I was surprised he didn't yell at her."

"Hurry," he commanded, his voice strung out and shredded. "Damn it! I was supposed to be sure she put it on. Paddle hard!" My pulse pounded in both ears and a lump the size of a baseball wedged in my throat. I no longer swallowed without concentrated effort; every breath thick as wet cement.

I couldn't watch what was happening on the sand bar and concentrate on paddling at the same time, so I stared into the water and with each dip and pull I told myself everything would be okay. Gabe was fine. Maybe it was her arm, or her knee, or her ankle. It would heal in no time. With every stroke, I told myself everything would be fine.

And then when I looked up again, I saw Scarlett collapse to her knees, overcome it seemed, by helplessness. The crowd slowly parted, and there sprawled out on the sand, at the top of a grassy knoll, lying under the jagged shadow of one lone fir tree, lay Tuffy.

His golden fur was full of dirt, but it was my Tuffy.

He's okay, I told myself. I had to keep going, climb out of the canoe and push my way through the mud and up the sand bar to where he was. I had to believe he was okay, but the thought hovered weakly and rendered little strength.

Dennis cupped his hands around Tuffy's snout and began to blow. He pushed on his chest next and I swore at that very moment that I would love Dennis for the rest of my life, because he was saving Tuffy, and by saving him, he was saving me. Then I was next to him, leaning over his motionless body. And as if I didn't live inside myself anymore, I heard a stranger scream, "Wake up, Tuffy! Breathe!"

Scarlett's arm came around me, drawing me back toward her. She pressed the side of her face against my shoulder and squeezed a surge of hope through me. "Dennis got to him as fast as anyone could, honey. Tuffy wasn't even under the water that long. It all happened so fast."

But I knew it didn't happen fast at all. I believed Tuffy had been pleading with me, telling me he needed me. And that I ignored him because I cared more about a boy who would never think of me as anything but another little sister. My mind was on Tom, more than Tuffy, who never stopped longing for me, even as he slipped under. Tuffy accepted all of me; even the Max-mean parts that didn't deserve such a loyal dog. How could I not hate everything about myself? Every cell in my body knew I had betrayed the one I loved most.

I asked out loud, for anyone to answer, "Was he coming

back for me? Was he struggling to stay alive? Before he went under?"

"No," Scarlett told me. "He slipped under like he was taking a dive. He just never came back up."

Dennis blew into his snout again. He was determined to give Tuffy life, and for that alone, I forgave him for all his mean ways and hurtful behavior, past, present, and future."Just save my Tuffy," I whispered, half wish, half prayer.

Dennis caught my eye for an instant, his position never changing, but in that fleeting link, his face told me he was trying and that as long as I was there, he would keep trying.

And then a rush of certainty washed over me. Tuffy had stayed by my side, and only my side, since I lost Mother. He was a warm presence with a beating heart that remained with me every night, breathing soothing sounds around my face while we slept. When no one was there to read, pray, or sing to me at night, Tuffy kept breathing, and never left me alone. So, he wouldn't leave me, I told myself. He didn't want to leave me. It was too soon, and he had to know I wasn't ready.

But the two strangers on the scene stepped back. "Nope. I'm afraid that pup ain't gonna make it," one said, hands tucked under his armpits. And then, "He's gone," both declared in unison.

"You don't know that!" I screamed, the words sharp as razor wire against my throat. The men dropped their heads, slowly turned, tossed their condolences over one shoulder and left.

And still, Dennis did not quit. When he looked up at me again, I saw tears in his eyes. I didn't want him to believe it was too late, because I couldn't believe it was too late. And he did not give up. He kept going for me.

Dennis had a heart like a geode. It was a rough, cold exterior that looked like an uninhabitable planet of stone. It was hard to even pick up without gloves on. But crack it open, even a little, and thousands of diamonds sparkled on the inside and spilled out to anyone who needed them.

Scarlett would be a fool to leave him.

I walked away, taking exactly ten steps, and stopped. I said in my mind to an unknown God, *Please save Tuffy. Let me hear him breathe. Bring him back—let me turn around and see a miracle right before my eyes. Then I promise to believe again and never stop.*

GABE STOOD NEXT TO ME, HER FACE SO SOLEMN I HAD TO glance away. "I'm relieved it wasn't you, Gabe," I breathed. She had been crying, but sucked in air, calmed herself, and said, "Zetty—I'm going to give it to you straight."

Tears, hot as acid burned in my eyes. Gabe took another deep breath, "Here's the deal—Tuffy is gone. *Long* gone. But my dad won't give up until you give him the okay. You need to tell him it's okay to stop trying." She moved in close to me, leaned her head against mine, and then wrapped one arm tightly around my shoulders. Her head turned to face me, her words soft like feathers, "Let Tuffy's body rest now; it's time for him to rest." She inhaled, her breath turned into jagged shards this time when she let it out. "None of us want to let him go, but we need to. It's time," she said.

I turned, wiped the lines of tears racing down my face, and saw Tuffy's limp body, his paws flopping around like a rag doll, his eyes empty. I can trust Gabe even when I'm not sure of something. But I was sure then. She was right. I turned around and walked straight to Dennis.

I stood awkwardly, arms dropped at my sides, heavy and limp, like Tuffy's. "Thank you for trying so hard, Dennis. It's okay—you can stop. Thank you for doing your best. I'll never forget it. You don't know how much—" I couldn't finish because my throat shut down from a flood of emotion.

"Okay, Zetty," Dennis replied, resignation in his voice. Tenderly, he lifted Tuffy and moved him farther into the shade. I knelt and held him in my lap still feeling warmth in his body. I cradled his soft face in my arms, brushed specks of sand away from his eyes, and pretended he was asleep. Surely he would feel the comfort I was giving him, and would find a way to come back.

But he was still gone. And I knew it when I laid my face against his belly and felt the absence of his heartbeat. Wherever the part of Tuffy was that loved me, it was gone now. And yes, I believed it was his soul. Grief attacked hard and deep. I didn't make a sound even though I was crying. The waves of sadness were so powerful, I felt they actually had the strength to kill me. And I hoped they would.

A part of me held on to the miracle idea. The one where Tuffy came back to life, just like the story where Jesus raised a man from the dead. But the only gasps for air that rose up came from me. I rocked back and forth, holding Tuffy because it was all I could do. That, and apologize. If only I could have known when I turned my back to Tuffy, I was making a life-altering choice to never see him alive again. His last moment was watching me paddle away without him. The lifelong bond we shared was over. It was, frankly, unforgivable.

"Let's get him back to camp, Zetty," Dennis said. Tom offered to carry him for me, but I was clinging too tight.

"Let Zetty take him, Tom," Dennis said, understanding he was mine alone to carry.

Tuffy was heavy, but I was determined to bear his weight every step of the way back to camp. Tom walked near me, ready to catch either one of us I think. I imagined this must have been how Jesus felt lugging the cross, walking to his execution. It wasn't right for Tuffy to go under without me, I concluded. I should have been right there with him.

Gabe and Jack were talking to Scarlett when I stepped under the big tree shading our tent and collapsed with Tuffy below it. The warmth was nearly gone from his body and even though his eyes were as dull as tarnished metal, they were half open and looking straight at me. For a moment, my heart flipped and I thought this was it. The miracle. "God" was supposed to be able to do that sort of thing, so why not then, for me? It wasn't right that he didn't, but he didn't. Probably, I reminded myself, because God's not real to begin with.

I embraced Tuffy and erupted again, waiting for a critical organ inside me to explode.

I didn't know the mind and body were capable of doing whatever mine was doing to me, but to my disappointment, I was surviving it—physically anyway.

I fell apart in bed the night Mother left, but never like this. I felt a little guilty for believing I could drop dead over my dog, and not my mother, but after all, Father assured me that with a little more time, she would come home. It was there for only a moment, but a surge of longing to tell Mother came over me. She should know, I told myself; she loved Tuffy, too. And then as quickly as she did, the thought fluttered away and vanished. It was replaced by anger and the realization she wasn't there for me.

Scarlett told everyone to give me time and space with my boy. I was relieved, because I never planned to leave him. I would be there with him for as long as he needed me. I sounded like I was out of my mind, even to myself, but I thought it anyway; I planned to take him with me everywhere from there on. I promised him I would never let him out of my sight, or ignore him again.

I remembered Tuffy lying next to me after Mother vanished. Following the verbal lashing and little kick I gave him that night in the kitchen, it was a surprise to find him sticking so close to me. He climbed into bed next to me, holding his yellow tennis ball in his mouth, mollycoddling it as if it were his own flesh and blood. I felt a sharp sting of regret, asked for his forgiveness, but the guilt pressed like a fifty-pound weight on my chest. So, I let him eat a small bag of ruffled potato chips, and three peanut butter cookies. But it wasn't until I spoon-fed him vanilla ice cream—soft serve in a cone—that my shame fully lifted.

This time, there was no chance for atonement.

I don't know how much time passed before Gabe asked if she could sit with me and Tuffy. She brushed dirt away to make a flat spot on the ground and set down two tall glasses of iced tea with lemons floating at the top. I wasn't thirsty or hungry or tired. I just felt numb and heavy, like Tuffy.

Gabe was still crying, too. And I loved her for that, but I couldn't find the words to tell her. She asked if she could hold Tuffy, so I offered him like a sacrifice to her waiting arms. It wasn't easy though. Tuffy was turning heavy like cement. It took all of our strength to lift him into her lap.

"Wow," Gabe said, "He won't bend. I wonder why that has to happen."

"Because he's dead, Gabe." I sounded like her. He was stiff as a board. Now I knew where that expression came from.

"Well, he definitely is. I mean, there's no question really that he's gone. And Zetty, I'm sure he's in heaven."

The tears filled my throat again and I had to choke the word out like a chunk of steak, "Why?"

"Because golden retrievers are Christians."

"What?" This sounded like something stupid coming from Gabe.

"Think about it. They're loyal, obedient, happy, faithful, loving, wise, and at our service unconditionally. Everything we're encouraged to be, is exactly who Tuffy is. I mean, was." Shame was strapped to my back, tied up with guilt. "Well, then I'm going to hell, because I was none of those things to him at the end. I killed him." I dropped my face into my knees and curled into a ball, weeping.

"You did not kill him. He was old and tired is all." Her tone was convincing if I hadn't known better.

I lifted my face so she could hear the full confession. "No, that's not all. He tried to tell me but I didn't listen." I gasped for air before I could continue, "I was too interested in my own selfish life. I didn't go back to him. It wasn't like him not to follow me, but I didn't care enough to go back to him. This is my punishment."

Gabe raised up on both knees, scooted directly in front of me, then rested her rear on naked heels, both hands clutching my arms. "No. It isn't punishment. You were given Tuffy because you deserved him. You did, Zetty. And you were a gift to Tuffy. I've never seen a dog love a person the way he loved you. My dad says so, too." She squeezed my arms a few times and then announced, "We'll give him a funeral fit for a king and lay him to rest."

My back jerked, "What are you talking about? No one is laying Tuffy to rest. He stays with me, forever."

She let go and leaned back a little. "How's that going to

work? He's not exactly easy to look at anymore. Or simple to haul around."

"I want to keep him, Gabe. I don't care how stiff and fake he looks. I can't part from him. It would be wrong. I want him stuffed. I'm going to call a taxidermist and stuff him."

"A dog?" I practically heard her eyeballs rolling to the back of her head.

I wiped my eyes again with the back of my hand. "What's wrong with that? Why not a dog? I saw a woman once on television who did it to her cat. It sat right there in her living room looking as real as ever. Except for its position never changing, of course."

"I don't know, Zetty," she shook her head, "is that what you really want? Tuffy made into a stuffed animal, like Herbert? Tuffy looking at you with glass eyeballs and probably stuck in a ridiculous pose?" She ran her hand along his spine down to the tip of his tail. "I mean he was too real to make fake, wasn't he? Think about it, do you really want a dead Tuffy sitting around stuffed and staring at you all day? Personally, I don't think he'd like it."

I watched her pet Tuffy, as if he could feel every stroke. "It's just that if he's stuffed, even if he's dead, he's still here. If I bury him, well, then I never see him again."

"I know. But the part of him you really want to see is already gone."

I had an image of trying to warm my feet under his stiff, newly stuffed corpse.

"Yeah. It's a stupid idea," I admitted.

Gabe's face relaxed as she took another long drink of tea. But I couldn't leave it at that. There was more I needed to say. "I just want to go back and do it over. This time I would listen to Tuffy, take him back to shore, or pull him into the canoe with us. But I didn't. It was so easy, but I didn't do it. I knew he wanted to be with me, but I didn't go back. I rejected him, Gabe! I killed him! My oldest friend and the most faithful one I've ever had, next to you."

Gabe's eyes were fixed on mine. "Look. People never know what to say at times like this, Zetty. But I do. I know exactly what to say. So listen to me—you have to let this guilt go."

I was ready to salute her, this side of Gabe that was there again, the take-charge general.

"You didn't kill him," she said firmly. "You didn't know what was going to happen. If you would've known, you could've made a different choice. But you aren't psychic, you have no crystal ball, and you're not God."

And just like that something shifted inside. I was almost in control again. She continued to talk for at least five minutes straight and barely took a breath. She could've stopped much sooner; she had already convinced me. Gabe startled me back into the here and now, "Do you hear me, Zetty? I mean it."

Loud and clear, Commander, I was thinking. But I just looked at her and nodded.

She took a drink, a slice of lemon bobbing under her lip. "Okay, then."

We sat quiet. Gabe drew in the dirt with a rock, and I combed Tuffy's fur with a pronged twig. "I don't understand it, Gabe," I finally broke in, "it's not right that we lose people and things we love. It's cruel and I have to say if there is a God, I hate him for it."

It took Gabe aback a little, but not much. Her head straightened with confidence. "I'm sure God gets hated all the time, but I don't think this has anything to do with him. But I do think your bond with Tuffy was meant to give you a glimpse of what's to come. The kind of love we'll have in heaven. Have some faith, Zetty."

I've heard people say faith is like the wind. But think about it. When was the last time you felt faith ripple against your skin, lift your hair, press at your back, or spill over your face like a cool silk scarf? When was the last time you saw faith move a mountain in your presence, or watch it waltz through branches, or lift a blanket of heat when the temperature soared? Have you ever seen faith carve the sand dunes into sculptures?

That is exactly my point. There is evidence of wind, and not a bit of evidence of faith. As far as I could see, trying to find faith was like chasing the wind—downright point-less. It hadn't done a thing to help Father bring Mother back, either.

I heard what Gabe said, and I was amazed at how fast she could go from sounding like an army general to a real nun. Either way, things always made better sense when she got a hold of my tangled thoughts and straightened them out into a perfect line with one beginning and one end.

Gabe had no idea how truly brilliant she was. We were equals when it came to hearts, but not when it came to brains. The thing is, she never made me, or anyone for that matter, feel less than she was. She never put herself above anyone. And, in my opinion, that was the really brilliant thing about her.

I told "Sister Gabe" I was ready. I wanted her to officiate over the funeral fit for a king, the funeral that would lay my royal, precious king to rest.

I WAS PRESENT FOR THE CEREMONY, BUT AT THE SAME TIME I was somewhere else. Disconnected, the way Tuffy was. I appreciated the wildflowers collected, and prayers and honoring everyone did for Tuffy at the hole the boys dug for him. It was a long way from camp, but Tom made a cross that would help us find his plot the next time we came to the lake. In black permanent marker it said, "Tuffy McGee: 1958-1971— Gentle and True, Loyal Lover of Zetty—swimming in the lakes of heaven."

I wanted to leave before the boys put Tuffy's body into a large, white, heavy-duty garbage bag and laid him deep in the ground. But before I turned to walk away, I tucked Tuffy's tennis ball under his chin as best I could. Then I placed the brand new one I was saving for him right between his paws, only I had trouble bending his rigid legs to hold it against his heart the way I wanted. People tried to help, everyone's hands fumbling. Out of nowhere came laughter, my laughter— gushing like a geyser. Seriously, I doubled up and almost fell down. It was a sight; the circle of us fiddling with a dead dog's paws—trying to make him hold a cockeyed pose with his tennis balls. It hit me like slap-stick, and when I burst out laughing, everyone else busted up, too.

And then I went right back to crying.

Tom leaned over, and one last time adjusted Tuffy's front legs, and positioned the tennis balls so it worked. Scarlett burst into tears and Gabe followed, and everyone was right back where they started. Dennis wiped his eyes and Jack coughed a couple times.

Scarlett bent over Tuffy with a small pair of scissors and clipped a few chunks of fur from behind his ears. She slipped off his collar with the gold metal identification tag and license attached, and placed everything in a harvest gold Tupperware bowl. She sealed the ridged cover shut and handed it to me as a keepsake. I tied his purple bandana around his neck, and then quickly untied it and wrapped it around my own.

I don't remember the walk back or anything I saw on the trail. I do remember I peeled back the Tupperware lid half an inch and inhaled Tuffy's scent as if it were the only air left to keep me alive. I hurried and sealed it shut again to preserve his smell forever. The idea of being able to smell Tuffy for the rest of my life struck a chord of pleasure in me, and brought me a second of happiness. I tucked the bowl under my sweatshirt, where, all the way back to camp, it beat like a heart.

I returned to the same tree that had been sheltering my heartache all day. I planned to sit there in my beach chair, overlooking the spot where I last saw Tuffy alive. I saw his death happening repeatedly in my mind, which felt like torture, but I didn't seem to be able to block it. I heard joyful children playing on the other side of the lake and a dog barking now and then, too. They're happy, I thought, the way I used to be before Mother left, before Father grew silent, and before my Tuffy went under without me.

Dennis was the first one back. He knelt next to me. "Zetty." He said it so soft, even his deep gravelly voice felt like a down blanket surrounding me, "Don't think I don't know how much you loved that pup. That ol' hound was a good one. But sweetheart, it was just his time. You did nothin' to make it happen. Now you gotta believe that because—"

"But he was too old for all that swimming. I should've brought him into the canoe with us; I should've never left him, Mr. Taylor."

"Honey, for Pete's sakes, call me Dennis." His voice grew strong-minded again, "The only thing you're guilty of is letting ol' Tuffy spend his final day doing the two things he loved most: going camping with you, and swimming. The way I see it, you gave that ol' hound his final wishes. A send-off to be proud of. He outlived himself for you, and he knew it was his time. He went when he wanted, and how, Zetty. Don't ever doubt it."

And then Dennis wrapped me in his arms and let me cry.

EVERYONE WENT FOR A WALK BUT I REMAINED STATIONED in the same place, unable to separate myself from the soil where Tuffy's body last lay. Sacred ground, now. I was grateful to have the camp completely to myself and I planned to enjoy the freedom to scream right out loud whenever the mood might strike. And I intended to do it without a pillow.

Tom stayed behind just long enough to bring me some campfire stew in a little foil bowl. He pulled apart the top of it and the carrots, potatoes, and meatballs inside were so hot the steam rose up like a sauna for my face. I thanked him and told him I was going to let it cool off a little.

He sat down beside me. "I'm sorry I didn't see him in time, Zetty. I'm really, really, sorry. Jack is, too." It was the most sincere thing I ever heard him say.

"I don't blame anybody but myself," I told him.

"Well, you shouldn't blame yourself. My dad was right. Some things he really is right about." We both smiled.

He stood to leave, and I turned to check on the stew. I was a bit hungry and thought I could eat a little.

And then I felt Tom's face floating against my left cheek. His lips pressed gently and sweetly on top of mine. Magnet to steel. And he didn't stop, which was fine with me. He looked into my eyes and I came undone—entirely unstitched.

I was at the top of a Ferris wheel, floating. And it all felt heartbreakingly good. Pretty soon he was on the ground next to me. And he was still not stopping, which was also fine with me.

If ever there was a cure for grief that was it.

The Scent of Remembrance

IT AMAZED ME REALLY, THAT A KISS COULD SO POWERFULLY ease the ache of the worst moment of my life. It was as if my grief lifted up in mid-air, just high enough to make it easier to bear. But when I walked through the front door of my house, I felt a twinge of guilt for letting myself indulge in the reprieve it gave me. Tuffy was dead after all. Leaving camp without him felt nothing short of impossible.

The scent of him lingered in the living room. Father was in his recliner reading the paper. Sorrow poured over me again when I saw the sun mopping the floor, a big circle of it drenched on the spot Tuffy liked to stretch out on.

Father slowly folded his newspaper and carefully creased it into a napkin-sized square before he set it aside. I fell into the davenport, and he told me Dennis had given him the sad news and, naturally, it was okay if I didn't want to talk about it.

But here's the thing: I did want to talk about it. I wanted to tell him the whole story. I wanted him to know the truth. It took everything out of me to relive Tuffy's last moments, but I did it anyway. It was odd, but I felt like I would have been dishonoring Tuffy if I hadn't. I felt compelled to empty myself of the thoughts and images forcing themselves on me. Somehow putting the experience to words helped diffuse the shock.

Maybe it was just that simple; what you can't put to words, you can't put to rest.

Father sat silently, listening with one elbow on the armrest, head propped against his hand. His pointer finger rested at the outside corner of his eye and I saw him stretch it to a slant, trying to squeeze the evidence away. But I saw the glistening of wet tears anyway. He wouldn't let himself cry, but he was crying. Especially at the end when I told him about the burial. I skipped the part about all of us laughing over the ball. I don't think he would have found it funny, only because he didn't laugh much anymore.

"I'm still expecting him," Father said, leaning forward as he pushed himself out of the chair. "I keep waiting for him to come barreling through that screen door." He went to the coat closet, pulled out a beige cardigan, and put it on. "He sure was a good dog."

"Yeah," is all I could say before more waterworks put a choke hold on me again.

"It could've been worse." He walked to the television, turned it to Walter Cronkite, and reached for the hankie in his front pocket. He blew his nose, and wiped the insides of his nostrils like he was cleaning out bottles. "At least he didn't suffer. He's in a better place, now."

I looked up, incredulous at what I heard. "What makes you think that?"

He got situated in his chair again, and inspected my face. A thread of surprise ran through his voice, "You doubt it?"

"I was there!" I bounded off the davenport, rummaged through my dirt-covered backpack for the Tupperware bowl. "Of course he suffered! He's dead!"

"But he's in a better place—the good Lord has him."

I stood with hands on my hips. "Right. That makes it all better, doesn't it?"

He held himself calm and steady. "Well, of course it does," he said matter-of-factly.

Something pent-up inside me forced its way out. I paced back and forth in front of the fireplace. "Go ahead! Paint yourself a pretty picture, Dad, so you don't have to see things as they really are." I turned on my heel and embraced the dramatic quality of my words. "Tell yourself all the lies you want, about God, about Tuffy, even about your wife. But don't tell them to me."

Father shook his head, eyes downcast. He reached for the folded newspaper again, and held it in his lap without looking at it once.

"And I'm sick of all of this. Sick of the way you are. *You*, Dad." There was no stopping now. Rage kept building. "You're a liar! You've never been honest with me. Not once since she left. Not once!" And then someone pulled the plug. Just like that my anger lost all its steam. I was worn out, every word tired. I added weakly, "I'll never forgive you," but it wasn't very convincing.

Gabe told me all the time I should mouth off more often, so there you go.

Father was speechless. But there was a second or two when he glanced at me and something crossed between us. I remember seeing it, an expression of hurt—my words painfully engraved in the lines on his face.

I didn't want to hear or say another word, so I disregarded Father the way he did me. I found the bowl at the bottom of my pack, took another whiff of air out of it, clutched it to my chest, and moved numbly down the hall to my room. I kicked the door closed, crawled into bed with filthy clothes on, and made a vow to carry Tuffy's bandana with me for the rest of my life.

And I wondered if, deep down, Father blamed me for

Tuffy's death, too.

I admit, the temporary exodus from pain I took pleasure in with Tom still conjured up a little "yippee" in my heart when I remembered it. I decided then and there, if the opportunity ever came my way again, to sample even a drop of joy in the midst of heartache, I would go after it, hold on to it, and let myself savor it for as long as I could make it last. I realized, moments like that are minor miracles when one is trudging through the sludge of grief.

In the middle of the night, Tuffy used to sit next to my bed, lay his chin near my face and pant until his disgusting breath jolted me awake. I would roll out of bed in one fell swoop and help hoist his rickety old bones up into my bed. He would promptly sprawl out over every square inch of my sleeping space. I had to worm my way under him, and fight for the corner of my pillow and enough covers to get comfortable again. It was our routine.

And now life stood motionless, the empty rug a bitter reminder of Tuffy's absence.

The comfort and familiarity of all I knew in my bedroom was gone. Even the air was not right. It closed in on me. Suffocating and heavy like toxic gas. I've never hated my aloneness, or the darkness of the night, or the stillness surrounding me more.

I curled up on the edge of my bed into a perfect fetal recovery position and faced the wall. A large tuft of Tuffy's hair unexpectedly came into focus against the wood baseboard. I tumbled to the floor, grasped hold of it, got back into bed, clutched it against my cheek, and sobbed my heart out again.

LATER THAT NIGHT A WINDSTORM SWEPT THROUGH TOWN that made the swollen floorboards in my room squeak and the walls snap. Wind ghosts. When they came spooking, they were bone-rattling loud, tearing through the trees, whipping them into confusion and pressing all their weight against my window. Every now and then, an angry gust blew so hard I shuddered and had to cover my head—as if the edge of my sheet could save me. It's coming for me, I thought. It's after me.

The mother I used to know would've helped me through this. But that was back when I trusted the big fat lie that love never ends.

It took every bit of my courage, because not one muscle or nerve wanted to cooperate, but in between the howling wind ghosts, I stepped out of bed to click on the nightlight in the corner of my room. I tried not to need it anymore; I was seventeen for crying out loud. But I was a mess.

It was time for an appointment with Dr. Id.

No one knew I met regularly with a highly distinguished, well-regarded psychiatrist. Not even Gabe. She referred to Sigmund Freud as Sigmoid Oscopy and said all psychoanalytical gibberish was a "bunch of horse shit," so why tell her.

His initials stood for "imaginary doctor." That's right. Dr. Id was fake.

According to what I researched in the library, Freud said "id" represents the part of the personality that's impulsive, immature, and driven to immediate satisfaction—usually through unconscious drives. He said "id" wants to find pleasure fast, usually through food, or of all things, "copulation." I suppose I should have chosen a different name, but I never did. He was simply the imaginary doctor I created based on Gregory Peck's character in *The Three Faces of Eve*.

"So Zetty, what brings you here?"

That was the way I imagined all therapy sessions began. "I don't have a clue," I told him.

"Well, give me your best guess."

"I'm afraid. The wind makes me think about death." I pretended to be on a black leather couch instead of my bed.

"Interesting. Tell me more."

"My Tuffy is gone. My mother is gone. They both left me."

"I see. And how does that make you feel?"

"I told you already. I'm scared!" I readjusted my pillows, closed my eyes, and the biggest questions I had suddenly appeared. I asked him, "How does a person who you know loved you once just leave and stop loving you? Isn't it true if that person still loved you, they'd want to come back? Especially if that someone was your mother?"

"Go on."

"The bond between Mother and me was severed in an irrational, random act of violence where, without warning, she was snatched out of my life forever."

"And?"

"It was like an abduction where Mother's soul was simply ripped out of her and replaced with aliens. They painted her face a pale and sickly shade of yellow, fake and pasty thick like wax. It scared me, the way she looked that day on the sidewalk. I hated thinking of her as a monster, but the truth is, I did a little."

"I see."

"No, I don't think you do. In fact, you don't get it at all." Since I had nothing better to do, I dropped my thinking like a lump of dough and rolled it out for him: "Mother went away, Father doesn't talk, my Tuffy died, I'm still afraid of windstorms, and I think I'm developing a gruesome fear of death. I mean, what's the point of life if this is all that happens?"

I heard Gabe in my head; *Put it in a blues song, Zetty.*

"I'd like you to think about that and we'll talk about it next time," Dr. Id said.

And that's the way it always went. No real answers, just more questions. The good doctor never came through for me. From what I read, it sounded like all psychiatrists operated this way. Which is why I vowed never to go to a real one.

At least Dr. Id listened, I told myself. It was something.

When the wind calmed, I laid my cheek against Tuffy's bandana, still saturated with his scent. I like to think he was there. I imagined he was until I finally fell asleep.

Marjorie

THE WORST THING THAT CAN HAPPEN TO A PERSON IS TO be different. Believe me, I know.

I tried to remember why I was. I searched for clues from my past that might explain it. Was it really so odd, for example, to see flying squirrels outside my bedroom window swinging through the trees like Tarzan?

Well, yes, I decided. It was.

I sat on my bed absolutely entranced by a circus of them when an orderly interrupted the show and my knotted up thoughts. "Time for group, Marjorie," he announced, "Come on down!" he said like the TV show that droned on in the group room every morning. "Doc has something special for you, today." He winked the way he always did. Like a real joker.

This was my life now. I was supposed to sleep, walk, shower, swallow pills, socialize with others, and eat. Simple, yet more complicated than you can ever imagine.

"Pills will help erase the voices," they told me. I swallowed them and kept hoping. I liked getting the round yellow ones that made me feel light and floaty. Sometimes they made the voices quiet to a slow drawl.

I hated leaving my room, but that morning the wind booted up and howled against my window with such force, I knew I had to get away before they took me again. The evil ones had been gone a while, but they were always lurking.

It would be just like them to hide behind a blustery squall and wait for their moment to break through my window.

I noticed a shuffle in my step when I reached Sophie. Her tummy round as a bowling ball, her brunette hair ratted in a wad at the back from knots. She needed the de-tangler spray I used on Zetty's hair. "Your baby is getting big, "I told her.

She beamed. "I hope she goes full term."

"She?" I asked.

"Oh, yes," she said proudly. "It's the baby girl I've always dreamed of."

And that's when the world went black.

"Margie, look at me." Eleanor's hand gently tapped my cheek. "Open your eyes; take a deep breath."

Her two black eyes came into focus. The air around me sweetened. I followed her directions and took a slow, deep breath.

"Good. That's the way, honey. Everything's fine now. You were walking with Sophie and something upset you. Can you tell me what?" Eleanor rested two fingers at the pulse point on my wrist.

She waited. Stroked my forehead softly and waited.

I started to cry, remembering.

"It's okay, Margie," she consoled. "Let it out. Tell me when you're ready."

"She's so afraid of wind. She shouldn't be alone."

"Who, Margie? You?"

"NO! Not me! My baby, girl! She needs me. I've left her alone. She's screaming!" I pushed off the floor, ready to run through steel if I had to, just to reach Zetty.

Mama! Mama! I remembered her screaming in the dead of night when she was four years old, *Banana slugs! Choking my neck!* She clawed wildly at the neckline of her nightie until I took scissors and hacked off the blue satin ribbons dangling from the collar. It was the only way to help her. Zetty had nightmares when she heard the wind.

Soft hands cradled my face. "Margie. Look at me, honey. Your baby girl's okay. You have nothing to worry about. She has Hank."

She has Hank, she has Hank, I repeated to myself. Eleanor always helped me. I pushed the hair off my face. "Yes, of course," I told her, and turned toward the group room. "And Tuffy, too," I said. "She has our sweet Tuffy."

I shrank into the unbending plastic orange chair, and suddenly felt Tuffy's nose nuzzle my lap, beckoning for my attention. A warmth spread over my feet, and I saw him there. He let me hold his face and I embraced him. When he slowly sauntered away he turned, wagged his tail, told me he was well, and said goodbye.

I studied my place in the circle, and stared at the board next to the medicine desk. It said it was summer. Paper beach balls were taped on the walls as if we were all having a bouncy, rollicking good time. *Happy Birthday to Rita, Gail, and Frank* hung on a poster. Patriotic metallic garland shimmered from the inside of the glass window separating us from staff. If the garland had been hung on the outside of the window someone would have wrapped it around their neck and been done with it. Believe me, it's happened.

Frank stood next to my chair and bent down to my ear. "Maybe we get gold pins today for giving them ten years of our life here!" he chortled as if it was humorous. The funniest thing he'd ever heard.

He was wrong though. Someone told me it hadn't been ten years for me, only eight.

"Group time is beginning," a nurse announced on the

loudspeaker. Every seat was filled. We waited to do as we were told.

"Marjorie, this is for you." the doctor handed me a clean tablet that I immediately fluttered under my nose to smell. "Keep trying to write something every day," he said, and placed a sharpened black crayon in my hand. I practiced my shorthand with it on the first page to tune him out.

"I'll begin as soon as possible," I precipitously blurted. "Thank you! My stage scenes need work," I said, still ignoring the talk I interrupted. "The cowgirl's daughter must shine in her part."

Even when the medicine did quiet the voices, they were soon replaced by a strong sense of shame and loss. Familiar, and yet foreign sensations all scrambled up inside me. I couldn't remember any reason I should feel this way. Only that it must be because I didn't have Zetty anymore.

"Sophie," I asked on the stroll back to our rooms, "can anyone use that new phone down the hall? I have a baby girl, too, and I really should call her."

"You should Marjorie, call her right away. They won't like it, but I'll stand guard. I'll make sure no one stops you."

"Thank you, Sophie. I knew you'd understand. Maybe tomorrow when I feel better."

"Whenever you want," she said.

We lumbered closer to our rooms. "How will I ever dance again if I can't walk right, Sophie?"

"You can, Marjorie. I know you can. I've seen you dance," she said. Sophie veered left and we parted ways.

But no matter how I concentrated, I wasn't able to change my gait.

Another part of me is gone, I said to myself when I entered my room. *Sophie lied.* But I knew I could trust her to help me call Zetty. I crawled into bed, heard the wind howl against the window and wanted to run to the phone right then. But it was no use. I stiffened like a dead person, and didn't blink or move. I was trapped in my bed—chased into a dark hole by the wind. *Soon*, I told myself, *I will call her as soon as I'm able. I have a plan now, and it's to call Zetty.*

Did I mention the squirrels were purple? It was the strangest thing. They just up and left and I never saw them again. Simply disappeared. I told my doctor I thought the wind was responsible for scaring them away. "Poor things," I told him. "They were just babies trying to get along without their mother."

Undercover

THE NEXT MORNING, FATHER AND I WERE FRIENDLY TOWARD each other again. It was artificial friendliness, but it worked. We simply moved on from what happened between us as if it never occurred. And I have to admit, it was a relief to tuck it away, like an unflattering photo you want no one to see.

Outside, palm leaves as big as sails were splayed around the yard and dangled off the roof. I went outside to help Father drag them one by one to a pile in the driveway.

"It's a dangerous business having to climb these palm trees to prune them," Father said, sounding like a teacher. "Men get killed doing it. Mother Nature helps us out sometimes. Brings em' down all by herself."

That was one way to look at it. A good way, I thought. It gave some purpose to bad wind storms.

Father pulled off his crusty brown leather gloves, one at a time, gave them to me, and went to the garage for others. I wanted to work that morning. I lifted, dragged, hauled, and tossed chunks of brown shredded debris onto the pile. It was a chance to get my mind off Tuffy and show Father I was good for something.

And then, in between heaving one palm leaf and then another into the pile, an idea struck. An idea so good, it just about bowled me over. *Maybe there's a way to see a psychiatrist without having to be a patient.*

So far, snooping hadn't produced any evidence of mother's whereabouts. But if this idea worked, I thought it might be the way to find answers. And if I was doomed to Mother's same fate, maybe I could find out if there was a pill I could to take to escape it, or a vaccine to prevent it. Who knows? And best of all, I wouldn't have to be a mental patient to find out.

A single idea can change everything. I had to test the plan on Gabe.

THE SMELL OF SUMMER POURED OUT OF OUR GARDEN HOSE, musty and warm. I could hear it; a rhythmic, constant stream moving through the plumbing just outside my bedroom window. A relaxing sort of hum.

Every morning, at the same time, I heard Father move the sprinkler from one section of the yard to another so it would pelt the grass and hedges in just the right places. The sprinkler head twitched across the lawn and spit out drops that sparkled like liquid diamonds. Then it shuddered for a second as if to re-load, and continued to spray out jewels that covered the grass. I always liked smelling the faded green rubber hose, cracked and burned up from the sun. The water coming out of it never tasted like anything that should go in your mouth, but the smell of it was pure comfort.

It was a barefoot, sprinkler morning like that when Gabe walked into my house and went straight to the fireplace mantel.

She picked up the framed photo of my parents' wedding and began dusting the glass with the bottom of her T-shirt. They had a big church wedding with a total of sixteen bridesmaids and groomsmen. The girls in the photo were in floor-length deep teal blue satin dresses holding burgundy roses and baby's breath. There were ribbons tied around hurricane glass lamps holding lit candles. Flowers were floating on a long vine on both sides of the white satin aisle. Mother and Father were walking down it, arm and arm, their faces lit with smiles. I have searched Mother's face regularly for any sign of what was to come. There was nothing I could see in that photo, only pure happiness and joy.

"My dad's being a jerk again. I had to get out of there," Gabe said.

"Sorry," I told her.

She played with the picture frame, swinging it around like pizza dough. I worried she'd drop it, but I did my best to ignore the thought. Gabe plopped herself down on our beige slip-covered davenport, still spinning the photo, this time between her two pointer fingers.

"It's been a long time, Zetty. But your house looks like it's still ready for your mom to walk right into, you know? Everything's right where it was when she left. Even her books haven't moved, or her reading glasses. Weird."

Gabe was right. Mother's belongings gave our home an almost ghostly presence; glimmers of someone once there, but who was completely untouchable now. Even when I picked her things up to dust, it felt odd to set them right back down as if they were part of the décor. But that's what they became. It seemed sacrilegious to even consider removing them.

"You should see their bedroom. Father keeps her wedding ring on his end table next to the last grocery list she made."

Gabe lifted her eyes up and gave me that look. If expressions spoke, hers would've said, "You've got to be kidding."

"I'm not joking. Her slippers are still right next to his in the closet, and her toothbrush is in the cup right where she left it. It's been eight years and he hasn't moved a thing. He still believes she's going to come back. In fact if she were to walk through that door tonight, I think he'd be expecting her."

I wanted to hold on to that belief, too. I worried that someday I wouldn't be able to remember her. Like her smell for instance: Chanel Number Five. I watched her dab it on her wrists and at her neckline every day.

Or her voice, like creamy hot fudge over vanilla ice cream. When she sang soprano in the church choir, her notes hovered like a swan gliding over swells on the water. It gave me goose bumps to see her head lifted upward, eyes closed, and mouth open wide. Mother was known for giving the chills to the whole congregation. Sometimes she made women cry. They say time can erase what you never planned to forget, so I thought about these memories and tried to hold on to them the best I could. And I have. Even now describing them to you, they fill me with unmatched pleasure.

I hijacked the wedding photo from Gabe, and inspected it again under the full light pouring in from the window. "I agree with Father, we can't get rid of her things. But it's a little creepy, don't you think?"

"I think your dad needs to get real. Seriously, he's not in touch with his feelings about any of this. But whatever you do, don't tell my mom."

Gabe was right; Scarlett might try to help him with her wacky therapy. But, I theorized, what if Mother did come back and all her stuff was gone? Assuming she was still alive, anything could happen.

"She could come back; it's possible, Gabe." I tried to

remove the doubt that began to creep around my words. "I mean, I know it's possible she won't, too. Trust me. I saw her face before she left. But how do we know? I know I've said it before but she could be better now. Living her life on stage."

"No offense, but I think she *was* living on stage."

Gabe had a point.

"And anyway, I don't think she'd give you up for Broadway, Zetty. No way."

"If she was confused she might."

Gabe gave a so-so nod. "Look, it's in the realm of possibility, of course. But it's better not to expect a thing." She pulled open the coffee table drawer and ruffled through the papers, books, and magazines inside. "I trust you've searched through all this, already?"

"This room and every other one. Didn't find a thing."

"Let's go to the movies tomorrow and figure out another way to get answers. The afternoon matinee. We'll think about it there."

"Can't," I told her.

She snapped up like a slingshot. "It's a western, your favorite; and guess who's in it?"

My eyebrows arched waiting for an answer, forgetting every other detail of my life. Gabe knew I had a thing for cowboys.

"Robert Redford and Clint Eastwood," she said with an excited edge.

"In the same movie?" I hardly believed it.

"Together! Both good guys," she said and flung herself over the edge of the davenport gaping up at me.

"Can't go." It killed me to say it, so I walked out of her range of view and started wiping down the dinette with a dishrag. It was time to test the plan I had already set in motion.

"Why not?" she practically whined.

"Have to meet a psychiatrist," I said in a something-I-do-everyday voice.

"WHAT?" Gabe banged into the coffee table and scrambled up behind me.

"You heard me." I shook the table crumbs off the dishrag over the sink, slapped it over the faucet, and gave my hands a few swipes back and forth on my jeans instead of searching for a towel.

"A shrink?"

I cringed inside; everything sounded silly after Gabe got a hold of my ideas and put her spin on them. "It's a doctor, and yes," I said primly, "I need to interview one for my summer school class: Exploring Careers in the Health Field." I grabbed a dust cloth, rushed to get the can of lemon oil from the cupboard, and began wiping down everything in sight.

"Since when have you ever been interested in summer school?"

A lie launched from my lips, "Since I found out I could graduate early if I knock off a class, or two, or three." Gabe's all-knowing gaze flustered me; I kept dropping the dust cloth.

"Have you started this so-called class?"

"Not technically. But our teacher mailed us a packet of handouts. I'm getting a head start. Good researchers do this sort of thing." I set everything down, took a seat at the piano and plunked out a few chords of "The Blue Danube," thinking it might shut her up.

"Since when do you like to conduct research? And what is there to know about shrinks we don't already know?" She paced around the piano bench like a high-strung cat.

"Lots of things, Gabe." I was getting mad at the way she was attacking my plan.

"Okay, so people get committed," she began. "The doctors come in wearing white coats, shoot people up with drugs, hook 'em up to electrodes that shock the living life out of them, analyze all their quirks as if that will change anything, and that's what they do, Zetty. You feel the need to research that?" She scooted down next to me on the piano bench, budging me over with her hip to give her butt more space.

"That's not true, Gabe." I had no idea what was true, of course, but the thought of mother going through any of it was unthinkable. I rested my hands in my lap. I impressed myself by the sound of my voice—very authoritative, "Well, anyway, it's too late. My teacher gave us a list of people to call for an interview and I already have an appointment." If I had been honest with Gabe, I would've told her the appointment filled me with absolute dread. But I had already decided not to be honest; I didn't want her to talk me out of it.

And then there was nothing but fragile silence. We both sat looking at Gabe's fingernail picking at the chip on one of the black keys. I was afraid to move, because if I did she'd see it in me. The big fat lie.

I spoke before she could. "It'll be interesting. I'm taking my notebook so I can write down everything I learn about what psychiatrists do." The left edge of my upper lip started to twitch and the more I tried to make it act natural, the stronger the spasm.

Damn, I thought. *I can't get away with a thing.*

Gabe leaned back, sucked in a gallon of air, and then blew it out so forcefully her bottom lip shuddered. Her face softened as she started tapping one key lightly in front of her and then stopped. "Okay, look. We both know you aren't taking this class to graduate early. You know, and I know, you think you need a shrink like your mom. You're worried you're next." Gabe stood up, lifted a leg and straddled the bench facing me. "Would you like me to go with you?"

"Of course not." But what I really wanted to say was, *Would you go instead of me, because you're the brave one and then you can come back and tell me what it is I really need to know.*

I hated it when Gabe saw the truth. I grabbed hold of a stack of sheet music, my mind racing for a way to save myself, and started ruffling through pages, pretending to organize them. Gabe stayed next to me; so close I could feel the warmth of her body radiate down the entire left side of my body.

"Zetty, remember what your pastor said to your dad?"

I rolled my eyes. "No."

"You were eavesdropping, remember?"

"It was eight years ago."

"He said there's a reason for everything. And we're never given more than we can bear. I think that's what you have to believe, no matter what happens."

It wasn't my place to burst Gabe's little make-believe religious bubble she floated around in. Otherwise, I would've asked her this: *Why do you think people have nervous breakdowns and kill themselves? Because*—I'd tell her, *things happen for no reason at all, and people get way more than they can bear.* It was the truth.

Gabe hopped up, sat in her favorite chair, the one that looked like a small barrel and started spinning, pushing herself off from the edge of the end table with her big toe. "I believe what your pastor said, Zetty, but listen. My advice is to interview a dentist and go into teeth. There's a lot of gum disease out there."

I lifted my upper lip to expose my gums in protest, and sprawled across the davenport where a breeze was circling. The sound of the sprinkler helped me relax.

I remembered the night Gabe was talking about. At the time, I resented the pastor's intrusion and, if I had been completely honest with her, I would have said in true Gabe-like fashion, "Didn't believe it then, don't believe it now." But I didn't say that, either.

Gabe held on to her Catholic faith the way I held on to Tuffy; it was the thing that mattered most. At that point, I was still fairly successful in keeping my newfound religion, a thing called *nothingness*, private. But not for long.

Gabe set both feet on the end table. "Zetty, I'm sure shrinks help some people." Her voice was full of caring. "And I'm sure not everyone needs electric shocks. I didn't mean to scare you."

"It's okay, Gabe." I closed my eyes sinking into the kind of trance you fall into before falling asleep.

"No, it's not okay. But you are."

Her words snapped me back; I was alert and listening.

"Trust me. You're not going off the deep end. You're the furthest thing from it; you're perfect. You don't need to talk to or 'interview' a shrink, or whatever you want to call him."

I opened my eyes and saw her use two fingers on each hand like rabbit ears and make quotation marks around the word "interview."

I decided to fully confess. "There's no class, Gabe. I mean, there is, but I'm not in it."

"Got it," she said.

"But that's how I have to explain it to the doctor I'm meeting with," I explained. "I had to test it on you. The truth is, I was thinking a shrink—I mean psychiatrist, might also help me understand what was wrong with my mother, not just me."

"Oh," Gabe stopped to fully consider the idea. "Maybe. I guess it's worth a shot." She got up and arranged the picture frames in a new way on the mantel. "But anyway, I support it," she said. "It has a high likelihood of helping. I'm just not sure what yet."

I remember shopping one time when a gray-haired couple crept across a department store like two tired inch worms. The man had a cane in one hand and held his wife's hand with the other. When he got to the door, he put his hand on her shoulder and she stopped. It took all his might to push the swinging glass door open, and he used his whole body to hold it back while she stepped gingerly past him. I turned to Gabe and said, "It's a lot of work to be alive, no wonder we're old and worn out at the end of it all." She looked me square in the face and said in the nicest way possible, "No, Zetty, it's just a lot of work being you."

I couldn't deny it. Mother knew me better than anyone alive for the first nine years of my life, but for the six years following, it was only Gabe. We were two years old when her family moved to the cul-de-sac across the street from us, but we became best friends on the second day of school in the first grade.

"I have a cowgirl hat," I announced proudly. I touched her Roy Roger and Dale Evans' lunch pail, tracing Dale's boots with my pointer finger as if I could feel the leather poking through the tin.

"Can I come over to your house and see it?" she asked, and I said, "Sure." And then splat. My plastic pack of ketchup split and the red sauce landed on the front of Gabe's new mint-green polka-dotted dress.

I was certain the play-date to view my cowgirl hat was over, but when everyone at the table squealed and hollered, Gabe started giggling, too. Completely unfazed, she got up from the table and in her matter-of-fact way, said, "Follow me."

We went to the bathroom, poured water over about a hundred scratchy brown paper towels, pumped out dry, pink, powdered hand soap, and did our very best to scrub it off. But the stain altered into a watery orange psychedelic design that took on a life of its own. The more it spread, the bigger our eyes grew, and the harder we laughed.

The lunchroom monitor stomped in and chewed us out. "Girls! Stop horsing around! Knock it off and get back to the cafeteria. Now!" Which only made us hoot louder and double up into complete hysteria.

That was the day we became soul mates. Mother told me if you can't laugh with someone until your stomach hurts, it wasn't the real thing. She was exactly right.

I made up my mind to do whatever it took to go undercover successfully and plunge myself into the world Mother had. It seemed like a good place to start. But first I let what Gabe said sink in.

Especially the "perfect" part.

IT WAS EASIER TO BE AN ACTRESS WITH STRANGERS, THAN next to someone like Gabe, who saw through me like a window. But it helped to carry her on my shoulder to my first appointment with Dr. E. Sperling.

The bus was on time that afternoon. *Too bad*, I thought. If I was more than ten minutes late they might have to move on to the next patient. That's what I heard about psychiatrists anyway. They didn't tolerate lateness, because it meant "resistance" on the patient's part. They called it resistance, but I think it was just bad for business.

I read something once that said everything we do is for some deep unconscious reason. If I remember right, Freud said people don't really make "mistakes." They respond to unconscious drives to avoid or "resist" things. Basically everything you say or do is something you're doing or saying on purpose, even if you don't realize it. It made sense until Gabe read it aloud to me in her best Austrian accent. This, of course, made everything about it sound silly and none of it rang true after that.

But I wanted the bus to be late, so I decided there was nothing unconscious driving my own mind. No problem there.

The driver pulled up exactly on time. He was an old fifty-something man with a neck the size of a redwood. His jet-black crew cut was greased up and standing at attention like quills on a porcupine. When I stepped past him and said "Hello," the stench of sour cigarettes filtered through my nose. He looked back at me with a vacuous expression and said nothing. I was used to feeling invisible so it came as no surprise. I listened to my quarters clink their way down the shiny silver pay slot. He lurched away from the curb so fast I had to grab a hold bar and steady myself. I glanced at him and wanted to mouth off to everybody like Dennis would and ask, "What the hell is his problem?" But I didn't. I tottered my way to a seat near the center exit. Just in case I had to get out quick. *You never know*, I thought.

My stop came faster than I expected. I pulled the string that signaled Mr. Picklepuss with a bell, checked my watch, and saw that I was still right on time. *Too bad*, I said, talking to the part of myself ready to abort the mission. I knew if I didn't go through with the plan though, I may never sort out the turbulence inside me.

When I walked into the office building, I discovered suite 307 was on the fourth floor, not the third as you'd expect. I took the extra flight of stairs, grateful for another chance to be ten minutes late and have to reschedule in another week or two. I felt my underarms dampen and sweat moisten my temples. I suddenly became self-conscious at the decision to wear orange Bermuda shorts. Why did I choose something so unprofessional? *Because,* I answered myself, *it was too hot to wear anything else. It's supposed to hit one hundred. He'll understand.*

"Dr. E. Sperling" was chiseled in gold on a sign mounted to his door. Whirligigs were spinning in my stomach, but I pushed through it and stepped inside anyway.

It was surprisingly noisy, even though all the leather sofas in the waiting room were empty. A fan in one of the windows was making a terrible racket. It appeared the good doctor couldn't afford air-conditioning, and didn't exactly have a thriving practice.

What a quack. I sat down on what I discovered were fake leather sofas before seeing a chipper woman sitting behind a white and gold French provincial desk with an avocado-green phone to her ear.

"Good morning, Doctor Sperling's office, may I help you?"

I heard the same southern hospitality that scheduled my appointment. A name plate in front of her phone said, "Anna-Victoria: Secretary." She had that teased-up kind of silver blonde hair that wouldn't budge in a wind tunnel. It was piled high, finespun like cotton candy, held up by backcombing and secured with a coat of lacquer. Frankly, she looked like someone from outer space. To make matters worse, bright yellow clip-on earrings in the shape of seashells bobbed violently from her earlobes, pinched pink. In my opinion they clashed with the hair and blue eye shadow that screamed for attention. She was wearing a sleeveless white cotton shirt with the v-neck open as wide as possible.

"No, I'm so sorry, the doctor is not available at all next week. Yes, sir. We do have a cancellation list."

Okay, I thought, *he might be somewhat successful.* And his receptionist seemed cheerful, despite her loud looks. When I crossed my legs, I felt the skin on the back of my thighs already sticking to the brown plastic sofa. As soon as she hung up the phone, it rang again. She looked over at me with a here-we-go-again expression.

"Oh yes, of course. Yes, ma'am. The doctor is confirmed to arrive August 30. One o'clock in the afternoon, that is correct. Yes, the fee is two thousand more for three hours. Will you send the contract or will Harvard?"

For that much money he had to be good. Good enough conceivably to see through my fake plan—my deceitful interior motives—and, Freud would probably add, my pathetic cry for help.

"No, the doctor is scheduled to present in Copenhagen on Wednesday, so that won't be necessary. But the limo would certainly be of use. We want to avoid the press until after the conference."

So. He *was* a big shot. I needed to reevaluate my plan. First, what was I thinking? Who would care if I left? I wasn't really enrolled in a class. Who would know? And besides, I rationalized, Gabe said I was perfect. She should know; her mom's a therapist. I convinced myself the whole idea was stupid. I had to get out, but if I ran, it would make me look like someone who needed to be there—someone with real problems.

"Yes, ma'am. Thank you so much. I will. We appreciate you confirming. Y'all have a nice day now. Bu-bye." And then, as if waiting to resume a conversation we had already started, she turned to me and said, "I am so, so sorry. This phone just keeps me hopping! You must be Zetty McGee."

As quick as I nodded, she continued, "I'm Anna-Victoria, hon. And I tell you what—we certainly do apologize for this heat today. It's already hotter than billy blue blazes out there, isn't it? Land almighty!"

Her accent came on strong when she hung up the phone, as if I had just tuned in to an episode of *Hee-Haw*. My goal was to act sane. "Oh, that's okay. You can't control the weather," I said like an idiot.

"The air-conditioning system is being worked on this week and wouldn't you know it's s'posed to hit a hundred today."

I shook my head sympathetically, and Anna-Victoria and I made more small talk, the kind I've hated my entire life. Another reason Gabe was my friend. She never, not once, used small talk with me. But I did it then because if I hadn't, Anna-Victoria would've known what a mess I was inside.

"Yup, it's hotter than hinges outside," I added. In case she didn't think it was funny, I also said, "That's what my dad said today." It was a lie, but it made her laugh again, even though I didn't find it one bit funny. However, if she liked me, I imagined she'd give Doctor Sperling some advance notice that I wasn't his average disturbed-type person and remind him I was merely a student, only here to fulfill academic requirements.

An unhappy woman sat down across from me and rested her head, the size of a small watermelon, in both hands. She was getting herself all worked up over something. She shifted her elbow from one knee to the other and heaved sighs as heavy as cement. She decided to make an announcement to the entire office: "How could she do it? My own daughter. She doesn't care if it kills me." She leaned back. "It's going to, you know. But I'm not gonna say another word, I'll say no more. I just can't take it anymore."

I found a magazine, opened it, and pretended to read the first thing I set my eyes on. My plan was to ignore her and hope she didn't do anything, well, crazy. There was no telling what she was capable of. Not in a place like this. "Where is the doctor?" I jumped from the clang in her voice. "I'm on the verge of a breakdown! Do you hear me? A breakdown."

Please don't let her have a breakdown. I had no desire to witness another one. I did my best to concentrate on a *Ladies Home Journal* when out of the corner of my eye, I saw Anna-Victoria approach her.

"There, there, Wilma," she said in a babyish voice. "There will be no breakdowns for you today. Doctor Sperling will see you here pretty soon, but only for five minutes between appointments. Let me get you some of your favorite tea while you wait."

"I don't need any goddamned 'tea.' I need Valium!" Wilma erupted.

"As you wish," Anna-Victoria said, turning on her heel.

"And four cubes of sugar! Not just one!" Wilma said nearly hissing.

Anna-Victoria shook her head in the affirmative, and reached for the teapot sitting on a plug-in warming tray.

Wilma laid her head back against the wall, fanning her neck with a newspaper. She was wearing a brown hairnet over a short puffy ball of light brown curls. Her pink zip-up top and white cotton pants were in the plus-size range and judging by the food stains, and thick black shoes, she was a waitress at some greasy diner. She blew out a lungful of air and started sobbing, not unlike I did the day Mother left. Every square foot of her shook up and down and I wondered if she was going to have a convulsion. Then she took two deep breaths; I think to try and slow it down.

Anna-Victoria set a mug of tea on the coffee table in front of her and moved a box of tissues within range of her right hand.

A crinkly, timeworn woman with white curls peeking from under a red floppy hat walked in and gingerly took a seat next to Wilma. She smiled sweetly at us and tucked her shiny lilac purse next to her hip on the sofa. It matched her round clip-on earrings. Wilma snorted back a wad of phlegm and in a pitiful, faltering voice, asked, "Would you ever sell your eggs to a man of science?"

Even before I glanced up, I felt Wilma's beady brown eyes bore into my head. She was fixated on my face, and my face alone. Her cheeks sagged from wearing a perpetual frown.

"Would you ever do such a thing?" she asked. "For a scientific experiment?" She sniffed back more snot.

"Excuse me?" I said, as politely as I could. I didn't want to be the one to push her over the edge.

"You know, EGGS!" she suddenly barked. "Targets for a man shooting SPERM!" You wouldn't dream of doing such a thing to your mother, would you?"

Now I understood why people made small-talk and yammered incessantly about the weather. "To my mother?" I didn't know what she was talking about, but I could tell she was going to start bawling again. She sucked in air so fast she practically choked on it. All the sniveling was getting annoying. Way too dramatic if you asked me.

Anna-Victoria sprang over and pulled a tissue from the box, handed it to her and said calmly, "New fertility treatments are the wave of the future, Wilma. Think of it this way: your daughter is helping people."

"Fine, she can help all the people she wants, but not with her eggs. Those eggs are part of me! Don't you see what this means? I could have a herd of grandchildren float-ing around in petri dishes! PETRI DISHES!" she shouted, repeating words that were like poison to her.

Wilma regained an ample supply of oxygen and aimed her words at me again, "I'm not gonna say another word. I'll say no more. Just tell me this, would you do it?"

"Well, I don't know a lot about that, actually," which was the wrong answer.

"Well, let me tell you." She revved up her speech, and took off like a race car. "As soon as they ripen up in your ovaries, they harvest—*harvest* your eggs! Can you imagine?"

I wished she would stop making me try.

She stopped again, trying to calm thoughts that seemed to erupt like bad heartburn. "They suck fifteen to twenty of them right out of you and squirt them into a bowl with some strange man's sperm. *Sperm!* So some damn woman can try and get pregnant!" She sighed, sat back and muttered, "I'm not gonna say another word. I'll say no more."

This time I saw real tears streaming down her face. I hoped Doctor Sperling would find Valium fast or tie off her arm with a plastic band and shoot her up with something. I saw it done in a movie once, and in my opinion, it was exactly what Wilma needed.

The petite elderly woman in the floppy red hat didn't seem fazed by Wilma's ranting.

She sat upright, perfect posture, and watched every-one talk back and forth as if she were enjoying a match at Wimbledon.

Anna-Victoria came back again. But it wasn't to get me. She had her eye on Wilma. Understandable, but still. For a moment I forgot about my nervousness; instead, I felt irritated that Doctor Sperling seemed to have overbooked his appointments. It was my turn to go in, but I didn't see how that was going to happen in a circus like this.

"Come on back, Wilma. Doctor Sperling only has a couple minutes, but you understand that, right?"

"Oh sure," she said dripping with sarcasm. "I wouldn't want the good doctor to miss a *donut* break." Wilma's voice went up a notch, announcing to everyone, "Better make it fast, even though I'm about to *drop dead.*" She used both arms to hoist herself up. It was slow going, like she had pain in her butt, which would not have surprised me in the least.

"It's okay, sweetie," Anna-Victoria consoled. "You just come with me and hang on to my arm. And we're not gonna let you drop dead. No siree. No dropping dead in the office today."

"I'll drop dead if I goddamned feel like it," Wilma muttered as she scooted down the hall, Anna-Victoria escorting her like the Queen of England.

The woman in the floppy red hat shifted to face me. She grinned politely, "I have eighteen hens and I get twelve eggs a day from them. Twelve every day! Way more than Wilma's daughter. Nice eggs, too. I'm Lottie, and I have plenty of eggs. Practically coming out my ears!"

This one was out of her mind, too, I thought, but only because she was hard of hearing. That was the moment I declared myself sane. I told myself I didn't belong there, and had no business thinking I did. It was official then. I was cured. If only it had been that easy for Mother.

I began to push myself up off the plastic sofa and realized my thighs were stuck. Almost permanently bonded. I had to rip them off, one at a time. It made an awful racket.

"Merry Christmas, dear," Lottie smiled.

"Merry Christmas," I said, now understanding there was

more off about Lottie than her hearing.

And then like a secret agent, I slipped past Anna-Victoria's empty desk and out the door. It was back to the normal world where I belonged.

Marjorie

WHEN I OPENED MY EYES, I GAZED AT ZETTY'S PAINTINGS as I always did. Every morning, and at the end of each day.

They were still beautiful after all these years; full of living color, only slightly faded now. The moment I set eyes on them, I felt better. The acrylics she used filled me with the kind of indescribable joy that had long since been squeezed out of me. There, taped to a muddy wall, with frayed and crispy curled edges, were the still tangible, physical parts of her I could hang on to. My Zetty shrine. Every piece like gold.

The sun put a spotlight on the one with a blue meadow next to the sea when the doctor entered. "Good morning, Marjorie."

I made up something promptly and in a sing-song voice recited, "I'm going to make a phooone call, and yooou caaan't stop me." I plucked the sheet up over my breasts and giggled.

"How are you today?"

Keep quiet, I heard a voice order. *Don't make things worse.* I had to keep myself to myself. I slid Dolly, the rag doll Eleanor gave me, from under my pillow and clutched her to my chest. "As soon as he leaves," I whispered to her ear, "we'll find Sophie and call Zetty."

"Is there anything you'd like to say to me, Marjorie?" he asked.

I shook my head, no.

He stood at the foot of my bed. "Okay. Well, I wanted to let you know you'll be leaving us. Not right away, but I wanted to prepare you."

"Home?" I asked the doctor stupidly.

"No Marjorie, not home," he said kindly. "We're waiting for an opening at a hospital that can help you more."

His eyes widened until they crawled around both sides of his head and disappeared.

I loped out of bed, scrambled to the drawer, reached for socks, underwear, and a paper gown, piled them in my arms, and hurled them across the floor.

I kicked them against the wall, screeching, "No! I belong here now. I can't do it!"

The palm of his hand flattened against my back. "We'll help you, Marjorie. You won't be alone." He gestured for me to move back to my bed and sit.

"Don't take me away from her," I whimpered. "She's the only one who helps." I clutched Dolly and bent in half, my stomach wrenched with aching. "I belong here, now. With her." I began rocking. "I want my mother."

"I understand, Marjorie," he grabbed a chair and sat across from me. "We don't want to take anyone away from you. Especially Eleanor. I'm sorry you feel afraid."

His golden eyes looked okay again when I raised my face to his. I believed him.

"I know it's hard, Marjorie, you've been here a long time. But you're in need of different help now. That's all."

A flash of insight appeared. "I'm not well, I know," I told him.

"No, you aren't Margie. Your condition is worsening again," he said. "We're taking steps now to be sure you're in a place that can care for you the right way."

"What does that mean?"

"As your condition changes, your care needs to, also."

"And the voices?"

"They may eventually stop. We aren't sure."

"What about medicine? Sometimes it makes the voices leave. Is there something I can take to stop all this?"

"We're trying, but right now there's no cure."

"There's *nothing*?"

"I'm afraid not. I only tell you this so you might prepare."

"Then I need to go home!"

"I only meant you might want to talk to people, and write," he hesitated, "or have someone write letters for you, speak to someone to be sure you have your affairs in order. I'm sure your husband will help."

"You sound like I'm dying. How can I be dying from a little confusion and hearing things?" *The evil ones are truly going to win*, I thought.

"I understand, Margie. I know this is hard."

"What do you mean you *understand*? Am I dying or not?!"

He looked away ever so quickly.

"*What?!*" I demanded, "Am I terminally *crazy*?"

When his face turned back to mine—his mouth began melting like wax. It moved slowly, bending and twisting so that I couldn't understand his words. And then the heckling started. And with it, sniggering. The words castigated, and banged around against my brain, echoing from ear to ear.

"Sophie!" I screamed. "Help me call her! Before it's too late!"

Strangers tramped across the floor of my room; not one of them Sophie. The doctor stepped back and prepared a syringe. When hands flattened one hip against my mattress, one sane thought rolled past: *I will get to the phone.* But the voices beat it down. I couldn't hang on to it.

Oh, how I missed my music. I can tell you the touch of ivory under my fingertips saved my life more than once. It was spiritual for me—my life-line to something sacred—something sane. If ever I needed my music, it was that day. I never understood why it had been taken from me.

I wrapped my arms around the sides of my head, trying to muffle the clatter. But it didn't stop until the needle went in and put me to sleep.

My Good Fortune

I BREWED A CUP OF TEA AS SOON AS I GOT HOME. NOT ALL natural organic tea, because I wasn't in the mood to play around with loose leaves to see if they spread out into a word or picture. I liked to "read" them sometimes like the gypsy did at the Halloween carnival. Sometimes the leaves told me I was destined for fame, a beach house, a rich husband, or a sexy convertible. Once the leaves told me I would make it on *The Carol Burnett Show*, and in my more religious days, they spelled out N-U-N.

After my grueling day spent at the shrink's office, I decided to make it easy and soak a ready-made tea bag in a mug. I carried it to my bedroom, lightly stirred, and noticed a fortune printed on a little pink tab at the end of the string. It read, "You are a living existence of light. You need not seek anything."

I pushed the pile of laundry on the floor that somehow made it back on my bed, stretched out, and considered my good fortune. I read it again, and then a third time.

Okay, I thought. *This is good. More confirmation. Exactly what I needed to hear.* I was done seeking, done trying to inspect my mind, and done worrying about going insane. I was perfect, just like Gabe said. No need for Jesus, Buddha, Freud, or some dumb shrink. I was all I needed—yup—a real ball of light. I took a deep, cleansing breath and heard the phone ring.

"Zetty!" Father yelled from the kitchen. "It's Gabe!"

I sprinted down the hall so I could take it in his bedroom for privacy.

I grabbed the phone on Father's end table next to the bed. "Yeah?"

"It's me. Tell me all about it."

I waited to hear Father hang up the other end and then asked for clarification. "All about what?" I bounced backward on the full-size, neatly made bed and spotted a shriveled-up daddy longlegs lying inside the glass light fixture on the ceiling.

"The shrinkologist! You went, right?"

"Yeah." It suddenly bored me to think about it. After all, I didn't even see the man.

"Zetty?" She sounded suspicious. "Did you go?"

I sat up cross-legged, as if being upright and alert would help me make this sound good. "Of course I went. His secretary, Anna-Victoria and I got along great. We laughed the whole time."

"Really. Anna-Victoria? Well, what about the shrink? You know, doctor-what's-his-name."

"It's Doctor E. Sperling." I coiled the receiver around my pointer finger so tight it started to pulse red.

"Okay, so what was he like?" she asked intently.

"Well, at first I thought he was a quack, but as it turned out he's some big shot! Very famous. He gets paid thousands and they drive him around in limos and everything."

"Wow," Gabe paused as if she was really impressed. "So what did he say to you?"

"Not much."

"What do you mean?"

"I mean, I met Anna-Victoria, we laughed, I heard all about Doctor Sperling, met a couple of real cases in the waiting room, realized I shouldn't have gone, you were right—so I left."

"I was right? You left?"

"Yup. Walked right out." I crossed the room and started poking around through Mother's clothes in the closet. "Like you said, it didn't have a high probability of working anyway."

"I didn't say that."

"Well, like you said though, it would never work to go in there as a student."

"I never said that, either."

"Well, close enough. Honestly. I don't know what I was thinking."

"I don't believe it, Zetty. You walked out?"

"Pretty much. His waiting room was packed with people who needed him more than me. I gave them my slot, because some were having meltdowns. I mean, really bad off."

Gabe sighed and then said nothing.

"Look, it was a stupid idea, okay? I bolted. I didn't belong in that place, Gabe. Even you said that." I slammed the closet door shut.

"Okay, okay. Don't get so touchy."

"The truth is I was an awkward mess, okay?" I caught my reflection in the mirror and cringed. "So, I'm done with shrinks. Don't need to talk to one, ever. I'll go to the library, educate myself and research all the psychiatric hospitals in New York. That's probably where she is."

"It would explain why your dad stopped visiting."

"Yes it would."

"So you research stuff—then what?"

I didn't know what to say.

Gabe waited.

"I don't know." I flopped on the bed. "Maybe it's a dumb idea."

"I don't think so, Zetty. But listen." Gabe was a little breathless, "I need to come over after dinner. We need to talk."

I could tell when Gabe had something whopping to share. She changed subjects way too fast. But the next thought made my insides twist like a cap. Maybe it was something bad about Scarlett. Maybe it was that kind of news.

I hung up the receiver, slid open Mother's side of the closet door again, and pulled out my favorite dress of hers. I sat on the faded purple carpet that went wall to wall. When I looked up, I saw familiar skirts, blouses, and dresses hanging above me in the same lifeless positions they had been in since the last time I sat there. It used to bother me that they never moved, so I rearranged them once and shook the hangers around to rumple them up a bit and make them look lived in.

I didn't have clear memories attached to many of Mother's clothes, except for the black lacy dress I laid carefully over my folded legs. She and Father were going to a fancy dinner for their anniversary. The large black satin waistband fell in five thin tiers around her waist, and the bottom flared out past her knees. It was sleeveless, so she draped a short black stole made out of fake fur around her shoulders and twisted her hair up like a little tornado. Very Audrey Hepburn.

When Mother emerged from the bedroom and strolled down the hall, she was undeniably elegant. She had shiny black high heels on with openings cut out at the toes. I told her that night how beautiful she looked.

She knelt down, gave me a smile, and her face turned rosy pink from blushing. She hugged me, kissed my cheek, and told me it was kind of me to say such a nice thing to her.

Father gave her a whistle, the kind male construction workers do when they see an attractive woman. Only, coming from Father, it was nothing you felt bothered by. He told her, "Honey, you look absolutely radiant!" She smiled in a way that made me wonder if she believed it. But being the man of few words he was, even then, Father always meant what he said and everyone knew it. It surprised me the way she turned so shy sometimes, especially with compliments and beauty pageant crowns. But put her on a stage with me, and she could do anything.

I used to hold that dress across my face and breathe in, trying to catch a long lost scent of her. Which I did sometimes. I can testify to the fact that Chanel No. 5 scent lasts at least seven years. But it was more than perfume I smelled. It was her clean skin, too, and an occasional waft of her hair. It was there somehow, memorized in the very weave of the fabric.

So, there I sat. Pining over a dress. I scrambled up and had the idea to try it on. I dropped it over my head, pulled the hem down around my knees and saw that it fit me perfectly over my shorts and t-shirt. I turned sideways to look in the mirror attached to the narrow blonde wood dresser when father walked in.

A strangled gasp hung in the air. "How dare you," he started.

I felt I hadn't heard him right. I couldn't make sense of his words. I stiffened, my own words suspended somewhere out of reach.

"What do you think you're doing?!" he erupted. A hostile silence lunged between us; his face turned motionless, pallid.

"Just trying it on," I finally said, my lips suddenly limp.

"Take. It. Off." Bright crimson began to creep up his neck.

"Dad, I was just—"

"No excuses," he said. "Take it off, Zetty." His fury surrounded the both of us like a thunderstorm. "Now!"

Father slammed the door behind him so hard, the wall shivered and a little piece of plaster fluttered off the wall. It was the first time I witnessed him so full of rage. Until that point, I never thought such a force existed in my father. Or that he was capable of ever using it against me.

I waited for a moment shaken and embarrassed, like I had been caught committing a cardinal sin. I stood frozen, my heart pounding, and then chased after him, refusing to take her dress off.

"It's only a dress!" I shouted. "Look!"

Father grabbed the glasses off his face as if ready to brawl. "It's your mother's and it's not to be played in!"

"Dad, I'm *seventeen*. I don't 'play' dress-up anymore."

"It was a disrespectful thing to do, Zetty,"—he set his glasses back on his face—"insensitive and cruel."

"What?!" I planted my feet on the floor, ready for battle. "Yeah. That's right. I'm sooo cruel, Dad. What a mistake I was. You wish I had never been born. Go ahead! Say it!" And then he left me standing in the kitchen by myself. "I hate you more and more!" I shrieked, knowing he could hear me from the garage.

When my throat loosened, tears rolled out of everywhere: eyes, nose, mouth, maybe even my ears. My face was drenched.

When the lawn mower blasted on, I went back to his bedroom and tugged at the dress gripping my neck. I slipped it carelessly back on the hanger and shoved it back in between the other clothes. I slammed the door shut and vowed never to set eyes on it again.

Father was methodically pushing the mower up and down the lawn, when Gabe appeared at the back window. She crashed through the screen door into our kitchen, took one look at me, and started interrogating. "What happened?"

"Who knows!" I snapped.

Gabe sat at the aqua blue dinette, and reached for a green grape from the wooden bowl centered in the middle. I sat across from her, dropped my head and ran a fingernail along the silver rim around the edge of the table. She pulled off another grape from the stem, popped it in her mouth, and chewed sloppily. "You're crying. What's going on?"

"I tried on one of mother's dresses and it made Father furious. He blamed me for who knows what. I screamed and yelled at him."

"Is that all?" She plucked a handful. "I yell at my dad all the time."

"Well, I don't."

"Well, maybe you should."

"I told him I hated him."

"They know we don't mean it." She spat out a rotten one. "What's your news?"

"Not so fast." She crossed her arms. "So what if you tried her dress on! What's wrong with that? And so what if you got mad at him. You know what I think?"

Of course I wanted to know, but sat waiting.

"I've said it before and I'll say it again. You need to mouth off more often." She rolled up the sleeves on her blue-checked cotton shirt-tail. "No one is going to die from it. Your dad's the type that needs you to get in his face and tell him like it is. Someday, you need to do that, Zetty. I mean really do that."

"Well, I thought I did."

"Not good enough."

She was right. I wished like anything Gabe could've seen me when I finally did.

"I just wanted to try her dress on, Gabe. I loved that dress. I still miss her, you know? I really do."

Gabe stood and instantly wrapped me in a cocoon. "Of course you do," she squeezed. "I don't know how you've done it Zetty. Really, I can't imagine how I would survive without my mom. But you have. And you've done it with grace."

"Grace?" I shot a look at her that must have teetered between terror and complete absurdity.

"It's true," she said. "I think it's because you're a lot like your Dad."

"I'm nothing like my dad."

"Well, the good parts you are." She leaned back and knew I didn't believe it. "It's like your dad has this inner compass that always directs him in the right way. He is a predictably good man, at heart. He is, Zetty. You know he is. And so are you."

"So was my mother." I went to the counter, tore off a paper towel and wet it. I dabbed around my eyes and sat again.

Gabe fell forward and rested the top of her skull in both hands, as if straining to channel new brain power.

We both sat motionless through three rounds of an ice cream truck's jingle creeping down the street.

"Maybe it's time I accept it. I'm never going to know what happened to her. I can't keep,"

"That's it," she said so softly, I hardly noticed she inter-rupted me.

"I can't keep," I said again, "Wait, what did you say? What's it?"

Gabe's head lifted. "Our plan."

Marjorie

EVERY DAY THE STAFF DIRECTED ME TO SOCIAL HOUR IN the rec room to play Bingo and participate with the others. I tried to find someone to play with the way I was supposed to. But everyone played games I didn't understand.

"War!" someone shouted at a table near me, slapping down cards feverishly in a long line.

"That's not war," Frank objected. "A king beats a queen."

"Times have changed. They're equals now!" the curly blonde shot back.

"Only in your world, dyke!"

She stuck her tongue out at him and growled.

You can understand why it wasn't easy to join in and play. The shouting scared me. I wanted it to stop, so I undressed next to the Bingo table.

People screamed at me from every direction. "She's getting naked! She's stripping! Bad, bad girl! She's exposing herself! Indecent whore! She's flashing us!"

I didn't understand why they shouted the way they did. I had only removed my clothes. That's all. I hurt no one.

"You're in fantasyland, woman!" Frank yelled in my face.

I could've used the sharp gray scruff on his chin to scrub my frying pan.

"Stop coming on to me!" he bellowed. "I'm not interested."

I didn't know what to do. I thought he was my friend.

"Well, cry me a river!" a woman built like a tank ejaculated. "You're not some la-dee-dah movie star, and no hot shot beauty queen, either!" She flounced her sunny curls back with just enough melodrama to make you think she was a beauty queen herself. "No stage director, no prima ballerina—nothing! You're a nobody!" She shuffled cards and then gave them a snap in my face. "Get used to it!" she commanded. "And don't you try coming on to me, either," she glared. Her voice dropped, "Ain't no one gonna get it on with me, sis. Not unless I say so."

"Spare us, Gladys," Frank grumbled. "And you Marjorie, all you do is lie," he complained. "Haven't you heard? Sinners go to hell."

I was so ashamed. I never meant to lie or do bad things. "I'm sorry," I repented. "Forgive my sins. I want to go to heaven. Please, you have to believe me. I didn't mean to do anything wrong."

Mother approached, swaddled me in a blanket, and when we moved away from the others, she helped me sit. "Margie," she pleaded, "Listen to me." She yanked a chair from behind and plunked down close. "You are a good, *good* girl, honey. You always will be. You are not going to hell. You've done nothing wrong; it was your illness that made you forget the rule about keeping clothes on. It wasn't right for the others to speak to you that way."

I started to disappear.

"Margie. Look here, right at me." She leaned in closer. "Look at my eyes."

I wanted to please her so I did as I was told.

"Fight back, just the way you told me you would. If you're hearing voices, I want you to sing or talk right back to them. Try and make friends with them, too. Listen to what they want to say, but tell them they must be kind. If they aren't, tell them they'll have me to reckon with."

Her words made me grin. My mind went quiet.

"You know I don't lie to you. I'll never lie to you," she promised.

"I know." It was the truth. "This time it wasn't the voices, Eleanor."

"Okay, sweetie. The other patients get confused sometimes, too. Do you understand?"

"Yes," I said, to please her again. "I want to go to heaven, Eleanor."

She took my hand and rested it on top of hers. "Honey, don't we all. But listen," she brightened, "if anyone's goin' to heaven, it's you, Margie." Eleanor raised her brows, "And let's hope me, too," she muttered. "Oh boy, let's hope me, too." Eleanor helped me up. "But you, sweetie," she added, "you'll be first in line."

I reached out and felt her arms wrap around me. I smelled the clean, sweet scent of green tea and verbena resting against her chest, and knew I was safe.

"I love you, too, honey." She placed a tissue in my hand. "You remember that."

I nodded, happy she could read my mind. I wiped my face even though I had no memory of when I started crying.

Eleanor held my hand while we walked to my room. My mind wasn't right, I knew that. But something inside told me to fight. When our hands released, she went to the desk and I heard it again, *You must fight your way back.* I recognized this voice. It was my own.

Eleanor unwrapped the blanket around me, helped me put on a clean gown, and then wrestled the yellow tablet out of the rickety wood drawer. She placed it on top next to a sharpened red crayon. When she left, I planted myself in front of Zetty's paintings, admiring the texture and grace in every lovely stroke. I rested my fingertips on the ocean scene. I slid them across the velvety smooth waves of color, a thousand shades of blue, as if they were strands of her hair. I hoped she felt it—my love coming through. I turned and decided it was time.

I peeked down the hall to see if anyone was on the phone and then set off to find Sophie.

"It's all clear," I told her. "Will you come now and stand guard while I call?"

"Yes, and Frank and Gladys said they'd help, too. We're going to protect you Margie. We'll make sure you get to talk to your baby."

"Thank you." I started to weep.

They took their positions down the hall, one on each corner. Sophie stayed near me, pretending to visit. She blocked the view of what I was doing by twirling her gown out in front of me. The receiver trembled in my hand when it lifted. The numbers were foreign to me. I didn't understand what to dial at first. And then BR7 came to mind. I dialed it but nothing happened. The next four numbers came too, so I dialed them. Still, nothing. "I would give anything to talk to her again," I told God. I only hoped I was remembering right and there was one.

And then a connection was made. It started to ring.

The Plan

THE WALL VIBRATED FROM THE BLARE OF THE PHONE. THE volume was up so Father could hear it ring from the garage.

I ignored it. My eyes solely on Gabe.

"Aren't you going to answer that?" Gabe asked.

"Forget the phone. Tell me what plan you're talking about."

"Just answer it!"

I grabbed at it in a huff. "McGee residence," I blasted.

Someone fumbled on the other end.

"Hello? Who is this?"

I heard someone's breath near the mouth of the phone. Almost a whimper.

"Hello?!" I yelled.

Still more racket. Like the phone was being thrown against a wall.

"It's the nosey party-line," I said, and slammed it down. "So what plan, Gabe?"

"The plan to find your mother."

"Okay. Explain." Whatever it was, I was already reeling from the idea.

"You said you were going to research New York hospitals, right?" she asked.

"Well, yeah, that was the idea. But—"

"We're going to call all of them if we have to," Gabe said.

"And theatres on Broadway, too, if she's not in a hospital. Once we find her, we're flying to New York. We're telling everyone it's our 'graduation trip.' But we're really going there to see her."

To this day, Gabe remains my greatest ally.

I tried to remain calm but every nerve inside me was standing at full attention, waiting for more.

Gabe started to pace. "It can work, and it will, but—" She started to say something and then stopped herself.

"But what?" I demanded.

"Well, I hate to say it," Gabe said reluctantly, "because you're not going to like it."

"Why?"

"In fact, you're going to hate it."

I waited for the tripwire that was about to blow up the plan.

"Because," she finally said, "I think you need to go back to your first plan, too."

I couldn't speak at first, and then, gradually, I did. "What—the plan to see the *shrink*?"

"Yeah, that one," she nodded. "He might be able to help."

"I don't know," I said. "Not if she's in New York."

"And what if she's not in New York? What if she's still here?"

I went to the cupboard and pulled out a box of animal crackers. "Well," I said, "it's not likely. But maybe someone in that white house could tell me something." I poured the box of animals in a bowl, and set them between us. "I need to be certain she's not there. Then find out where she went."

"My thoughts, exactly," Gabe said, wild eyed. She lustily grabbed a handful of animals.

"But how would I get the shrink to get me in the 'white house'?" I asked. "I mean, besides the obvious way." I rifled through the bowl for all the horses, as if they tasted best.

"Zetty, your 'student research', remember? Pretend to be a student."

"Oh," I said thoughtfully. "I like it. No sense in being mentally ill until I have to."

"You'll have to come up with something convincing. But I know you can do it."

The excitement buzzing between us could have generated enough power to light up the city.

Gabe heaved a gallon of milk out of the refrigerator, reached for a glass and started pouring. "Okay. So, you see the shrink, get in the 'white house', and snoop around a little. Then, if you get nothing, we hit the library and start calling every hospital in New York. After that all the theatres. And then we go to New York to see her face to face. Nothing's gonna stop us, Zetty."

"Nothing." I repeated. "Unless she's dead—" I counted on Gabe to know. I needed her to take away the very thought of it. She didn't disappoint.

"Nah." Gabe shook her head, "We would've heard." Her glass clunked down on the table and she sat. "You can't hide death. Just secrets."

Her ease at dismissing the idea completely calmed me.

"Ready for my news?" she asked.

I had almost forgotten. "Tell me!"

"I got a job. Hired at the Lucky Seven, working the cash register in my own check-out line."

An audible gasp flew out of my mouth, "A cashier at the Lucky Seven?" I started feeling woozy.

She held one hand up. "There's more," she said, as if the shocking news would never end. "This is big, Zetty," she said teasingly. "Guess who got a driver's license today?" She chugged her milk.

"You finally passed?!"

"Sure," she belched. "Seventh time's a charm."

"Far-Out!" I felt my face flush from the excitement.

"And I've just decided," she added, "the red Mustang can wait. I'm saving every penny from my job for our airplane tickets to New York." She set her glass on the table and tossed a giraffe in her mouth.

It was so much to take in. I dropped my head between my knees.

"What are you doing?"

"Trying not to pass out."

"Why? What's wrong?"

I elevated warily. "Too much excitement. And you know I'm not a good flier on big jets—after all those near misses."

"You've taken one trip on a big airliner, Zetty."

"Yes, and it had multiple near misses!"

Gabe rolled her eyes.

"What's wrong with taking a train to New York? There's a lot of bad karma around me and flying." I bounced upright and fiddled with the plastic orange arranged in a fake fruit basket on the window ledge. It was covered in a sticky gray coat of dust now, not oiled and shined since Mother left.

"Where did you get that stupid idea?" Gabe snapped, "A train would take forever!"

I had good reason to ask. My phobia wasn't, after all, totally irrational. Even Father agreed I had more than my share of bad luck on my flight to Idaho.

She continued, "Those were hardly 'near misses' Zetty. And don't start with the 'karma' crap. If it's your time, it's your time. You've flown a million times with your dad and loved it, so what's the deal?" She crossed her arms, waiting.

"It's not the same. I like small planes; it's different flying with my dad."

"Well, what sense does that make?" Gabe asked.

"None." I started bouncing the orange off the wall. "It's dumb. I admit it."

My gruesome thoughts about death weren't anything I cared to describe to Gabe. Even I didn't understand them entirely. I only knew they started after Mother left. And not just with flying. I didn't want to be behind the wheel of a car, either. Sure, I saw ghastly flashes of myself torn apart in mid-air collisions, but I also saw myself flattened on the freeway. I could imagine these things and didn't know how to make them stop.

Later that year I learned all my thoughts and feelings, even the graphic ones, were natural based on everything I'd been through. And I was reminded that on most days, and even on most flights, nothing out of the ordinary happens at all. I was told, "If you choose to reside in the 'what-ifs' of the future and you plunge into despair, you miss out on the joy that is now. Save it for when it really happens, Zetty. You'll have plenty of time to grieve and react anyway you want if it does."

It was true. Trust me. "Out of the ordinary" things kept happening to me and I had more than enough time to feel lousy about all of them.

I tried to convince Gabe I was right. "But they *were* near misses, Gabe—all on that one flight! I'm telling you, the wind practically blew that plane to pieces! Even the stewardess screamed and fainted. The plane was bucking through lightning and thunderbolts which practically killed us! By the time we landed there was one broken arm and a head injury. So much for seat belts! And don't forget the kid behind me who projectile-vomited his tuna fish sandwich all over the ceiling above *me*." I was even more convinced I was jinxed after reliving it for Gabe.

"Okay, that part was vile, but it was fate, Zetty. It obviously wasn't your time." She grabbed the orange out of my hand, pitched it back over my head and straight into the basket.

"I hate when people say that. And besides, I promised myself I'd *never* fly on an airliner again. I can't do it. And I won't."

Gabe stared at me the way I had wanted to stare at Wilma. I dismissed the thought as soon as I had it. This was different, I told myself; I am not a hysterical middle-aged woman crying over lost eggs.

But before she could eat the three fat grapes she tugged off another stem, she bolted out of her seat and flung them back in the bowl. "Holy Mother of God!" she blurted. "What is your problem?" She made the sign of the cross against her chest again the way she always did when she said God, Jesus, or Mary. "We finally have a plan, and now you're gonna let this stop you from finding your mother?! What are you so afraid of? I'll tell you what it is. You're not afraid to die, Zetty. You're afraid to live. You are! You're afraid to have the life your mom can't. And that's a waste. You're on a guilt trip and you're not even Catholic."

"I'm not anything."

"Well, great. Don't believe a thing. That's a big help."

I ignored the sourness and continued, "Lots of people think I'm jinxed. So, for the safety of everyone, I shouldn't fly." And then added, with my flair for drama, "But fine. Since you don't think it's a problem I'm going to fly anyway— with *you*." I hastily wiped the table with a towel, shoveling all the grape stems and half-chewed rotten ones into my cupped hand. "Prepare yourself. I guarantee something nasty is going to happen."

Gabe pranced out the door practically crowing. Stepping on nothing but determination, she turned and hollered, "Okay then—we're going to do this!"

Maybe I wasn't so different from Wilma. I wondered if I sounded just like her, panic-stricken, irrational, so wrapped up in my own thoughts and fears that I couldn't see beyond them. Maybe Gabe was right. Maybe there was a part of me that was afraid to live. Maybe my problem also was the way this implacable, unmerciful fear prevented me from doing normal things most people did all the time, like getting a driver's license or flying to New York with their best friend. Granted, we would be on a mission to find a runaway mother. Not your usual itinerary for a graduation trip. But I had to face it: sometimes I was a walking case of cold, stagnant, gloom and doom and it had taken root in my heart. Every corner I turned I expected the worst to happen. The awareness unfolded somewhere deep inside me, and, for the first time, lay quietly open and exposed.

But I resolved to do it anyway. I would fly, and I would go back to the shrink. Because, the truth is, the desire to find Mother was bigger than my fear of crashing in a plane, or being overcome by the wicked force that took her away. Wanting her in my life again was bigger than my fear of anything.

I made the call to Doctor Sperling's office and accepted another slot from the cancellation list for the next day. Then I found the book from the library I had hidden and went to the chapter on "Neurosis." It was time to rehearse lines for my bit part as a student researcher. I had to convince this shrink that's all I was.

Marjorie

"WHY DID YOU PITCH THE PHONE LIKE THAT?" SOPHIE asked. "Gladys can't stand guard much longer. She has to pee." I glanced back and saw her holding her crotch with both hands, bouncing like a pogo stick.

"It rang," I told Sophie. "But the phone wires inside the handle got too hot. Look! It melted right in my hand. I had to drop it!"

"Okay, Marjorie. Calm down. It's not melting. It's okay."

"The number was right! I know it was. The evil ones won't let me talk to her!"

"I'll handle the evil ones. Now Marjorie, you have to calm down," Sophie said. "You're shaking so hard you can't think right."

"I forgot the numbers, Sophie. They left me. I can't remember what I dialed!"

"Try again and let me watch."

My shaky finger pulled each hole around the circle while she leaned in next to my ear and listened, "The number you have reached is not in order at this time. Please check the number and dial again."

"The numbers won't come back!" I began to weep and dropped the phone. "I can't touch it! It's melting again!"

"Quiet, Marjorie!" Sophie shushed me. She grabbed the receiver. "I can call information. That's all we have to do," she said excitedly. "You're shook up, that's all. We'll get the number again, Marjorie. Don't worry." She took the phone, and dialed the operator. "Yes, please. I need the number for Mr. Harold McGee. In Windansea." Sophie gave me a thumbs up. "BR7," she repeated, and closed her eyes to commit the rest to memory. "Thank you," she said briskly and hung up. She lifted the receiver again and started dialing. "I got it Margie. I'll hold it for you, so you don't get burned."

We leaned in together and heard it connect. It started to ring when a loud, long toothless whistle blared between Gladys's two front teeth.

"Incoming!" Gladys hollered.

Sophie flinched so hard the receiver launched into the air. I dropped to my knees so it wouldn't hit me in the head.

Frank followed, "Stand down! Do you read me?' He flailed his arms as if redirecting a jet on a runway. "I repeat: Stand the hell down! Abort Mission!"

Sophie helped me up, fumbled with the receiver, laid it back on its cradle, and we moved away from the phone.

An aide rounded the corner. "Ladies and gentlemen, your meals are ready and waiting for you," he announced like the royal butler.

"I know the number now," Sophie whispered. "We'll call her after dinner." She held her gown out like a party dress, twirled around, and winked at me. We parted and I shuffled to my room.

Eleanor lifted the cover off my dinner plate as soon as she saw me at the door. "What were you all doing in the hall, Margie?" she asked.

"I can't really say. Please don't make me."

"Of course, I won't," she said, handing me a napkin.

But when I lifted the spoon to my mouth I knew something was wrong. The food smelled like poison. I dropped everything and wanted to disinfect my hands as soon as a piece of corn beef hash landed on my palm.

"It's okay to eat, Margie," Eleanor reassured. "The food is safe." She tasted a spoonful to prove it. "Try a little." Her smooth, dark hand fell over my face and made me feel safe. She stroked my hair lightly. I relaxed. I believed she was my mother until the black skin against my sheet reminded me I was being stupid. I kept forgetting though. It made me sad to know she wasn't mine, and since I wanted her to be, I pretended. At first I pretended, and then it became real.

I still wouldn't eat though.

My mind went fuzzy, out of tune like a television screen full of snow. I wanted to play with Zetty. The cowgirl's daughter. Or was she my daughter? Or my mother? Or just a friend, I wondered. I only knew we were cowgirls once. And she could be trusted. I remembered sometimes. I knew that I loved her and always would.

When Mother was with me, the voices usually behaved. They hid from her. The evil ones knew it was harder to hurt me when she was near. But they still used their trickery to upset me. When I reached for my knitting, my hands went stretchy, the skin rolled down over my wrists like ruffled sleeves. All part of their plan to disrupt progress on my net.

"Margie, what is it? Not feeling hungry again, tonight?"

My thoughts darkened. I missed the cowgirl's daughter.

"How about a few bites before you go to bed?"

I lay back and closed my eyes.

"Okay, honey. Rest." She carried the tray away. "I'll be back later."

I could sense when they were about to come out. As soon as Eleanor left the room their words filled the room: *We know what you're trying to do and who you're trying to call and we're really sick of you.* I searched the room for music again. Just in case. My clock radio, my record player, my piano. But the room was still barren. As always, I knew music was the only thing that would've helped in the quiet dark of night when it always got worse.

Keep quiet.

I tried to do as I was told.

You don't want to be in this life.

I tried not to listen.

Coward, they continued, *we want you dead. Both of you. You don't deserve a mother.*

You have no idea what this did to me. You have no idea until an evil being you can't see, is at your ear and taunts and terrorizes you whenever it feels like it. And you know he will do what he says he will, whatever he wants. In this extreme state, I can only tell you there seems to be no control anywhere in your mind. You believe you're at the mercy of the voices.

I rolled to my side, pummeled my face into the pillow, but it was no use.

Someone must have heard me; the room filled with light, commotion, and the surge of hurried footsteps danced around me. Hands pressed against my arms and thighs until the hot sting of metal filled my mouth. And then I went under and never saw Sophie, or the others again.

To the 'White House' Please

I STROLLED INTO THE OFFICE WHERE WILMA HAD MADE SUCH a commotion and the mad hatter had chippered away about her hens. I was in full character when I arrived—a student researcher. There for scholarly pursuits. Nothing more.

"Nice to see you again, hon!" Anna-Victoria bubbled. "Have a seat, sweetie, and Doctor Sperling will be with you shortly. May I get you something to drink?" I read a novel once about a shrink who called her patient "sweetie" a lot. I wondered if it was a common thing they said to keep disturbed people calm.

"I've had plenty," I lied. The truth is I was feeling jittery again and didn't dare take a sip of anything for fear I'd throw up. Although, as Dr. Id pointed out, I only vomited dramatically in my fantasies.

I was relieved she hadn't asked the obvious yet. Like, "What in the world happened to you last time?" or "Why did you run off like that?" or "Do you have a problem with nerves, hon?" Although highly unlikely, it occurred to me that it was possible they didn't even notice. Just in case, though, I was ready: bad case of diarrhea.

I smoothed out the smocking on the Hawaiian print shirt I was wearing and sat.

An old man, at least thirty, came down the hall and passed by me. I was surprised to see he looked perfectly normal. Not like a mental patient at all. He had a sport shirt on, black slacks and put a pair of sunglasses on top of his head as he walked away. "Have a great day, Anna," he said, like normal people do.

"Zetty, come on back, hon. Doctor will see you now." Anna-Victoria was wearing an A-line skirt and blouse the color of a mushroom. A little drab, I thought, for such a lively personality. With every stride down the hall, I felt I was one step closer to the electric chair. Anna-Victoria opened the door, ushered me in like royalty, and then swooped out.

And there, sitting at a massive Mediterranean-style dark mahogany desk, was a woman.

I thought there must be some mistake. I turned to see if I was in the right place. It's okay, I quickly informed myself; Scarlett would approve; and so should I. But if you asked me, the desk was a bit over-stated.

She had a dark shade of red hair. Like a rich, strong wine. It fell just below her shoulders—soft looking, and flattering to her face. She was around my mother's age, which would have been about forty, give or take. And she had the same color of emerald green eyes, too.

Doctor Sperling seemed bouncy and energetic when she stood, leaned across her work space and extended her arm to shake my hand. I held out my right hand to hers and felt a sturdy grasp wrap around my moist palm and fingers. She did the shaking; I went limp.

"Hello, Zetty. I'm Doctor Sperling. Have a seat wherever you'd like."

I noticed her cream-colored crepe blouse had green embroidery on the collar and down the front on both side of the buttons. The closest thing to me was a long, black, leather chaise sofa. I knew full well that was the place where everyone lay down and spilled their guts. I could only imagine all the things that had been exposed there. I scanned the seat for anything that might stick to me and never come off. I'd rather catch the mumps again, I thought, than be exposed to something that sucked you out of reality. Then again, it was already too late for that, so I sat on the edge and kept my feet flat on the floor. The decision to stay upright was firm in my mind, even though it was incredibly uncomfortable and hard to hold my posture straight.

Doctor Sperling watched me as she sat effortlessly in a navy blue crushed velvet chair. "Is that comfortable for you?" she asked.

"Perfect!" I said, even convincing myself a little. I straightened my back again and held both hands in my lap, on top of my school binder. She crossed her legs, and relaxed both arms on the sides of her chair.

"So, Zetty, what brings you here today?"

Bingo. Dr. Id had that part right. I tugged on my pant leg a little, trying to keep it from bunching up in my crotch.

"Well, only my class, of course. I mean the project I have to do. You know, the paper—a term research, a term paper I'm researching, I mean. For school." I sounded like I had spit for brains. Everything went blank.

She sat in the same relaxed position, while I leaned my hips nervously to the right and then the left and had to straighten myself up again.

"Yes, your class, that's right," she said. "What aspect of my job do you want to research?"

I cleared my throat, "Mental asylums. I want to see what happens after you have a nervous breakdown. Could you send me to one?" I said it so fast I wasn't sure what I said, or why. She raised both eyebrows, I imagine a little alarmed.

"What's the focus of your research?"

"Well, I want to know what it's like to live in one. And see what goes on in there. And how people get out, if they ever do. Or where they go if they don't get better. And also, how do shrinks, or excuse me—I mean psychiatrists—figure out, or I mean tell if someone, or determine if there's actual insanity in someone." I unclotted my words, "Sorry. I'm not usually so nervous." Which, of course, was a complete lie.

She looked at me in a warm sort of way. "Okay. Tell you what. Let's switch places. I'm thinking it might help you relax. This is where I sit to interview patients, and it'll be easier for you to take notes next to the good lamp." On top of the table sat a hefty amber glass ball, the pedestal for a lamp glowing with bright light. Very mod.

"Okay," I shrugged.

The corner of my four-inch-wide white plastic binder nearly jabbed her in the hip when I maneuvered myself over to the navy blue, crushed velvet chair with a strong back. My bell-bottoms matched the chair perfectly. I heard the soft sigh of the cushion beneath me and for a moment felt I had just sunk into bed.

Doctor Sperling pushed a small gold leather hassock out of the way, and shot an apple core into the waste can. She was wearing what looked like Italian leather pumps. When she took a seat in the chair across from me, she adjusted her long flowing green skirt, so it draped elegantly over her legs. "Okay—fire away. Ask me anything."

I was starting to feel more relaxed and, to my surprise, a little bold. "They say psychiatrists pick this career because they really need to fix themselves. Do you think that's true?"

"Fix ourselves? Most of us aren't that smart," she chuckled. And then added, "Listen, everyone needs to ask for help sometimes. Getting better is a combination of helping yourself and letting others help you. It's true for most of us at some point in our lives, including psychiatrists."

I was thinking, *Sure, I bet they all say that to make you feel better, but what they really mean is, you really need help—so I'm going to make you believe it's normal for everyone to be as big a mess as you are.*

"How did you decide to become a psychiatrist?"

"Someone told me once that I've been one my whole life, so I may as well get paid for it." She laughed again. I didn't expect her to be full of jokes. But then she explained it was a career that came naturally to her. She told me she started out wanting to be a surgeon, but after seeing how poorly patients were treated when they had mental health problems, she changed her mind. She said she never regretted making the switch. Most of all, she said, and I took out my pen, opened my binder, and wrote this quote down: "I consider it both a privilege and honor to work with my patients. I receive much more than I give."

I wondered what in the world someone with problems could give her, except more problems, but I didn't want to seem unkind, so didn't ask.

"So, what happens first?" I turned the page to a clean sheet of paper and wrote down the word—First.

Doctor Sperling leaned forward, opened a drawer on the lamp stand, and reached for something. "Do you like popcorn?" She pulled out a red-and white-striped bag that looked like it came from the carnival.

"Sure," I told her, and watched her pour some into a paper cup.

"Help yourself," she said handing it to me. "I hate the stuff." She sat back again and continued.

"Okay, so for patients who come to see me here, or for patients assigned to me at the hospital, I conduct a diagnostic interview which includes a full psychiatric evaluation and testing. I assess the patient's history, what's going on currently, and how well they're coping with their symptoms. I also find out how much support they have from others. Hopefully family and friends."

She kept explaining, but her voice trailed off. My mind drifted back to Mother's life. She had lots of friends and family, but it wasn't enough. She hated popcorn, too, but made it for me anyway. Mother was every bit as nice as Anna-Victoria, and even this Doctor Sperling, and it made me wonder if they could lose their sanity just as easily, or if it was just people like me, related to people like Mother, who were in danger.

And then a question flew out of my mouth so fast that it interrupted her. "Can you tell what's wrong with someone right away?" I greedily tossed popcorn in my mouth; the kernels disappeared so fast I wasn't sure I was chewing.

"I might have an idea. Sometimes behaviors and mannerisms tell me a lot about someone. But the more information I gather, the clearer it becomes."

I closed my binder and set the cup of popcorn on top of it, trying to slow down the pace. My heart sped up when I asked, "So, do you have a hunch about me, for example?" I quickly corrected myself, "Well, what I mean is, can you ever tell *that* fast?"

She leaned back with folded arms across her chest. "It's more than first impressions."

I took hold of all the paper in my binder and flipped all the pages at once, like shuffling cards. And then to my surprise, I said even more, "I probably have some mental illness, like we all do I suppose." I was waiting for some reassurance, but she didn't exactly jump at the chance to give it to me.

She leaned forward with one hand on her chin, elbow to her knee, "What do you mean?"

"I'm in your manual."

"My manual?"

"Yes, the book you guys use. I found it in the library. I'm pretty sure I'm in quite a few of the chapters. So was my mom, I think. Before she left." The cup was empty now, but I caught myself grabbing for more popcorn anyway.

"Really. Well, some people think they have things figured out, but they aren't always right." She sounded sure of herself, pulled the bag of popcorn over and handed it to me.

I reached for a handful, chomping way too fast again. "Well, it wasn't that hard," I explained in-between bites. I lifted my right foot and set it on the edge of the coffee table stationed between us. I couldn't help but admire my new white sandal at the same time. Then I slipped it off so it wouldn't scuff up the glass and rested my bare heel on the glass top. It was only against the coolness of the glass, that I realized just how hot my feet were. It didn't seem normal, but nothing about me did that day. I wondered if having one sandal on and one sandal off told her anything. I was thinking it was an odd thing for me to do. Too late now, I thought, but pulled my foot back quickly anyway, just in case I exposed something dirty on the bottom of it. "I think I show symptoms of a neurotic type hang-up. And other things."

"Really. What else besides the neurotic hang-up?" She sat back as if she'd wait for me to answer no matter how long it took.

"Let's just say if I had time and money, I suppose I'd be in here as a patient, instead of doing this class." I chuckled casually, but felt my insides tighten.

Doctor Sperling gave an I-don't-care-shrug. "Talk about whatever you'd like to, Zetty."

My head went iron heavy. I stretched my neck backward and examined the ceiling while I thought about what it was I could say to her that wouldn't take hours to explain. "If I did that, you'd probably sign me up for life. But don't get me wrong. I'm not like, on the 'edge' or anything."

"The edge?"

I kept my eyes on the ceiling, focused on the white bumps covering it like the surface of the moon. "Or 'ledge,' you know. Like ready to jump." It was easier to talk if I didn't look at her.

"You mean you're not ready to kill yourself?"

"Oh no," I said abruptly, watching her face. "I mean, yes! I'm not ready. I mean I'm not trying to get ready—the idea scares me to death. Ha!" I hoped she could see I could be funny, too. She wasn't laughing, but she didn't exactly look serious either.

"So you've never wanted to end your life," she concluded. I saw a glint of levity in her eyes, which helped me keep talking.

"Not really, no," I said.

Her eyes squinted some and she tipped her head.

"More than end it I want to start it—to get to fully live it," I told her. "My best friend Gabe, agrees that's my problem, too."

"I see. So you aren't living the life you want, is that right?" She stood, grabbed her mug off the desk, walked to a long console against the wall, and poured hot water into it from a glass carafe sitting on a portable electric burner.

"I guess not," I said nonchalantly. I could've added, *living life with morbid fears isn't what I had in mind, either,* but I didn't want her to get more out of me.

"Would you like a cup of tea? It's English Breakfast, my favorite," she asked.

"No, thank you."

I watched her drop a tea bag and one sugar cube in the flowered mug, give it a quick stir and walk to the window. She sat on the wide windowsill, one arm crossed, supporting the other hand holding tea.

"What's your 'neurotic hang-up' Zetty? If you don't mind my asking."

"Love."

"Love?" A puzzled expression rolled across her face.

"Yes. The unrequited kind, mostly." I started flapping my binder open, fanning my face. If I had been honest I would've added, *From the mother who doesn't love me anymore.* But, of course, I knew better than to be honest.

"Ahh, yes. That kind." She went to the chair and sat across from me again. Her eyes shone kindness, if such a thing is possible. "So, your mother left."

"Well, yes. She did. And left my father, too. But here's the thing," I said, shifting directions. If I continued to talk about mother, something told me I'd come undone myself. It was prudent, I decided, to move on. Leave the truth in its tomb.

Her face spread open like a welcome mat, ready to receive whatever I had to say.

"Can you send me to the hospital that looks like 'the white house'?"

"The white house?" she asked somewhat bemused.

I set my binder on the gold carpet and twisted my back to the right until it cracked, and then to the left a few times, too. "I prefer to call it that instead of what everyone else calls it. You know, the 'funny farm.'"

"Yes, sadly, they do call it that. We clearly haven't evolved enough to understand that having a mental illness is no different than having diabetes or heart disease. But don't get me started."

"I don't mind."

"Well, good. I have a lot to say about it. And you'll have the opportunity to educate people in your paper, too. I hope you will."

"Me, too. And I'd like to go to the white hospital because it looks like a grand southern estate. I like the tall pillars and flowers all around. No need for a padded or locked room though. I'm not that brave." I checked her gaze to see if I needed to stop rambling, but she sipped her tea and gave me a go-on nod. "Solitary confinement wouldn't be necessary on account I'm not that bad off, right?" It was obviously a failed attempt at humor because she didn't laugh. "I'm only doing research. So a nice room with a view would be fine."

She stared out the window and I thought I lost her. But then she asked, "For what?"

"For the paper. You know, a bird's eye view. A look from the inside out. Zetty undercover," I said it sweeping my right hand out like a wing. "It's original, don't you think?"

Her lips folded over on each other as if pressing something hard between them. But then she smiled. "It's original, yes. But tell me what else, Zetty. What else are you looking for?"

She was good.

"Nothing," I fibbed. But she seemed so sincere I had to say something of the truth. "Honestly, I'm not sure. But I want to go inside and see what it's like for myself."

"Okay. Tell you what." She set down her mug with care on the coffee table, opened her appointment book, and began jotting down something with a new, sharp pencil. "We can send volunteers to join in the activities in the social/

rec room where you want to go. It's the state hospital. But first you'll need to go through an orientation for volunteers and your parents or guardian will need to sign permission forms."

"So, let me get this straight. I'm not too young to go inside?"

"No. Not as long as we have your parents' consent."

"What about a nine- or ten-year-old going in with a parent?"

"It's fine. They have special visiting rooms for children and families."

"Interesting." I filed that one in my "Proof of Father's Lies" folder.

"I'll get you the paperwork." She rustled through a file cabinet and pulled out a packet of forms. I saw father's impeccably forged signature on them already. It was my turn to be shady now. She handed me everything and sat again.

"Perfect!" I said.

"Well, not exactly, Zetty. You need to understand the inside of this hospital isn't what you seem to be imagining." She laid the cowhide-bound book on her lap and tucked the pencil behind her ear. "It's not a southern mansion with luxury suites. It's not a resort called 'Sunshine Acres' with country views from the windows, either. Really, nothing like that. And you won't be able to spend the night. They're overcrowded as it is." She reached for her mug again. "But I know you can spend at least half a day there, maybe more, and you'll have the opportunity to assist staff in some group activities if you'd like. It's really the best way to see if you enjoy working in a hospital environment."

I nodded in agreement but was disappointed. "So, you definitely can't commit me like the real thing?"

She sipped her tea and carefully placed her mug back on the coffee table. "No hon, hospital rules." She smiled a little when she said it, stood and walked over to her desk. "Our time's almost up, Zetty."

"Well, it'll have to do then." I picked up my binder off the floor, tucked the packet of forms and my pen inside, and took a few steps toward the door. "Oh, one more thing. Do you practice batting pillows and rolling into fetal positions here?"

She guffawed. "No, I just do it without practicing." She opened her top drawer and handed me her business card.

I found her humor a little annoying. "No, I mean 'inner fetal', something or other. Batting pillows and stuff."

"If you mean the latest 'inner fetal recovery work' fad, the answer is no." She shook her head like she meant it.

"Why not?"

"Because, quite frankly, I think it's, pardon my French, 'horse shit'. Don't get me wrong—if someone wants to wail at a pillow for fifty minutes, go into a fetal position, and pay someone to do that, and it helps, well, be my guest." She scribbled something down fast in her book, then closed it. "But do I think it's the secret to happiness, and good mental health? I'm afraid not."

"Are you a women's libber?"

"Well, I don't know how you define it, but yes, equality is good for mental health." She arched down, pinched a paperclip from the shag carpet and tossed it on the end table. "It's as simple as that."

I stood and started toward the door, but stopped. "One last thing. Sorry," I said briskly, "do psychiatrists think there's a God?" The question was a fascinating one, I thought.

"Some do. Some don't," she said matter-of-factly. Then pushed her desk chair back and walked briskly to the door with the same perky gait.

"Well, I don't." I said it so sure of myself I wondered if I had any doubt left about it at all. I hugged my binder against my chest like a shield and followed her.

"No one can make you," she said.

"Nope." And I hoped I hadn't just purchased a ticket to hell.

She opened the door. "Anna-Victoria will let you know when the next orientation is. We'll meet again after your visit—okay?"

"Sure!" I exited her office, practically sprang down the hall, waved goodbye to Anna-Victoria, who was on the phone again but, as I passed, she looked up, flashed a big smile, and gave me a wink. I climbed down all four flights of stairs, aware that I was practicing a little bounce in my step like Doctor Sperling's.

It was almost dinnertime when I stepped off the bus to walk the rest of the way home. A wave of salty night air washed over me, the breeze cool and refreshing again. The heat wave had broken while I roamed the downtown library, rode in the glass elevator in the swanky hotel next door, and window-shopped the entire length of Mission Valley Center Mall.

For the first time in my life, I felt important. Like someone on a mission, ready to risk up to eight hours of her life inside a real mental ward. The place Mother had lived, and maybe still did. If I could do this, I thought, I could fly to New York, too. Gabe was right. Father couldn't prevent me from seeing Mother forever. I wasn't going to let him.

Everything that evening made me feel happy to be alive: the rustling trees, the bus engine roaring off in the distance, even the cracks in the sidewalk. The world was unfolding in front of me; I sank my teeth into it like a candied apple. That evening, the crisp night air made everything taste delicious.

And then like the sudden shock of hearing some awful news, I understood why I felt this way. The last time I felt truly happy to be alive was when I was with Mother, wearing my red leather cowgirl boots, talking to Aunt Julie about our show. Nothing was wrong with life when Mother was in it. She was the buffer between me and everything bad that ever happened. I could believe in God, because I could believe in her. I could believe in love everlasting because she personified it.

I closed my eyes, remembering the formation of her hand cradling my own, the crooked, shy smile I saw all through the day when I was with her. And kindness. Not just to me, but to anyone fortunate enough, on any given day, to pass through her life.

I knew those streets, every square inch of the sidewalk leading home, because Mother and I used to walk them together. That night, my path took a momentous turn and moved me closer to her again.

The decision to seek out Doctor Sperling had to be divine providence.

By the time the calendar flipped over into September, the fluttering trees were still green, only sprinkling one or two leaves if the wind stepped up. Heavy, sharp palms fanned the sky with little more than a soft swish and sway. Camellias bloomed and red roses, the size of softballs, filled the air with aroma so velvety sweet, any nose that passed had to make contact. The only fall colors to be found in Windansea in September were draped on people.

I grabbed the silver rail and pulled myself up the steps of the bus, dropped two quarters into the slots, and told the bus driver, "California State Psychiatric Hospital, please." At least that was something I learned at the volunteer meeting. I was too distracted to notice the name of Mother's hospital the day I sat in the parking lot. But the two-hour orientation they held outside under a fancy gazebo prepared me for little else than that.

I ascended the stairs to the top of "the white house" mansion. It did make me feel a little like a queen at first, but I wasn't prepared for what hit me when I reached the summit and stepped inside.

A wall of sickly air permeated the atmosphere and blocked me at the entrance. Just like that, the happiness that had surrounded me like a cloud, dissolved. I spun around when my stomach turned sour and went back outside. I had to. Getting to fresh air was the only way not to puke. Even now, as a grown woman telling you this, the memory makes my stomach bloat. Doctor Sperling was right. It wasn't what I was expecting. The grand pillars were all a front for what was inside.

Of course, Mother was in New York, I rattled to myself. She had to be. Father would still be visiting if she wasn't. The idea I might find her, or discover "clues" to her whereabouts, suddenly seemed ludicrous. I took a deep breath, pushed back through the doors, and told myself that surely the nose would adjust and if nothing else came of the trip, I could always check myself in. There was always that.

I followed the signs to the Volunteer Coordinator, a sparrow of a lady perched at her desk. "Good morning," she greeted.

"I'm here to volunteer," I said, knowing I had probably stated the obvious. The air quality was only slightly better where she sat.

She pushed her chair back, grabbed an official looking

badge from a drawer and toddled toward me, aiming it at my neck. She clipped it into place. "There you go!" she said in a jovial way that sounded like I might be entering Disneyland, instead of where I was. "You're all set. Go right through the double doors down this hall to your left." She pointed me toward a waxy, hollow corridor. The same color, actually, of mother's face the day I last saw her.

"Okay," I said, and then added as dispassionately as possible, "I wonder, could you tell me which room my Aunt is in? I want to drop by and see her again before I leave."

"She's a patient?"

"Yes, Marjorie McGee. Can't remember the number."

"Let me check." She scrolled down a long list of handwritten names in a large ledger that looked like a guest book for a wedding. "Hmmm," she stopped mid-page. "I don't see it. Oh wait."

My heart flip-flopped into my throat and I started feeling faint again.

She pulled down her glasses from her head, "Here she is. Oh!" She startled me when she glanced up abruptly. "She's been discharged. You can see her at home now."

"Discharged? Or do you mean transferred?"

"No," she rechecked the list. "I don't know when, but it says 'discharged.' That means home. Nothing here about any transfers." The phone rang at her desk, and she waved me off with a satisfied smile which I reflected right back at her, as if it were true.

When I reached the end of the greasy hall, the six-inch thick double steel doors clicked open when I approached. A man in a blue uniform stood guard holding keys. When I passed to the other side I heard them shut with force and latch behind me as if I had entered a bank vault rather than a wing of a hospital. Several nurses stood at a long counter, flipping metal charts open, scribbling furiously, and then slamming them shut.

Patients wandered about wearing paper clothes in shades of the same sickly yellow cast off in the hallways. Feet shuffled in paper slippers up one side the hall and down the other. Like ants in formation. I felt my pulse quicken every time a woman passed. At some point, maybe not that long ago, she had been somewhere inside these walls. I took everything in as if she were a part of everything I saw.

I made a mental note to ask Doctor Sperling why the hospital looked the way it did. Why couldn't they paint the walls soothing colors and hang beautiful art? Why not have music playing, too? If people had to live here, it seemed to me they should try to give them the feeling of home, not to mention adequate ventilation. And why had Mother chosen to stay in a place like this rather than come home to us at Christmas when she had the chance? None of it made sense.

I tried not to stare. The first time I did, I caught the face of a young woman with drool coming down both sides of her mouth. Or was it snot from her nose? It was hard to tell except it did seem crusted over the way it does when children have head colds and walk around the park with it plastered on their cheeks. It was the snot and drool that made me want to hurl again. That, and the odor of ancient smoke and pee that seemed to follow me everywhere.

The memory of something Mother and I did snapped into place like a slide dropping into a projector. "You have an extra sensitive nose, Zetty, you're always the first to smell anything," she told me once while hiking through a canyon. I was first to detect the mint growing on the side of the trail. I held it to both nostrils, rubbed it into the tips of my fingers, and enjoyed returning to the scent all morning.

I had to get my mind off the drool, snot, pee and smoke.

I tried to focus on other things. Like the lingering memory of fresh mint. And then a short, portly man with a chin full of gray stubble unexpectedly turned and stared into my eyes. "What are you looking at me for?" he asked sternly.

"I didn't mean to. Sorry."

"What right do you have to be here?"

"I volunteered to help today. That's all." If I learned anything from Wilma, it was to answer all questions simply.

He stared back at me with a controlled intensity. "Stop walking around here acting like some smarty-pants. It pisses me off."

I broke eye contact and examined a scuff on the top of my boot, "Okay," I said and focused on his face again. "I didn't mean to piss you off. Sorry." I wasn't sure what I'd done, but at that very moment I knew it was a good call not to wear the white lab coat Father gave me. I went to work with him once and wore it around his lab pretending to be a scientist. I actually considered wearing it—just to be sure no one thought I was a patient. Just to be a real smarty-pants. I was ashamed I had even considered it. As if I was any better, or saner, than anyone else here.

Around the corner was a middle-aged woman with stringy hair standing like a pink flamingo at the San Diego Zoo. She was frozen stiff. I could stare at her all I cared to, and it didn't matter because she never moved. I didn't see her blink once.

I couldn't carry on a normal conversation with anyone it seemed, which reminded me of Mother. The more disconnected I felt from everyone, the more my mood sank. I no longer wanted to take notes, or pretend to do research, or study anyone.

I spent the next half-hour sitting in the recreational group room feeling awkward and out of place. When I tried to play cards with a few patients, they stared blankly back at me, nonresponsive. It was like being at the sixth grade dance again without any friends.

But then I met Sophie.

"Morning Social starts in five minutes. Five minutes until Morning Social, please." The announcement screeched over an intercom just off center from the nurse's station. Patients began to roam in from the hallway. Staff directed them to the circle of chairs where I had already found a seat.

A girl about my age plopped down next to me. "Hi," she said. "You look nice. I'm Sophie."

"Hi. I'm Zetty," I said. "You look ready to have a baby."

"Oh yeah, I am. I'm ready alright," she said, like she'd done it a million times. "They don't have maternity clothes here so I have to untie these pants and do the best I can."

She was a tiny little thing, except for the baby belly hanging all the way out.

"God, I hurt," she moaned. "I keep having contractions and they're getting harder. Have you had a baby?"

"No, I haven't."

"Well, don't. It's hell. Don't get me wrong, I love all my babies, but labor is hell!" She clutched her belly, and started to moan and groan something awful.

"Are you okay?" I asked alarmed.

"Nope," she grunted. "They're coming hard and fast! Piggy-back style!"

"Sophie's in labor folks," the head nurse announced. "Somebody start the Bingo game," she ordered, and then left.

"She must be getting the doctor," I told Sophie. I tried to reassure her. "I'm sure they'll be right back." Sophie pushed herself up with a robust grunt and waddled into the bathroom just off the circle area, clutching the underside of her baby belly. She started moaning even louder, nearly screaming by the time she reached the sink. I followed behind her figuring someone should. She pressed her back against the wall and slid down to the waxy flecked floor and crouched. She was breathing way too fast. "Get a towel," she ordered. Her face went purple from pushing, she spewed saliva, and through clenched teeth yelled this time, "I need a towel, Zetty—hurry! She's going to be an eight pounder!"

Normally the spitting would have made me feel like barfing again, but I didn't have time to focus on it. I twisted to the right where several other patients hovered around us. "Someone get a towel for Sophie, I don't know where they are!"

"Here you go Miss Zetty." A hefty woman chucked a towel in my face. "I'm Gladys. I'm here to assist you."

"Assist me?"

Gladys bobbed a head of yellow sausage curls violently up and down.

"Oh no. No one's assisting anyone," I assured her. "The doctor will be right here. I mean, we're *in a hospital.* There's plenty of them, right?" I snickered, trying to keep everyone calm. Especially myself.

I handed the towel to Sophie and bent down next to her. "It'll be okay. The doctor is on his way." But as soon as I said it, I witnessed three nurses glance in at us, and then leave not seeming one bit concerned. Which started to piss me off.

Two of the patients began chanting, "You can do it, Miss Zetty, you can do it!"

Before I could ask, "Do what?" Gladys ran toward me in a frenzied ball of motion and knocked me to the floor shouting lines from *Gone With the Wind,* "I don't know nothin' 'bout birthin' no babies! Don't know nothin' 'bout birthin' no babies! Please, Miss Zetty, help us!'"

I saw the fear race over Sophie's face. "The baby. Please save my baby," she begged.

Gladys sluggishly bent her frame all the way down to my ear. "Ain't goin' to be no doctor, Zetty. You is it." And then she straightened and went feverish again. "Help us Miss Zetty! You gotta help Sophie save her baby!"

Sophie pleaded, "I want her, Zetty. Please help me. I want this baby girl more than anything."

"It's a girl everybody!" Gladys shouted. "Zetty, please, for the love of God, help Sophie deliver her baby girl! Please!"

I moved straight in front of Sophie, and scanned the crowd that had formed. "Everyone calm down. I know all about birthin' babies." I thought it would shut them up until help came, but Gladys kept going.

"Oh, thank you Miss Zetty. Thank you," she said hugging and swooning all over me like Scarlett O'Hara herself.

I gently removed the thick hand Gladys had gripped around my arm and scooted closer to Sophie, ready to help catch the baby in, of all things, a muddy-colored hand towel. Her pants were down to her knees when she gave a massive heave ho.

"I did it!" Sophie cried nearly out of breath. "Look at my sweet baby girl."

I leaned forward, inspected the ground between her legs and saw nothing. I picked up the towel, and just like that, I was a hero. The sweet baby girl, all eight invisible pounds of her, lay in the muddy hand towel in my arms. The patients cheered my name and shook my hand over and over again.

Well, I thought, *I guess I've made some friends.*

"Maybe you should go to your bed to rest now," I told Sophie.

"Oh yes, please. What a good idea."

I pulled her up, still amazed at the size of her belly. I

led her by the elbow to her room. "Here, Sophie," I gently handed her the towel cupped in my hands after she climbed into bed. "You can keep your baby girl right by your side."

"I love her, Zetty. I'm a good mama. I promise I am. A wonderful mama. I would do anything for my baby. I love children. You have to believe me."

"I do believe you, Sophie," I said, covering her with a sheet. "Now try and rest—"

"Wait!" she screamed, "I'm not done!" She spread her legs and pushed herself up. "I'm not done!"

"There's more?!" I said, thinking this could be the real one.

"Yes, another one's coming! Oh God, please don't leave me."

Gladys screeched again, "Don't leave her Zetty, don't leave!"

"Gladys," I insisted, "I'm not going anywhere." I stuffed two pillows behind Sophie's back, scanning the door anxiously for a real obstetrician. Gladys leaned in over my shoulder when I asked Sophie, "You're having twins?"

"Yes, it's twins!"

"Oh my God, everyone!" Gladys announced, "It's twins!" and she burst into tears, one hand cupped over her toothy grin. But almost as soon as her joy erupted, the tears turned to raw panic. "My God!" she yelled. "We need incubators! They never make it without incubators!"

"Gladys, please," I said, sounding like a mother myself, "we're in a hospital. Incubators are everywhere. They're going to make it. You and I know what we're doing, remember? We're a team. Now go get more towels, okay?"

"We're a team, Miss Zetty. Miss Zetty and I are a team everybody! She and me goin' to save Sophie's babies!" she bellowed all the way to the linen closet.

I put my attention back on the mother-in-labor. "Okay, Sophie. Keep breathing and keep it going steady," I told her. "I saw Walter Matthau do this once in the movie, *Kotch*. Only he helped deliver a baby in a gas station bathroom. Can you imagine?"

"Did you watch that whole entire scene?" she asked.

"Yes, I did."

"Good. Because it's happening now!"

The way Sophie and everyone else continued to carry on, it was clear there were a lot more than two babies I delivered that afternoon, but I lost track.

"Congratulations for an excellent job of baby birthing, Zetty!" someone told me.

"Will you deliver my baby too?" another asked. "I'm planning to get pregnant tonight."

When I left Sophie's side, I saw the staff peering in her room. I could hardly believe they did nothing through Sophie's "labor" but play Bingo. It was aggravating. Then the head nurse told me, "She goes into labor at least twice a day. I almost thought you believed her by the way you responded, Zetty. You had me fooled!"

"Well, with a belly like that, who could know?" I joked. Of course, my acting skills must have helped, but the truth is I did believe Sophie. One hundred percent, almost right up to the end. But I kept that to myself. What I wanted to know and asked her was, "Did I do something wrong?" My stomach tightened in an old, familiar way. It was the same ache, an almost interminable companion since age nine.

"Not at all," the nurse defended. "It was brave of you, Zetty, you showed a great deal of compassion supporting her the way you did. It helped all the patients feel safe around you."

Her words, to my relief, bolstered me. She affirmed my ability to trust my instincts. Before long I would need to use them again in ways I never imagined.

When I said goodbye to the patients and staff, Sophie and Gladys gave me the longest hugs of anyone.

"I'll come back and visit you both as soon as I can," I told them.

Gladys jumped up and down with a two hundred pound thud of enthusiasm and then the thrill left her face. "I'm set to sail, Zetty. I'm tard of people pickin' fun with me. I'll be over the Indian Ocean by midnight."

"Oh," I let the words sink in. "Okay, Gladys," I said. "Thanks for all your help."

Gladys beamed and stepped in close to me, her shoulder leaning into mine with nearly all her weight. I had to brace myself against the bingo table to stay vertical.

"And I'm moving tomorrow," Sophie announced. "Leaving for China to work in orphanages. I have to do it, Zetty. So many babies need me."

"They do, Sophie. The babies will love you," I told her.

"Okay, then," I said, when I reached the steel-plated doors that felt like they belonged on Alcatraz. "Don't forget to write when you get where you're going; I'll never forget you guys."

"Promise?" they asked.

They waved to me from the window at the corner of the building where they told me to look when I went outside. Sophie held her babies up high, well, the muddy colored hand towels, and I blew them a kiss, flashed the peace sign and waved until I couldn't see them anymore.

I've kept my promise. I've never forgotten Gladys or Sophie. I've often wondered what became of them. For a long time I imagined Gladys with a bamboo orchid draped over her left ear, swinging in a hammock on a tropical island, sipping rum from a glass with an umbrella in it. And I saw Sophie traveling the world, gathering all the babies without mothers, rescuing them from a life of poverty and abuse, like Mother Teresa herself. The conceived notion that my own mother might be living in a New York pent-house performing on a Broadway stage, was starting to sound just as unlikely. But denial did have its perks. I started to understand why Father was so fond of it.

In a strange way, a new and different way, my trip to 'the white house' had brought me closer to Mother. I was glad I went, but the word "discharged" bobbled around my brain on the stroll back to the bus. My trip confirmed Mother had in fact moved, as Father suggested she might. And I knew she hadn't been sent home. That much I knew.

It was a start.

In My Mother's Footsteps

DOCTOR SPERLING WAS WEARING DARK, CHOCOLATE brown trousers and a plaid shirt with pumpkin colored shiny metallic threads woven through it. To complete the look, she wore an expensive-looking forest-green suede fitted jacket. Her red hair fell to one side and shined like a jewel against it. The hem on her jacket stopped just below her hips, Katherine Hepburn classy.

"I'm glad to see you again, Zetty." Doctor Sperling exuded the same energy as last time, bouncing around her desk, springy like. She had a happiness about her that made you feel like everything you were about to say would be easy. Like nothing she heard would ever scare her. She gestured to me to take her chair again.

She grabbed a flowered mug from the desk and sat in the chair opposite me. "How did your visit go?" she asked.

I glanced at her desk, looking for any frames of family photos. "Well, you were right about it not being a five-star resort. But you know, it should be. They deserve a resort."

She nodded, "Couldn't agree more," and propped her feet up on the gold hassock.

Doctor Sperling's wire-rimmed glasses slid down her nose and she set them on the table next to her. She reached under the lamp shade and switched on the light. "Wasn't quite what you expected?"

"Not exactly. I didn't expect it to smell the way it did, and all the patients shuffled around like they were on another planet. Well, I'm sure I don't have to explain it. Not to you."

She folded both hands in her lap. "No, you don't, but I'd like to hear what it was like for you. And answer any questions."

I told her everything. When I got to the part about the dumb idea about the lab coat, she asked me what line of work Father was in.

"He's an aeronautical engineer," I said proudly. "The only one around who repairs the same kind of airplane Amelia Earhart flew. And he's building his own French designed airplane in our garage, too. My mother bought him the blueprints and plans for Father's Day a long time ago." I reached into the front pocket of my jeans and checked to be sure Tuffy's purple bandana was safe. I gave it a gentle squeeze, pulled out my hand, and relaxed. "But anyway, that would've been silly to wear a white coat and try and dress up like a real shrink. I mean, 'doctor,' sorry."

"It's okay." She refilled her cup of tea. "May I pour you a cup, too?"

"Sure," I said, and tore open a pack of sugar in the bowl on the coffee table.

"The woman you said looked like a flamingo was in a 'catatonic state,'" she explained. "Physically, people can completely shut down." She handed me a yellow mug with a white peace sign on the front with a long name of a drug written underneath it. I thought about asking for some.

She reached into the drawer next to her and handed me a bowl. She ripped open another bag of popcorn. "Help yourself if you want any," she said. She went to the glass carafe and carried it over like a waitress warming up both our mugs for a refill and I was thinking, *Gee, we're practically friends.*

When she sat again, her voice rose with new energy, "So, go on. Tell me more about Sophie."

I wiped five buttery fingers on my jeans, being careful not to touch the bare skin that showed through frayed holes, and described everyone's reactions after I helped deliver a throng of babies. I felt a happiness rush over me when I told her how the nurse complimented me about the way I handled Sophie's labor.

"She was right, Zetty," Doc Sperling said. "It was brave and compassionate of you."

Her words raised me up at once; almost like another Ferris wheel ride.

The truth is, Mother was the reason I treated Sophie, Gladys, and the others the way I did. I tried to give them the same care and respect I would have wanted for her.

And then, as if reading my mind, Doctor Sperling said, "Zetty, tell me why you're really here." She set down the mug, kicked off her right pump, and casually folded her leg under her reinforced toe. "It's not about the class, or a career, is it?"

I said the truth before I had time to make up a real whopper. "I wanted to see the place where my mother went. You sent me to the first hospital they put her in." I rolled up the bag of popcorn and tucked it between my thigh and the chair. "I haven't seen her since I was nine. And I'm not in the class you thought I was in. Sorry."

"Not a problem, Zetty. Tell me more."

And just like that, our appointment to discuss my field trip changed. And her usual fifty-minute hour, which she seemed perfectly punctual about, stretched out to seventy-five minutes. It happened every time I told someone the story of Mother's last Thanksgiving with us; it stopped everyone in their tracks. Even, Doctor Sperling.

At one point she told me, "Mental illness is not something people choose, Zetty." Apparently, something I said made her think I needed to hear that. "But Sophie made herself look pregnant! She chose to do that," I argued.

"Maybe she needed to believe it was true," Doctor Sperling explained. "She may have wanted it so bad she tricked her body into believing it. Or, sometimes people reenact events, trying to undo something traumatic that happened. They may do things over and over again, trying to resolve it, or make it turn out differently."

"Oh," I said, struggling with the idea of reliving pain, over and over again. "Can you help them?"

"Yes. We can. But some forms of mental illness take a long time to overcome. And some forms, right now anyway, are incurable but are managed with the right help.

It'll improve someday, as we learn more." She adjusted the pearl necklace around her neck. "What else do you remember about your mother?"

"Things." I sat back and a happy memory bubbled up. "The red leather cowgirl boots I wore every Sunday night when we watched *Bonanza*. I broke them in galloping around in circles to the opening theme song."

Doctor Sperling's head tilted back and she smiled wide.

"Sometimes Mother joined in, and we laughed til' we couldn't breathe, which sounds strange, I'm sure. But she was silly and fun that way. I guess you had to be there." I felt lighter. Somehow the memory of Mother had prevented Tuffy's memory from intruding.

"It sounds like you shared a very special bond. What about your dad?"

I had to think. She sat quietly and waited. "I remember Father sitting in his chair, smiling at Mother and me. Every time we danced, put on a show, or practiced our numbers, he stopped whatever he was doing and sat to watch. He smiled the whole time, and clapped. Once he gave us a standing ovation we were so good."

I felt like I had described a completely different man, the father he used to be. I rolled down the bag of popcorn, sealing it shut for freshness. "And I remember her giving me pennies. You know, to throw into wishing wells and fountains. I wished for the same thing every time. The same thing I begged Santa Claus for each year, too."

"What was that?" She sipped her tea.

"A baby sister or brother. It never happened, of course, because Mother had already messed up when she had me. I was a huge mistake."

"Really," she said. Her face questioned the idea.

"I was. Trust me."

"Why do you believe that about yourself, and your mother?"

"My mother?"

"Yes. It can't be easy."

From what I had read, Freud was stuck on the mother thing, so I wasn't surprised she decided to hone in on that again. "I've accepted it," I said it in a brand new voice I just invented, hoping it would prevent tears from falling. I didn't want to be a bawl baby in a shrink's office. Not like Wilma.

"It can't be easy," she said again.

I felt my mouth start to quiver, I didn't want it to give me away. I wasn't ready or eager to return to that dark place inside me where I hid both my mothers: the normal one and the extra-terrestrial version. "It's just Tuffy. I'm still not over it," I said, flapping my hands like fans against my eyes, as if air could stop tears.

"Tuffy?"

I burst into tears and finished off her box of Kleenex when I told her every last detail of his entire death scene. She reached under a cabinet and handed me a new box when I pulled his purple bandana out of my pocket to show her.

"Zetty," she said with care wrapped around her voice, "would you consider coming to see me as a patient?"

So, this was it, I thought. It came as no real surprise. She had to see the evidence of my own crazy, mixed-up mind. Or perhaps the hereditary problem she knew I was doomed for. I wiped my dripping eyes. "Do I have a choice?"

"Of course you do."

But I knew I didn't, not really. It was time to face facts. "Sign me up," I said, resigned to the inevitable. But I was about as eager to be a mental patient as I was to run head-first into a brick wall. I told her in a voice as flat as I felt, "Admit me to the unit. Whatever you have to do."

"You're not being hospitalized, Zetty. You're starting therapy. All we have to do is find an open slot and schedule weekly appointments. Anna-Victoria will take care of the paperwork and billing information. Have your dad read and sign what she gives you, and of course have him come in or call if he has questions. Then, we're good to go." She said it so chipper, you'd think she had just sold me a car. By the time this was over, I figured I would have bought a car, a brand new sexy convertible for her.

The "have your dad sign" part wasn't going to happen. I could forge his signature easy enough, that wasn't the problem. It was the insurance billing I was worried about.

But Gabe figured that one out: "Ask Anna-Victoria to give you the statements instead of mailing them," she said. "All you have to do is explain that when you were learning to drive, you crashed into the mailbox. Tell her it wasn't repaired yet, so everything has to be hand delivered." It worked the way most of Gabe's ideas did.

Doctor Sperling escorted me to the door. I stopped, built up my nerve, and then said it: "Better get your textbooks out and study up. As far as I know, I only have one personality, but the one I have is going to be a real case."

She flashed a smile, but the only thing she said was, "I look forward to working with you, Zetty. See you next week."

She thought I was kidding.

A House With Soul

"Zetty? What are you doing?" One sluggish lid lifted and I saw Gabe's head wedged between the door and my bedroom wall. "You gonna mope around all day?" she asked.

Gabe's head twisted, her hair swishing like a horse tail. She froze when she spotted the piles of laundry, shoes, dirty plates, cups, and candy wrappers scattered over the brown tiled floor. Then she stepped to the window, grabbed the bottom of the roll-up blind, gave a fast yank, and let it rip. As soon as it snapped, the room flooded with eye-aching sunlight. I pulled my feather pillow over my face and felt the roses Mother cross-stitched on my pillowcase against my nose.

"Well, are you?"

I uncovered my mouth. "If I feel like it, yes! What's it to you?" It felt good to unleash my sassy side now and then, especially to Gabe. She always knew what to say, no matter what I flung at her.

Gabe plopped down on my bed, picked up Herbert and stroked his ears. "In a matter of days school starts and yay, we're going to be seniors. But our freedom is twirling to an end so let's go do something."

"Next year at this time who knows where we'll be. You'll probably leave and go to college and I'll be stuck here alone."

She smacked me lightly on the arm with Herbert. "Don't be so melodramatic," she groaned, "we'll always be here for each other."

It made me feel better at the time.

Gabe bent to the floor and picked up *Our Bodies, Ourselves*. It was Scarlett's gift to us for summer reading. "I've read and seen all I care to about our vaginas," Gabe said. "I've got stuff to tell you so let's walk to the beach. You can take Tuff," she braked. "I can't believe I just said—"

"Happens to me all the time," I broke in. "Let's go." I bounded off my bed, grabbed my moccasins and we left.

We walked slower than usual down the hill lined with pickle weed. I took a deep breath of salty air when the beach came into view.

"It's weird not to hear Tuffy with us—the jingle of his collar. It's too quiet," Gabe said.

I nodded. "I lost my childhood when I lost him, Gabe."

"What do you mean?" she asked, with an edge of sadness.

"I counted on some things never changing. And yet everything has."

"Lots of things won't. But you have to move on when they do."

"Well, I don't like it," I said, ignoring every crack in the sidewalk my moccasin landed on.

"No one does. But listen, we have another problem."

"We do?" My stomach took a nosedive. Gabe was serious when she said it.

"It's my mother."

"What?"

"I've been reading her journal."

"How?"

"It wasn't hard. Trust me."

"And?"

"She *is* having an affair."

"You waited to tell me this? With who?!"

"A blue barn."

My face went blank trying to interpret what she said.

"Yeah. She's having an affair with a blue barn she fell in love with years ago in Vermont. Some dumb place up on a hill with acreage all around it and a rolling paddle-wheel. She said it was a 'house with soul' that was 'always meant' for her. She's leaving to start a new life. Alone. I remember she wanted to buy it when we lived there, but my dad wanted nothing to do with it. Now it's for sale again, and she's planning to run off to live happily ever after with a blue barn."

"What is she thinking?"

Gabe went to the curb and balanced it like a tightrope. "She's in la-la-land," she said. "Probably went to a phone booth that night to buy a ticket to Vermont."

I stopped in front of her. "Do any normal mothers even exist, Gabe?"

Gabe took hold of both my shoulders for balance. "None. Is she crazy, or what?"

The question was, sadly, all too familiar. And yet, I knew enough about Scarlett to see she could only be pushed so far. There was a limit she reached before she set things straight with Dennis. No-nonsense, Gabe-style, and with the kind of wisdom that comes from knowing who you are and what you want, completely, and only after forty-odd years of living.

Gabe let out a deep breath and told me, "She referred to it as 'the one that got away.' When we get home I'll read it to you. There's something about us in there, too. How she feels 'invisible' to both her daughters."

"I'm a daughter, too?" A sense of pleasure spread over me and softened the moment.

"Of course you are," she answered, not surprised in the least.

Gabe leapt off the curb. "Come on, let's jog to the cliffs."

When we reached the rock where I had sat next to Tuffy and heard the voice, I shuffled my feet over the spot where he had lain, hoping to kick up his scent. Hoping, maybe, to hear *him* this time. It was a silly thought, but I seemed to be full of them.

"Let's go to your house, Gabe. Your mom asked me to stay for dinner."

When we rounded the cul-de-sac, Gabe sped up, kicked in the screen door to the kitchen, grabbed two spoons and snapped off a lid. We dipped them into a jar of thick chocolate fudge sauce and continued up the stairs. After Gabe cleaned the last of it off her spoon, she reached under the mattress and pulled out Scarlett's red spiral notebook. She leaned back on an olive-green corduroy pillow with side arms and crossed her legs with the journal propped open on one knee.

"I forgot to tell you what Doc Sperling said about inner fetal recovery work."

"You talked about that, too?"

I watched Gabe's face before I said it. "Called it 'horse shit.' Said it's a fad." Gabe's lower jaw dropped and then closed as her whole mouth arched downward, as if to say, *I don't believe it.* Gabe paused, staring at the cover of her mom's journal and then with a high step in her voice she said, "I like your shrink, Sperling."

I turned up the radio and plunked down across from her.

"So, is she actually helping?" Gabe asked. "I mean, you know, to contact hospitals."

"Not really."

"What's the hold up? We need to rule out all the hospitals first, right?"

"The problem is Father. If she's going to search for her, he has to be involved. Otherwise her hands are tied. She explained a bunch of legal gobbledygook. I'm not sure I'll be able to do a thing."

"Now hold on, Zetty. We'll do it with or without her," Gabe said, her voice decided and strong. "We have a plan and we're sticking to it. Get me phone numbers and I'll start calling myself."

"Who's going to tell *us* anything?"

"We'll have the same little lapse in memory you had at 'the white house,' Zetty. We'll forget what room she's in. But we'll convince them we've seen her there before. That was a brilliant move by the way."

"It worked, yes. But to do it again means a lot of long distance calls."

"I'm a career woman, remember? I've got money," Gabe said.

It was only then, concentrating on my hands, nails filed just the way I liked them, that I realized something I needed to say to Gabe. My eyes met her gaze. "To think you would do all this for me is unbelievable, Gabe. I don't deserve it."

"Of course you deserve it. And always have."

I dampened the edge of my sleeve when I patted the corners of both eyes. I didn't feel I warranted such a perfect friend, but was grateful she felt I did.

Gabe straightened next to me. "All we need is one lucky break in this case. Just one." She turned to me to be sure I was listening. "It'll happen. You'll see. Opportunities will come our way, they always do. Somebody's gonna mess up and tell us something they shouldn't. And when they do, we'll be ready to run with it, Zetty. Honestly. I'm not worried. Nothing can stop us."

I loved it when Gabe refused to give up.

"So. Why-oh-why, does your mother feel invisible?" I asked. "Do tell." I folded my arms behind my head and waited for Gabe to start reading.

But before Gabe turned to the first page, two loud knuckle raps startled us into full upright sitting positions— two crooked pillars of guilt. The red spiral took a reckless plunge over her shoulder.

Even though Scarlett appeared calm, the moment I saw her I knew it would be easier to face an armed swat team. "Anyone happen to see my red notebook?" Her arms were folded below a pin stuck to a black vest that read, "Women Hold up Half the Sky." Scarlett's right foot started tapping. "Alright my dears," she continued, "gig's up. Hand it over." It sounded like a hold-up by someone really nice. Scarlett could handle even the worst situation with a velvet fist.

Gabe pulled the notebook from behind her back and nervously handed it to Scarlett. It bent open as she passed it, sprinkling small pieces of scratch paper with notes on them, which only infuriated Scarlett more. Gabe fumbled to pick them up and stuffed them back in.

"I can't believe you stole this. It's private property, Gabriella." Scarlett twisted the volume on Gabe's radio as low as it would go. "How would you like me to steal your diary and read it with your dad and brother tonight around the dinner table? Huh?"

There was really no need to respond to that question since we all knew the answer.

However, I was glad to hear she expected Tom for supper.

"And by the way. Nice try with the 'dream'. You know—the one you shared around the campfire. Honestly, did you really think I would fall for that?"

Again, there was no good answer worth offering.

"Reading my journal once wasn't enough?" Gabe and I looked at each other in disbelief.

"Yes," she affirmed. "I know. Why did you do it?"

"Why do you think?" Gabe stood, ready to defend herself. "You got up and drove off at three in the morning. Why'd you do that?"

"You had no right snooping on me."

"Well, unless you're Clark Kent, it's a little odd to take off like that, don't you think? We almost called the cops thinking your car was being stolen, didn't we Zetty?"

"Yes, that's completely true; I actually recommended calling the police twice, Scarlett."

And then Gabe detonated like a small grenade. "Just be honest! What were you doing?" Before Scarlett could answer, Gabe launched into more. "We know you're moving to Vermont and abandoning everyone, including Zetty, who has already been down this road, Mom! How could you?" Gabe's face turned red hot, her eyes like blistering sparks.

"Now wait just a minute," Scarlett said with a catch in her voice, "what are you talking about?"

Gabe lifted her head, took a slow, deep breath and spoke at an even, steady pace, like a prosecuting attorney. "You're 'invisible' here, remember? You're in love with a blue barn! Just tell the truth."

"That was a rough draft for a short story I'm working on. It was an assignment for my Wayward Women's Writing Circle. I'm supposed to describe a discontented middle-aged woman. Who is actually starting to look a lot like me. But that's beside the point. I would never leave you, or you, Zetty. Never!"

Okay, I thought. *We can relax about that one.*

"And as far as my taking off in the middle of the night, honestly, you won't believe it." She shook her head as if talking to herself, took a deep breath and then looked right at us. "Girls, I went to a phone booth for a live radio interview after some of my work was recently published."

"What?" Gabe said.

"That's right. My writing is gaining a lot of attention and the media want me for interviews."

Gabe frowned. "I don't get it."

"I needed privacy," she explained. "They were calling from the east coast. If I had taken it from home, no telling what would've happened. Not to mention Tuffy." Both Gabe and Scarlett made the sign of the cross over their chests simultaneously. "May he rest in peace," they said in unison. "Anyway," Scarlett continued, "I couldn't risk a barking dog, and husband, and kids listening in or interrupting me. I was nervous enough!" She pulled out the chair from Gabe's desk and positioned it closer to us. "I was waiting to tell everyone."

"But Mom, you got published?"

She dropped with a thud. "I know," she smiled playfully. "It is exciting."

"What story did they publish, Scarlett?" I hoped it wasn't going to be the dumb one about the blue barn.

"Noooo, not a *story*," she corrected. "They wrote about my Inner Fetal Recovery work. I'm considered to be a bit of a pioneer!"

It fell like a bomb in our lap, but we tried not to let Scarlett see the jolt it gave us. We both nodded carefully up and down. "Ohhhh," I answered. "I seeee," Gabe said at the same time.

Someone needed to break the awkwardness. "Congratulations, Scarlett," I said.

"Yeah, Mom. Have you told Dad?"

"No," Scarlett hesitated. "You know him, first he'll ask if they're paying me, and then when he finds out they aren't, he'll begin his lecture on the 'ridiculous' profession I'm in."

I remembered what Tom said and it was true; there were some things his dad was right about.

When the timer went off in the kitchen, a loud and annoying buzz, Scarlett hopped over record albums scattered on the floor and trotted downstairs. It wasn't long before we could smell the garlic-roasted chicken she pulled out of the oven and heard the clatter of silverware in the drawer.

We went downstairs and watched Scarlett put her favorite Jimi Hendrix album on the turntable, shift the automatic lever to "on," and crank up the volume. With a shock of black curls, she shook herself up and down, Woodstock style. It wore us out just watching her. We collapsed on the gold and green brocade sofa and Gabe turned to me. "I know my mom's smart. And she can be fun, I admit it. And I really am happy for her, I am. But she's craaaaazy, Zetty! She does this work that's making her famous but no one knows how completely weird she is at home."

"What mom isn't, Gabe?" *Look at mine*, I thought.

"Most of them aren't therapists Zetty. You can cut them some slack. All my mom does is talk about feelings. Talk and talk and talk and try to help people figure themselves out, like that's gonna help. Which of course it doesn't, so she makes them beat pillows and go back to the womb. So weird."

"Well, she's not that bad. Most mom's think Pat Boone is still in the top ten."

"Yeah, but come on, she rocks out and grooves all over the house singing, 'Come On Baby, Light My Fire'! She said someone researched it and it speeds up housework. And okay, she's not a bad dancer, I admit that, but she's not young enough anymore to act like this. Yesterday, she stood out in the cul-de-sac counseling the neighbor women about loving their bodies! Talk about sick."

I grimaced in agreement.

"Sorry," Gabe said in earnest. "I know how you hate it when people bitch about their moms."

"You have no idea how good you have it."

"I know," she said and leaned against my shoulder. "I've almost saved enough for our plane tickets. We're making progress." She sat straight again. "Hey, what has the shrink said about your fear of flying?"

"Told me it sounded like displaced anxiety—symbolic of Mother leaving me."

"Hmmm," Gabe considered. "It's a little out there, but okay."

Dennis walked over to the stereo and changed the record. He looked at Scarlett. "Darlin', you're a damn dandy fine woman. We're gonna dance." He wrapped Scarlett in his arms, and they folded their hands together, pointed to the left. "You watch, girls. This is real dancin'," Dennis crooned.

A flamenco guitar started playing along with a mariachi band, and Dean Martin started singing, low and sultry. Dennis twirled Scarlett around and they swayed to the music as if they had rehearsed a million times. They were good enough to be on stage, I thought. I liked seeing the romance sparkle between them as they pulled in together, Dennis's hand pressed to the small of her back.

"A regular Ricky Ricardo," I told Gabe. "What got into him?"

"Beer," Gabe simpered.

And then, the front door opened and Tom walked in. My face must have shown something.

"Zetty—it's just Tom."

"Oh. Okay."

"For a minute there I thought you went starry eyed," she said.

"Hey Zetty, how's it goin?" Tom tossed his keys and wallet on the table in the entry.

Gabe's head jerked up, her eyes studied Tom's face.

"Goin' good. How 'bout you?" I asked.

Gabe's head jerked again, this time toward me.

"Good," he replied.

Gabe crossed both arms. "What's with the meet and greet stuff? You guys never do that."

Tom flashed her a big-brother reprimand. "Zetty went through a lot at the lake, Gabe. I was there, remember?"

"Yeah, duh, but—"

"I'm checking to see if she's doing okay, is that a problem?"

"Well, no. It's just that you sounded so, well, really nice."

"Well, I am nice. When there's a reason to be." He bolted up the stairs, and I turned to Gabe, trying to look stunned.

I grabbed a throw pillow and clutched it to my chest. "People with dead dogs make him nicer I guess," I told her.

"Yeah. I guess."

During dinner, Tom and Dennis heard all about Scarlett's newfound fame. After the wisecracks died down, Tom signaled me into the garage. We only made out for a minute in the dark, but I memorized every curve of his lips, the rounding of his ear, the taste of his skin, the smell of his neck, the sound of his sighs, the light touch of his fingers circling my naked shoulder that turned my skin to goose-flesh. I replayed it in my mind the whole night long. And every day after, too.

IN-SESSION

I JUDGE THE COMFORT OF ALL NEW SHOES BY THE WAY THEY sound. Yes, that's right, how the heels sound when they hit different types of pavement for the first time. I listened on cement sidewalks on the way to school, beige tiles in the cafeteria, black tar pavement on the playground, and the wood floor of the gym where I learned to square dance in the sixth grade. How the heel hits the ground is like a piano chord in my mind. Solid, soft, pleasant. It has to sound right, or I've never been happy with them.

I listened to my heels that morning when I took four floors up to Doc Sperling's office wearing the new pair of Mary Jane red suede shoes. They completed the look with my red and orange paisley dress with long puffy Juliet sleeves, the "in" thing that year. It was a test-run for the first day of school, only three days away.

The linoleum tiles on the stairs sounded good underfoot, but they lost their tone when they hit the carpet beyond the entry where Anna-Victoria sat. My shoes lost their appeal; too dull and quiet. Practically invisible, until Anna-Victoria saw them.

"Morning, hon! Well, would you look at you in those adorable shoes! You look like you could tap dance right across the room! Just adorable, sweetie." She reached for the phone, and in a hurried whisper said, "Have a seat, she won't be long."

And then I saw her. It was Wilma again, head down, sitting in the spot I usually do.

When her face lifted, I could see she looked absolutely dreadful. Like someone who had lost her best friend or, maybe, her dog. In which case I completely understood. Whatever it was, she was subdued this time. And she avoided eye contact. I was scheduled to see Doc Sperling next, so I hoped Wilma wasn't going to have another emergency that would cut into my time.

I actually wanted to see Doc Sperling even though I had become a real tested, assessed, and diagnosed mental patient. I couldn't help but notice I was ten minutes early, which I also found interesting. I suddenly heard Gabe shouting in my mind, *Stop with the Freudian analyzing, Zetty! Enough with that nonsense!* Anna-Victoria came around her desk. "Zetty, you can come back now."

When we were down the hall she turned her chin over one shoulder. "By the way, Lottie stopped by yesterday with four dozen eggs her hen laid. She asked me to give you and Wilma some. Bless her heart," Anna-Victoria sputtered, trying to remain professional. "They're by the door, so help yourself when you leave." When she turned, I saw a smile as big as pie plastered on her face.

As we reached Doc Sperling's office I told Anna-Victoria, "It's nice Lottie has so many eggs to share. Thank God none of them are in a petri dish."

Anna-Victoria cupped one hand over her mouth and held her stomach. We both gasped for air laughing. It was the way I used to laugh with Mother. But as soon as I thought of her, I wrestled the memories to the ground and kept them quiet so it wouldn't interfere with my session. It wasn't what I wanted to go in thinking about even though

I didn't know what I should go in thinking about. It just wasn't going to be about Mother again.

I went into Doc Sperling's office feeling somewhat relaxed. Laughter can do that to a person.

"So, where do we start today?" I asked her.

"Wherever you'd like to begin."

"Oh. Well, in that case I'd like to discuss whatever you think would help me the most."

"Let's talk about the secret in your family."

"The secret?" I said it as clueless as I felt.

"No one in your family likes to discuss what happened to your mother and where she is, right?"

"Right."

"Tell me what you think happened, Zetty. I want to understand how you made sense of all this."

Doc Sperling sat quiet, relaxed, waiting.

I told her everything I could for twenty minutes straight.

She glanced at the time. "Okay, Zetty," she said. "I want you to make a list of what I'm about to tell you. Keep it to remind yourself of what I'm going to say." She handed me a tablet and pen and I wrote down:

1. *Mentally ill people are not crazy.*
2. *Mental health exists on a continuum we all live on. Some people need more help finding their balance on the continuum than others.*
3. *A combination of difficult experiences and hereditary factors can make it hard for anyone to cope.*
4. *Mental illness is not contagious. My mother lost touch with reality. I have not. A vivid imagination is not the same thing.*
5. *Mother may have a rare form of schizophrenia. Her child-like behaviors were a part of her illness when she stopped connecting to me.*

6. *I'm not "bad" for feeling frightened of Mother the day she left. It's natural that I would feel afraid and confused by how she changed.*

7. *Mother was not able to control what happened to her. No matter how much she loved us and no matter how much she wanted to stay.*

8. *The loss of my mother has affected my heart, mind, body, and soul.*

"What do you mean my soul?" I asked, as I scribbled down what she said.

"How did your mother's leaving change your beliefs?"

My eyes met hers and I was blunt when I answered, "It didn't change them. It ended them." I felt a sea of sadness begin to engulf me. I was getting worse talking about this instead of better. I think she could tell I couldn't continue down the road we were on.

"What happened between you and your father, Zetty? After that visit?"

I was relieved. I would have changed the subject if she hadn't. "Nothing," I answered, "except he seemed mad at me."

"Did the two of you talk about that?"

"Not really," I responded. "Like I said, there's a law against discussing her. Sometimes I'm glad. I don't always want to talk about her either. It makes going to bed harder. There's something about being alone in the dark that makes my thoughts go squirrely."

"Squirrely? Tell me more." She jotted something on her tablet.

"I knew you were going to say that! Just like Dr. Id."
"Who?"

I decided to tell all, and be done with it. "It's probably a delusional problem."

She tipped her face down, eyes peering over a pair of

new wire-framed granny glasses, the small oval kind psychedelic rock bands were wearing.

"You know," I continued, "delusions of grandness, or something like that, where I've invented a make-believe shrink, I mean an imaginary doctor, for myself, for the purpose of discussing all my problems with him."

"It's not 'delusions of grandness.'"

"What is it then?"

"An imaginary shrink you invented to help yourself sort all this out. Clever, actually."

I did a double-take on the word "clever." All this time I had been clever instead of mentally ill? Well, I decided, that was probably pushing it.

"Go back to your thoughts. Tell me what scares you at night," she said.

"Death. Plane crashes. Losing it like Mother, or that poor lady, Wilma, only doing it at school."

"What else?"

"Feeling like it's only a matter of time before what happened to Mother, happens to me. And going under and never coming back up. I like to pretend that I drown. Almost the way Tuffy did, but it started before that happened. My drowning dream doesn't scare me in the least by the way. I only mention it because it's something Gabe said I should definitely tell you about."

"Okay." She lifted her glasses and waited.

"I'd rather tell you about my aunts. I'm concerned about all of them."

"So you want to put aside the drowning dream. Do you know why?"

"Because. I just don't want to talk about that. Or any God stuff."

"Okay. Tell me about your aunts."

"They giggle about nothing, like Mother did. What I mean is, it's not like *real* laughing, like the time a large section of wallpaper lining our dining room slumped down over our heads while we ate banana cream pie. Now that was funny. When they laugh, it's fake. Polite, but pointless. They spend hours discussing the latest gall bladder gone bad, herniated discs, ballooning thyroids, and toes that caught the gout. But not one word about what made Mother change. In the world they inhabit Mother is as unmentionable as their age."

Doc Sperling's eyes widened. "I bet," she said and flipped over a full page of notes to a clean page. I wondered if she ever wished she knew shorthand after sessions with me. "It's like you said, Zetty," she continued, "thinking about your mother makes it hard for you to sleep at night. Maybe it's the same for them. Talking about her may be too hard. Just like it's hard for you to talk about your drowning dream, and 'God stuff,' do you see what I mean? We all do it sometimes. When we're uncomfortable or afraid."

I readjusted my head against the built-in pillow on the couch and stretched my arms straight toward the ceiling, wrists circling in mid-air. "This stuff is deep, isn't it?"

"Sometimes," she answered.

I realized the very thing I was determined not to take into session with me that day was the very thing I ended up talking about. Classic textbook behavior as far as Freud was concerned.

"Until now, it's been up to me and Dr. Id to figure everything out," I told her. I smiled inside, thinking of the word "clever" she used to describe him. My frosted pearl fingernails shimmered against the backdrop of the ceiling until my arms turned to heavy metal, and slammed to my sides. "Some help he was. Look where I ended up!"

Doc Sperling unfolded her arms, grinning. "Our time's up, Zetty."

Doc Sperling sprang from her seat with her usual vim and vigor. She opened the door and I felt a slight twinge of unhappiness at being directed out. She did stick to her schedule whenever she could, that's for sure. I told myself I couldn't expect to be important to her outside our fifty minutes; it's just not the way it's done. She was a doctor, not a friend, not a teacher, not my sister, not my mother. She was my shrink.

Nothing more. But, still.

"Thank you, Doc Sperling. I really like you. I mean I like that you're trying to help me and all." She was becoming important to me. I was afraid she might think it was silly—see it as some kind of mother complex I was developing. Freud said patients could get all mixed up about that. Something I certainly had no intention of doing. I did wonder if Doc Sperling had a daughter, though. Or if she liked me in that way, just a little.

Ferris Wheels

By the third week of school I was bored again in every class but one: Senior Art Studio. I loved the smell of it.

You know how it is. When you crack open a brand new can of hot pink play-dough and breathe in. Or lift the lid of a clean box of new, perfectly sharp crayons and sniff. Or untwist the cap on a new jar of creamy peanut butter and inhale. Or grab hold of the aroma when you dip your nose inside a bag of freshly ground coffee. That's what a bottle of acrylic paint does for me. I'd soak in a bathtub of it if I could. Preferably midnight blue.

Senior Art Studio was the only class you had to be selected for. A committee of art teachers went through a process and hand-picked twelve of us. I can't say exactly why I was chosen to be in it. I'd like to believe it was my talent, but, it was more likely my psyche, which on canvas must have looked a little frayed my junior year.

Naturally, the selection committee would take pity on someone like me. I was, after all, "the poor kid without a mother." I did earn an "A" in Art last year, and my final project, a painting, won a blue ribbon. But as soon as I saw it spotlighted in a six-foot-tall glass display case at the school entrance, I had the feeling it was picked for other reasons.

The theme of the exhibit was "The Genius of Madness." There it was, my pointillism scene made up of at least a million dots hanging right between two famous paintings, one done by a guy who lopped off his ear and another who liked to paint pictures of people screaming bloody murder. Both of them—duh—a little "disturbed." So you have to wonder. Was it something about the lone tree on the hill at sunset in my landscape that concerned them, or was it the back of the girl hunched over on a swing dangling from the largest limb that appeared disturbing, or the clouds hanging low, dark and heavy, that contributed to their doubts about my stability. Or maybe it was the lightning bolts and rain in the sky, or the girl's head of electric blue hair that looked like it came in contact with a light socket. Maybe that gave them the wrong idea. At any rate, I was one of the first in my class to be selected for Senior Art Studio, and as Gabe said, "If it got you in, who cares."

Sweet Baby James was playing on KCBQ the second day back. Since they inspired our creativity, James Taylor and Joni Mitchell played the whole period. We set up our easels, poured out delicious paint colors on clean palettes, and began dipping soft horsetail brushes into a rainbow of liquid velvet paint. I held a brand new bottle of emerald green and watched it flow out like syrup, full bodied and flawless; it calmed me with just one whiff.

The floor smelled good too, freshly waxed and polished. The tone, by the way, was perfect under my new beige, suede desert boots. Sue Willy ran up to me with a giant hug, sporting a flaming red crocheted beret and string of love beads.

"What did you do all summer?" I asked. "You still haven't told me a thing." I smeared emerald green paint across the corner of a creamy white canvas.

"After the Woodstock trip," she said again as if she had actually gone, "my mom met another asshole of a boyfriend. He tried to cop a feel on me, so I let him have it. Knocked the holy sheeet right out of him." She laughed triumphantly. "Knocked him senseless, un poquito tontito! Of course my mom didn't believe he reached down my shirt and grabbed my boob, or my ass, so she was pissed at me."

"What?!" My brush froze, suspended in mid-air. "Why would you make that up?"

"Oh, I know." She dipped a stick into my paint and stirred. "But he paid for it. Pathetic Senor Pequeno!"

Sue Willy had a zaniness about her that was infectious. There was beauty in her plainness. A natural vibrancy she seemed to emit, and always a spark of chaos in her eyes. Sue Willy had a personality that was over the top, and boys really fell for it.

We all knew why Sue Willy made it in the class. Her art was as wild as the life she lived. Like the one she did of a giant bottle of whiskey with a pot plant propped up against it. That was nothing though, compared to what she entered into the student exhibit at the county fair. She painted a woman's overwhelmingly large naked breast on a bigger-than-life canvas. That one launched a community uproar.

Parents were outraged mainly because it was so lifelike! The entire PTA threatened to sue the school district for condoning sexual content, but Sue Willy refused to paint over it. "I'll take it straight to Congress, if you don't allow it in the art show," she threatened. "And," she added, "I'll add more nude body parts and design a whole exhibit around sex if you don't allow me free expression! And that's a promise." She made it into the morning paper and by that evening she was the main story on the six-o'clock news. For about a week, Sue Willy was famous. She told a reporter, and I quote, "You have to paint true to who you are, man. I paint what's real, what's happening. I don't hold back; if I did, I wouldn't be a real artista." Sue Willy always had a flair for throwing in a little Española when she spoke.

The thing is, Sue Willy had a mother, but sometimes I think it would've been better if she hadn't. And Gabe was right. Even though she was a little dodgy, in your face dramatic, and seen by many as sluttish, you couldn't help but like her in her own outrageous sort of way. Scarlett agreed. In her opinion, Sue Willy needed more friends like us to be a better influence on her. Maybe that's true, but I never knew what she could learn from me. My friendship with Sue Willy was more about me getting to learn from her.

"Is there any red over there?" Sue Willy asked. Something hooked my attention when she turned her head toward the paint table.

"Sue Willy, did someone beat you up?"

"Oh, my gawwwwwd!" Her head fell back rubbing her neck. "They're just hickeys, Zetty!" Sue Willy leaned her chair back on its two hind legs and balanced herself with one hand in front of her on the edge of the table. "You always think the worst about everything! Some stoner gave them to me at a party. That's all!"

I wanted to tell her to stop rocking her chair back because she might fall and crack her head open, but that would've proven her point.

Sue Willy didn't understand what it felt like to be on a Ferris wheel the way I had with Tom. A Ferris wheel where you love every second of the ride and feel a happiness too big for words. That first intimate moment with Tom imprinted itself permanently on me, implanted itself and happily took roost in my soul. I wouldn't have changed it for anything.

Sue Willy started mixing my green paint with some of her yellow. "I can't wait to go to Shell Beach again. You need to come Zetty and loosen up, a little. It'd be good for you."

It took me back, the idea I might be seen as slightly

uptight. I wasn't having it. "Going to a nude beach doesn't bother me in the least," I lied.

"Are you sure?" she glanced at me sideways, not buying it.

"You really think I'm such a prude?" I said, convincing her more this time.

"It's totally liberating Zetty, really, the most amazing experience. Trust me. It'll blow your mind."

But that was precisely the problem. A mind like mine couldn't risk it. I thought of Father's reaction to this if he knew I was even considering the idea, and ran from the thought before I could fully see it.

"Listen, you don't need to convince me of anything. I'm all for free love." Whatever that meant.

Sue Willy's face perked up. "Then come on! Let's skip next period and go!"

I tried to close my gaping mouth and relax. Sue Willy laughed like she always did—full of the devil himself.

I wasn't a "trouble-maker" at school. I'd never been expelled, given one referral, or ordered into detention for anything. I hadn't even been marked tardy. Not once. So, when I made the decision to cut class with Sue Willy, a splash of bravado hit me. It was a little exciting—the idea I may have hung up my goody-two-shoes. Still, I really had no intention of running around a beach buck naked.

And yet, that's exactly what I had agreed to do.

Marjorie

TIME PASSED, BUT I CAN'T TELL YOU HOW MUCH. I ONLY know that at some point, to my absolute relief, I traveled somewhere. I remember the drone of engines and floating in a swaying motion, jostled by bumps in the air, or from a long, strange road, I wasn't certain which. I remember trusting it was Hank sitting in the pilot's seat flying me away.

"What is it, Margie?" Eleanor asked.

I gripped mother's hand tighter to tell her.

"It's okay, honey. I'm right here," Eleanor said. "I'm staying with you."

I lay my cheek against the back of her hand and felt secure. *We are escaping the evil ones,* I thought. *Hank and my mother will save me.*

I was frightened when I awakened in the night and didn't recognize anything around me. I sprang up, squinted hard, and tried to get my bearings. The fact I had no bearings didn't stop me from pretending I did. My new room was smaller than the last one. It seemed darker at nightfall, but quieter, too.

When I screamed for her, Mother appeared. "Margie," she said quietly, "everything's fine. You're in a new hospital now. Give it some time, honey. You'll get used to it."

Not without Hank, I remember thinking. *What's the use of going to a new place if it's not with him?* But these thoughts rarely transformed themselves into speech. Only dreams.

It was well after midnight when I closed my eyes and tried to fall back asleep. I clenched Dolly to my chest and sang her songs to help us both relax. I tried to sort through the nursery rhymes I remembered. They didn't come easy anymore the way they used to, so I made up tunes and sometimes the words. "Zetty's here with us," I told Dolly. Pretending made me happy. "We're going to sing to our baby girl."

"You're my puddin' pie/I love you to the sky/I'm gonna tell you why, why, why/cuz you're my puddin' pie."

That was the song I remember chanting before I hurtled down a long, strange, rabbit hole. I suppose I went to sleep. There's no other explanation I have for the exquisite memory that came floating back to me in what had to be the perfect dream. It was so vivid, so real, so sane. I can't tell you the freedom I felt in going back to a time when I was in full possession of my sanity.

It began at the county fair. I was propped up against a metal post holding up a white canopy over a large wooden dance floor when, out of nowhere, he approached me.

"Would you like to dance?" he inquired. "It's only taken me an hour to work up the courage to ask, but now that I have, what do you say?"

I turned from the cool breeze against my face and answered the striking man in uniform, "I'd say, thank you very much, I'd love to."

We snaked through the crowd, his arm parting the sea of dancers until a space opened up and we came together, amazingly, in perfect sync. I wasn't sure what was more uplifting, the band playing my favorite Glenn Miller song, or the unbelievably handsome man spinning around me.

We pulled in together. "What brings you to the fair?" he asked.

"I never miss it!" I said loudly. "I came down with friends this morning from Hollywood."

"Hollywood! What do you do there?" He collided with another dancer before I could tell him. "Excuse me, miss," he offered apologetically. "I'm so sorry." He looked back to me, shrugged off his obvious embarrassment, and waited for me to answer.

"Well, at the moment I'm in a bit-part in a stage play. Only one of the dancers, but I love it."

"*Only* one of the dancers? I'm dancing with a professional? Great," he chuckled.

"I hope to be a stage director someday, but it'll do for now. It pays my rent."

"Why a stage director?" he asked.

"The challenge, I guess. To be able to realize an artistic vision and shape the concept and interpretation of the play. It's a hard field for women to break into, but I won't let that stop me."

"Well, you shouldn't let that stop you. I think that's great. If you have a passion for something, you need to pursue it. Absolutely."

His response was refreshing. Most men I knew scoffed at the idea and said it was silly to even consider it. "Stick to dance pageants," they'd say, "you're too pretty to do a man's job." I glanced at the emblems on his uniform. "Air Force?"

"Sgt. Harold McGee, 106th Installations Squadron, 22d Air Base Group. Friends call me Hank."

"Pleased to meet you, Hank. I'm Marjorie and I've never been in an airplane before. But I'm sure it's a thrill!"

"Never flown?" He backed away in disbelief.

"No, but I'd like to someday. Why did you choose the Air Force?" He pulled me in for a spin under his arm.

"To fly. It's all I've ever wanted. Well, that and build my

own plane, someday. One that's fully aerobatic—I'm an amateur stunt pilot, too." He dipped me cautiously backward in his arms. "Anyway, that's my dream. I'm living the flying part every day though."

"Well, I envy you—you're doing exactly what you love."

Hank dropped his face, grinning. I felt at home immediately with the sense of humility that made his face flush. "Yes, I am," he confessed. "I'm dancing with you." He smiled.

I was so taken aback, I didn't know what to say. For the first time in my life I fell victim to stage fright. It's ludicrous to say really, but right away there was something about him I started to love.

Hank lifted his neck over the top of jitter-bug bouncing heads and pointed to the Ferris wheel. "Look!" he shouted. "Isn't that a sight?" The entire circle was lit up. All the buckets were outlined in yellow lights and rolled against the black sky. "You want to take a ride?" he raised his voice next to my ear.

"Yes!" I shouted back. I never expected that evening to be celebrated as one of the most romantic nights of my life, but that's exactly what it turned out to be.

Hank took my elbow as we dodged the floor of dancers and made our way out to whiffs of popcorn and cotton candy-scented air. The sound of wooden balls clunked down rows of Skee-Ball alleys, children squealed on spinning rides, and carnival vendors called us in to win life-sized stuffed animals. A Dixieland jazz band played in the distance, and a bell rang every time someone had the muscle to hammer it to the top. All of it filtered together through the air making happy noise.

The carnival man wiped the grease from his fingers on the red bandana wrapped around his forehead, and slammed the bar down on our open bucket. Hank immediately rechecked the latch and made sure it was properly secured. I gathered the skirt of my coral, cotton eyelet dress and tucked it under both thighs. The night air made my shoulders cool to the touch, but comfortable at the same time. We floated to the highest point, descended lightly, and moved around to ride the crest again, and again. A few times we came to a dead stop at the highest point. The bucket began to sway, but I hardly noticed through the steady stream of our conversation and the amazing views we captured. To the right, fluffy rippled waves lit up on shore from all the lights, and to the left was the Del Mar Racetrack where just hours earlier, throngs of people had cheered their horses to the finish line.

We handed the operator more tickets to keep riding until we both emptied our pockets. Then Hank pulled out cash. The carnival man with predictably unpleasant body odor, and a few shots of Jim Beam on his breath, adjusted his grimy bandana and, like a beggar, held out his hand for payment. It worked; he let us stay on as long as we wanted.

I'm still not sure if it was the push over the top that made my stomach fall or if it was the attraction to Hank that was the real kick. I only know when he took one of my hands as we made another drop, that I loved him. As I said, it's a crazy thing to proclaim after only a few hours, but I felt as if someone I was waiting for had finally shown up.

"Your hands are sweaty," I teased. "You're a pilot, and your hands are sweaty on a Ferris wheel?"

"Sorry," he said, wiping them on his pants. "I can't fly these buckets. I guess I like to be the one operating things. That," he hesitated, "and I'm a little nervous with you."

"Why?" I asked, hardly believing it.

"Afraid I won't see you again."

"Me, too," I said in all honesty.

He gave his hand another quick wipe, clutched mine again, and this time wove his fingers securely through mine.

"Maybe if we kissed, that would help," I suggested.

"I think it really would," he smiled. He leaned in and as soon as his lips touched mine, all my organs shut down. I can't quite describe the spark between us, except to say it was strong enough to short-circuit the entire city. It certainly short-circuited something in me.

We were the last ones off the Ferris wheel when the rides closed down.

"Feel like walking?" he asked.

"Sure," I said, and ran to a bench to take my sandals off. "Let's feel the water. But just so you know, I don't walk alone at night with just anyone."

"Well, you shouldn't. But I know you can trust me, so I'm not going to talk you out of it."

We strolled for hours, huddled on the sand under his chocolate brown leather bomber jacket, and revealed everything inside us until sunrise.

When the sky opened in full light he asked, "Want your first plane ride?"

I sprang to my feet with a jolt. "You mean it?"

"My Cessna 120 is only an hour away. I've racked up 250 hours in it and have about 4,000 hours of flying time total. I promise to keep you safe."

It would've been a reckless thing to do with any other man. But I already loved Hank. As soon as I climbed in next to him in the two-seater plane, and he spooled up the engines, I knew I wanted to be with him for life. And with every take-off and landing he showed me that day, he thrilled me more. I never wanted to leave him.

That was our beginning.

And not one day went by that I regretted leaving Hollywood to marry him. Not one day.

A voice pushed through the flashback and light flickered over my eyes.

"Marjorie," I heard some distant ghost whispering. I ignored it and fought to stay where I was. Where I longed to be. The reminiscence that played out in my dream was like a special offering, a chance to be who I used to be. But when I did awaken I wasn't sure if I should be thankful or enraged.

Hank never left me. But by some wicked twist of fate, I was forced to leave him. Somehow, I ended up here alone in a bed with metal side rails with chums who lived inside the idiot box on the Romper Room show.

I wanted Hank to know how deeply sorry I was. I wanted to tell him I had never, ever, meant for this.

Whatever this was.

Good night—I was only going for potatoes.

Invitation to Betrayal

Sue Willy was one of the most convincing people I knew. She could tell you a space ship landed around the block and by the time she finished telling you about it, no matter who you were, you'd go running to see it. She was easy to believe on account she believed all the things she said herself. I didn't blame Sue Willy for "making" me go to a naked beach, but unlike Gabe, I did allow her to have ample influence over me.

We climbed down the long, winding dirt path toward nakedness and I took my own sweet time. I stopped a lot and dilly-dallied. First, to look at the pickleweed's blooming little pink flowers, and then to pick a blossom off the honeysuckle bushes to suck out a drop of nectar. Next, I planned to search the bushes for ladybugs. If I can postpone our arrival long enough, I thought, maybe some reasonable excuse will come along to cause us to turn back, or I'll just get lucky and die.

"I'm telling you, Zetty," Sue Willy said, "it's no big deal." She stopped, one hand on her hip humped to the side. "They warned me you'd chicken out."

My head jerked toward her. "Who? Chicken out of what?" I asked in a huffy voice.

"Going naked! Where nobody cares!" she trumpeted. "Everyone knows you're too uptight."

I picked up my stride, just to show her I wasn't the prude everyone thought I was.

The sand was so hot and dry it almost squeaked when I stepped into it; the soles of my feet nearly blistered as soon as they sank. But when I looked up, there was no one running around naked at all. Unless you count one elderly man in a lawn chair with a big book, thank you very much, modestly propped over his lap.

While my day just got better, Sue Willy's disappointment was palpable.

My navy blue hooded sweatshirt and blue jeans remained firmly and happily attached to my body. But Sue Willy was fuming. "Shit. What fun is this?" she complained. "Where the hell is everyone? Damn it." She grumbled, kicking sand up like a soccer ball. "There's no one even here." And then she did what she's done a hundred times before. She went quiet on me.

Emotionally, Sue Willy had a way of spacing out in a distracted sort of way. She was tense, fidgety and I could almost see the aura of wrath that orbited around her. I realized Sue Willy had an appetite for attention, and when it wasn't there for her, she practically split into someone else. We had an unspoken agreement that every time she got like this, she could count on me not to tell anyone. Like the time I caught her in the bathroom squashing smoldering cigarettes on her forearms. And another time when I found her behind the Lucky Seven chopping off her hair with sewing scissors and swearing at herself like a sailor.

I had to agree that if people saw this glowering side of her, it would be bad for her image. So I learned what to do when she got like this. I tiptoed around Sue Willy with careful words, like a parent trying not to wake the baby. Speaking to her was like picking up broken glass off the floor. You had to carefully set each response you got out of her gently aside, being sure none of the pointy edges cut you. One wrong move, and you'd have worse problems on your hands. So, I let her be.

We sat beside each other on the sand in silence and watched the ocean roll over on itself, like the ruffle on the edge of a dress. The waves dissolved almost as quickly as they built their strength. They melted into the sand and then rushed backward, reincarnated for another ride.

I finally broke the silence. "You're mom is pretty wild, isn't she?" I asked.

"Hell, yeah. But it's cool. At least she's not flipped out like yours. Your mom really lost her noodles!"

Shame wrapped around me as soon as she said it. And then a side of myself tip-toed out without permission. "Yeah, I'm glad she's gone," I told her. "Honestly—I don't even want to be related to her anymore. Who needs a crazy mom living in a funny farm anyway?" I hugged my knees. "She was no ordinary mother, that's for sure."

I dropped my face into my arms and felt the guilt chip away at me. Not my best moment.

"None of them are ordinary, Zetty. Not even Scarlett."

Sue Willy was right. What would an ordinary mother even look like? I had no idea. Maybe she was right and so was Gabe; none existed.

The sun was overrun by billowing white clouds, puffy and swollen from the salt air, the most annoying kind when you're trying to tan. I lay back, but felt cold one minute, then hot the next, depending on how fast they moved. A burst of sunlight briefly brightened the beach, so I peeled off my sweatshirt and used it as a pillow. My eyes stung when I closed them, and the sun welded them shut a little tighter each time it broke through. I listened to the waves, like a rocking lullaby, rolling in, washing out, and wishing I could go under one right then. I imagined it; the force of the sea pouring over my body, the salty fizz clinging to my skin. Floating untethered, drifting slowly below the surface, back into nothingness.

A seagull squawked close by as if coming in for an attack and startled me back to the surface, to the strong bank of sand cradled beneath me.

I turned to my right to see if Sue Willy was asleep, but saw a pile of clothes instead. Her clothes, with a pair of tie-dyed bikini underwear folded neatly on top.

And there she was, straight ahead, prancing down to the water's edge. Her naked heinie, white as a curd, strutting like some kind of fashion model on a runway.

With sensuous abandon she stretched both arms up behind her head and then ran one hand up through the back of her wavy-brown, tousled hair, just before diving in.

"Welcome back, Sue Willy," I said to no one.

Two guys straddled their surf boards, just beyond the breaking waves. It was the whole reason for this little show.

Sue Willy swam out to meet their Popsicle-wide grins. Her head popped up like a mermaid between them. She tread water like she was stroking the back of a Persian cat in a gentle circular motion. It was faint, and garbled, like a low volume radio station with static, but I heard enough of the tone to know she was pleased to have their full attention.

I saw Sue Willy take hold of the edge of one surfboard, and with both hands she pulled her breast in close, then pushed back a little, and then drew herself in again. Back and forth, tipping her head back under the water every few minutes and smoothing back her hair with one hand.

It occurred to me that Gabe was right again; Sue Willy was filled with a dangerous combination of too much rage and desire. I needed to find a ride home, because whenever Sue Willy was ready to leave, I knew it wasn't going to be with me.

Beige metal blinds rested against the open window in Doc Sperling's office. They started to breathe in and out when a little breeze began to stir. The back-and-forth clang on the inhale was soft and predictable like the ticking of her clock. It didn't annoy me in the least.

I relaxed into my chair waiting for Doc Sperling to take a seat. She set her tablet and pencil on the end table, tossed the pillow from her chair to the chaise, and settled back, looking comfortable. Then she dropped a bomb.

"We have plenty of time yet, Zetty, but I wanted to prepare you."

My stomach hit the floor. I sensed something bad was about to hit and wanted to duck and cover like the drills we did in sixth grade for earthquakes and atomic bombs.

"I'll be leaving for Europe on a lecture tour early spring. Doctor Rohal will be covering for me while I'm gone."

"No problem," I smiled. "I mean it won't be that long, will it?"

"A few months, actually."

My smile retracted itself.

"Tell me what you're thinking." Her pant legs rustled when she crossed her legs.

I tried to sound logical and carefree. "It means your work comes first. I understand."

"Comes first over what?" She held her gaze on me.

I picked off a few pills of fabric from the pillow at my side before I could answer, "Over me."

Old, familiar, pent-up sensations began to spill out: sadness, hurt, panic, fear, and believing I wasn't important enough to her, just like I wasn't to my mother.

"This is an opportunity for us, Zetty," she told me. "I want to help you cope differently with situations that feel like abandonment to you."

"Okay," I nodded. My head dropped and I let out a long sigh.

"What's troubling you?"

"Something I did."

"Do you want to tell me about it?"

"I got naked on Shell Beach," I announced, pushing a gold tasseled pillow behind me. It sounded daring, even to myself. Doc Sperling lowered her head and gazed quietly over the top of her wire glasses. She waited like she always did when I was supposed to keep talking.

"Well, I almost did," I admitted. "Well, okay, I wasn't even close to getting naked, actually. But my friend did before she ditched me for two surfers and left me stranded."

"Some friend," Doc Sperling said casually, removing her glasses. She pulled a tissue, huffed on each lens, and started polishing.

"Oh, she's alright," I assured her. "She's different, but who wouldn't be when the only parent you have gets in as much trouble as you do. Sue Willy just needs friends who understand her."

"So you volunteered yourself for the job?"

"It's what I do," I said, shifting my weight from one hip to the other, wondering if what she had said wasn't a tad rude.

Doc Sperling tipped her head to the right as if angling for a different view.

"What are you thinking?" I asked boldly.

"What do you mean by 'it's what you do'?" She quickly put her glasses back on.

"Well—" I hesitated, and then hesitated again. "It's definitely what my mother did."

And off we went. Another fifty-minute round analyzing Mother. This time it was about her big heart for outcasts, a few of them real odd balls.

I told Doc Sperling about the lonely widow without kids who wanted to give me things I had no interest in whatsoever. "I had only meant to be polite when I admired a bulky metal anchor on a chain around her neck that looked like it had been dredged up from the sea," I explained. "She took it right off her neck and handed it to me. And then I had to wear the thing."

Doc Sperling's head tilted to the back of her chair and she smiled.

"She pushed my head into her hot, blubbery stomach all the time, too."

"Oy vey," Doc groaned.

"Yeah," I confirmed. "I hated that!"

"What did you do?"

"What could I do? I had to grin and bear it."

Doc Sperling held her pen and tablet poised to jot down notes, but so far hadn't written anything.

"Oh, and then there was Gerdie." I couldn't wait to tell her about Gerdie.

Doc gave her pen a hard shake, scratched it back and forth across the paper, and then tossed it in the trash.

"She was the scary one." I continued, "Drove Mother and me to the bowling alley once. Moved slow as a snail with a frozen grin on her face. I assumed the wild ratting in her bleached-blonde hair was a result of trying to gas herself in the oven one too many times, but Mother said it wasn't."

"So, you went bowling with Gerdie?"

"Oh yeah. And we were lucky to make it there alive. I fully expected she was going to run us off the road and kill us all. I was scared to death! But I have to say, Gerdie really could bowl. Way better than Mother or me, so you had to admire her for that." I stood and stretched and then plunked my bottom down again.

"Did your mother know you were afraid?"

I shrugged. "She didn't ask. I knew we had to be nice," I said stroking my legs a little, noticing they could use a shave. "Mother was nice to everyone—no matter how different they were."

Doc Sperling sprang up and leaned over her desk to snap up a new pen. "How old were you, Zetty?"

"Maybe seven or so."

Doc wrote something down, and clicked the pen shut as she tucked it over her ear. "Well, you had a lot of training," she said.

My face went blank so she explained, "You've had practice reaching out to people who needed friends. Extended yourself to them. And, I suspect, learned from your mother to be nice, no matter what."

My hands crossed and clutched the coolness of my upper arms. "Sometimes it isn't a good idea?" I asked.

"It depends," she started. And then she set her tablet aside. "It depends on whether or not you lose yourself in the process."

I had the sinking feeling that's exactly what I had done.

"I did something else at Shell Beach, Doc."

"Yes?"

"I told Sue Willy I was glad Mother was gone and that I didn't want to be related to her anymore. Called her crazy. Stuff like that." My face drooped from the sick feeling that rolled over me when I remembered using the term "funny farm," too.

"You don't look happy."

"I'm not! It was awful. I didn't even want to go to that stupid beach to begin with. I hated the idea. But I lied about it. And then I decided it was easier to lie about Mother, too."

"You must have had a reason," she said.

My throat began to ache from emotion. "No good reason. None at all. I did it because I was trying to prove I wasn't a prude. And I was embarrassed when Sue Willy reminded me my mother was a flipped out mental case."

"Are you ashamed of her?"

"Well, yes, a little." I glanced away and then met her gaze again. "Maybe, a lot."

"Do you believe her illness is a reflection on you?"

"Well, yes! It is!"

"You aren't your mother, Zetty. And your mother is still the woman you love most in the world. Her illness will never change that. Her illness will never be all of who she is. Only a part."

That was the whole truth, right there. "And I betrayed her," I said.

"You betrayed yourself, too." Doc reached for her teacup, ran a finger around the rim and went on. "Zetty," she said slowly, "I suspect it wasn't always possible to express your feelings as a child, or react the way you wanted to, but it is possible now. The more authentic you can be, the less likely this will ever happen again." Doc Sperling held her cup in both hands under her chin. "Being your true self prevents depression, too," she added. "It's important for everyone, but especially for women. Too many of us have grown up with the pressure to please others, or change ourselves in order to find acceptance and a sense of belonging."

"I did learn to grin and bear a lot of things."

"Yes, you did."

"And tried to be something I'm not at Shell Beach."

"Yes."

"I hope I can change," I told her.

"You're changing right now," she said.

I didn't see Sue Willy for months after Shell Beach, but only because she was on the road again. Rumors roared across the school like wildfire; Sue Willy and her mother supposedly had dropped acid, been arrested, and joined a hippie commune. Gabe and I were a little uneasy about the gossip, but didn't take it too seriously. We knew Sue Willy would call us if anything drastic happened. But I made up my mind that I would never say or do another thing that betrayed Mother, or myself, again.

Marjorie

I CAN'T GET TO THEM FAST ENOUGH, I SAID TO MYSELF.

I can't tell you the thrill I felt. I entered the scene from our play in another lovely dream. It was the part in the saloon where Tuffy took a bullet to save us, but survived. *I'm better now*, I thought. *I remember! I must get home to Zetty, to Hank, to our precious Tuffy.* The dream convinced me I was fully intact again. Back to my old self.

It was so clear. And yet, once more it evaporated like steam when I awakened.

I lived for those dreams, and yet died a little more each time I had one.

I tried to tell Eleanor about the cowgirl's daughter so many times. But my words locked up and changed on me constantly, so I couldn't be sure I had. I wanted to tell her about this scene I dreamt about, too, and ask if she thought I might, at long last, be improving. Even though I knew I wasn't. Not really.

I was fully awake when the door flew open and a gaggle of medical coats swarmed around my bed. They discussed lab reports and vital signs. Meaningless numbers to me. And then I heard one lab coat say to another lab coat, "You'll note that the patient appears disturbed by her surroundings and yet there's a peculiar indifference to it all. As you can see, she's been robbed of human connection."

Students, I supposed, stood at my side. Their faces

stretched like chewing gum to the ceiling. It was impossible to see who they were.

"The patient doesn't realize what's happening, of course, but her thoughts, feelings, and behaviors continue to regress."

I wanted to scream, "You think I don't realize? You think I don't know I'm different?" Everything in me tried to squawk at the big expert know-it-all, but nothing came out.

Then he leaned over. "Don't be afraid, Mrs. McGee," he said, "we're going to do everything we can to help you. We'll take good care of you. Your husband has made sure of that."

His words shifted around inside me. The rage let go and went back into hiding.

"Mr. McGee will be here shortly," he told the circle of coats. "We'll meet with him after his visit with his wife."

My dear, sweet, Hank, I thought.

The sun was too bright through the window, but I hoped it would help the doctors see the spiders crawling over my arms and legs. No one seemed to notice. I remained flat on the bed now as much as possible; I had no choice. When I sat up I began shrinking. I used my feet to kick the bedspread over the top of me, just in time. I didn't want Hank to see the scorpions and worry.

"Hello, sweetheart," he greeted. "Do you know me?"

"Why would you ask me such a thing? Of course I know you. And I knew it was you flying the plane I was in. I was right! Oh, thank God, you took me away, Hank. It's better here. I'm more relaxed. Thank you for flying all the way back here to see me again."

"Honey, I'd go anywhere to see you, but—"

"Hank, please. Listen," I broke in. The words were there. Suddenly there. I had to use them. They were making sense, even to Hank.

"Honey, you're speaking clearly today." A wave of excitement pushed through his words. "Are you feeling better?"

There was my proof. "Listen while I can say this!" I pleaded.

"Sweetheart, what is it? Tell me, please."

"You don't deserve this, Hank. I want you to move on."

"Marjorie, what?"

"Listen to me!" The words rushed out, "I keep having dreams. Wonderful dreams. One was about us. When we first met. It showed me how much I've changed. How much we've changed. Go on with your life without this. I mean it, I don't want you to come back."

"Marjorie, don't—"

"Hank," I cut in, "I want you to be happy, again. That's all I want. If you love me, do this for me."

"But —" he started.

I held my hand to his face. "It's harder on me, this way. Please don't let me shoulder the weight of having taken away your life, too."

"Honey," he said taking hold of my hand, "now, you listen to me. If you believe that, even for a second, you're more confused than we thought."

And then laughter echoed in the room like a beautiful symphony. It was his, and it was mine—lively, the way it used to be. And for a moment, my stomach took a dive as if we were floating on the Ferris wheel again. I clutched his hand to my chest and wriggled my fingers through his. It was still there—his bond to me. And selfishly I held on and didn't let go.

My words never flowed so freely again. Not even briefly. I didn't regret saying to Hank the things I did. I only regretted that I couldn't have told Zetty what was in my heart, too. I never stopped trying to put into words what I wanted her to know. But it was never clear if I had. My telepathy skills were useless here. I attempted, but the currents didn't work over my new room. *If I can't see you again,* I wanted to say, *at least I want you to know that the last thought I held, in my final moment of sanity, was of you. It was always of you, and the play we didn't have time to perform.*

STARRING: MY TRUE SELF

NEXT TO TOM, THE PLAN TO FIND MOTHER WAS THE ONLY thing that kept me going.

Gabe's voice was on the other end of the receiver when the phone picked up.

"Hey," I told her right away, "I have a list of hospital names and numbers. You won't believe how many there are. We'll start with the big ones. There's a place called Pilgrim State that has 14,000 patients in it!"

"Wow," she said, "that's a small city."

"I know, and there's other big ones too, like Kings Park, Central Islip, Edgewood, and tons more. I'll bring over what I have. But man, Gabe, I had no idea. With thousands of patients in these places, how are we ever going to find her?"

"We will, Zetty. Good job. I'll start calling, but listen, have you heard from Sue Willy?"

"No. She's still not back in class. Why?"

"My mom talked to her. She's been trying to reach us for a month. She didn't sound well at all, Zetty. We're really worried."

A sense of dread filled my chest. "This isn't good, Gabe."

"Nope. And I saw her mom's car in the driveway today when I went to work."

"I don't get it. If Sue Willy's home why wouldn't she come see us?"

"Let's go find out," Gabe said.

Father was bent over the fuselage of his plane, the way he was most Saturday mornings in the garage. It was showing more like a real airplane now, complete with a tail section attached. In case it mattered, I told him where I was going, and turned to leave.

"Zetty," he called out so that I'd stop. "Thanks for your help this morning. It's been nice to have you around more, honey."

I didn't know what to say. The truth is, I had been so bored with Gabe working all the time and Tom away surfing with his college team, that I started helping Father hold clamps, and glue, and bend wood, just for something to do. It was such fragrant work, I started to look forward to the sweet, dry scent of fresh-cut lumber. It was like standing in a forest of Sitka Spruce. I didn't mind sweeping up the sawdust either, just for the pure pleasure of smelling it longer.

Father added, "It's been good to see you, that's all. Whether you help or not, it's just nice to have you around."

"Okay," I said in a semi-state of shock, because the thing is, it sounded like he might want me around more.

"You kids be careful and have fun."

More niceness. Working on the plane did make Father happy, that was clear. And it seemed to help him relax, too.

Gabe turned the key and her dad's truck rumbled awake as I climbed in. She still didn't have the best use of the clutch, but this time she remained solemn when we lurched twice in the middle of the intersection, killed the engine, stopped traffic, and a swarm of cars started honking in unison. And then something switched.

"Okay! Okay!" Gabe hollered out the window. "Give me a break!"

A guy in an old Rambler laid on his horn again, and wouldn't let up.

"Geez!" She turned to me. "Like they never had a bad clutch in *their* trucks?!"

"Apparently not," I said. And then, as soon as Gabe pulled away, I leaned out the window, stared at the guy honking, and flipped him the bird.

"Zetty!" she hooted. "What was that?!"

"Exactly what it looked like," I said.

"Oh my God." She crossed her chest. "I can't believe you did that."

"Well, believe it," I said. "I have to practice being my true self. Part of therapy."

"I'm not sure that's what your shrink meant."

The truth is, I wasn't either. As soon as I did it, I had the uneasy sense I hadn't responded from my true self at all. I had reacted instead. It wasn't who I wanted to be, so I made a personal vow not to flip off anyone again, if I could help it.

Gabe grated the tires against the curb in front of the Williamson's house so hard I smelled burnt rubber when I got out. I ran to the front door and quickly knocked, leaving Gabe behind.

The door sprang open so fast and wide it bounced off the wall behind it and started to close until Mrs. Williamson stuck her foot in front of it. She was wearing a purple and lime green tie-dyed granny dress, obviously bra-less, her sagging breasts swirling like the cubes in her three-inch-tall glass of whiskey. "Well, looky here. It's Susie's little friends!" she shouted. "What'd she do? Call and tell you what a *bitch* I am?" She backed away and stumbled against a chair.

Gabe came up behind my left ear, and hushed her voice, "She's tanked."

"Duh," I quipped.

We trod forward cautiously at first, and then Gabe moved confidently ahead. The sour, rank smell of alcohol breath lingered in the doorway. The walnut wood end tables were covered with a layer of soot, the carpet filthy like the insides of a smoker's lung.

"Is Sue around?" Gabe asked.

Sue Willy's mom plopped herself down on a saggy sofa with a burnt orange-colored slip cover. One corner didn't stretch far enough and exposed the raggedy pink cushion hiding underneath. Her hair was a frizzy, bottle blonde; black roots ran down the top of her head like a zipper. She plunked her glass down, pulled a cigarette from her bosom, cupped it in her hand, and lit up.

"Well, is she?" Gabe repeated glancing down the hall.

Mrs. Williamson took a long, slow drag, tossed her lighter across the coffee table, and looked at us like old friends. Smoke poured out her nose and mouth when she said, "We've had more drama around here than on the silver screen, girls." She tittered and danced her cigarette through the air like a fairy, flicking the ashes wherever she pleased. "By the way, did she tell you what a little whore she is?" My insides tightened every time she dumped a sewer of words in front of us. She drew on the cigarette again, deep and slow. Mrs. Williamson, her face crazed with madness, blurted, "I really hate her. You know that?"

"I know you do," Gabe said, "and I've always wondered why."

Mrs. Williamson scooted to the edge of the sofa, her whole body tipsy, and tried to find a way to push herself up without falling. I noticed then, shattered glass against the wall that looked like it had once been a hand mirror.

I inched my way back toward the front door.

Mrs. Williamson tucked an arm on top of her stomach and propped up her smoking hand. A Marlboro was growing a long stream of ash that soon would be dangling dangerously over her breast. It was almost shaking loose with every sassy word she pelted out. "That's right, don't worry about *me*, Little-Miss-High-and-Mighty-Gabe, you think Suzie-Q is so perfect, and I'M the bitch, don't you?"

"What a trip," Gabe muttered.

I stood tight-lipped, but Gabe tried again, "Do you happen to know where your daughter might be? If not, we'll just go."

But Mrs. Williamson wasn't done. "DON'T YA, GABE? She's the little whore-bag, *not me*, but you wouldn't know about things like that now would you? Not a nice, perfect little do-gooder like Gabe!" She fell backward into a chair and ash sprinkled over the carpet. To my relief the red in it burned out as soon as it hit.

Gabe flashed her a tired look, unfazed. "Yeah, yeah, yeah," she droned, just like Dennis. "Okay," she added quickly prodding me farther back to the door, "we'll be leaving now."

Mrs. Williamson grabbed for her glass and launched herself toward us.

"Let's get out of here," I said, and backed my way into the door knob.

Her head dropped back with raucous laughter, and I saw silver fillings all the way to the back of her throat. In a drunken blather she spit out, "That's right, run for your life, Phhhh-etty! Sweaty, Freddie, whatever the hell your name is. Run for your lives, my little pretties!" She nearly toppled over a chair.

"You're a good-for-nothing drunk. No wonder Sue Willy doesn't come home," Gabe said.

Mrs. Williamson teetered, raised her glass of whiskey into the air as if ready to say *cheers,* but instead blasted more polluted breath in our direction, her face twisted up ugly like Satan himself. "She doesn't come home cuz she's a fuckin' little cunt."

Her words pierced like a dentist drill attacking the one raw nerve it shouldn't. And something snapped. I still can't tell you what it was, but in that moment, I left another part of my old life behind, and went head first into a new one.

I pushed Gabe aside and stood directly in front of Sue Willy's mother—close enough to see the bloodshot of her eyes. "What kind of mother are you?"

"Not a nutcase like yours!" she shot back.

My voice turned fearless. "Don't ever say that again. *Ever.* Even at her worst, she was a better mother than you'll ever be."

She flicked her cigarette and then smashed the butt against an ice cube, her lips lifted into a disfigured snarl. "Why, you little bitch. Fuck you, *Setty!*"

It was our cue to leave. The door slammed behind us with such force, I thought it had broken from the hinges. I made it halfway to the truck before I spun around and charged back.

"What are you doing?!" Gabe asked.

I pushed the door open and stomped back inside. It felt like my favorite saloon door scene in the cowgirl show with Mother, a scene I had perfected, perhaps for that very moment.

Mrs. Williamson had dropped on the sofa like a bag of laundry. My eyes centered on her when I said it, "A part of me wants to say, fuck you back, but I won't. I don't believe in using violent language that perpetuates a culture of rape. Scarlett Taylor is right." I turned in time to see Gabe's eyes bug out and then I drew the sign of the cross against my chest. It was the "F-word" after all, and technically it was the second time I used it that day.

"Stay right there," I told Mrs. Williamson, "and don't say another word."

"Zetty, what're you doing?" Gabe asked from the porch.

"Making sure Sue Willy isn't lying dead somewhere in this house." I marched down the hall, kicked open the doors to both bedrooms and the bathroom. I checked every closet, too. You never know.

I traversed piles of paper and trash and slowly positioned myself on the lumpy cushion next to Sue Willy's mom, but with enough space between us, just in case. Her head was cranked all the way back, eyes frozen open like a dead person. The room went quiet.

"I've always liked Scarlett," she said softly to no one.

I took a deep breath. "Look," I told her as I swallowed back on a mountain of dry rock, "I may be wrong, but I don't think you mean the awful things you say about Susannah. Or any of us for that matter. I think you're really saying how you feel about yourself."

"What, you're a therapist now?" she asked without moving.

"Hardly," I answered and straightened out the slip cover between us. "What I really want to say is, just be there for your daughter. Be grateful you have the chance to be her mother."

Mrs. Williamson dropped forward, rested her forehead in one hand and started to snivel as I went on, "Sue Willy will do okay without you. She already has. But she doesn't have to, you know? Not like me."

Mrs. Williamson hugged her stomach and half-heartedly suppressed a belch. "I know I'm a goddamned mess," she said, her voice growing weak, "believe me, I know." She lowered her brown eyes to the floor, black eyeliner wept across her cheeks.

"Yeah, well, look where my mom is," I said point blank. "Assuming she's in a mental ward somewhere, let me tell you, that's messed up, too. But *you* have a choice. You don't have to keep being a mess. You don't." I pushed up with both arms, my toes inched back into both flip-flops, making squeaking sounds. "Sue Willy wants you," I said. "If you can't be there for her, well, then, you lose out too, you know. You lose your only daughter. So, don't blow it." I arched my back, unwinding the tension that had roiled up my spine. "Now, can you please tell us where she is?"

"Don't know. Maybe L.A., maybe Mexico, hell, maybe took off for Canada with a draft dodger. No idea."

A careful silence settled around us but only for a moment. When I stepped away, she wept louder, her nose dripping. I didn't know if that meant I should stay longer, but I thought about Doc Sperling and the time limits she put on our talks, and I decided I had said all I needed to say. So, I walked through the open door, closed it softly behind me, and stepped into the afternoon light.

Gabe stood slack-jawed on the front porch, her eyes big as baseballs. When I crossed the lawn, she came up alongside me smiling and said, "Way to go, Zetty."

"We still don't know where she is."

Gabe put a hand on top of each shoulder, stopped us both, and turned me directly toward her. "No. We don't yet, but don't you see? You can do anything you need to. Anything," she told me. "This is why you're going to find your mom. And we'll find Sue Willy, too." She took hold of my right hand and pulled it across my chest. "But it goes like this: *Father, Son,* and *Holy Ghost.* You never get it right."

"I know," I said with total peace. Because I knew I had finally done something exactly right.

On the ride home, my mind kept returning to something I said to Mrs. Williamson. Something I knew was true for me, too. I realized, it wasn't just about *my* loss when mother left, she lost me, too.

My mind kept returning to it, rewinding the words, *my mother lost me, too.*

I handed Gabe the first list of New York hospital names and numbers. "I'll work on mine tomorrow when I can get to a phone booth," I told her.

"It won't be long, Zetty."

I shot out of the truck, opened the front door, and was engulfed by the smell of mother's pot roast recipe baking in the oven. It felt like a hopeful sign.

IT WASN'T THE FIRST TIME SUE WILLY WENT MISSING. SHE usually showed up after a few weeks and, like a stray pup, Scarlett took her in and dished out plenty of food and love as if she were her own and never once complained about it. Dennis could be a mean son-of-anything you want to call him, but when it came to Sue Willy, he went soft-hearted, too. We were all worried this time.

Booze didn't make the best parent, and Sue Willy got a bottle of whiskey for a mother, no fault of her own. But booze wasn't all. Sue Willy told me once her mom's boyfriend gave her a line of cocaine, and it was the best high she ever felt. She said to try it if I ever had the chance. I didn't tell her then all I had to do was snort a nostril of testosterone off Tom's neck for the same result.

When he was around, Tom found ways to pull me wide-eyed into someplace private at the Taylor home, like the storage closet, or the bathroom, out to the backyard shed, or the pantry. Once we even fit in the broom closet for a full ten-minute make-out session. When the phone rang once, it was him. Our signal to meet at the side of my house for as long as we could steal away. I knew the sneaking around we did would eventually change and we'd break the good news of our relationship to everyone, but until then we kept it a secret, and I held on to it like a charm.

"Maybe your talk with Sue Willy's mom will do some good, Zetty. Maybe our little love-fest knocked some sense into her," Gabe said. "Things might get better, now."

"Maybe," I said. But I wasn't convinced of it.

TIME MOVED SWIFTLY THROUGH THE EARLY MONTHS OF the New Year. My attention was less on school and more on Father's airplane and researching the hundreds of hospitals in New York. Gabe and I didn't have any leads yet—not one lucky break.

I hung out with Father more, even when I didn't have to. I started to enjoy helping him build the Super Emeraude. And he gave me the honor, he said, of being the one to select the color scheme for the three-striped design that would wrap the fuselage. I chose three shades of blue: navy seal, midnight jazz, and skylark, in that order. He told me he loved the choices, which made me feel like my skills as an artist had finally been put to real use. But mainly I felt satisfied, because I knew Mother would have loved them, too.

It was on my mind all the way home from school—Father needed my final approval after we sampled the colors. I explained it was absolutely essential to see them directly on the plane in bright daylight before he purchased gallons of them for the professional painter.

I hurried past brown leaves rotting in mushy clumps against the street curbs, trying to get home while the sun was still high. But when I arrived, kicked off my Mary Janes, and dropped three notebooks on the counter, I found a bulky letter propped up against the wood fruit bowl on the kitchen table and forgot all about navy seal, midnight jazz, and skylark.

The envelope was frayed, the corners starting to tear from the sheer bulk of it. It was postmarked, March 10, 1972, addressed to me, and in the upper left hand corner it simply read:

S. Williamson
The Sisters of St. Mary Convent
Los Angeles. California

HOLY-SUE-WILLY

BEFORE GABE FINISHED SAYING, "HELLO, TAYLORS' RESI-
dence," I broke in, "Sue Willy's had a 'calling' and wants to
be a *nun*." I gripped the phone so tight, my knuckles went
white.

"What are you talking about?"

I wrestled open the letter bent stiff in two places, and
held it down with one elbow. "I have it right here—a letter
from a nun convent in L.A. It's where she's been all this
time."

Gabe switched to sensible logic, her tone dry and
annoyed. "She couldn't be 'called' to be a nun. They're
virgins and they stay virginal. She can't be either."

"I'm just telling you what she wrote. I haven't even read
the whole thing. It says here it's like living on the set of *The
Sound of Music.* 'You would love it, Zetty. That is, if you
were PG like I am.'"

Gabe and I both gasped. I continued,

"You read right, Zetty, I'm PG. Or as they say here, I got
myself into 'trouble.'"

Gabe was still riding the same shock wave I was. Breath
caught in my throat and started to quiver as I read more:

*My Mama-seeta deserted me after I couldn't go through
with the whole coat hanger thing, do you blame me? First,
she took me to a clinic in Tijuana but I ran out when they*

called my name. The floor looked like it had been pissed on, and the lady doing my paperwork had dirty nails. The whole thing made me barf, which I do regularly now, by the way. My mom was pissed and yelling at me, as usual! So she said if I didn't go through with it, I had to leave. She carried on and on about how she couldn't take care of me and a baby. Blah. Blah. Blah. She took off and left me there so I hitchhiked my way out. Ended up in L.A. So, here I am. Saying Hail Marys three times a day to a statue wearing a long, flowing blue gown! Yeah, we really do that every day.

My mom quit the booze for a while and really changed! But it didn't last. Now she's trying to get back on the wagon again. Once she does, I know she'll want me to keep the baby. I hope so, anyway.

I'm so bored; and I can't smoke, not exactly a dream vacation! I hope, hope, hope, you and Gabe can come see me! I'm enclosing directions. Gabe blew out all the air from both lungs. "Why am I not surprised?" She sighed and then guzzled something from a glass.

"Oh, but that's not all," I said.

I am scared to death about getting a baby out. It's not like a dick, you know. Even a big one. This thing's gonna be a seven to ten pounder with limbs.

Something sprayed violently out of Gabe's mouth. Then she hooted. I kept reading:

The girls here say labor is so bad, you can die. And now don't panic, but I've taken a razor to my arm once. It wasn't enough to bleed to death, and it didn't really hurt. The nuns told me it was a sin to cut myself, so I had to promise to never do it again. But if I can't keep it (a he or she, who knows), I don't know what I'll do because I know I really want a baby to love and love me back! It would be so cool. I'm coming up with names, just in case.

By the way, I have no idea who the Papa is, but I know it's not the surfer because I was already pregnant when we went to Shell Beach. Can you believe it?!?! I had no idea.

One more thing, it feels really weird to be PG. I feel mostly sick. But I do feel it kick and that part is a little creepy. Say hi to Gabe! And it's okay to tell the Taylors, since I don't think they'll call me a slut the way my mom did.

I have to warn you guys though. I'm as big as a whale and my TETAS are getting HUGE! Oh my god, do they hurt. Gotta go. The nuns make us take naps! Ha ha. Sister Carmelita is the only nice one here.

"The end," I announced.

"Wow," Gabe said numbly. "Sue Willy having a baby."

"Sue Willy can't be a mother," I said in the black-and-white manner Gabe was famous for.

"Well, she's about to be one, Zetty. Any way you crack this egg, it's gonna be a mess. And it wouldn't surprise me in the least if she keeps that baby."

"I know, me neither. What should we do?"

"Go see her I guess," Gabe said. "Maybe my mom will have some ideas." I heard a juddering intake of breath. "Write the little señorita, well, technically a señora, and tell her we'll come as soon as we can."

OUT OF BODY, OUT OF MIND

GABE AND I SPENT TIME WITH SUE WILLY BEFORE THE BABY came, but not at the same time, and not in the way we ever imagined.

A week after I received Sue Willy's letter, I remember being startled awake in the darkest crease of night. I bolted upright in bed, gasping for air, sure of only one thing: Tuffy couldn't breathe. I remember telling myself that he needed me but I had left him underneath the gelid, damp dirt, alone and smothering in the middle of nowhere. How could I? What was I thinking leaving him out in the woods by himself, in total darkness?

And then I said to myself, *He's dead, you fool.*

My skin shriveled every time I remembered Tuffy's death; it ran like a movie that kept re-playing in my mind, even when I didn't mean for it to start. I asked for his forgiveness again, forgiveness for not giving him what he needed. I felt such a stronghold of guilt for believing I had abandoned Tuffy, I wondered for a long time if that night, reliving it the way I did, wasn't an omen of some kind.

The next night I went directly to my room after dinner to complete take-home make-up exams. My teachers gave me second and sometimes third chances after someone spread the word that my mother was still suffering from some dreadful mental problem.

Having someone in the family out in left field seemed to make grown-ups skittish. Regardless, having someone in the family who was out in left field did have its advantages. So did Gabe's brains.

After lending her assistance to me, and trying to get the clunky concepts of math and government through my head, Gabe agreed that the likelihood of my failing these classes would be exactly the same, with or without a psychotic, or as I preferred to believe, a runaway mother. She pushed back from my desk one night, and told me straight, "Even if your mother was June Cleaver herself, cooking a pot roast in the kitchen right now, you would not get this. Because your brain works best in paint, music, and dance moves. That's just the way it is," she said, erasing more of my work. "Yep," she blurted, "very high probability of failure no matter how you look at it."

As long as I stayed in the room with Gabe, kept Led Zeppelin playing, gave her a boxing ring-style shoulder rub now and then, and only left to pee or cook her an exploding silver dome of popcorn, she was able to fly through all my homework with ease. "I will not let you sabotage your graduation and our trip to New York by failing math and history, Zetty. Not gonna happen."

I lay back on my bed reading *Emma* by Jane Austen when she said it, stuck a finger on the page to mark my spot and told her, "*No*. Do *not* let me do that." Then went back to imagining *Emma* as a stage play, starring me.

But this particular evening I was on my own, my impatience with math building to atomic levels. I was hoping Gabe would call any minute to offer help so I could tell her I really had tried, but was stuck again.

"Honey?" the door cracked just a sliver as Father gave it two light raps.

"Come in," I said without looking up, all ten fingers raking my hair over a useless brain.

"Wanted to let you know that Dennis just called, and everything's fine, Gabe is fine, but—"

"What?" I closed my book and studied Father's face. My heart bucked for a moment even though I heard the part "Gabe is fine," but somehow it hadn't fully registered.

"It's a miracle, but she's fine. A drunk driver hit her in a head-on collision tonight and she was taken by ambulance to the emergency room."

"What? When did it happen?" My heart was racing now faster than I could think.

"Several hours ago. She was on her way home from work, had just left the Lucky-Seven. She's already home—it's just a miracle she's alive. She's pretty banged up, but she's okay."

"And you're sure she's okay to be home? Can I see her?"

"The doctors checked her over, she had x-rays, and yes, she is just fine. Lots of bumps and bruises and she'll be sore awhile. Dennis said she wants you to come over when you can. I thought we could take her some flowers."

I dropped my book, raced to the bathroom and tried to pee as fast as I could, but it seemed to stream on forever. I clasped my hands around bunched-up toilet paper to still the trembling. My knees started shaking, too. Gabe was okay, but my stomach turned somersaults and made my dinner turn sour inside me.

The evening had grown chilly. A gust of wind blustered up the street from the ocean. I pulled my sweatshirt tight, my hood over my ears, and hurried to Gabe. I was still shaky with a million questions when we reached her bedroom. "Gabe, are you okay? What happened?" She was lying on her back, the lamp turned on low next to her bed. Father set down the vase of flowers, kissed Gabe on the forehead.

"I'll let you two girls talk, but I'm glad you're okay, honey. Really relieved."

"Thank you, Mr. McGee."

"Honey, call me Hank." Gabe and I flashed a look of astonishment at each other when he left, but Gabe only wanted to talk about what happened to her.

"He aimed his headlights right at me, Zetty. Right at me! I knew what was going to happen, and I thought this was it."

I felt my eyes double in size. "You remember everything?"

Gabe spoke easily, quickly, sure of herself. "I remember everything. And this is the thing: it was okay to die."

Gabe's bluntness startled me this time. Her words didn't seem like her own, though I didn't know who else they could possibly belong to.

She raced on, "I wasn't scared once I shot up into space and was leaving. I left Zetty, and I was excited. I knew it was my turn to meet God. This was it. I was ready, and I wished my parents and Tom and you knew I was okay, because I was! Look at me." She held one hand out in front of her. "I still shake like a leaf just talking about it!"

"Did you see anything, I mean when you shot up?"

"No."

"A white light?"

Gabe's eyes darted right and left. "No."

"No tunnel?"

"No." She flashed a stop-being-dumb look. "Look. I'm just saying there *is* more, Zetty."

I began to doubt the shooting up into space part, but didn't say so.

She continued, but the speed of her thoughts made her breathless, "I figured I'd be in the headlines on the front page tomorrow. I mean, who survives a head-on collision?"

"You, Gabe. If anyone could, it's you."

"Well, all I can tell you is I was going up into darkness, propelled like a missile, and I was ready, and excited, and I was fine. We don't have to be afraid of dying."

"But you didn't die, right? You didn't see anything."

"Well, no. I came back too fast. Like I dropped back into my body, BAM! And I was disappointed because I was ready, you know? But then I thought I was going to die a slow death, which made me huffy at first, until I realized I wasn't dying at all, and it was all one big, fat, false alarm. My time wasn't up." Gabe flipped off a prescription cap and sprinkled two yellow pills into the palm of her hand. Then she froze.

"Gabe? What is it?" Her eyes slammed shut. "Are you alright?"

"I keep seeing it. The headlights," she said weakly. "I keep hearing the crash of glass and metal. It keeps happening over and over." Her shoulders shuddered. "It's so real." She looked to me, it seemed, for an answer.

"How awful, Gabe. I had that happen to me, too, after Tuffy. But nothing like this. Living through it once is enough." I led her hand up to her mouth. "Better take your pills and fast."

She tossed them both to the back of her throat and gulped water from the glass sitting next to the flowers.

"Are you sure you're okay?" I asked, worried for Gabe in a way I had never felt before.

"I hurt. My chest especially," she said struggling to complete her sentences.

I took the glass for her and returned it to the end table. "The whole steering wheel bent completely in half." Gabe gingerly lifted the lavender clematis-covered sheet lying on top of her and showed me bruises starting to appear down the entire left side of her body.

"Thank goodness you're okay. It could've been worse."

"It's not a bad thing to die, Zetty. I know that for sure now, even though it sounds weird."

"Well, sorta, but you are in shock still."

"No, this is not shock. I'm telling you, there is nothing to fear. God is there." Gabe said it like a speaker in a Billy Graham crusade. Or maybe the first woman priest in the Catholic Church.

"Okay," I said, partly to appease her. "Good to know."

"What's good to know? Hey, sis." I heard the bedroom door swoosh open and slide against the bushy shag carpet. Tom's head leaned in, "Hey, Zetty. Man, you got wiped out, huh, Gabe? Okay to come in?"

"Sure," Gabe said as she tried to scoot herself up higher against the pillow. When her face scrunched in pain, I slid both hands behind her back and gently raised the pillow and added an extra underneath to keep her upright.

I was about to say something to Tom, something casual but with a hint of intimacy that only he would catch, but when I turned to him I saw a girl. A beautiful, tall, blonde, flawless, picturesque piece of art, holding his hand. I felt the blood drain from my face and the room start to swim.

"I came over as soon as I could—hope it's okay I brought Annabelle with me. Annabelle, this is my sister Gabe—Gabe, Annabelle. Oh, and her best friend, Zetty."

Oh, and her best friend, Zetty whirled in my mind. I was already an afterthought. My knees felt loose and I swallowed back a sickly wave of nausea that rose in my throat.

I watched Annabelle lean into Tom's side, clasping his hand tighter. "Hiii," she practically sang. "it's nice to meet you, Gabe, but sorry it's like this. I'm glad you're okay."

It must have looked like my insides had been scooped out, my core left hollow. Gabe took a double take and wondered if I needed water. "No," I told her, "I'm still getting over the shock of all that happened to you," which was not a total lie.

I rearranged Father's flowers in the vase as they talked, and didn't hear a word of the conversation until Tom let go of Annabelle's hand and leaned in to give Gabe a tenuous hug goodbye and patted her weakly on the back. Then he stood tall next to me and leaned awkwardly down into an angular, prickly, no contact, embrace.

Childhood memories with Tom flashed before me like I was about to die myself. First age six, then eight, then ten, and twelve, and finally seventeen. And then I realized Tom and I were destined to be family; it could never be anything more than family. His new counterfeit embrace told me the little sister's best friend would never be more than just that.

"Hey, we gotta run, get better soon, sis."

Annabelle dragged behind Tom, clutching his hand again. She rotated her head toward us, "Nice to meet you Gabe, get well soooon. Oh, and nice to meet you too, Betty!" The cheerful sing-song crap was grating on me.

"Zetty," I corrected harshly.

"Oh," she said, sounding surprised, "*with a Z?*" Her face wrinkled up in confusion.

"As in ZEBRA, yes. *ZETTY.*"

"Oh, alright. Well, bye." She took Tom's arm, smiled a perfect Pepsodent-white flash of teeth, and was gone.

When the door shut, I smirked, "Can you believe her?"

"Annabelle?"

"More like Tinkerbelle," I chided.

"People always mess up your name. What's the big deal?"

"It's just the way she said it."

Gabe's heavy-lidded eyes fought to stay open even a slit. "Wow, these pills make me spacey." Her words rolled out like boulders, slow and heavy, "By the way, you know the kind of doctor I want to be someday?"

"An emergency room doc?" I slunk down on the chair next to her bed.

"The shrink kind, Zetty. That's what I've decided."

"What? You said psychoanalyzing is all horseshit, and Freud was full of it—"

She cut me off, her words slurring probably like the drunk who hit her, "Yup. I'm going to be a different kind. For someone like your mom. A good kind, like your Sperling sounds like. I think there is a *real, real, real* need. I do. And Sue Willy. We have to do something to help, don't we? We need to go see her. And about your mom, Zetty."

I halted, trying to take in everything she was saying, "What about my mom?"

"Don't give up."

"Of course we won't, Gabe. But I'll work on all the calls now until you're better. You need to rest."

Gabe grinned in slow motion. "Okay," she sighed, "I'll give you more money soon. Only use the phone booth, Zetty."

"I know, I am."

"Good. And Zetty, tell your dad thanks for the flowers and coming over. And sorry—I know you love him, but it'll be okay."

"Don't worry about me and my dad, Gabe. Really, it's better," I assured her.

Gabe's eyes were only open to a slit. "No silly," she said, "I meant with Tommy. I *know everything*. He—" And just like that they shut and she was out.

"Hey! What do you mean, you know everything?" But it was no use. She was asleep, and of course she knew. There was never hiding anything from Gabe. But I figured the wanting to be a shrink part must have been a side effect of the pills she was on.

Although, later that night, as I sat with the gloom and doom of another gut-wrenching loss, thanks to Annabelle's existence, I realized Gabe was a natural for the shrink profession and I planned to tell her exactly that the next day. If she really did mean it, I thought she might be able to help patch up the hole in my heart Tom left that was so big even Tuffy could've driven a tractor through it. Doc Sperling had just left for Europe and who was more perfect to take her place than Gabe, I thought.

In the meantime, wrangled-up questions caught to my insides like barbed wire, and tortured me all night. How could I, yet again, believe someone was there for me, believe they loved me, and be so wrong? How could Tom kiss me for months the way he did, and not care? How could people not care about hurting someone, even someone who was as close as family?

And in mother's case, *was* family.

It was still in the realm of possibility, I reminded myself, that Mother ran away to follow her dreams once she felt better. So far, we weren't getting anywhere with hospitals, it couldn't hurt to start calling theatres now, too. I added that to the list of crucial things Gabe and I needed to talk over when she was clear minded enough.

However, what had seemed so vital to discuss with Gabe that night, became absurdly trivial the next day.

Marjorie

IF I WOKE UP EARLY AND MADE IT TO THE COMMUNITY room in time, I got to watch cartoons. "Little Lulu" and "Bugs Bunny" were my favorites. But some mornings a fog girdled around me and it seemed impossible to move. My mind so fuzzy and dull, at first I could only hear the echoes of shoes on the floors. Clomping, like horses. Nothing came into focus but sounds. So I would wait for help. I would wait for my mother's arm to lead me.

The hallways grew longer and narrower each time I strolled down one. The walls here were made only of paper. *Such a strange place*, I thought. It was too late for cartoons, and even Romper Room, so Eleanor took me to the window, already cracked open next to my bed, and I listened to the children outside playing.

Two children. Young girls pretending to be spies. I liked hearing them play in their make believe world of daring escapes, life or death adventures. It helped me feel alive again.

"No, Zetty," I heard one say. "Get on the ground like this, and crawl. Take cover!"

"Ten four, Gabe, I mean agent 99. Copy that."

"You don't have to say ten-four and copy that at the same time."

"Why not?"

"Never mind. Now be quiet or they'll hear us. Use the moon necklace. It's our secret microphone! Tell the good guys were coming in to save them."

"When we grow up, let's be real detectives."

"Yeah, like *The Mod Squad*."

"Whatever we do, Gabe, let's be sure we do it together."

"We will, Zetty."

"Now, you be Calamity Jane, and I'll be Annie Oakley."

Their voices always faded away too soon. I loved my girls. I was pretty sure they were mine. I wished they would've come in and eaten warm crinkle cookies with me. I used to invite them in to join me. "Gray Squirrel, Gray Squirrel, swish your bushy tail," they sang. I watched them dance the moves with the children's circle on Romper Room once. "Little squirrels!" I'd say, "Time to eat!"

They played outside all the time after that. I slept, tasted bits of food, swallowed juice and water, tried to color in books, sang songs to music, and dreamt of days when I used to live somewhere else.

A new, loud voice blasted in my ear, "It's time to take your shower this morning, Marjorie. Or we can run a bath for you. Do you hear me, dear?"

I covered my head and started to cry. The tears spilled so hard, they dropped like bricks to the floor. I had to pull away, I wanted to run, but my limbs congealed, thickened like rubber.

"What is it, sweetie? Let me help you," the stranger offered.

"No!" I screamed. "No!" again I yelled. She didn't hear the rest. I wanted to say, *You don't understand! I will lose myself down the drain if you make me go in there!* Running water terrified me; it threatened to dispose of me completely.

Covering the wall just outside my room, there were

faces in the wallpaper pattern. They knew what I wanted to say. They tried to help, but they couldn't either. Like me, they were entombed.

"Anything I can help with?" It was mother's voice.

"She's refusing the shower again, Eleanor."

"Not a problem. I'll take it from here." The stranger left the room. "How about a sponge bath today, Margie? We'll take a break from the shower until we figure out how to help you feel safe in there. Okay?"

Yes, Please, I said in my mind. I gripped Eleanor's arm with gratitude. Her eyes told me she understood.

After a warm, soft, sudsy cloth massaged my limbs, Eleanor kneaded lotion into my skin. When I was dry, she skillfully lifted my hips and wrapped me in a diaper. Some days she took extra time brushing my hair before she knit a long braid to one side. By then, I was so relaxed, she tucked me into bed for a nap. She adjusted the curtains, switched off the light, and squeezed my hand goodnight. I liked it when she kissed the top of my head, too.

"Just rest, Margie," she'd say, "We'll play when you wake up." She tucked Dolly under my arm and quietly stepped away.

The line between sleep and waking wasn't as clear anymore. Sometimes I was able to stay in my dreams, even when I was awake. It was liberating. I was released, unbound, emancipated into a world I belonged in again. I looked forward to that, at least. And to cartoons and play time with Mother.

That morning, I had the most pleasant dream about a woman I used to know. A grown-up. She was a beauty queen once—and a rising star on stage, but that wasn't the most important thing about her. She was far more than that; she had strength of heart and mind. Her most important role wasn't on stage at all; it was being in the role of a mother. Because, for this woman, the love of family gave her life significance. Being a mother filled her with the deepest love there is.

When I closed my eyes, I understood she had the life I created; the life I wanted back. But, she was farther out of reach than ever. I knew she was leaving and it wouldn't be long before I'd never see her again.

I remained grateful to her for all she gave me. For everything she had once been. I promised to carry her with me for as long as I could.

In the Safety of the Ocean

In the morning, I lay in bed trying to imagine the secret language of birds. Their chatter woke me with high-pitched chirping and low rolling screaks that seemed to bounce from the telephone wire, to the palm trees, to the rooftop and back. But it wasn't just chirping; I heard the rustle of wings caught on the leaves of branches—flutter-ing, busily foraging for food, and maybe collecting twigs for nests. Whatever was going on, something was up in bird land.

It was an odd way to begin the crisp spring day that would surpass all others and take its place in history as my worst. Maybe the jays, California towhees and yellow-rumped warblers sensed something was about to crack; maybe they knew the world was going to split apart and never come back together again; maybe they felt it in the air.

Somewhere between my shower and breakfast, Father broke the news.

"There's something I have to tell you, Zetty," I think he said. I remember his arm around me, guiding me to a living room davenport. "I'm just going to say it." He stopped and choked back crying.

"Dad," I said angrily, "stop talking like that." He was scaring me. But then I read it on his blanched face—it was about Mother. The slow burn of dread spanned my chest. Mechanical breathing replaced the natural, spontaneous airflow we forget to appreciate.

Father looked at me, his face a mixture of fear and sadness, "Zetty," he fought to continue, "during the night a blood clot traveled to her lung."

We're too late! I screamed inside. *Gabe will be crushed! Now Mother is dead and Father is to blame for it all.* When I pushed him away, he embraced me and whispered in my ear.

And just like that I heard the words from Father that Gabe was gone.

I tried to organize my thoughts, reject what he said. But when I saw Father's eyes swimming with tears and his hand wipe slowly across his face, I remember the ache that began to rise in my chest. Like the baying of a tortured, dying animal, I heard, "No! No! No!" and I could not stop screaming it.

Father sat close to me, weeping brokenheartedly, unable to gain control for either of us. Under the weight of our grief, my soul shattered—I honestly felt there was nothing left of it. I was a floating particle, attached to nothing and lost. I had no one left.

THEY TOLD ME THE NARCOTICS GABE HAD TAKEN FOR PAIN gave her a peaceful death. As if that would somehow comfort me. All I wanted to do was take the same thing and follow her. She had told me not to be afraid of dying, and now I could honestly say I wasn't.

Father called our family physician who prescribed sleeping pills. "Take one to start, Zetty. You need to sleep," he instructed. But all I could say back to him in my mind was, *No. I don't need to sleep; I need to die.*

But sleep I did.

The first night I dreamt that Gabe came back. We were riding on a train, standing outside on a platform at the front, speeding forward as the wind flattened our faces, rushed up our noses and whipped our hair in a frenzy. We watched excitedly as the rails rushed under our feet. And then a short, but deep valley appeared in front of us and I told Gabe to hold on, because I didn't think we could make it. She told me, "It'll be fine Zetty. See?" And we rolled down and right back up as graceful as a sailboat.

And then the train stopped. "It's time to go, Zetty," she told me.

"Okay," I said, and followed her to the steps to climb down.

"No, not you," she told me. "Only me. I get off here, but you need to keep going. The journey isn't over for you," her voice tranquil and confident when she said it.

"No, Gabe, you have to stay and go with me," I said in desperation to keep her there. The train started to move, she stepped off, and waved goodbye. She shouted happily, "Keep going, Zetty; It's okay! I'm fine. You just keep going! And don't forget!" she added, "your mother is waiting."

"But I can't do it without you, Gabe!" I hollered. "I'll never find her if you leave."

She waved until I couldn't see her smile anymore, until she dissolved in the half-light.

I believed what I told her. I believed that without Gabe, without our plan, my search for Mother wasn't to be. I believed I would never know anything more than I did.

But I didn't believe it for long.

THE PANG OF WAKING UP HURT. I HAD BEEN WITH GABE and then was without her again. The dream was brief; it carried only a glimmer of peace before it fluttered away. But she was alive when she left me. And that gave me the tiniest flowering of hope, if only for an instant. But something else was waking me. Breathing—a steady rhythm of it. I bolted straight up expecting, wanting, wishing, begging someone, anyone, to put her there in front of me again.

But it was Father. Sitting on a chair next to my bed.

"I'm right here, Zetty, you just had a bad dream."

"No. It wasn't bad; waking up is," I said, and started to cry again, hoping all the tears would drain the life right out of me.

"Take two of these Zetty. It will help you sleep better." I placed them on my tongue and took a gulp from the glass of water he lifted to my mouth and washed it back wishing it were cyanide.

My eyes blurred when I reached for the bottle. I wanted more. I wanted to go to Gabe and Tuffy, and finally rest, never having to feel the pain of waking again.

But Father's hand blocked my reach. It was warm and gentle and strangely familiar. I saw his knuckles on top of mine. He was still sitting by my side. He squeezed my hands, wrapped every finger in an embrace, and the comfort it gave made me think for a moment I had taken the whole bottle of pills after all.

I drifted out again slowly pushing away from shore and I heard him calling from a distance, "I still need you here, Zetty. I love you."

And then I went under, suspended in a pool of blackness, floating into the liberation of pure nothingness.

"Zetty, it's time to wake up. You need to open your eyes."

Nope, I thought. *I don't need to and I'm not going to.*

"Zetty, wake up, honey, you've been in bed for days. You're going to see Aunt Julie. You need to get up."

I opened my eyes a sliver from the shock. "What did you say?"

"You need to get up,"

"No," I said. "What about Aunt Julie?"

Father jostled my foot with one hand. "You're going to go stay with Aunt Julie for a while, to get away. It's for the best right now." He lifted a small suitcase off the floor made of a floral pink tapestry, and set it gently on the foot of my bed. "It's not good for you to be here where everything is a reminder. I know you won't fly, so I bought train tickets; you're leaving today."

"Are you kidding me?" I sat up on both elbows wondering if I was dreaming again.

Father straightened. "No, Zetty. I'm not kidding, now hear me out. Sometimes the best thing we can do at times like this is to get away, and you know how much Aunt Julie loves you. She can be real good to be around at times like this."

"But, why Dad? Why would you want to send me away? Is this what you did to Mother, too?"

"Of course not. I'm not sending you away; I'm helping you leave all this behind. You can be around your aunt who I know you can talk to."

"I haven't spoken to her in ages. Why would you think I could talk to her?" I paused and decided it was time to risk everything. "I have a shrink. She's the one I talk to, if I'm going to talk."

"I know, Scarlett told me." Father seemed unaffected by the revelation, unzipped the cover and flipped open the suitcase. "But you haven't gone anywhere, or seen anyone since this happened—"

I broke in, "Doc Sperling's in Europe and she won't be back for a while. I'm not talking to anyone but her. Not the guy covering for her, not the on-call person, no one."

"Okay," he said gently, "you can stay with Aunt Julie until she comes back. I think the change will be good."

"For me, or for *you*?" I said sharply.

Father looked at me disapprovingly and shook his head.

"Fine," I said. "I'm leaving. Hope it helps you to have me gone," but what I really thought was, *I'll bring that bottle of sleeping pills with me and take as many as I like.*

It took all my strength to push back the weight of quilts and blankets over me. I staggered out of bed, adjusted the knee-length black tee-shirt I had been wearing for days, and mindlessly threw things into the small suitcase lying open on my bed. Toothbrush, underwear, deodorant, and when Father left the room, the bottle of sleeping pills he had left behind. I tucked them carefully in a side pouch within easy reach.

Yes, I told myself, I was ready to go now.

ROUND TRIP TICKET

I SLUMPED INTO THE SEAT NEXT TO THE WINDOW AND SET my suitcase and backpack on the two empty spots next to me. The train lurched forward and I saw Father standing below the other side of my window, waving. Then he blew a kiss.

I craned my neck to watch him for as long as I could, and as he turned to walk away he pulled a white hankie from his pocket and rubbed his eyes with it.

I had an overwhelming urge to run to him, wrap my arms around his waist, and climb up into his arms like I had a million times as a small child. I imagined his hold on me, not wanting to let me go. I wondered why growing up had to change everything.

I didn't waste any time. I opened the prescription bottle and held the little white fish of a capsule in my hand and made sure no one was watching. I slipped it into my mouth like I had just smuggled it over the Mexican border. I pooled as much spit in my mouth as I could, swallowed, and pretended it tasted delicious as it slid down like sand. But then I gagged, my eyes watered, and I had to start over. This time it was soggy and spreading like clumps on the back of my tongue, but I didn't give up. Before long I was singing along in my head to The Rolling Stones, "Doctor please, some more of these...what a drag it is getting old—"

Conversations spun around me from all directions. A mother and daughter were in front of me. The little girl's face rested in the crack between the seats. Her wide brown eyes peeked through at me. She reminded me of myself at that age. Her eyes didn't dart away when I met them; they kept staring, as if examining a big new bug never seen before. Her mother started to read to her. Something about a twinkling star stuck in a frozen sky. She flipped over and swept her fingers up and down the window, as if jumping over every tree, boulder, and telephone pole we passed. Then she pressed her nose on the glass and breathed out two foggy spots on the window. She drew on them with her finger, then discovered her mouth could blow an even wider spot for an even larger canvas. Her mother admired her art.

A woman across the aisle chatted with her friend, saying she was "just ducky" and "having big fun," and a younger woman behind me argued with her boyfriend and complained, "You never spend time with me anymore. You've changed. Do you want to break up? Well, do you?"

And there I sat. Listening to drivel fly at me from all sides with no one to keep me patched up and sewn together as I came apart, to keep me in one piece so I didn't have to swallow little white fish-shaped pills. No one could do that for me except Gabe.

Great timing, Doc Sperling, I thought. *You're off sailing the seven seas, whooping it up European style—not giving me a second thought.* I knew I sounded a little like Wilma again, but, *oh-well*.

The clickety-clack, clickety-clack rhythm of the train distracted my thoughts and changed them into abstract ideas, the kind that race around in your mind just before sleep. Then the brakes screamed as the train cars shook into the next small town, and the next one after that. Flashing red lights and the steady beat of bells played over and over. My eyes closed to a long stream of shadows, light, shadows, light, darkness through tunnels, and more shadows and light. I was going under to sound, motion and flickering darkness. Down to a place where no memories of Gabe had yet formed. Under a frozen sky of little stars, everything finally went black.

"NEXT STOP, BOISE, IDAHO—BOISE, IDAHO, NEXT STOP, PLEASE!" The rustle of the conductor's uniform brushed past me.

The sun was high in the sky. I slept through the morning and could have kept sleeping if only we hadn't arrived so quickly. Outside the window were happy people awaiting our arrival. I wondered if I would be able to recognize Aunt Julie, or she me.

I spotted a military man in a white bell-bottomed pant sailor suit leaning against a light pole, lustily eyeballing each woman up, down, front, and back as they passed him. I stumbled out of the train, wondering if I would be of any interest to him. I wasn't.

I looked him straight in the eye and not once did he look back. He was too caught up in the black mini skirt in front of me. In a perfect imitation of a turned on Jimi Hendrix, I heard, "Foxy lady," as she passed him.

But then I looked him in the face again. "Max?"

"Yeah," he answered clearly unimpressed with who was asking.

"It's me, Zetty."

"Well, I'll be damned. I didn't even notice you." He tossed the butt of a cigarette in front of him and stepped into it like a giant cockroach.

"Yeah. No kidding," I said flatly.

He tossed a piece of foil on the ground and started chewing a wad of gum like a Guernsey. "Hell, you look awful," he chuckled. His head bent around my backside, searching my ass. "You could stand to lose a few pounds," he smirked.

Alright, I told myself, *enough of this.*

What I did next still amazes me.

Without any warning at all, I raised my fist and popped him in the chin. "Shove it up your ass, Max," I told him.

It only took him back a little, not enough, so then I boxed him on the ear with my bag. He flinched, raised both arms like a shield, and the skin on his neck turned angry, like the sun striking the cheek of a tomato. Rage flickered in his eyes. "Why the fuck did you do that?!" He glared at me, stroking his jaw.

"Because now I can," I told him.

With suitcase in one hand, and backpack resting comfortably on my shoulders, I turned in the opposite direction, and went straight to the first train car going west. When I climbed up the steps into car 48, I heard him shout, "What the hell are you doing? Hey!" I released the backpack from my neck, took a seat, gulped back more sleeping potion, and settled in for the ride home.

I was in no condition to deal with the likes of Max-Mean in his hotshot white sailor suit. And then, as if she were sitting right there next to me in the flesh, I said aloud, "Max-mean is history, Gabe."

FATHER WAS AT WORK WHEN THE TAXI BROUGHT ME HOME. I was aware of a little shuffle in my step when I walked through the front door. I wondered if it was the effects of the medication, or fatigue, or a bit of Mother's plague coming over me before I popped two, or three, or maybe more pills, and went to bed.

The dull ache of grief carried into sleep.

I don't know how much time passed when I heard a conversation float in the airwaves past me. It was Father, his words coming in and out, "...My daughter is Doctor Sperling's patient... Yes, I understand. I'm trying to reach someone who can help us."

Has Doc Sperling died too, I wondered? *Why not*? I thought. *Let's all go together. What's the point of anyone staying alive anyway*?

"Zetty?"

Yes? I thought I had answered.

"Zetty! Open your eyes. Wake up, Zetty."

What was the big deal, I wondered. *And aren't my eyes open? I see everything, don't I? Oh well, leave me alone. I'm fine.*

But there he was again, saying things in the distance. "I'm calling about my daughter...she's not responding....Yes, she is breathing. She's like a rag doll, though. Yes, she does... No, she is not speaking... Yes, her eyes are open sometimes... but she can't speak... I think she needs help... Her mother had the same thing happen....no, she looks like it though.... what should I do? Okay, yes, I can."

And then, I remember being moved. Slowly moved, and I wasn't happy about it at first. I had been perfectly comfortable after all. Why disturb me when I finally didn't care about anything? I was rolling on something that felt like a wagon. Little bumps and bounces now and then, but securely swaddled in it at the same time. It seemed to go on for miles and by then I didn't mind it in the least. Nothing bothered me. I was heavy like a brick, and not worried about anything. It didn't matter where I was going, or who I was with. *Just everyone, let me go under, please.*

It took all my strength to lift both eyelids, but when I was able to boost them halfway up, I happened to see them: big, white, majestic pillars at the top of a long train of steps. *Back to the white house,* I told myself. *Maybe this time I'll meet the president. Or maybe this was the room Doc Sperling said she couldn't get me into, until now,* I thought.

I'd like a private room please, I rehearsed in my mind, *unless of course I have to have a roommate, in which case I would like my mother, please. I would really like my mother.*

Hurting is Part of the Cure

It was just another awakening.

Something in the room signaled it was morning. The drugs had worn off and I knew I had to come back to it yet again. I came into consciousness kicking and screaming, fighting against the reality of another day born without Gabe in it.

The first thing that came into focus was a familiar navy-blue leather clog. And it moved because a foot was in it. And attached to that foot was Scarlett's leg. She was there, sitting next to my bed in a hard metal chair. Lightly pumping her clog, up and down. It was a comfort when I saw her. Immediately comforting.

"Hi," she said softly. When she leaned forward, the chair cushion squeezed together and sighed.

"Hi," I strained to say it back. And then without warning I bolted up, heart pounding like a jackhammer. "What's happened?" I asked, panic coursing through my veins. *What now?* I thought, *where am I?*

Then the memory of the pillars surfaced, and I knew. "Have I gone insane, Scarlett?"

"Honey, no," she reassured, "you have not gone insane. Nothing else has happened. Your dad is here. He let me come in first." She clutched my hand and squeezed. "You're only here until you feel strong enough to go home. You're okay, Zetty, but the pills you were taking were awfully strong."

Heavy metal bars were bolted across my window. It was impossible to reach in and drive a fist through the glass. I wasn't interested in trying, but believe me, I did look forward to the colorful pills dropped into a doll-sized paper cup with my name on them.

Every hour a nurse, an orderly, or a shrink stopped by to ask me something, like, "How are you feeling today?" "Ready for a walk?" and "Do you have any thoughts of wanting to hurt yourself, Zetty?" Then, two pills flew down the hatch. After that, professional eyes spied on me through the window of my door at regular intervals.

It was a gloomy room, everything concrete gray, including my blanket. The bathroom only held a ten-inch sink, and toilet. But it was all I needed.

I pulled a lever to raise my bed. "I look the way Mother did when she left us, Scarlett. Maybe I'm becoming her."

Scarlett leaned forward, her eyes like black marbles beneath her sunglasses. She tenderly placed both hands on my arm. "Honey, you're not your mother. This is not happening because you have her illness. This is grief."

"I hate that Gabe's not here. And I always will. She left me, Scarlett."

"I know, honey. I know. But we'll live through this, Zetty. Somehow, we will." Scarlett pushed up her sunglasses and rested them on her head. Her eyes raw and swollen at the corners.

"How do you know?" I asked.

"I don't. The truth is I can only put one foot in front of the other right now. And today it got me here, to you." She crossed her legs slowly, as if weights were tied to the bottom of her jeans. "Death is a natural part of life, honey, and—"

"Gabe didn't think so," I said, as a matter of fact.

Scarlett planted her eyes on mine. "What do you mean?" she asked looking like a statue.

"She thought our brains were wired for eternal life. And that's why grief wrings us out until we're torn to shreds. It's really not in our nature to leave one another. That's what Gabe said."

"Huh," Scarlett considered.

"I think she was right, Scarlett. I've never felt anything more unnatural in my life."

Scarlett stared up at the black iron bars against my window. She nodded weakly, her face weary from the weight of sadness.

I pulled an abrasive blanket up over my bare limbs. "I've stopped going to school, missed all my appointments, deadlines, and I haven't left a bed for weeks, or has it been months? I don't even know. I've lost all track of time."

"I know," she said kicking off her clogs and resting navy-blue socks on the edge of my bed. "Let me tell you how it happens, Zetty. First you only make it to the toilet and back. Then, you go to the kitchen and drink orange juice one morning and maybe sit on the sofa. Then one day you put on your favorite jeans and keep putting one foot in front of the other. Because you have to. You go through the motions like the living dead, but you keep living."

"I'm glad you didn't say we had to bat pillows, but I have to admit, I've found myself in a fetal position without even trying."

"Me, too," she grimaced. "To be honest, it seems my therapy is not all that helpful."

"Really?" I tried to sound shocked. Gabe would be relieved her mother was coming to her senses about that.

"Yes," she said sheepishly. "Don't tell anyone."

"Never," I promised.

"Right now I wouldn't half care if they threw me into a bed next to yours," she said. We both expelled a tepid "ha" because it was all the energy we could muster for a real laugh. It was the first almost-smile my cheeks had felt in weeks.

"I made a to-do list for survival last night," she said. "It helps. Coming to see you was number five. Number one was: get up. Two: go to bathroom. Three: put clothes on. Four: swallow coffee. Five: go to Zetty."

She poured water from my pitcher into two Dixie cups. "As soon as I can pull myself together, I'm going to focus on something new, Zetty. I'm joining Mothers Against Drunk Driving, MADD for short. Great name, isn't it?"

"Perfect." I wrapped my hand around the Dixie cup, but it felt too warm to sip. "Can I join, too? I want to help." A sense of urgency pounded in my heart; I wanted to throw myself into the cause if I could ever find energy to get out of bed again.

"Of course. Whenever you're ready." Scarlett turned her face away, leaned back in her chair, and we both closed our eyes.

"Every year on Santa's lap, I asked for sisters and brothers, and Gabe used to ask for her own babies. She said she wanted to be a mom all the time, Scarlett." Our eyes opened again.

"Oh my goodness," Scarlett looked flustered. "I had no idea. I wonder why? She always said she wanted a career."

I looked at Scarlett dumbstruck. She really didn't know. "Because she had you," I told her with one hundred-and-fifty-percent certainty. "She wanted both because she had you."

Scarlett reached for the box of tissue on my hospital tray, pulled out a wad, and buried her face in them.

After Scarlett left, I was tied up with guilt. For a mother who had lost her only daughter, I was humbled that she would find time for me. I didn't even thank her. It was as if someone had reached down my throat, snatched all my words, and made a run for it. But only because I felt so undeserving of having that place on her survival list.

And then I heard Doc Sperling ask, *And what about the daughter who lost her only mother? And her only dog? And her only best friend? And in a certain way her father? Isn't she important, too?* Oh, I thought to myself, *when you put it that way, I suppose she is.* But on that day, the guilt raised only as high as a carpenter ant could lift.

TO DO LIST FOR SURVIVAL

1. *Put both feet on floor.*
2. *Walk (or shuffle) to bathroom.*
3. *Pee (sit as long as I want).*
4. *Shower when they come and get me.*
5. *Put street clothes on.*
6. *Get day pass from head nurse.*
7. *Drive home with Dad.*
8. *Eat lunch with Dad (pretend).*
9. *Meet Scarlett out front and go for walk (short).*
10. *Eat dinner with Dad (pretend again).*
11. *Drive back to hospital with Dad (in time for pills).*

Scarlett and I schlepped across the cul-de-sac and hugged when we met in the middle. "You're number nine on my To Do List today, Scarlett."

"Wow. You've done more than me. You're number six on mine."

The day had clouded over and a thin mist hung in the air, floating around our words. I couldn't help but notice that she didn't look like her usual self. I tried to keep my gaze on her and not on the Taylor house. I didn't want to see Gabe's bedroom window, or Dennis's truck, or their front door, or the porch. The whole house was a trigger for another meltdown if I let myself fix my eyes on it for too long.

"One thing is certain, Scarlett," I told her as we stepped up on the curb and followed the arch of the sidewalk out of the cul-de-sac.

"What's that, honey?"

"We both look like hell." I almost said, "'Like death warmed over,'" but my stomach turned sickish, stopping me in time.

"And feel like hell, too." She laughed weakly. "What a sorry pair we are."

I had a ripped-up pair of jeans on with an old button-down flannel plaid shirt and hand-knit black beret that hung down over my ears. Scarlett wore stretch pants that bagged at the crotch and a zip-up sweatshirt, her hair messily pushed under the hood.

"Do you mind if we only go around the block once?" I asked. "I can't take much more than that. I have eleven things on my list today, and it's way too much."

"That's fine, honey. Have the doctors said when you can come home?"

"No."

"You feel ready?"

"I dunno. How's Dennis?" I asked, and didn't care how obvious it was that I changed the subject. "Has he gone back to work yet?"

"He tried," she said, tucking both hands in the front pocket of her sweatshirt. "Only made it a couple hours and came home. He's suffering so—I hardly know how to help him."

"You can't, Scarlett. The only thing that would help any of us is if she came back."

"True enough."

I avoided all the cracks and crevices in the sidewalk as we ambled in silence. "What about Tom?" I finally asked. The hole in my heart from Annabelle was a mere pinprick, compared to this. It all felt so silly now, to have felt the least bit sad about something so trivial.

"He went back to his classes. He's thinking of moving out and living closer to campus, but I think it's just too hard for him to be home. He told me to tell you hi and hopes you're doing better."

"So, he's okay?"

There was a little hitch in Scarlett's face when she looked at me. "It's hard to tell. You know how he and Dennis are. They don't exactly show their emotional side."

"Or my dad."

"*Yes*," she said. "Your dad, too. But that never bothered your mom."

"What do you mean?" I felt my pulse quicken for the first time in months.

"She used to tell me it was part of what was so endearing about him."

"Huh?"

"Well, you know, she knew your dad was a sensitive man. Kind and gentle—never a harsh word. And a generous heart—showed it all the time. So even though he didn't show his feelings, at least you could tell he had them! We talked a lot. Your mom always listened when I needed someone to talk to."

"She listened to *you*?"

"Yes," she said, hesitating in mid-stride. "A lot. Why are

you surprised?"

"I thought it was the other way around. That's all." We came to a complete stop.

"No." She faced me. "Your mom gave me lots of good advice when it came to my marriage."

"Really. Like what did she say?" I picked up the stride again, and she followed.

"She told me not to accept the critical, rude ways Dennis talked to us. She said to leave him if I needed to, you know, to make a point. But she said, 'If you stay with him you *must* do something for yourself.' She was the one who encouraged me to go back to college."

"Was my mom 'making a point' when she left us?"

Scarlett broke her stride again; I braked abruptly alongside her. I cast my eyes away from her face, staring at a high-climbing magenta bougainvillea bush when she answered, "No, Zetty. Nothing like that. Your parents had a great marriage. Your mom felt nothing but love for you and your dad. It was her illness that took her honey, nothing else."

"In one day?" We started moving again.

"I'm sure that's how it seemed, but she was struggling off and on for a long time. Didn't your father tell you anything, Zetty?"

"No. Actually, he didn't—hasn't. I mean, thinking back, I can remember things—her crying, acting strange, and being silly in odd ways. Things like that. But we had so much fun, I didn't think anything of it."

"She concealed it well for a long time, but she had periods of being depressed and easily confused. I wish I knew more to tell you, but I don't. I only know your mom may have gone to long-term care when her condition worsened. Back east, maybe."

"Is that what my father told you?"

"He mentioned it was a possibility years ago. But he's never said where, or mentioned it again. I didn't want to pry—it seems too painful for him."

Scarlett was right. Asking would have cut into him too much. "Yeah, I heard him say 'New York' to my Aunt Julie, too. But it's not like my father to give up on her. At least not the Father I used to have. Sending her away seems so drastic. So cruel. Mother would've never done that to him."

"Don't be too hard on him, Zetty. I'm sure he had good reason. It's never an easy thing losing a loved one, no matter how you lose them."

"Well, if Gabe were alive, you wouldn't stop seeing her. Not for any reason. Not ever."

"It's not the same thing, honey. Nothing is ever that simple. Right or wrong, your dad has done the best he could. His intentions are good. Remember that."

My legs turned weak and shaky, and I told Scarlett she would have to carry me home if we didn't turn back.

"I admired your mom, Zetty," she said, making the turn toward home. "She was an inspiration. She never called herself a feminist, but, honestly she could have led the women's movement, and she worked tirelessly for the civil rights movement at church, too. She was really something."

I noticed her scan the sky while we strolled in silence.

"What happened to all that, Scarlett?"

Scarlett wrapped her arm around me. "I'm not sure, honey. It's a helpless feeling, I know."

But being helpless was not something I aspired to be. A surge of defiance began to pump its way up my spine when Scarlett put a name to it. No matter what I'd been through, I was not willing to accept powerlessness as a side-effect. I wasn't having it. I would not give up when it came to

Mother. And not, I realized, when it came to my own life. A renewed source of energy was filling my core; I started to feel alive again.

"We made it around twice, Zetty," she finally announced. "Let's get our sorry asses home."

Before Scarlett and I began to part ways, I blurted, "I can't believe I missed Gabe's funeral, Scarlett. I should've been there." It pounced out of nowhere but it wasn't until I said it that I realized how heavy it had weighed on my heart.

"Oh, Zetty," Scarlett enfolded me. "Honey, it's okay. It couldn't be helped! Don't blame yourself, please. We missed you, but Gabe would understand. We all did. You know that."

I could have said, yes, I did know that. But I watched my tennis shoe claw at the curb knowing this would remain another albatross I would carry permanently, something I'd never be able to change, like Tuffy.

Scarlett held me. "Listen, I know how hard it'll be to come back inside our home again. Especially the first time. But could you try to come over for just a few minutes after dinner? We have something to give you—Dennis, Tom, and I."

"Tom?"

"All of us, yes. But I'll explain when you come over, if you can do it, okay?"

"I'll try. And Scarlett?" She turned to me. "Thanks for everything. The things you shared about my mom. It means a lot. Everything else does, too. The way you've wanted to spend time with me, and be with me." She smiled, blew me a kiss, and we parted ways.

I edged backward against the horizon and for the first time since Gabe's death, stared at the Taylor house. I let my eyes rest on the two big branches on the tree in the front yard that Gabe and I climbed as kids, pretending to be sitting atop a wagon train. I moved to the brown two-toned truck sitting in the driveway whose clutch she never got the hang of, the front door we ran through a million times over the years, slamming our fingers more than once, and finally, I let my gaze fall on Gabe's bedroom window, but the only reflection standing there was the sky pressed against the glass.

I couldn't step back inside. Not yet.

After a slow-moving dinner, circling chunks of lumpy meatloaf around on a plastic plate as hard as a turtle shell, and pushing cold clumps of sticky mac and cheese here and there to appear at least partially eaten, I set my knife and fork down and left the table. Father picked up the newspaper, turned on the nightly news, and went to his recliner.

Same old stuff, I thought.

"Dad, could we work on the plane for a little while tonight? Before I go back?"

The newspaper rustled with delight between his fingers. "You bet we can. You feel up to it?"

"I'd like to sit and just watch if that's okay."

"Sure it's okay," he said eagerly. Father folded the newspaper in half, tucked it into the magazine rack, grabbed the aqua, cushioned step-stool from the kitchen and carried it to the garage. He pulled out the bottom step and set it next to the washing machine directly in front of the evolving semblance of an entirely solid two-seater cockpit. The Chevy stayed outside at the side of the driveway now.

"I used to sit on this stool at the bread board, stick my finger in a bowl of water, and paste blue-chip stamps into mother's booklets for her, do you remember?"

"I sure do," he said, closing the lid on the washing machine so I could lean one arm on the top if I wanted.

"You know, this whole plane will be made from scratch, except part of the engine and the landing gear," he said excitedly. "And you know, she's going to cruise at 140 miles per hour with a range of 800 miles. Isn't that something?"

"It is. But can you fire up the table saw?" I asked. "You know how I love the smell."

"I'll get her runnin' just for you." But before he could center a piece of plywood against the guide of the blade, a thunderous crash hit against the house. My first thought was lightning, the second was a bomb, and then we watched in horror as the garage door violently splintered down the middle, and instantaneously reshaped the fuselage of father's plane into an accordion. Father stumbled to the side door, broke through the gate, and yelled like I never heard him yell before.

Scarlett and Dennis came running, and all the neighborhood doors flew open. When I caught up to Father, I saw it: a flashy gold sports car about the size of a beer can, whose back end missed our car by mere inches but lodged itself into the center of our garage door. The bronzy-haired woman at the wheel, pie-eyed and sloshed, stumbled out, her orange tent dress billowing and flapping like wings under her arms.

Nine years of work was reduced to rubble in mere seconds. And Father's dream buried with it.

"How dare you, how dare you, *how dare you!*" I screamed, my arms flailing, flying toward her ruddy cheekbones, ready to box her one, just like I had done to Max.

"Whoa! Back it up, Annie Oakley," Dennis ordered, his voice loud and scrappy. "Simmer down!" He pulled me back and pinned my arms in place, but I kept yelling at her.

"Do you have any idea what you've done? You wicked, selfish, evil woman! Did you even think about what you were doing? You could have killed someone, just like Gabe!" I screamed, "She died because of a drunk like you! This is why she died!" I bent at the waist, dry-heaved, but nothing but spit emptied out which made me thankful for not eating. I heard her kitten heels slapping against the asphalt all the way down the street.

Father kneeled next to me. "Zetty," he said firmly, "no one was hurt here. No one."

"But your plane, Dad! Your plane—all our work."

"I know, but you didn't get hurt, no one did. That's what's important. Everyone is okay. I'm just thankful you were sitting on the stool and not near that door. Thank the Lord," he said.

I didn't stop sobbing until I reached the hospital, swallowed two pills, and went back into nothingness, putting a hold, temporarily, on the self-determination I had felt so confident about just hours earlier.

It was only a temporary setback because Gabe was right. I did have an inner compass like Father. I used it regularly, too. And each time I did, the radius expanded. "Healing happens even in the hurt," Doc Sperling used to say. "Hurting is part of the cure."

THE LIGHT BEYOND OUR REACH

"MISS MCGEE?" A STRANGE MAN'S VOICE SPLINTERED THE stillness of my perfect sleep. "I'm Doctor Rohal. I'll be treating you for another week until Doctor Sperling returns."

"It's *Ms.* McGee," I corrected, knowing Scarlett would be proud of me.

The light felt like acid to my eyes; I rested my arm part way over them and looked at him through the cracks. He was tall and lanky; a bald spot on his head shone under the fluorescents. His feet, when I peered downward, were mammoth. Absolute dinosaur-sized. I said nothing.

"How are you feeling today?" he asked.

I didn't reply.

"Is there anything you'd like to do?"

I knew it was best to control my crazy ideas the way disturbed people didn't, but what can I say—I loved being an actress. "Sure," I said, "how about you let me out of here so I can go play in traffic? You could also double the strength of my pills if you want, and I could stock up on those for a midnight cocktail, or better yet, why don't I get on that plane to New York and leap off the Empire State Building and rocket up into space with Gabe?"

I rolled over and covered my head with blankets.

"Betty?"

It's a sign. I'm done here. I uncovered my face.

He flipped back the chart, two fingers sprinted up and down each page until he reached the front. "It says here you tried to overdose due to complicated grief reactions."

"Nope. It wasn't like that at all. I took my pills as I needed them, not all at once. It was completely normal."

"Oh," he said, like a big fake trying to act surprised. "I see." He brushed his hand along a short bristled beard, flecked with red. "Well, let's give you a few more days of rest, join an activity group as soon as you can, and then we'll see how you feel in a couple days."

"But I do feel better," I assured him. "I'm feeling great right now! Don't need any more 'rest,' trust me." I kicked off the blankets with renewed energy, swung my legs over the edge of the bed, and sprang up to prove it. "I'm ready to hit the road."

He didn't look up from my chart, so I tried again. "I'm okay now. Really. And I appreciate everything you've done. All the drugs were great. A real blast."

I made a mental note to myself: *Do not use sarcasm and humor, no matter how subtle, or funny. Also no movie lines. Gladys went overboard with those.*

"Nurse!" he shouted toward the door.

"Yes, Doctor?" A sizable woman leaned in, her bosom straining against the door frame.

I didn't convince him enough. He seemed determined to keep me.

"Let's give Miss McGee—"

"*Ms,*" I interrupted, a cold sweat crossing my forehead.

"Pardon me again, yes, *Ms.* McGee, her first new dose intravenously please." A dryness in his tone told me he was through with me. Perhaps Mother had been held against her will, too.

"Yes, sir." And she walked away.

He slapped the metal chart shut. "Get out there for some Bingo now as soon as you can and—"

"No, really," I pleaded, "I need to leave—it's—"

"Take care now," he cut in. And out he went.

"—not good for me here, anymore," I finished anyway.

I felt a guttural scream climb into my voice box and release itself, as if Jack the Ripper had just slipped in and put a knife to my throat. "NO! Do not shoot me up with anything! I don't need it!" I felt my eyes watering, hot as acid. Dread surrounded me like a black cloud.

It only took two people to restrain me to one side, but I continued to plead, "Please, call Doctor Sperling. She wouldn't do this! She knows me! Please," I begged. "I'm not my mother!" I felt a sharp exhale when I said it, and knew it was true. But the shot was in and out of my left hip and no one cared.

Everything went into a vortex. Faces leaned over me; eyes wide with compassion, or so it seemed until they multiplied and melted into globules of shifting shapes and sizes. I tried to fight it, blinking hard. *I need to stay awake,* I told myself, *just stay awake. Scarlett will be here soon, I need to stay awake.*

DAYS PASSED BEFORE A CONVERSATION DRIFTED BY, BREAK-ing through the drug-induced stupor my body was in. "She had a setback when she went home for the day," someone bemoaned. "Hasn't been doing well since."

"Poor kid," someone countered sympathetically.

I heard the food cart clunk down the hall, doors open and close; trays clanked like a train track against the metal shelves inside it.

"Zetty? Are you awake, dear?" I looked up at the same bosomy nurse hovering over me. "I have your medicine. It's time for you to take these, please."

"I'm tired enough," I told her.

"Well, swallow these or we'll have to give you a shot again. Then I want you to eat some breakfast. Will you do that for me?"

"Sure," I said compliantly, knowing full well now how to play this game. She smiled, handed me a paper cup with four pills this time, all different colors and another cup full of water. I shook them back to the side of my mouth. "Thank you," I offered politely, tilted my head back and pretended to drink.

As soon as she left, I spit them into my hand and tucked them down my underpants.

I picked at the orange gelatin cubes just to watch them bounce like rubber, stirred a bowl of cream of wheat, but managed to actually swallow some apple juice when Scarlett walked in.

"Zetty, what in the world is going on?" she said, worry wrinkling her face.

"I don't know Scarlett. Thank goodness you're here." I pushed the tray table away. "They think I'm suicidal and shot me up with something that would knock a horse out."

"I know. You've been out of it for days. I just talked with your dad."

"He knows?"

"Well yes, the doctor spoke to him right away. What's going on?"

"I'm bored, Scarlett. And sick and tired of sleep. They analyze every little sarcastic comment you make! I can't take it anymore! Now they're feeding me more pills and shooting me up with things and trying to get me into the

Bingo group. I went once, looking for Sophie and Gladys, but they're long gone."

"Who?"

"Never mind. Just some old friends."

"Well. Enough is enough," she said, sounding agitated. "Now you look at me and you tell me the truth." Her eyes locked on mine. "Did you, or did you not, deliberately overdose on your sleeping pills and try to kill yourself?"

"I did not. Not on purpose. I kept taking them because I don't want to go through this. That I admit. But I don't really want to die. Honest. I just couldn't face it yet, my life without Gabe. And it brought back everything I felt about Mother again, Scarlett. And then Father's plane. It's all too much!"

"I know, sweetie. I understand," she said convinced. "It's Gabe's birthday, you know. You slept through the last four days, so I didn't get to tell you the plan."

"Four days?!" She nodded. "What plan?" I sat up to get my thinking straight.

"We need to spend today doing something she loved. Are you with me?"

"Well, sure—do I have a day pass?" My voice shook with excitement; I hardly recognized it.

"Not exactly." Scarlett went to the door, shut it completely, then turned to me, her voice hushed and hurried. "Help me grab all your stuff and throw it in here." She opened a large fabric shoulder bag, grabbed my underwear and socks from a shelf, and motioned me to do the same. Then she untied Tuffy's purple paisley bandana from around a vase of flowers Father gave me and handed it to me.

"Why do I need all this?" I asked, confused.

"Because," she said like a spy, "you're not coming back."

"I'm not?" I hurriedly slipped my jeans on and rolled up the ankles. "You mean we're busting out?"

"That's exactly what I mean."

It was as close to a miracle as I'd ever been. Scarlett was every bit as good as Gabe. Or Gabe was every bit as good as Scarlett.

"Psych-*a*-delic," I said.

Scarlett curled her arm around my shoulders tight and led me through the hallways like the hospital's head honcho. My hand tightened around the strap of my burlap bag as we made the auspicious voyage down the hall. And then a nurse innocently blocked our path.

"Oh, Zetty," she seemed surprised to see me. "You're going out today?"

"Yeah," I said, smiling like a fool. "Isn't that great?"

"Are you sure that's been approved?" she asked suspiciously.

My brain churned for something to say, producing nothing.

"Oh yes," Scarlett broke in, "and we have a wonderful afternoon planned. I'm Scarlett Taylor," she rambled off quickly. "So nice to meet you. I'll have Zetty back by three o'clock. Four at the latest." Scarlett nudged me forward, cautiously moving us along.

"Well, that's terrific!" she said turning to see us off. "Real progress, I'd say." But then the friendliness fell from her face. Her eyes shifted, as if she caught a glimpse of our plan. "Wait a minute," she commanded, "hold on."

I'm here for life, I told myself.

She marched up and blocked our path again. "You're Scarlett Taylor? *The* Scarlett Taylor, who does Inner Fetal Recovery work?" She went star struck.

"Yes, I am." Scarlett reached out and shook her hand.

"Oh, gosh, I am such an admirer of your work. I would love to talk with you sometime about it. In fact, I've mentioned that we need one of your groups here!"

"Well, I'd be honored to help in any way I can," Scarlett said. "In fact, I'd be happy to call and set up a time to come and speak with staff."

"I'd love it! Thank you so much." She craned her neck while turning, eyes still on Scarlett, and knocked on the door behind her. "Hey, do you have a book out yet?"

"Working on one," Scarlett lied.

"Well, I can't wait. Zetty, you're in good hands. Have fun today!" and she disappeared into a patient's room.

We both released the tension wired to our faces and kept in step with one another. I focused on Scarlett's feet, and, with increasing speed, we practically skated out of the place like Olympians.

We coasted down the broad concrete steps into a warm sun. I almost forgot how delicious it smelled. The outdoor lilac bushes, clipped into perfect-shaped domes, fanned the air with their perfume, too.

"Where's your car, Scarlett?"

"What was Gabe's dream car?" she asked coyly.

"A red Mustang convertible. Why?"

"Looky there." She pointed to one parked almost directly in front of the pillars.

I felt exhilaration well up. It was an old familiar pleasure I had once known that came back for a visit. "It's yours?" I asked, hardly believing it.

"Ours, I rented it for the day."

"Neato!" It was the first word of true happiness I had spoken in months.

Scarlett tossed the bag to the back seat, and in we went. The white leather bucket seat felt swanky against my rump. Scarlett cranked the key, grabbed hold of the wheel, and made a tight circle around the main entrance. Gunning the accelerator hard and fast past the tightly pruned gardens, she shot out of the lot and with a rush of air we took a flying leap over a massive speed bump just beyond the gate. We careened around the curve so fast, the wheels squealed. I turned back to see if we were being chased. "All clear!" I shouted.

Scarlett drove nothing like Father.

I pulled Tuffy's purple paisley bandana out of my pocket, pressed it over the top of my head and tied it at the back of my neck. Scarlett slid on a baseball cap, but locks of black curls continued to dance over her ears. She grabbed at them peevishly, until she finally wrangled them under her cap and secured them.

"Turn on the eight-track, Zetty. And crank it up loud so we can hear it on the freeway!"

When I pushed the "on" button, Led Zeppelin serenaded us with one of Gabes' favorites—a song about needing to "ramble on." Perfect for the occasion.

"Where we going?" I yelled excitedly.

"No idea!" she hollered back.

We sailed down the highway, along an ocean that sparkled under blue skies again. We were on our way to nowhere, and it felt just like home.

WE SWAPPED TAPES BETWEEN LED ZEPPELIN AND CROSBY, Stills, Nash and Young and kept driving as if we were never going to stop. Sometimes we sang along, and sometimes we just listened. I watched hundreds of people and places pass by, scooped up the air with the cup of my hand, and watched it ripple against my skin as if I had just discovered the feel of wind for the first time.

The waterworks never stopped coming, but we laughed through them sometimes, too. Like when our convertible beat the train parallel to us; we cheered crossing an imaginary finish line. There is a thrill that comes from feeling alive and free. I remember thinking it must be what Father felt every time he went flying. And why he never gave it up.

"Gabe would approve, Scarlett," I told her confidently. "This is the best celebration we could have given her. Happy Birthday, Gabe!" I yelled. A red traffic light winked in the midday sun, and Scarlett thought better than to run through it.

"Happy Birthday, Gabe!" Scarlett echoed. "I only wish I had thought to do it while she was still alive. Can you imagine the three of us doing this together?"

"Well, you *have* done this for her," I said. "There's no way she isn't here. There's no way she would ever miss a day like this."

Scarlett clutched my arm and a bittersweet smile swept over her face.

I reached down into my underpants, snagged the pills I had stashed, and pulled up six of them; not the four I remembered hiding. I clenched them between my fingers straight up in the air and released them to the wind so this time they'd be smashed to smithereens on the highway, instead of me.

The sun dove gracefully into the ocean as we drove north past the rocky cliffs of Windansea. The wind was nowhere, the beach sand combed smooth, and the smell of the infinite expanse of sea was the only medicine I needed. We turned up Led Zeppelin full board for the song "Stairway to Heaven" and I imagined Gabe in the clouds that stretched across the sky like batting. She was holding on to a banister, climbing one stair at a time, looking down, smiling on us. We drove until pale golden shafts of sun faded against blushing rose sashes in the sky. I tried to let the colors of the sunset penetrate my skin, as if Gabe lived inside them now.

When Scarlett pulled into our driveway and stopped, she turned to me. "I left a message with your doctor's office this morning with the funniest lady. Someone named Anna-Victoria." She pulled out the eight-track tape and tossed it in her bag. "I told her you were going AWOL with me and I was taking full responsibility with your father's written permission."

"Father agreed?"

"Yes, he did. I asked him to trust me."

"Thank you, Scarlett."

"I love you, honey. We'll be okay. I promise."

"Okay," I said opening the door. Before I swung my legs out, I reached for Scarlett. First to hug her, and then to grip her hands in another wordless thanks. When I stepped out, Scarlett leaned up toward the open window near me. "The Anna-Victoria lady said, 'Whee-doggies! Get our baby-girl outta there!' She sounds like a character!"

I grinned, imagining the country twang of Anna-Victoria's words in my mind. I closed the car door, waved to Scarlett, and recognized the warmth of light spreading through the closed curtains across the living room window. My shoes felt like velvet underneath the steps going up to our porch and when I walked through the front door, I felt the comfort of home.

New hope awakened inside me; though I couldn't tell you why. My mood shifted into brightness and I only knew I felt alive again, and was never going back.

I BARELY TOOK THREE STEPS INTO THE ENTRYWAY WHEN Father buttonholed me in a full embrace.

"You're home," he said and tightened his grip until I struggled a little to breathe. "Are you okay, Zetty? I've been so worried." He didn't loosen his grip.

"Yeah," I exhaled when he released a little. "I'm okay. I mean definitely okay not to be *there* anymore. They drugged me up with all kinds of stuff, Dad. I think they were going to schedule brain surgery next."

He pulled back, and I felt my lungs expand freely again. He held both sides of my arms, and scanned my face. "They wanted to keep you safe, Zetty, that's all. And I'm grateful they did. You look good. I'm glad you got through it."

"Oh, I haven't gotten through anything, Dad. And I never will," I told him straight. "I'm just taking one step in front of the other. Like a living-dead person. And it will never be perfect again, because Gabe's not here, but it doesn't have to be to keep going. That's what Scarlett and I decided."

Father listened, nodded his head in agreement. "True enough," he said, and went to the kitchen to prepare a dinner out of breakfast foods.

I sat at the table to keep him company. "Dad? What about your airplane?"

He whisked four extra-large eggs in a yellow mixing bowl for omelets. "The front two-thirds of it was demolished, Zetty." His head dropped, shaking. "Unbelievable. The whole thing."

"So, what now?"

"I get back to work on it." He poured the runny slime into a buttered-up fry pan.

"Really?" I asked, feeling in awe of his fortitude. That's when I was reminded again that this was what made Father "zing."

"Already started," he said rolling the mixture lightly around in the pan. "Like you said, Zetty, we keep going. This was just a plane, not a life. And so, I can go back to it, and after a proper mourning period, I have."

"Did Mother die?" I asked point blank.

Father's hand tripped over the side of the searing pan—he flinched in pain. He reached for an ice cube out of the tray in the freezer, sounding flustered. "Your mother's alive, yes."

"Then why haven't you gone back to *her*?" I tried to keep my voice light and friendly so he'd tell me something of the truth. "You went back to the plane, why not Mother if she's alive?"

"I tried, but it wasn't possible, Zetty. Right now we need to focus on you."

The phone rang and Father hesitated for a moment, as if he didn't know if it was the right time to end our conversation.

"Go ahead," I told him, knowing full well we were done anyway. "Answer the thing." He picked up the receiver way too fast.

AFTER FATHER FINISHED HIS CONVERSATION, WE ATE cheese omelets sprinkled with tomatoes, onions, and green peppers. Someone wanted to volunteer to help him repair the plane. He spent the entire meal talking about how grateful he was to those who had spread the word of the crash and agreed to come to his aid. Father was never a glory-hound; years later when he did complete his plane, he never stopped giving that team of men all the credit.

I was happy for Father and could see how the news of their generosity, and my being home, had brightened him up. I didn't press any further about Mother, but his response nagged at me like a sliver to the foot I couldn't see, or get to. It stabbed somewhere with every step. It always seemed that mentioning Mother's name broke a spell, and cast an even worse one on me for doing it.

After drying the dishes, and wiping down the kitchen counters, I told Father I was going over to the Taylors' but wouldn't be gone long.

Part Three

1972

My Moon Necklace

When I am dead my dearest
let the party start
scatter my ashes north and south
as friends beat on their drums
I'll dance away on gusts of wind
and twirl along the ground.

When I am dead my dearest
fly to a Grecian Isle
visit the temple of Artemis
to laugh with the nubile maids
choose the one with downcast eyes
who stands alone in the crowd
protect her youth and budding breasts
with the gift of my crescent moon.

—Diana Griggs

THE GIFT

I MISSED HAVING TUFFY BY MY SIDE WHEN I SAT ON THE Taylors' gold brocade living room sofa. I wondered if his presence would have been enough to save me from going to the hospital, and I concluded it would have.

There was no Mother, no Tuffy, and now no Gabe; the emptiness never left. It was as if someone pulled my heart out by the roots and took all the plumbing with it. I caught a familiar whiff of fresh soap from the basket of clean laundry on the floor and for a moment thought Gabe had just passed by.

Dennis sat across from me. "You okay, darlin'?"

My face jumped. "I'm okay. But nothing is easy anymore," and then remembered my own noticed improvement. "But yes, I'm better."

"I'm not sure we get any easy moments from here on," Dennis sighed.

I stared at the golden amber suede-fringed moccasins laced up to my knees and wished Gabe had gotten a pair, too. She wanted chocolate-brown so we could wear them at the same time and not look like the double-mint twins.

"I do have regrets," Dennis said with a shudder, as if trying to shake something off. "Like not hugging her the last time she left for work the night of the crash. I was too damn lazy to get off my ass and just go over and give her a hug goodbye. She was so banged up after, I couldn't hug her then either. I'm always going to regret that." He leaned back in his chair, eyes downcast.

"I had my regrets about Tuffy, too, and you talked me out of feeling that way, remember?"

"Yes. And I stand by that. But I've caused a lot of trouble in this family."

"She knew you loved her."

"She knew I was a mean son-of-a-bitch too, Zetty. I want to apologize to you for that, too."

I looked at him, and waited. Doc Sperling style.

"Because Gabe was right," he went on. "It wasn't right to speak to you girls, oh, hang on now," he corrected, "I mean speak to you *women* the way I did sometimes." He scanned the stairs to see if Scarlett was about to jump him for sounding like a male chauvinist pig. "Gabe deserved better. I'm not the man Scarlett deserves, either."

"Then be who Scarlett deserves now. It's not too late." His eyes went watery, but it didn't stop me. "I mean it; be who Scarlett deserves, now. That's what Gabe would want."

Dennis unclogged his throat, and stood slumped. Pain concentrated on his face, like a raw, open wound. He pushed his hands deep into the front pockets of his jeans and numbly relocated himself across the room to the back window. I think he was trying to out-walk the grief welling up, but it wasn't working. I continued unafraid of his emotions.

"It's what Gabe would want," I repeated. "That, and have you go to Sunday Mass with Scarlett, I suppose."

Dennis flinched his shoulders upright and blurted, "Hey, I did that one already!" A gasp of humor came through. "It would've made Gabe happy, wouldn't it?"

"Sure," I said. "That was her bag. I think she knew the

rosary better than a nun." I picked up the *TV Guide* off the end table next to me and ruffled through it, smelling the clean scent of fresh newsprint as it fanned my face. "How'd she get so religious anyway?" I asked, knowing full well he had nothing to do with it.

"Beats the hell out of me," he said sadly. "I don't even know, Zetty." His eyes went moist again.

Tom and Scarlett came down the stairs. She moved decisively toward me, arms outstretched, and enfolded me in a long embrace.

"Hey, Zetty," Tom said, when Scarlett released me. He headed to the refrigerator, pulled out a small carton of chocolate milk, and started gulping.

Scarlett picked up a bright orange envelope off the counter, carried it over to the sofa, and sat next to me. "Dennis, Tom and I have something we want to give you, Zetty," and then she pulled out the silver crescent moon necklace that Gabe had been wearing when she died. "We want you to have this," she said in a rock-steady, heartfelt way.

"But Scarlett, it's yours now, it should be yours to have," I objected.

"No. This was between you girls, and I want it to stay that way. So, there is no changing my mind," she said as she fastened it around my neck. "And, we want you also to have this." She placed the orange envelope in my lap.

When I saw hundreds of dollars tucked inside, I stopped.

"It's the money she saved for your graduation trip," she explained. "She told us you were both going to New York to see as many Broadway shows as you could. We want you to have it."

I wanted to say, *No, you don't understand, I couldn't go without her,* but it was clear they didn't know about our "plan." It didn't have to be a secret, but I left it that way.

Somehow it kept a part of Gabe alive just for me.

Scarlett continued, "Dennis, Tom, and I agree. In fact we all had the same idea when we found it in her room. We want you to make that trip in her memory someday. When you're ready."

"You should go, Zetty," Tom said, "if you can get over your problem." My expression froze on the word "problem."

"You know, with big planes." His face registered the jolt it gave me. "Sorry, Gabe told me."

I went parchment-faced with embarrassment and wondered how Gabe got on that subject with Tom. "Well, for the record," I announced, "I'm not afraid of them anymore. I found an instant cure. It's simple—you have to *want* to die and suddenly the fear of crashing is no problem at all."

As soon as I saw awkwardness creep up everyone's face, I knew they didn't get it. "I'm kidding," I added, thinking they were as bad as Doctor Rohal.

Scarlett patted my hand, signaling she understood.

"So, it's a done deal, Zetty," Dennis said rolling up his sleeves.

"It's such a nice thing for all of you to do," I finally said. "All of Gabe's hard-earned money. And the necklace." I felt my eyes blur and my throat constrict again. "I don't know what to say. It means more to me than you'll ever know. I love you, all."

I hugged Scarlett, and then Dennis, and then when I reached toward Tom, he pulled me into the expanse of his chest and I felt the genuine warmth of a big brotherly hug.

It was all I needed.

THE NEXT DAY, THE BREEZE OUTSIDE WAS SO WARM IT

practically raised me up like a mound of bread dough. I could smell the fresh, clean aroma of pine scent, sprayed by the trees every time the wind lifted the branches like angel wings. My chin was resting on the top edge of my history book when I saw Tom cut across the cul-de-sac toward our house. I sprang up, swept my hair back, and grabbed my purse.

"Zetty," he said when I opened the door, "I want to talk to you."

"I see a shrink," I said, defiantly. "I have to catch the bus for my appointment," I told him, knowing full well I still had an hour to spare. I started to close the door.

"Let me drive you." He stopped the door with one hand. "Look, we need to talk. Please."

The last thing I wanted to hear was how poor Tom pitied poor me, for the terrible way he led me on. "Thanks, but everything's fine where we're concerned, Tom. Really," I said pleasantly enough. I inched the door toward him again.

"It's important, Zetty," and the way he said it made me believe it was.

"Okay," I conceded. I grabbed my keys, and followed him out.

"I told Gabe about us," he explained as we pulled away from the curb. "I told her, because I was all mixed up. And sometimes we could talk and she was like a normal person I could talk to. Once in a while," he smiled.

"Gabe was smart, Tom. I'm sure whatever she told you was right."

He looked over at me with a question on his face. "No," I told him, predicting what he was about to ask, "I have no idea what she told you, but it doesn't matter. Just forget it."

"But I need to apologize—tell you how sorry—"

"No, you don't," I interrupted. "Look, I mean it. It's fine.

Don't say another thing," and he knew I meant it, because he shut right up. Until we got there.

"Thanks for the ride," I said, opening the door.

"Sorry I was such a jerk, Zetty," he began again.

I ignored his words. "Listen, I hope you and Tinkerbelle will be very happy together." Tom's face reacted just the way I intended when I called her "Tinkerbelle."

"Sorry," I said in all sincerity. "She's perfect, Tom. I'm happy for you. Really, I don't care anymore."

"Thanks, Zetty, it's—"

The car door whirred shut and ended the conversation. I climbed the stairs to the fourth floor to Doc Sperling's office. And the whole way up, with every solid note my moccasins played on the stairs, I felt relief. Because I meant what I said to Tom. My best friend was gone. How could anything else so trivial, as a silly infatuation gone bad, ever matter again?

An audible gasp flew out of Anna-Victoria when she saw me. She sprang from her desk like a jack-in-the-box and rushed to my side. With one hand squeezing my arm she said, "I know this is against the rules, but if it's okay with you, can I give you a great big ol' bear hug?"

"Sure," I smiled, because it felt better than good to have her gushing over me again.

"I'll try not to squeeze the livin' daylights out of you, doll, but I'm just so happy to see you back," she said and grabbed me tight. "My land, honey, what an ordeal. What a terrible ordeal you've been through. Sorry doesn't even come close to how I feel about everything you've been through." Anna-Victoria's lip started to tremble, and she welled up in tears.

"Are you alright, baby girl?"

Normally being called "baby girl" would have irked me, but coming from Anna-Victoria, it only sounded nice and motherly. "Yeah," I said honestly, "I'm better."

"Land almighty, first a hug, now the blubbering. I'm just so tickled to see you, and now you listen to me, and I mean it, anyone in your shoes would have fallen apart. Anyone, Zetty. I am just so relieved you're back. I was calling that hospital every day checking on you for Doctor Sperling. We both were worried, sick."

"Really?" A rush of embarrassment flooded my cheeks.

"Sweetie, yes, we care about you. I'm just so glad you came back to us. Take a seat, doll," she said pushing the intercom button on her phone. "Let me tell her you're here."

I deposited myself in the navy-blue wing chair and closed my eyes against the window light. I clung to the box of Kleenex in my lap as I narrated the events over the past two months to Doc Sperling. I never fully expressed all that was rolling around inside me, until I told it to her. A lot like talking to Gabe, I noticed.

"Sorry," I told her, tossing wads of tissue into the trash can. Always apologizing, it seemed, for my very existence.

"You're apologizing for having feelings?" she asked, "For loving Gabe so deeply?"

"No," I told her. "You're right. It's all warranted."

I was wrung out from telling the story again, for living through the grief in a freshly churned state that seemed to never age or tire itself out. "I feel like a one-winged moth running in circles," I told her. "What now?"

"What do you mean, Zetty?"

"I mean, how do I move past this? I start to think I'm getting better, but it doesn't last. Not really. How do you crash land and rise from nothing but ashes?"

Doc Sperling tipped her head and leaned toward me with both elbows on the arms of her chair. Her hands gently folded like she was praying. "Zetty, there's only one choice in front of you, and it's this: let yourself feel, and then do whatever it takes to find joy again." She paused, holding her eyes on mine. "That's the only choice left. Keep moving toward joy."

"I'm not sure I can. I don't know where to begin."

"That's okay," Doc Sperling assured me. "Think about what the most important thing is—and then find your way to it. That's how you begin." Her face was a never-changing composition of kindness.

New York flittered into view. I felt myself unreservedly open up to the idea of completing the plan—of going alone to see my mother. *It's what Gabe would want*, I told myself. The idea rippled like a tiny wave in my brain and gave me a small dose of joy; only a tiny teaspoon of hope, but at least it was something.

"Starting with nothing, what do you really need to be happy?" she asked.

I would've let myself consider the question slowly, but the answer came fast. "Love," I told her.

It was settled, then. I was going by myself to New York.

Permission Granted

I was scheduled to return to school on Monday. I was nervous about going back—already jittery and nauseous, even though I still had two days. I would be bombarded by memories of Gabe; the school and every building in it was hers, too. The memory of Gabe's footsteps were left somewhere on every surface I would cross.

I found Father in the garage, measuring long thin pieces of the wing spar, a fresh, sharpened pencil resting on his ear. "Ready to go to work?" he asked.

"It might be the last Saturday I'll have the time," I told him.

"Well then, I better take advantage of your help while I can," he said buoyantly.

Father motioned for me to step around and hold the ends steady for him while he marked in measured spaces all the way to the end.

It was as good a time as any, I thought, to tell him what I was considering. "You know Dad, I'm not quite eighteen yet. But I think it's time that—"

"I know, I know," he interrupted. "And as much as I dread you being out on the road, I know it's got to happen. When do you want to take the test?"

"I don't want my driver's license," I told him. Getting behind the wheel of a car careening out of control was still one of my worst nightmares.

"Oh," he looked up slightly taken aback. "I have to admit I'm relieved. Take your time. You've got plenty of it."

"So, that's not what I wanted to talk about."

"What is it then?" His face met mine for an instant and then he looked down again.

"I need, I mean *we* need, well, I guess *you* really, need to—"

"Hold on. You lost me. Who needs what?" he looked up holding my gaze.

"I need you to give me written permission. To learn more about Mother."

And just like that, my former father walked back into the garage and stepped into the new and slightly improved model. "That's not going to happen, Zetty. I'm sorry." His head jerked down again, his hand stabbing the measurements into the wood with the chiseled pencil. "It can't happen. That's all there is to it."

"No, Dad, that's not all there is to it. I'm sick and tired of the way you dance around this as if I were a child. And for the record, if I ever have a child, I'll never withhold the truth from them the way you have me. No matter their age." I remained true to my word on that promise, and have never regretted it. "I have a right to see her," I told him.

"It's not about your 'rights', Zetty. It's *my* right to make this decision."

"But Dad," I pleaded. "I need to know. You owe me that!"

"Zetty, the answer is no. No more discussion. Please trust me on this."

I could taste the bitter acid of swallowed-back anger rising in my throat. "Trust you? Why would I? You've given me no reason at all! Look, I'm sorry I was born—I really am, Dad. I'm sorry. I apologize. I ruined your life and Mother's by coming into it, I get it. But I'm here. And I was born. No fault of my own."

"Stop it, Zetty. You're talking crazy." He tried to back up his words, but it was too late. "I didn't mean—"

"Like hell you didn't!" I dropped the wood from my hands and let it bounce to the floor. "Fine!" I couldn't help but notice I was delivering my words with a magnificent stage presence. "I'll forget she ever existed! I'll never mention her again! Finish your own damn plane."

"Watch your mouth, young lady."

The words came fast and hard, "Oh I do. All the time. I cuss now whenever I want! Ha! You should have heard me at Sue Willy's!" I stomped away, pushed the step-stool aside and went into the house to call Gabe.

Only of course, there was no Gabe, which rolled through me like a shock wave all over again. I detached from my body, unable to hold the truth of her death inside me again.

I went into my room, slammed the door, and cranked up The Rolling Stones. I blasted the song Father cringed at, always complaining in the same way each time, "What is all that screeching and hollering?!"

At the end of it, I picked up the needle and moved it back and replayed it over and over again, until even I got sick of hearing it.

I pulled out a suitcase and started packing.

TIME TO TAKE THINGS INTO MY OWN TWO HANDS, I TOLD myself. *Figure it out.*

So I did. I took things into my own hands and forged a perfect "Howard D. McGee" signature on a permission form allowing Doc Sperling to give me unlimited information about Mother.

Besides playing piano by ear, forgery was my other

hidden talent. People at school offered to pay me good money to sign excuses for them. I only took their cash once, and then felt too guilty, so did it for free after that. Then Gabe warned me I could face prison time pursuing that particular career path. So, I gave up my two-week life of crime and went back to staging shows.

Scarlett's voice came through the crack of my bedroom door when she knocked. She sounded rushed, a sense of urgency surrounding her words. "Zetty, can I come in?"

I panicked. "Just a second." I crammed the fraudulent note to the back of the top desk drawer in such a flustered state my palms turned sweaty. "Okay, you can come in."

"Listen," she said, "we have to go. You and I—to Sue Willy. She's in labor. She wants us there with her mother."

"What? She's having a baby, *now*?" As if I should be able to send back a circumstance that didn't work for me, or have Sue Willy choose a more suitable time and give us fair warning.

"Her contractions have started. Come on, I'll explain everything in the car. Your dad said we should go. Are you with me?"

"Well, yeah, I'm with you," I assured. "Of course. I'll get the directions she mailed me."

"Don't need them. I drove up when you were in the hospital. I needed to get away, so I went for you and Gabe."

"She'd be glad," I said. "I am, too."

Scarlett gave a knowing nod. "Meet you in the car," she said, turned a thumbs-up and left.

As I was leaving, Father stretched the phone cord as far as it reached and waved the receiver at me. "It's for you, Zetty," and then in a carefully hushed tone, just loud enough for me to hear him, "I was told it was something very important."

I covered the mouthpiece and hollered to Scarlett, "I'll be right there!" Her arm flew up to let me know she heard me across the driveway. "Hello?" I said, anxiety flooding my chest.

"It's me, Zetty. Now, don't hang up. Don't do a thing but listen."

Don't Look Back

Tom sounded remarkably like Dennis on the phone; his voice low-pitched, and broad. "I know you're leaving in a minute. So I just want to tell you I'm not with Tinkerbelle. And not anyone else, either. Because the thing is, Zetty, it's you I want to be with. Gabe told me if you felt the same way I'd be the lucky one."

I held on to silence for about five seconds while the tiniest shudder of pleasure rippled down my spine. When I was able to speak, I had just one word to say to him: "Good." And I hung up.

It was all I wanted to say. I was learning the art of authenticity, the very quality that defined Gabe's nature. And I loved Gabe more all the time for everything she thought about me, true or not.

I remembered something Doc Sperling said about Tom's kiss after Tuffy died. "You were right to embrace joy when you found it, Zetty. Always pay attention to those moments in life, no matter when or how they appear." Doc Sperling said a rabbi told her once that feeling that kind of joy and happiness is God's way of thanking people. "For what?" she asked him. "For loving," he told her.

I kept what Tom said tucked away, gently folded, and situated somewhere deep inside myself. It was only a corner, a small space where it lay, but even a corner one millimeter wide holding happiness felt like a great gift and I was grate-ful to carry it with me.

I yelled out, "I'm leaving, Dad!"

"I hope it goes well, honey. And Zetty, I'm proud of you for doing this."

"Okay," I said. "Maybe you'll see that a lot of things I do are worth being proud of." And because I had one foot out the door, I added, "Like having the guts to talk about Mother." I didn't stick around for his response, if there was one.

Scarlett and I piled into the rattle-can red Plymouth, rust crackling along its steel seams. Both of us stopped and stared at the interior, looking dazed as if we had climbed into the wrong car. We gave each other a glance that said, *it's not the same as being in a fancy red convertible Mustang, but it will have to do.*

Scarlett threw a handful of Gabe's cassette tapes on the back seat. "Music can help women focus," she said. "Go through them and pick some out that you think Sue Willy would like."

"What do you mean?" I asked.

"On getting through labor, honey. I'll explain it all once we get gas."

I told Scarlett what I learned from the Walter Matthau movie and the girl who had one baby after another on the psych ward, but she convinced me there was a lot more to it. After she added the missing details, I had to agree. "Sorry," I told her, "I'm not ready to see the real thing. You're on your own. But I'll keep the music playing for you, in the next room."

"Zetty," she laughed, "they have doctors and midwives there. All the sisters are trained, too. It's their job! Don't worry!" She pulled a candy bar out of the glove box and tossed it on my lap. "Sue Willy just needs our moral support.

And you know her mother—who knows what condition she'll be in."

"Oy vey," I said in a perfect imitation of Doc Sperling.

By then we were in Los Angeles. The smoke-polluted air cast a hot haze over the horizon. "Rain needs to scour this sky clean," I told Scarlett. She nodded and pulled into the parking lot of St. Mary's Convent where I imagined Sue Willy would be waiting breathlessly for our arrival. Literally. The poor thing, I thought, she was going to be in so much pain—her face scorched tomato red with each contraction, everyone shouting, "Breathe! Breathe!" And the fact is, I found out there isn't enough air in the world for anyone in labor. Even the polluted kind.

It didn't promise to be a fun visit. But, I reminded myself, I was getting out of school again. Based on what Scarlett told me, it didn't seem likely I would make it back in time for my first class Monday morning. And I didn't. Not even by Wednesday morning.

Oh, and the doctors and midwives? Let me tell you, Scarlett was mistaken on more than a few things.

SUE WILLY WAS RIGHT. SHE HAD BREASTS THE SIZE OF bowling balls. And gas coming out the wazoo. Childbirth is not a pretty sight. I noted that under *remember this, if you ever think about having a baby* file.

We traveled down a dark, damp, narrow hallway built of stone. A robust, cast-iron crucifix, at least six feet high, donned the wall at the very end of it. The body of Christ hanging limp on it, a crown of thorns resting on his head. His image filled me with sadness; no matter what else I believed, I always felt that.

Our shoes clippity-clopped as loud as Clydesdale horses, echoing in what felt like an underground tomb. The musty, dank smell of low, dirty earth filled my nose.

"This is creepy," I told Scarlett.

"It gets better once you get in her room," she said.

I heard music filtering down the hallway, growing louder with each step. Scarlett directed me to Sue Willy's door, and when we knocked, it was obvious she couldn't hear because the music was blaring behind it.

"I'm surprised they allow that in here," I noted to Scarlett.

"Well, it is Latin I think," she said.

"Santana, actually. You're right," I told her.

"Come on. I'm sure it's fine if we go in." Scarlett pushed the door open, but then we stood dazed for a moment, trying to take in what we saw.

Sue Willy was doing the cha-cha with a nun? It took a minute to register.

And then I noticed they were having fun. Sue Willy was unmistakably pregnant, but this did not look like a labor scene to me; it looked like a Broadway play; the nun was a groovy dancer.

"You're heeeeeere!" Sue Willy squealed when she saw me. The full-fledged nun in the black and white habit lowered the music while Sue Willy's arms wrapped around me tight as they could with her giant belly lodged between us. She was wearing a sleeveless yellow gauze cotton dress that flowed around her, soft and loose. On the front was orange embroidery and a pin stuck on the V-neck collar that read, "Make Love, Not War." Sue Willy was the poster child for that motto, I thought.

"Look!" she said to the nun. "They came! This is Zetty!"

"Nice to meet you, Zetty. I'm Sister Carmelita. And nice to see you again, Scarlett. Susannah talks about you both all the time. She's lucky to have you. Do either of you need anything?"

"No thanks," we both said in unison.

"I'll let you visit then. Let me know if I can do anything," and she slipped out the door.

"Bad news, guys," Sue Willy announced as she lowered herself down into a chair like a three-ton piling attached to a crane. "We think it was a false alarm." The vinyl cushion under her rump exhaled air for a long time after she came into contact with it.

"You didn't look like you were in labor," I said.

"Sorry, I tried calling, but you had already left," she shrugged.

"It's okay hon, we want to be here anyway," Scarlett said.

"Really? I'm so glad to see you. Are you okay, Zetty? You *look* normal. I'm glad you made it out of the sanctuary they stuck you in. Was it *de locos* in there?"

She was exactly the same Sue Willy, only in the plus size now.

I looked at Scarlett, and she shot me a boost of confidence. "I'm as normal as I'll ever be," I told her. "What was crazy was losing Gabe," I said.

Scarlett excused herself to the bathroom.

"No kidding," she said, with a sober face. "I still can't believe it. I thought I might have a miscarriage when my mom told me. She saw it in the newspaper and called me. I didn't half-care if I did lose the baby at that point," and then quickly added, "but not now."

She inched to the edge of her chair and leaned forward, legs spread open wide as the Hoover Dam.

"I've really missed you, and Gabe. I still can't believe it, Zetty," she said again.

"I know. I can't either. Maybe never will."

Sue Willy made a long stretch for her cup of ice chips on the tray table next to her chair. "I'm sorry you couldn't be at the burial service, Zetty, but in a way I'm glad you missed it. I swear, watching them hoist her casket down," she choked, "I can't get it out of my mind. It was the worst thing I've ever had to watch in my life. I think its good you weren't there."

"I guess," I sighed. "I might have jumped in and gone under with her at that point."

"Yeah, that's what I heard."

My face jerked, and part of me wanted to quiz her and ask, *from who?* But I didn't respond. I didn't have the energy to deny it. Besides, it was true.

"Have you been to her grave yet?" she asked.

"Just once with my dad. I haven't been back. Not yet." I felt my mood taking another plunge.

Scarlett slid through the cracked door. "So, your mom's not here yet, hon?" she asked, and plopped down on a chair.

"Nah," Sue Willy grimaced and rubbed both hands over her atomic belly in a slow-moving circle. "I tried calling her, so I don't know what happened."

"Are you sure this was a false alarm?" Scarlett asked suspiciously. She slanted her head and peered at her with squinty eyes. "You look mighty ripe to me."

"I feel like I'm carrying a block of cement," she said, pulling out a matchbook and scratching until a flame shot up. "Sorry, you guys, I have *gassy-oso*. It hurts so much I have to let it go." She waved the match around, blew it out and adjusted a small pillow at the small of her back. It reminded me of how grateful I was for matches on the nights Tuffy had it bad.

Sister Carmelita appeared holding a tray with a gold plastic cup and a matching pitcher of fresh ice chips.

Sue Willy lit up like a neon sign. "Sister Carmelita! Yay, you're back!"

"I'm back!" she bubbled, and then less bubbly said, "Your mom called."

"Where is she?"

"Stuck; just off the freeway. Her car broke down twenty miles from home."

"Oh no. Not again," Sue Willy droned. "She was going to spend the night and everything."

"I can go get her, honey. I'd be happy to do it," Scarlett offered.

"It'll all work out then," Sister Carmelita said in a chirpy way.

"But I'm not in labor yet," Sue Willy complained.

Sister Carmelita wiped her fingers on the white apron over her habit. "That baby is not going to wait much longer. Your mother needs to get here sooner rather than later. She's still on the phone, Scarlett, second door on your right."

"Scarlett?" Sue Willy said before she slipped through the door, "tell her I really want her to come, okay?"

"Of course I will. I'll go get her right away. Be back as soon as we can," she said, and hurried out.

"Even with all she's been through, Scarlett still worries about us," I said.

"Who could blame her? You in a loony bin and me in a convent for sluts."

Sister Carmelita shot a stern glance of disapproval at Sue Willy and motioned for her to lay back on the bed. She pulled out a blood pressure cuff. "How are you feeling?" she asked as she wrapped it around the top of her arm.

"Like a submarine stuck in quick sand," she said as the air pumped and then blew out of the cuff. Sue Willy's eyes shifted to the window, where long green tentacles of a willow tree swayed against the infinity of blue sky. "It should've been me, not Gabe," she said sullenly.

"It shouldn't have been *anyone*," Sister Carmelita responded. "Your life is no less valuable than anyone else's. Those kind of thoughts devalue yourself and the baby you carry, Susannah. They're no help at all."

Sue Willy and I arched our eyebrows at one another at the same time. But I had to agree with her.

"Now. Should we try dancing again?" Sister Carmelita asked, but only halfheartedly.

Sue Willy looked over to me and explained, "They say it helps bring on labor if you keep moving."

I nodded, but wasn't convinced it would make one bit of difference.

"Are you up for it?" Sister Carmelita asked.

"No," Sue Willy flat answered.

"I didn't think so. We'll try again later. I need to keep my girlish figure," she joked.

Sue Willy giggled, like a five-year-old.

For a moment, I could see them together, and wished Sister Carmelita could adopt Sue Willy. And maybe, her baby, too. If only she wasn't a nun, I thought, she'd be just the kind of mother Sue Willy needed. A mother like I once had. It was easy to forget Sue Willy already had one.

AFTER A SHORT NAP, SUE WILLY RUBBED HER EYES, YAWNED, and began to discuss the biggest decision of her life.

"Ay caramba. What would Gabe say?" Sue Willy asked, lying on her right side with a pillow between her knees and one against her back. It was a question we asked ourselves often.

"Oh, that's easy. I know exactly what Gabe would say to this one," I said with complete confidence.

"Well, what?" Sue Willy's eyes widened into saucers.

"She would say, 'Sue Willy?'" I stood, channeling Gabe's body language, sauntering nice and slow across the room with my arms folded and my voice steady and sure, "'Here's what you have to ask yourself: Are you willing to give up partying and running around with cute guys'?'"

"That means no more road trips or 'doing it' with anyone," I interjected. Sue Willy slumped, and I continued, "'Can you give the baby a home without a bunch of boozers and druggies in it? Can you clean up barf, the kind that sprays the walls all night?'"

I stepped out of character again, "How's your gag reflex?"

"Awful," she grimaced, her face turning slightly green.

I nodded disapproving, but continued as Gabe, "'Can you listen to inconsolable screaming and crying for hours on end without snapping? Get your baby to a doctor at a moment's notice? And do you know what to do if they swallow a rock or drink poison, or stick their drooled up fingers into a wall socket? All of which can kill them instantly, you know. And what about trapped gas? Do you know what to do then?' And last but not least, Gabe would ask, 'do you know how to change a foul diaper so loaded with diarrhea, the poop gushes all the way up the baby's back? Count on lots of butt rash, too.'"

"Oh. My. Gawwwwwwwd," she moaned. "Stop already." Sue Willy's face dropped lower than the floor. "I'm exhausted just listening to her."

"Sorry, Sue Willy. It's really what Gabe would've said."

"I know," she acquiesced, "that's the problem." She picked up a worn-out religious magazine and fanned herself with it. "One nun said it's God Almighty's will that I give it away— my punishment for 'sinning.' You shoudda seen what she did to me, Zetty! She grabbed hold of my whole cheek with her fist of fat fingers, pinched really hard, and then let go like I was a piece of trash! She was all high and mighty and said, '*Let this be a lesson to you!*' What a bitch."

"She should be fired," I said, feeling the slow burn of anger rise in my voice. "What about Sister Carmelita? What does she think?"

"She doesn't say. She mostly listens." Sue Willy pushed up and sat; both hands gripped the edge of the bed, her bare feet dangling three feet apart.

"I just remembered the most important thing Gabe would tell you," I said.

"Jesus, there's more?!"

"She'd say, 'Now here's the important part, so listen good: Don't have a baby just to have someone to love you. Because it never works. Worst idea, *ever.*'"

"Great," Sue Willy mumbled. "I suppose you agree with her."

"Honestly? Before seeing you, I hoped you would give the baby to a couple who dreamed of having one. Now, well, I just don't know."

"Really?" she said, her voice aflutter. "You think I have a chance? If my mom agrees?" Her arms stretched back and she twisted until she cracked her back.

And with blistering honesty, I told her, "I don't know. Maybe even if your mother doesn't agree. I mean I think anyone can do what they have to, if they want to. And you do have courage, I know that. And I can see you falling in love with this baby. And that's what babies need. If you really, truly, could sacrifice everything, like Gabe said, and still be happy, then you could do it, Sue Willy. I think, anyway." I pushed a foot stool toward her feet and helped her prop them up. "Do you think you're meant to be a mother?" I sat back down and waited in perfect silence, Doc Sperling fashion.

Sue Willy curled one hand under the side of her chin and rested her elbow on her swollen belly. She stared at her lap for the answer. She took a deep breath, and on the exhale she said, "I honestly don't know. I have a hoochie-mamma and a fugitive somewhere in Mexico for parents. So, what do I know?"

"What?" This was the first I heard anything about Sue Willy's father. We didn't think anyone knew who he was.

"My real dad lives in Mexico. I'm half Mexican."

"Is that why you're learning Spanish?"

Her head nodded weakly up and down. "My mom said we can go see him when I turn eighteen, so I wanted to be ready."

"That's cool, Sue Willy," I said.

"I heard her tell a friend his name was Mr. Casanova. But she lies, a lot."

This was not news, but I didn't want to rub it in. "Well, you have to decide if you can be a good mom, Sue Willy. Or if it's better to give the baby to a family who can shower it with love and attention. But whatever you decide, don't look back." The truth is, I had no idea how one couldn't look back. But it was the only advice I had.

Sister Carmelita walked in with an arm full of towels and linens. "Excuse me, girls, I need to drop these off."

Sister Carmelita had characteristically striking eyes. The light from the black diamond paned window next to Sue Willy's bed reflected their color, like the blue-green in an abalone shell. Her face was blessedly clean and untouched by make-up, but it was hard to guess her age. She wore a white cotton cap secured by a white wimple of starched cotton that covered her cheeks and neck. All the nuns wore black fabric tunics pleated at the neck and draped to the ground. Sister Carmelita wore a belt made of woven black wool. A rosary of wooden beads and metal links hung from her belt by small hooks and a silver cross hung from a black cord around her neck.

"We're just talking about the baby," Sue Willy offered, "and what I should do."

Sister Carmelita stopped. "May I sit?"

"Sure."

She dragged another chair over. "I heard some of what you were talking about. I didn't mean to eavesdrop, but it echoes around here, and anyway, I heard you."

"I don't care, Sister, you know I trust you with anything."

"That means a lot to me, Susannah." She swept her hands under her long flowing gown to straighten out the layers as she sank into the seat cushion. "Do you know what faith is?" She looked at Sue Willy, and then at me.

We both sat motionless with obtuse looks on our faces. I was dreading another let's-see-if-we-can-attempt-to-save-your-soul lecture. My faith was at low tide no matter how she defined it and, frankly, I was in no mood to listen to a religious crusade.

"Having faith is not a guarantee that everything works out, or that your choices will be right. But it's trusting that the outcome will make sense, because your choice made the best sense it could. You factor in everything you know, feel, and believe to make the best decision you can. And then you let go. In one way or another, I believe God will honor it. That's how I see it, anyway."

Sue Willy rolled her eyes. "But I don't know what the best choice is, I really don't."

Sister Carmelita tipped her head. "Sometimes you can only guess based on what you know and feel right now. You do the best you can."

I didn't envy Sue Willy.

"It's the biggest decision of my life," Sue Willy said, almost sounding like a real grown-up.

"Yes, it is," Sister Carmelita affirmed. "It's a decision that will change the course of this baby's life forever." She stood up. "You'll figure it out. It'll be clear when you do."

Sue Willy waved one hand as if to dismiss what she said. "That's because you're a nun. You don't have the same problems we do. It's easy for you."

"My sin is no different than yours," she told her.

Sue Willy shifted her bottom and then stared at Sister Carmelita with amazement. "Wait a minute," she said gingerly, "you're telling me *you've* done it?"

"Done it? Oh, you mean sex," she laughed. "I'm just saying we all make mistakes and fall short. Even nuns. No one has the right to judge anyone else."

"Some of your flock of sisters missed that sermon in their training," Sue Willy quipped.

"We all fall short," Sister Carmelita repeated, standing up to stretch. "Still no more contractions, Susannah?" she asked.

"Nooo," she groaned. "When will this ever end?" It took Sue Willy a while to fully lift her behind up. Clearly not the same little heinie I saw on Shell Beach, I thought. I watched her bend over as far as she could, one hand gripping the edge of the mattress. And then the strangest look crossed her face and shot out her eyes. I think it was sheer terror.

"It's coming!" she shrieked, "The baby is coming!"

MOTHER LOVE, MOTHER LOSS

I THOUGHT SHE WAS JOKING. I HOPED IT WAS AN ACT, UNTIL I saw a cascade of water gush as big as Old Faithful, down the center of Sue Willy's legs. Never saw that happen to Sophie, I thought. And that's when it registered; *this is the real thing.*

Sister Carmelita rushed to Sue Willy's side. "Okay, lay back, easy does it, looks like it's time after all."

"But my mom! She's not here yet!" Sue Willy said as if she were doomed without her.

And neither is Scarlett! I wanted to shout back, but didn't. My heart started galloping, but I told myself there was no need to panic. I wasn't going to be involved. Not this time, not for a real birth. I glanced down the hall, searching for a door that might lead to the waiting room. It was time for me to make my exit.

"This baby is ready and so are you, Susannah," Sister Carmelita said in a comforting voice. "You're going to do great." She helped Sue Willy spread open her legs, slapped on a white plastic glove, and her hand disappeared between her thighs. Sue Willy lurched back in pain, her head arched back on the pillow. I wanted to run, but something pinned me to the spot.

"Well, would you look at that!" Sister Carmelita exclaimed. "You're almost there." She whisked the flowing layers of her habit around, stripped off the glove, and swished herself across the room.

"Holy, sheeet! Oww!" Sue Willy's eyes practically flew out their sockets.

Sister Carmelita rushed through the door. "Wait!" I yelled, alarm oozing from my voice. "Where's the doctor and the midwife?"

"I'm it, Zetty," she winked. "Stay right there with Susannah." She scrambled to the hall, twirled around and recklessly rolled in a large metal tray of instruments covered by clear plastic. Sister Carmelita began ripping things open.

"Okay then," I said shakily, even though no one heard me in all the commotion.

Sue Willy was huffing and puffing and writhing in pain. "Zetty!" she cried. I repositioned myself to her side, feeling my face hot as a jalapeño. "I'm so scared," she panted. "I can't do it, Zetty. I can't! What if I die?"

With the sweeping certainty of a buffoon, I told her, "Statistically, it's not likely. Women do this every day. And so will you." But what I was really thinking was, *please, please don't up and die on me. I can't take it again.*

"Hold my hand!" she screeched, and then began laboriously breathing through her mouth.

And I hoped I wouldn't faint and drop unconscious right on top of her. I searched for help in my memory of "Kotch," and Walter Matthau, and realized it was truly no help at all. But some of the things Scarlett told me on our drive up did turn out to be useful.

Sue Willy cried out again. And again. Squeezing tight. It was then I knew I might have to sacrifice a few bones in at least one hand and not complain about it. It was time to grin and bear it, again.

"Yeeooowww! Sue Willy panted. "I can't do this! Don't make me do this!" Followed by, "Get it out! *Nooow!* Yeeooowww!" she let loose again.

I looked at Sue Willy helplessly, tears streaming down her red and twisted face, and was dumbstruck. Where was Scarlett? And why wasn't Gabe here? This was clearly a job for Gabe.

But now it's a job for me, I said, resigned to the fact I wasn't going anywhere.

Sister Carmelita wrapped the blood pressure cuff around Sue Willy's arm again and scurried to the cupboard for more linens.

Sue Willy cried in pain, unable to catch her breath. Her head rocked forcefully against the bed rail. "Don't let them, don't let them do it, please! Don't let anyone take my baby," she pleaded weakly, her eyes trying to focus on mine. "The mean one doesn't want me to have it." Another contraction took hold of her and wasn't letting go.

The whole room went under a glass bowl. The air still, and sticky. Sweat slithered its way down the matted hair at Sue Willy's temples. The window was up, but it made no difference. The thick air clung to our skin and wasn't going anywhere.

"Yeeeooowww!" Sue Willy burst out again. I leaned down with both hands clasping hers. "Focus, Sue Willy, Focus on me. Look in my eyes. Look at my eyelashes now. Each one of them, and count. Focus and count, one eyelash at a time. Keep breathing, keep it slow and steady as you count. In your nose, and exhale out your mouth, nice and slow," I instructed.

Sister Carmelita continued to press a warm cloth saturated with oil against Sue Willy's vulva, explaining it would help stretch her skin and prevent vaginal tearing. "It's a little extra work, but well worth it," she said.

Sue Willy gave me a desperate, almost dying expression and mouthed, "I'm scared."

Sister Carmelita was exuberant. "You're almost there, Susannah! You're doing perfect!" She announced.

"Yeeeooowww!" Sue Willy cried again.

"We need music," I announced. I let go of Sue Willy's grasp just long enough to turn on the player on the end table and hustled back. *Rrr, sabor!* it began. Santana was rocking the room in Spanish again and I was ready.

"Okay, Sue Willy. Focus!" I ordered. "Focus on each note of every word." Sister Carmelita repeated the sign of the cross, quick like a patty-cake game. I had seen it so many times now, I knew I could never get it wrong again.

"Okay," Sue Willy said earnestly, trying hard to ignore the pain. "Okay. Every note. Okay. I will. I am. Every note," she said, starting to calm down. And then she roared like never before, "I need to push! I. HAVE. TO. PUSH!" she said, clearly pushing.

Sister Carmelita threw back the sheet. "There's the head! Go ahead, Susannah! Give it all ya got!"

"It feels like a chunk of cement!" she hollered, her face full of perspiration and wrinkled up so cherry-red tight it looked like she was right; she might be pushing out a mountain of granite.

Only moments later, a gasping diminutive whimper sang in the air and a slippery little gus wriggled into Sister Carmelita's arms, and straight to Sue Willy's heart.

"Sue Willy, you have a boy!" I pronounced, as proud as if he were my own.

Sister Carmelita wiped at the beads of sweat dotting her brow with one sleeve, drew the sign of the cross against her chest at least two more times, and then a smile unfurled slowly across her face and spread around the room like a lighthouse beam.

It was a moment I have marked as one of my best days ever. *Wasn't it nice*, I thought, *that you could have both—the worst, and the best, and that they could co-exist in the same life. There was room inside for both.*

"Sue Willy," I said, "just look at him. He sees you, I think!"

She smiled, and cried, and laughed, and smiled. And then smiled more. She kept right on smiling through tears. I never saw her more radiant and joyful, so truly happy as I did in that moment in time.

We couldn't stop staring at his face. When he yawned for the first time, he softly pushed his rolled pink tongue out and, right at the tip, lay a delicate little bubble of spit.

Sue Willy sparkled.

Only she didn't look like Sue Willy anymore. She looked like a mother.

I shakily helped Sister Carmelita cut the cord. And I still didn't faint.

"Zetty," Sue Willy exhaled, "I'm so glad you were here. What would I have done without you?" She helped Sister Carmelita gently tuck the receiving blanket around her baby's head. The warmth of his newborn body, molded into her arms.

Sister Carmelita folded up the soiled sheets and towels, and then leaned in and kissed Sue Willy on the forehead. "God bless this precious new life, and the young woman who brought him into this world." Here it comes, I thought, and as soon as I thought it she flew the cross across herself again.

"Thank you, Sister Carmelita. Thank God it was you who delivered him." And then Sue Willy added, "You're the only one I trust him with."

"I'm honored, Susannah. I'm very proud of you. And you didn't tear!"

Sue Willy smiled and then checked the clock. "I wonder where my mom is, and Scarlett," she said sounding anxious again.

An exceptionally plump nun I hadn't seen before appeared at the door. She checked a paper clipped to the wall and then rushed toward us confidently. "The baby will go with me, now," she announced, her face puffy like dough.

Sue Willy stretched the blanket over her baby boy's head as if that could hide him. I placed myself like a shield between them.

"Step back, please," the nun said calmly. "The baby needs to be removed now. It's best for everyone," she said, wiping both hands on her apron. "It's not helpful for her to become attached."

"What?" I asked, astonished.

"This is not for you to worry about," she told me.

"But it's her baby. Not anyone else's." I parked myself on the edge of the bed, still blocking her from the baby.

"These are the consequences," she said, her head shaking with repugnance. "Let it be a lesson to you, too." She peered down at me. "I'm sorry. The baby must go with me."

"No, the baby will not go with you," I said in a civilized way. "The baby will stay with its mother until further notice." I stood to meet her face-to-face.

She gently placed both hands in the front pocket of her dress. "I don't expect you to understand, but it's easier on everyone if the baby leaves immediately. Miss Williamson should forget it ever happened." I stepped in closer, arms folded, glowering into her eyes, exactly the way they tell you not to when confronted by an attack dog.

She straightened her spine. "Now hear this," she said in a ratchety voice, "it's against our rules, I won't allow you—"

I stopped her. "Tell it to the pope, sister, because I don't care." I heard Sue Willy gasp and Sister Carmelita turned away toward the window, one hand cupped over her mouth.

"Okay, sorry," I surrendered. I probably only sounded a little sorry. "I don't mean to be disrespectful. Honestly, I'm usually not."

"She's really not," Sue Willy chimed in, cuddling her newborn baby with an unwavering grip.

"Well," the nun softened, "I can forgive, so I—"

"Oh no," I interrupted, "I'm not asking for forgiveness. Sue Willy must have *some* rights. It's rude to call her a sinner, pinch her cheek, and make her feel dirty like a piece of trash, as if she's not good enough to keep this baby! Well, she IS good enough!"

Sue Willy's face lit up so bright I practically saw it from the back of my head.

I was saying what I really thought, and the freedom it gave me felt amazing.

The sister, her puffy face tight as a knot now, bowed her head like a geisha girl and backed away. Her rosary beads swung violently around her hips as she marched out.

"You're as brave as Gabe was, Zetty." Sue Willy took a bottle from Sister Carmelita and fed her baby boy as if she'd done it a hundred times before. She was a natural.

"You're the courageous one, not me, Sue Willy," I told her. "You just pushed a human being out of yourself! You get the medal."

But the truth is, I did feel a braveness come over me. And it didn't feel like it was me, alone. It felt like I had help, but from who, I wasn't exactly sure.

If I hadn't been brave like Gabe, I thought, I might have fainted and landed right on top of her at the very beginning when the room really started to spin a little.

It was dusk. The curtains swayed like ghosts in and out next to Sue Willy's bed. The friendly noise of a fan hummed in the background moving the air over Sue Willy and her baby. The room darkened, making it hard to see their faces, but I could hear the steady purr of sleep.

Sister Carmelita tip-toed in and gently tapped my shoulder. She motioned to me to step out of the room.

"What is it?" I asked still keeping my voice low, standing in the hallway.

"I just spoke to Scarlett," Sister Carmelita sighed. "Susannah's mother wasn't where she was supposed to be. We don't think the car broke down at all. Scarlett's husband drove to their house and said the car was there, and no one was home. It appears it was all an excuse, Zetty. I feel just awful."

I had to press my mouth shut with the palm of my hand and hold it for two seconds, then dropped it and admitted, "If you weren't a nun, I would've sworn like a sailor right then, Carmelita."

"Well, I have to confess, a few words came flying out of me, too, in my mind of course."

"It's the same old story, every time. I can't tell you how many times Sue Willy has gone through this." My eyes welled up and anger pushed them over the edge.

Sister Carmelita put her arm around me. "Well, it's clear to me why you're in her life. You have everything you need to help her. And you will."

"I don't pray, just so you know."

"Oh?" she asked adjusting her belt.

"No. I always have too much agony to put into words."

"Your agony is prayer enough, Zetty—more eloquent than any words."

She walked away, and to my amazement I believed what she said. At least the part about having everything I needed to help Sue Willy.

I stepped back into the room; a chorus of crickets and bullfrogs croaked outside the window. The sounds of the night spread comfort across the room. A soft, low wattage of light glowed next to Sue Willy's bed. It was enough to see her eyes were open. She was inspecting her baby boy, fixated on all his parts, drinking in his every crease and curve. It was surprisingly restful to be around her.

"He's beautiful, Sue Willy," I told her, taking a seat next to the bed to watch them. "Do you need anything? Can I get you something?" I asked her.

"No—sit. Please stay and look at him with me. I'm so proud."

"Sister Carmelita just taught me how to change his diaper. It was easy! Nothing to it. She warned me it will get harder, but I want to do it, Zetty."

"Then you will," I said. I hoped she wouldn't ask about her mother again, but she did.

"Are they here yet?"

"No."

"My mother needs to see him. Once she does, she'll want me to keep him. I know she will. Do you know why they aren't here yet?"

"Not really."

The rosy color drained from Sue Willy's face. "She didn't want to come did she?"

"I don't know, Sue Willy. It's hard to say."

"She's bombed."

"Most likely," I said, "and if that's true at least we can give her credit for not driving here and killing people on the way."

"No kidding," Sue Willy slumped. "Tell me everything

you know. And don't sugar-coat it for me. I want it straight."

"Okay, so, Scarlett couldn't find your mom; she wasn't where she said she'd be. Dennis said her car was at your house, no one was home, and we don't know where she is. Scarlett's on her way back."

"Okay," she said. And the way she said it I knew she was done discussing it. She stayed quiet for awhile.

"I'm sorry, Sue Willy, I finally said. "It's never been fair to you."

"Or to you. We've both grown up with invisible mothers." She shifted the baby to the opposite arm. "I don't know what I'd do, or where I'd be, without you and Scarlett."

"Well, you don't have to do without us. And we mean it, Sue Willy; we'll support you keeping him. No matter what, we'll help. We're one hundred percent behind you, and always will be." I knew as I said it, I was wanting that baby, myself. At least to help raise him. We could do it, I told myself, with Scarlett's help, we'd take care of him the right way.

"I'm naming him Gabriel, after Gabe," she said grinning.

His little hand blurred from the tears welled up in my eyes, but I lifted it with one finger and told her, "It's perfect."

"And then," she said, "I'm going to ask Sister Carmelita to be the one to choose his parents. It makes the best sense."

My throat seized up and I couldn't find a way to dislodge the knot of words tangled up there. She saw my distress.

"I know," she said. "I hate it, too. I really do. But who am I kidding? I'm not the one who can raise him. He deserves a real chance in life." Sue Willy reached for a tissue box and yanked three out, one after another. "I've made the choice and then I'm going to have to let go, like Sister Carmelita said."

"Whoa," is all I could say back.

"My biggest fear though, the thing that really kills me, Zetty?"

"What?" I squeaked out, wanting, with all my might, to talk her out of giving him away.

"What if he thinks I didn't want him, and just threw him away? How do I live with that—always wondering if he believes that?"

I don't know where it came from but I knew exactly what to say. "Then let's make sure he knows the truth. Write a letter to him, and tell Sister Carmelita she needs to choose parents who will agree to be honest with him and give him your letter when he asks about you."

Sue Willy's eyes stretched wide. "That's exactly what I'll do."

"And," I added, "we'll keep a copy of that letter here with Sister Carmelita, in case the parents ever lose it, and you should keep a copy, too. Trust me. I know how important it will be for Gabriel to know the truth. All of it."

"I'll give it to him." she perked up. "I'll tell him how much I wanted to keep him. That I loved him the first moment I saw his face. That he *was* wanted, unlike me. And I'll tell him where his name came from."

"He'll love it, Sue Willy."

"Sister Carmelita told me all babies come into the world looking for someone who's looking for them. And that children are created with an emotional need to be cherished and delighted in. That's who I want for Gabriel. Parents who are looking for him and who will cherish him."

"I'm proud of you, Sue Willy. It's an amazing thing for you to do."

Sue Willy dropped her face into her hands.

"If you'd like," I offered, "I could take a picture of you with Gabriel. One for you, and one for the letter. He'll see you have the same wavy hair and brown eyes he does. And the dimple on the same cheek you do."

"I love that!" she said sounding light and rosy again all at once. "And I'll enclose the 'Make Love, Not War' pin I was wearing for him to remember me by. And maybe someday he'll want to meet me and I'll get to see him again, all grown up."

And then Sue Willy began to weep and when her chest shuddered, Gabriel started to rouse from his sleep. She extended him toward me like an offering. "I don't want to wake him. I don't want him to see me cry."

And then she whispered, "I hope he finds me someday," and tenderly released him into my arms.

I rested my cheek to one side of his face and unearthed his pure scent, instantaneously bonding me to him. There's no way to really describe it; except to say I had never breathed in anything more beautiful and perfect in my life.

The Most Important Thing

It must be a sign.

It was the first thought I had walking through Doc Sperling's door. There was a tunnel of light taking aim into her office. It positioned itself, quite unbelievably, on my favorite navy blue, crushed velvet chair. Month after month I had been taking that seat regularly, and not once had I ever seen the sun hit it like that. For a moment, I forgot everything else and imagined it could have been a set for a Broadway play—with my seat, center stage, directly under the spotlight. It gave me a little movie star thrill to move under it.

Or maybe it was celestial. A ray of holy light, a sign from Gabe, reassuring me I was about to do the right thing. Something Father would just have to accept.

Doc Sperling ruffled through the pages in my file. I noticed her burgundy hair and green eyes popped next to the deep indigo vest she was wearing. I filed the color combination away in my mind and labeled it: to be used in next painting.

Doc Sperling told me once she believed my creativity, whether painting, dance, or piano, was something I could trust in the midst of chaos and heartache. That my talents anchored me to something real in life, and gave me hope for something beautiful to emerge from the emotional wreckage around me. I could see now that Sue Willy and I had that in common; the drive for art and creativity was probably a survival tool. It was probably the reason we were friends to begin with.

I rolled up the colorful, embroidered puffed sleeves of my black cotton peasant blouse as high as they'd go and then rolled up my blue jean cut-offs higher, too. I positioned my head back to an optimal angle. Just in case I could tan from the sun beating on me through the window.

"I called your emergency line last night," I announced.

"Who did you speak to? I don't see it in your file." She turned a few pages again and clicked her pen open.

"No one." I closed my eyes and rested my head all the way back.

"No one got back to you?" She sounded alarmed.

"Yeah, they got back to me," I said reluctantly.

"And?" she pressed.

"And then I hung up because it wasn't you, so there was no point."

"Why not?" she asked.

"Because you were the only one I wanted to talk to."

"Was it an emergency?"

"To *me*," I said truthfully.

"Okay," she said calmly, and then got up for tea. "So what happened?"

I sat up and stared straight at her while she dipped a tea bag in a mug. My pulse quickened and my breathing felt out of whack again just thinking about it. "It just suddenly hit me. I wanted to tell you right away."

"You mean about Sue Willy and the baby?"

"Well yes, and also what hit me afterwards. I couldn't say it to just anyone."

"What hit you?" she asked, patient as ever.

"I realized my mother went through that with me; that moment of amazement when she first laid eyes on me, that moment she first took in my scent and said to herself, 'she's mine.' I watched Sue Willy with her son; and she sparkled, Doc Sperling. I've never seen her so happy. I don't see how that bond could ever go away—it's something she'll never forget. My mom fell in love with me that way, too. I felt it for the first nine years of my life. Giving birth is more than I ever knew. Together or not, that bond is for life. I don't think it can ever end, Doc."

The sun had already moved across the room and left a shadow over both of us. Doc Sperling switched on the lamp next to her. "Without a doubt, Zetty," she said, "you and your mother shared the deepest bond there is. What you experienced with her was very special. Love, when it's formed in such a way, does feel eternal, doesn't it?"

I nodded.

"Not everyone experiences it that way, though. It's not always possible. And we also know there are circumstances that make it impossible for early bonds to survive, no matter how deep the attachment was in the beginning."

"Do you think my mother has forgotten me? I mean if she hasn't recovered by now."

"I don't know." Doc Sperling bent forward, arms folded on her knees. "It's a possibility, based on what you've told me."

I took a deep breath, trying to gain the courage to come out with it. "I need to find out. And I can, now."

Doc Sperling took a slow sip of tea, set down her mug on the side table, and looked approvingly at me. "So, your father has finally agreed?"

"Yes," I fibbed. "I've convinced him. Can you help me find her? Gabe and I started calling hospitals in New York, but it's taking forever. And the calls are expensive."

"I'll do whatever I can." She pulled out a sharpened black pencil from the drawer next to her. "Zetty, are you sure your Dad has no idea where she is?"

"That's what he says."

"And he's had no contact?" she asked sounding incredulous.

"Says he hasn't."

"Okay," she sighed and nervously tapped the end of her pencil against her thigh. "I'll need her birth date, and all the information you do have—the dates she was admitted and released from the hospital here. Also, ask your father the names of her doctors. That would help tremendously."

I hoped my stunned expression hadn't given me away. "Zetty?" Her countenance changed. "He's fully on board with this, right? You know I need his consent before I can start."

"Yes. Here," I said, reaching into my purse, and handed her the expertly forged "permission slip." She unfolded it, pushed her glasses down, and rolled her eyes over it.

I listened to the ticking clock slice the silence exactly fifteen times before she continued. "Okay then," she said placing the note in my file, "when can I speak with him? Actually," she paused, "let's have your dad join us at our next session. I'll have Anna-Victoria move it up sooner."

"Sure," I said, like I was all for it, "that'd be great."

"Okay," she said satisfied, "I'll start researching and the three of us will meet to discuss the next steps."

We would not be discussing it with Father. That much I knew. And there was no way she was going to help unless he was in on it. The plan had just imploded and yet to me nothing had gone wrong at all. I heard the clock again, calmly ticking through the stillness as if there was nothing hard about this at all.

"I think you and your father are doing the right thing, Zetty. Regardless of her condition; it's important to know the truth." Doc Sperling tilted her head. "But I want you to be prepared for the fact that she may not know you."

"It's okay," I told her. "I don't need her to know me. I need to know her." Which was the truth now.

But what I didn't tell her was that I was ready. Ready for the golden opportunity to carry out our plan, because it was never just mine. Gabe would always be part of it. I had the money, a bag packed and hidden, and Tom on standby to drive me to the airport, any hour, day or night at a moment's notice. I just had to wait for one lucky break, just the way Gabe said. There was simply no turning back. When the opportunity came, and I knew it would, I would seize it and run. I would take hold of the reins on my runaway life and crack them in the right direction. The only direction I wanted to go now—straight to Mother.

That was our plan.

All the Gold We Can Gather

The birds circled the air over a large mound of seaweed on the beach. The sweetness of spring blew past me when I climbed down the hill from the cliffs and sank my toes in the sand. I didn't have Tuffy to lie at my feet, or Gabe to stroll with me, so I went to the edge of the water, waded through clumps of slippery gold algae with tentacles threatening to entangle my calves, and plunged in. The cold battered up my nose and against my chest and the salty fizz on my lips tasted delicious. I have to tell you, this time was better than ever before. This time I wanted to break through the waves and burst up like an opulent fountain in Rome—high in the air, expansive and free. With the rush of the sea came anticipation for something. I wanted to be fully conscious for whatever was coming next. That day, "going under" into nothingness lost all its appeal.

And that day my golden opportunity was closer than I knew. My lucky break was about to land in my lap. It started with a phone call that felt like snow had fallen in Windansea again.

When I heard it ring, I expected to pick up and hear the school counselor on the other end. She was supposed to call to discuss my graduation plan with Father. But instead, I heard a voice curiously familiar, and at the same time strangely out of place.

"Zetty, this is Doctor Sperling. Do you have a minute?"

My neck flushed to my ears. I scanned all the doorways for any sign of Father. "In my home?" I asked feeling my heart skip out of sync from the weight of deceit pushing on it.

"If it's a good time, yes."

"Okay, it's a good time," I said nervously, still wondering if I was completely private.

"Zetty, I have good news for you and your father. I've located your mother. In fact, her doctor is a former colleague of mine who I knew in New York."

"What?" My thoughts started to spin. "Really?" I rooted through the junk drawer and scrambled everything up inside searching for a pen and something to write on.

"So your friend knows her? And where she is?"

"Yes. She was very helpful. She hasn't been on her case for quite some time, but remembered her right away."

"Does that mean she's better? Living on her own now, or, what?" I waited, the air in my chest not moving, longing, wishing, nearly praying that the next words I would hear were, *she's performing on a magnificent stage on Broadway.*

"As suspected, she has the rare, regressive form of schizophrenia we discussed."

The air expelled from my chest. "So, she's in a hospital. Okay," I said, trying to steady myself. "She has childish symptoms then? Like giggling and not acting her age?"

"Right. Eventually patients with this diagnosis will go back to an infantile state. Your mom won't be who you remember, but the good news is her condition is fairly stable right now. You and your father can make plans to see her—the sooner the better."

I pulled out the phone book and a stubby pencil. "Okay, I'll tell him," I assured her.

"I need to speak to him, too. Is he there?"

"Why?"

"Remember Zetty, I won't keep anything from you that I share with him."

"I know," I said, as if that was the reason for my hesitation. "He's donating blood." My face twisted up as soon as I said it. Why that lie rolled off my tongue I still can't tell you. It simply appeared in my mouth before I could prevent it, and then I had to go on. "O-positive. Serious shortage right now."

To make matters worse, the saw powered up in the garage as soon as I declared it. I pulled the cord out as far as it would stretch and wedged my head inside the broom closet to try and block the noise.

"Okay, well, have him call my office when he gets in. We can set up the appointment for all of us to meet before we arrange the visit. I plan to speak with your dad about how he can best support you."

"I'll be fine," I said, wanting her to drop all the talk about Father and tell me where in New York I'd be white-knuckling it to.

"I believe you will, Zetty, but this is an important step you're taking, not just with your mother, but with your father, too."

"I know," I said plugging my other ear with a finger.

"I'll notify her nurse, Eleanor, ahead of time before your visit. I'll explain that to your dad, too."

"So where exactly in New York is she?" I hoped she wouldn't notice the muffled effect from being inside a closet, or hear the desperation dripping off my words.

"I'm sorry, what did you say?"

"I was wondering where in New York she is."

"Manhattan. For about six years."

"Six years? What hospital is she at?" I was getting light-headed again.

"I'm sorry, It's hard to hear you. Did you ask what hospital my colleague was at?"

"No, where in Manhattan is my mother?"

"Oh, no, no. Your mother isn't in Manhattan. My former colleague was. We both worked there at the same time. Years ago."

"Okay, so where in New York is my mother?" This was getting on my nerves.

"She's not in New York, Zetty."

"She's not? But—"

"No. She hasn't been back there at all."

"She hasn't?"

"No. She's right here. In fact, not far away at all."

"What?" I thought I might fold over on the spot.

"Yes. She was moved to the Good Samaritan Psychiatric Nursing Home."

There was my answer. Dangling in the air, finally within reach. It was a moment of release, as only the discovery of truth can be.

I wrote down, "Eleanor," shaking uncontrollably. "You mean the big green stucco building near the avocado orchard?" I tossed the pencil down and then wedged my head between the mop and duster knowing this was my providential break; an opportunity worth more than gold.

"Yes, that's it."

"Wow. All this time. Only a half-hour away!" It was getting harder to keep my anger toward Father from leaking out, but, like a sinking vessel, I plugged it up with everything I had.

"I know. It surprised me, too," she hesitated a little, "so, I need to speak with your dad as soon as possible."

"Sure. I'll tell him to call right away," I fibbed. "Thank you for finding her so fast. I'm really excited." And then added for good measure, "My father will be, too."

"I'm glad I could help. I know it's the right thing for you and your father to do."

"Me, too. I mean it, Doc Sperling. Thanks again."

"Of course, Zetty. We'll talk soon."

When I hung up the phone, I ripped out the page in the phone book I had scribbled the information on and took the lucky break, the golden opportunity of colossal proportions, jammed it down my pocket, underneath Tuffy's purple paisley bandana and reflected on Gabe's words. She was right again. And then I remembered to breathe.

Father was still in the garage, the saw screaming every time it pierced wood, then rumbling low as the motor idled after a cut was complete.

Then I did something I had never done before. I snapped up Father's car keys and headed for the door. I said to myself, if Gabe would do it, so should I. I wasn't going to let any opportunity skate past me. With nothing but gratitude, I gathered them all, mobilized myself, and ran.

The last inch of the front door was nearly closed when I heard the phone ring again. I stopped with one ear to the crack. Father's machinery was off and I heard him scuffle from the garage into the kitchen. "McGee speaking. Oh, yes, hello Doctor Sperling," I heard him say, and a buzzing shot up on both sides of my spine and I went numb everywhere.

Move it, Zetty. Now! I ordered myself.

To stay calm I reminded myself that I was only going to drive. Not fly on an airliner. It was slightly helpful. I piled into the front seat of Father's blue Chevy, turned the key the way I had practiced with Gabe, and pretended I was going for a nice and easy drive. It wasn't nearly as difficult as I imagined. Our practice sessions in the Lucky-Seven parking lot had been far more challenging.

But now I was on my own. In traffic. With an invisible co-pilot.

"I'll act like I know exactly what I'm doing," I said aloud to Gabe. "As if I've done this a million times. There's nothing to it. It's a straight shot!" I said with ease. "Just stop on red, go on green, and, as soon as I see yellow—gun it."

I repeated more of her driving tips out loud to myself: "Focus on the painted lines and don't worry what color they are. Just stare at them if the cars whizzing by make you panic, and go plenty slow, in case you have to stop fast. Get the feel of the brakes, and whatever you do, don't change lanes unless your life depends on it."

Nearly fifty-five minutes later, I crept into the parking lot of the Good Samaritan Psychiatric Nursing Home and parked horizontally across three spots, just to be safe. I peeled off my stiff fingers, clutching the steering wheel like claws, and stretched them out one finger at a time.

I did it, I told myself proudly. I practically heard Gabe cheering when I told her, *I conquered my fear of operating a massive piece of dangerous glass and metal on wheels, risking myself and everyone in its path. I did it, Gabe.*

It's time to see my mother.

THERE WAS A TEENAGER, NOT MUCH OLDER THAN ME, SITting at a desk where the automatic doors into the front lobby opened. She wore a pink and white striped dress with a white cap bobby-pinned to blonde hair. The badge pinned neatly on her apron said, "Sherie – Volunteer Candy Striper." She looked up pleasantly at me. "Hi there," she said with a peppy step in her voice. "May I help you, please?"

Must be a cheerleader, I thought.

"Yes, I'm here to see Marjorie McGee."

"Mrs. McGee? Are you sure?" She looked confused.

I nodded yes, afraid to speak.

"I'm sorry," she said, "but I don't think she can have visitors."

"Oh, I know, but Eleanor, her nurse, said it was okay, just this once, since I came from out of town."

"Oh, Eleanor. Okay."

I nodded affirmative.

She paused unsure of what to do. "Let me see if I can find Eleanor and let her know you're here."

I dug through my burlap hippie bag trying to appear distracted.

"Your name?" She started dialing.

I kept digging in a frenzy, as if I hadn't heard her. "Is Mrs. McGee still in the same room? Let's see I think it was, hmmm." I dug louder.

"Let's see," she ran a finger down a list taped to the top of the desk still waiting for Eleanor to pick up. "Yes, still room 217, but Eleanor doesn't seem to be answering. Let me try and find her. Be right back," she said in a perky way.

Yes! I celebrated with myself, *another perfect blunder that I will seize and run with.* I was almost giddy from the number of lucky breaks I was getting. *Maybe Gabe's helping.* It was a pleasant thought to hang on to.

I watched Sherie trot down a wide hallway, the perfect flip in her hair bouncing on top her shoulders. She probably twirled a baton, too, I thought.

I went to the elevators, and pushed the "up" button. When the doors opened, a frail looking woman in a white cotton gown was holding on to a man's arm like she was ready to march down a wedding aisle. When they stepped out, I couldn't help but notice the familiar shuffle, but I knew it wasn't Mother. The woman's hair was inky black and way too thick. She was an empty shell of a person, her face seemingly frozen into an almost malicious glare. But nothing about her, or this hospital bothered me. Having been through it myself, it almost felt like home.

But when I reached the second floor, I took it back. A wall of skanky air surrounded me. *Not this again.* For an instant, I was back at the state hospital entrance and couldn't move. No matter how I turned my head, I couldn't escape it. I made a mental note to myself: *don't take breathing for granted.*

The pungent odor of sour smoke, urine, and probably vomit yanked on my gag reflex several times before I reached Room 217. *It'll get better*, I promised myself, *it always does.* The door was open and I saw a nurse in white pants leaning over a thin, naked woman, wiping stool off her backside. Mother's backside. I knew it was her. I recognized the arch of her spine. I stayed back, waiting for my nose to adjust the way I told myself it would.

The nurse rolled her over and even from a distance I knew. She was still an empty version of the mother I once knew. Still gone—the plug pulled from the source that connected her to life. And to me.

Next to her lay an open, soiled diaper smeared with a vile color of feces. It was another, even worse smell now mixed in with the rest. I retched and this time I knew there was no holding it back.

I spun backward to a stairwell, threw up behind the door and hurriedly tripped down the flight of stairs in search of air. I bolted outdoors into the soft glow of the afternoon sun and directly into Father's arms.

All Doubts Swept Away

"Zetty, stop!" Father clutched me tight, and then his face drooped. "Sweetheart, are you sick?"

I inhaled, grateful for the fresh air that coursed through my veins like pure oxygen. "Yes, I'm sick! Why did you have to come?"

Father launched into a lecture. "What were you thinking doing such a foolhardy thing?" He pulled me toward himself and tried to hug me, but I stiffened and backed away. "If I wasn't so scared, I'd be mad right now." he scolded. "You could have killed yourself. Or been arrested."

"It was fine. I knew what I was doing."

He pointed at the parking places I had spread the car across and stabbed the air with his forefinger. "That is what you call illegal parking!" His other hand gripped my upper arm as if I were a thief trying to elude him.

"It's only a parking lot." I tried to shake his hand off my arm, but he wouldn't let go.

"Zetty, you completely disobeyed me. I never wanted you to come here, and now look what's happened."

"You've known all along. You've known she's been here and lied to me!" I jerked away from his grasp, sat on the edge of a stone wall planter box, and used two fingers to wipe off the vomit still stuck to my lips.

"Just sit here for a minute. And don't you go anywhere,"

he warned. He took two steps and then spun back around. "Give me those keys," he ordered.

I pulled them from my bag and dropped them carelessly into his hand. When he jogged through the hospital entrance, I took three slow, deep breaths and tried to erase the rancid smell from my memory. I could remember it at will and every time I did, it made me want to heave again.

Father stepped briskly back to me. "Take a drink, Zetty, and here's a paper towel to clean your face with. What happened?"

I wiped at my mouth, embarrassed. The water did nothing to erase the bitter taste in my mouth. "It's complicated in there," I said drily.

"Well, of course it is. It's no place for you to be."

"Oh, really," I said caustically. "It *was* the place for me to be not that long ago. A place like it, anyway." Father rolled his eyes, but I needed to explain. "It was just the air, Dad. I couldn't breathe. And then I smelled Mom's diaper. I feel so stupid for running off."

"Don't feel stupid, Zetty. It's not easy in there. It never has been."

"Why didn't you tell me, Dad? *Why*?"

"I couldn't, Zetty."

"You're still not answering me!"

"Now just hold on!" he bristled. "I didn't want you to know everything that happened. I wanted to spare you this. How can it help to know things that even your mother would never—and I mean *never* want you to know? Zetty, if she were in her right mind, she wouldn't want to put you through any of this."

"If she were in her right mind, we wouldn't be here. But since we are, I'm sure she would want me to know. So, if it's the diapers, I know it's awful, but I can handle that. It was just the smell at first,"

"It's not that, Zetty," he cut in. "It's not the diapers. It's more than that," he said with a withered look.

Father dropped next to me, both shoulders slumped. His body had grown suddenly fragile, his frame limp.

"She became violent, Zetty. Dangerously, so. It happened the day we went to bring her home for Christmas. Do you remember?"

"How could I forget? Of course, I remember."

Father grimaced again. "Okay. Alright." He shifted uncomfortably. "Well, she was terribly upset as soon as I arrived, but it kept getting worse and she actually became so distraught, she attacked me. It was—" there was a slow expanding pause, "—shocking," he choked. "They told me they had never seen her that way before. She swung at me and screamed and it took all of them to hold her down. And then she attacked them, too." He stopped, rubbed his hand up and down the side of his face, and pressed out the hard lines of stress carved around his outer eye.

He continued, "It was seeing *me* that set her off, Zetty. And there's more." Father sounded like he had rocks in his throat. He could barely get it out, "She had no clothes on."

"Naked?" I asked in disbelief.

"Completely," he said grimacing. "All the way down the hall."

I shook my head in disbelief, "Streaking? That's not like mother, at all."

"Of course it isn't. That's what I mean. It was devastating. And I was worried what might happen around you. Physically and emotionally. I couldn't risk it. Can you understand that?" He didn't give me time to answer. "More than anything, Zetty, I wanted your memories of your mother to be only the loving ones you had. I know, without a doubt, she'd want that, too." He studied my face. "Trust me, she would. It would've killed her to know you might ever see her this way."

I didn't know what to say. My eyes darted up and down rows of avocado trees and I wished I could be inside the orchard doing something simple like walking up and down each perfectly planted line. There was something calming about an orchard, no beginning and no end when standing in the middle of one.

"I didn't stop seeing her—not exactly," he admitted, "but it was hard after that. I worried I might cause another episode like that one again so I didn't go as often. It tore me up something awful, Zetty." Father gazed out at the orchard, too, both hands planted on his kneecaps. "Eleanor tried to convince me it was alright to keep coming, so I did. Just not as much as I wanted to. I wasn't worried for me, you understand, I was worried about her."

"You could've told me," I said with resentment heating up my words again. "All this time, Dad."

"Listen, Zetty—you're right. I probably did everything wrong. I thought I was protecting you. And, I still am. I have to forbid you from seeing her; it's what she would want. You need to trust me on that."

"But I don't, Dad. I'm sorry, but I stopped trusting you a long time ago."

Father's eyes began to glisten. Tears forming from what I said. Even though I meant it, I didn't want to cause him more pain. Clearly, he had been given enough. "I'm sure it was awful, Dad. I can't even imagine it, but does she become violent a lot?"

"I don't know. I don't think so because I've stayed away more. I know it's hard, but I have to insist you do the same."

"But—"

Father didn't let me finish. "It's not just the violence, Zetty. It's who she's become. Believe me. She'd never want you to see her this way."

"Stop saying that!" I shouted. "Doc Sperling agrees I should know everything and see her! She's said nothing about her being violent, and I know she would have. Especially if it wasn't safe."

"Your doctor was never on her case, Zetty."

"No, but someone she knows has been!"

"All I can tell you is what happened. I'm sure your doctor would've explained all this more fully to you when she met with *both of us. Together,*" he smirked. "If I hadn't been donating another gallon of blood."

I smirked back.

I picked a weed out of the planter and started painting my legs with it. An abyss of careful silence spread between us.

And then Father spat out a chuckle. "Guess who drove me here?"

"Who?" The mood lightened.

"The drunken lunatic who ran into my plane."

"What?! Why would you let *her* drive you?" I snapped.

"Because *someone* stole my car," he scoffed, "and no one else was home. She said she wanted to apologize, assured me she was sober. So that's what she did the whole way here—yammered on and on about how sorry she was. But the woman drove just as bad sober as she did drunk—a real crackpot."

My mouth dropped open and I tossed the weed back in the bed.

"Hit every curb," he continued, "and slammed on her goldarned brakes at every intersection. Never seen anything like it."

"Should've driven with me," I bragged. "I didn't hit one curb and I made it through every yellow light before it turned red. Except one."

Father rolled his eyes and then turned serious. His back tightened, both hands flat against his thighs. "Apparently I've failed you and I'm sorry. I can't take it back. I don't know what else to say but I'm sorry." Both of us stared at the pavement around our feet.

"I know the feeling," I said as if talking to myself. "I really don't blame you for resenting me when she left, Dad."

"What on earth do you mean?" he asked.

"Me being born!"

"Why would I resent that? You were the best thing that ever happened to us, Zetty."

"But I read the medical letter, warning her not to have children, Dad. It said it could hurt her. I found it at the bottom of the drawer in the hutch."

"Do you know how your mother wished for a daughter? Of course, she would have loved a son, too, but it was you she wanted. And she never stopped saying it, how grateful she was to have you. You were everything to us. You still are. She fell in love with you the moment she saw you. My God, the joy you filled her life with, Zetty. You have no idea."

I remembered Sue Willy's face all aglow when she first saw Gabriel and the fist inside me finally started to unclench.

"Having you didn't hurt her, Zetty, don't you see? She sailed through pregnancy without one problem! Her illness was going to happen regardless. Having you didn't give her this illness. If you don't believe me, ask Doctor Sperling. She can explain it, I'm sure."

"I thought you blamed me," I said full of relief. "I blamed me."

"I'm sorry, Zetty. I've been a blasted fool. I didn't know

how to do this very well, without your mother."

I nodded understanding. "It's okay. You did everything else good."

He pulled out his white, wrinkled-up hankie, dabbed at his eyes and quickly pushed it deep into his trouser pocket again.

I stood, adjusted my tee-shirt, and looked at Father. "I can do it, now. I don't think I'll barf again."

"Do what?" he said with alarm.

"Go back in. To see her."

"But Zetty, I just explained—"

"This is my decision now, not yours. I'd like you to come with, but if you can't, it's okay, I understand."

He blew out enough air to fill a barn and pushed the hair back from his forehead. "I just don't think it's a good idea."

"Dad. Did Doc Sperling tell you she thought it was good for me to do this?"

Father glanced away. "Well, yes," he said reluctantly, "she did."

"Okay, then." I swallowed the rest of the water. "It's a good idea. Look. I don't want to upset her any more than you do. Now that you've told me, I'm prepared for whatever happens. But I won't leave without going in. I won't."

"Okay," he conceded. "Your doctor is probably right; it's time I listen to you. She said I should, you know."

A warmth spread between my ribs as if Doc Sperling was right there making me feel smart and clever again.

Father adjusted the belt around his waist as he raised himself up. "Lead the way."

Before we went through the front doors, I turned my head and took in as much fresh air as I could. But this time when I went up to the second floor, the smell didn't offend me. The atmosphere was refreshingly clean.

And when we walked into Mother's room, the window was open filling the room with an unspoiled breeze of fresh-cut grass. Unlike the window I had been confined behind, I noticed there were no black iron rails fencing hers in, which I took as a good sign.

Father and I approached the bed Mother was asleep on. I remember it was a struggle, controlling my quivering lips, afraid they'd be no use at all. She was on her back, her face framed by a soft white feather pillow, and a crisp white sheet pulled snug around her like a cocoon. A rag doll peeked out from under her arm. She whimpered once, sounding like a small child, and winced a little, too, as if having a bad dream. But as quick as it started, it stopped, and she drifted down into a deep sleep again.

Doc Sperling warned me: Mother's emotions might be like those of a small child. But they would still be her emotions, I decided, and she was still fully alive. I only wished Gabe had been there by my side. I told myself, *maybe she is. Maybe she's right here watching everything.* The idea sparked a flame of joy inside me that never left.

The Listening Heart

CHALKY LIGHT FILTERED THROUGH THE IVORY RUFFLED curtains across the window in Mother's room. I noticed something familiar about them: the royal blue piping on the hems. "Hey, those are ours, aren't they?" I asked Father, anticipation lining my voice. Mother was still asleep, but being this close to her already made my insides quake with happiness.

"I brought them over to help things feel a little homier," he said, sounding pleased with himself.

"Good, I'm glad you did that," I told him. "She deserves to feel at home."

My burlap bag rested on the chair between mother's bed and the window. I swung the strap over the back of it when a petite-framed nurse, in white pants and a matching snapped-up shirt bustled toward us. A badge attached to her lapel read, *Eleanor, R.N.* Her face, smooth and creamy like dark chocolate, matched the tone of her voice. "Margie, you've got visitors!" she broadcast. "Oh," she said, shifting down to a whisper, "she's asleep."

Eleanor leaned in to Father, her voice low, but bubbling with exuberance, "So nice to see you again, Hank! What a wonderful surprise for Margie." She stepped to the sink to wash her hands. "And how do you do," she said to me with the same strong energy. "I'm Eleanor."

Father's face shuttered open, as if he realized some faux pas he had made. "Eleanor," he said properly, "I want you to meet our daughter, Zetty. Zetty, this is Eleanor."

"Hi," I nodded.

"Zetty," she said, her head tilted, a tentative line drawn around my name. "Might you be," she said, contemplating each word, "a cowgirl?" She pulled two brown paper towels from a wall mount and wiped at her hands.

"Cowgirl?" The word registered, of course, and with lightning bug speed, I knew what it meant.

"Yes," Eleanor continued, "back at the state hospital where I worked, too, your mom used to talk about her daughter, the cowgirl once in a while." She tossed the paper towels in a large trashcan next to the sink. "But she talks to imaginary people too, so I wasn't sure," she added.

"It wasn't her imagination!" I piped in. "I was the cowgirl's daughter," I said. "It was the musical stage play we were working on together. Dad," I swallowed abruptly, without warning and had to pause, "she remembers!"

Eleanor chuckled. "All these years I thought she had an imaginary friend, or a real daughter riding in rodeos, wrangling up cattle, or bucking broncos!" She went slap-happy; delight gushed faster with every word, "Maybe roping hogs!" She wheezed out a long muffled chortle.

A rumble rode up my insides, and I shook in a fit of giggles, too. Me, on a bucking bronco, roping hogs? The images were too nonsensical to ignore. Father removed his glasses to wipe his eyes, and there, plastered to his face, was the largest smile I'd seen in years.

"Oh, my." She slowed her breathing, "I am so pleased to meet you." Eleanor squeezed a warm, satin-soft hand into mine and an aura of calm surrounded me. Her humor gave way to genuine graciousness. The kind I felt right at home with.

Eleanor removed the tray off Mother's bedside table, leaving a plastic cup of four prunes next to the pitcher of water. Having seen the diaper earlier, I would've removed the prunes, too.

"She looks beautiful," Father said, cautiously moving closer to Mother. He reached down and gently lifted her hand into his own. She stirred a little. "I explained to Zetty I was afraid I would cause another violent episode, Eleanor." Father lightly stroked Mother's hand with the tips of his thick fingers.

"I'm going to tell you again, Hank, it wasn't you. She believed something else was happening. I don't know what, but Margie simply got confused. I've gotten to know her well over the years; she can't express herself in normal ways, but we help her with that, now. It's okay."

"Does she still get violent?" I asked.

"Your mother wouldn't hurt a fly, honey. Not intentionally. Like a young child, she has meltdowns now and then, and for good reason. Frustration, tension, things she's genuinely afraid of—it all builds up sometimes. She has to let it out. We can't underestimate the depth of her pain—even if she can't convey it. You learn to listen with your heart."

Attached on one side of Eleanor's badge was a shiny round gold pin with *20 Years of Service* engraved in the middle. Flanking the other side was a larger button sitting cock-eyed with the words *Black Power* printed in bright yellow letters against a black background. She caught me staring at it.

And then Mother's lids shuttered open. With some awareness, it seemed, her eyes, the same emerald jewels I remembered, danced from Father's face to mine.

"Now just look at the way she is all lit up right now!" Eleanor popped. "Bright as a Christmas tree!"

"Sweetheart, it's me, Hank. How are you feeling?" Father asked anxiously.

Mother blinked and looked toward me. "Mother," I said softly, "It's Zetty. I'm so happy to see you." I leaned my head down on her shoulder and there in the bones of her neck, I felt the mother I had always loved. "I've missed you so much," I whispered.

Mother's eyes widened when I came into her view, and I believe they sparkled.

"This is the happiest I've seen her in a long while," Eleanor said with sureness. "I'm so glad you both came."

"Eleanor," Father said with respect wrapping his words like a gift, "thank you for all you've done, and for all you continue to do. What you do is so important."

"It's my pleasure, Hank. Margie is very special to me."

"We can't thank you enough," Father repeated.

Eleanor closed her eyes momentarily, and nodded with respect. "Let's get you into a chair, Margie, so you can have a visit." Eleanor helped Mother stand and led her to the corner to a sheepskin-covered recliner. She moved in measured steps; the same shuffling gait I witnessed in the psychiatric hospital and a vacant expression had already replaced the sparkle I had just witnessed.

Once mother was seated, Eleanor went to the window and slid one curtain over to protect her face from the last blinding light of sunset.

And then without warning, Mother pushed herself up, bent down in a peculiar position, and rapidly rolled into a somersault before our feet. When she giggled, I recognized the same tinny, high-pitched titter I remember hearing as a child; one of the childlike symptoms Doc Sperling prepared me for. Only I didn't feel prepared for that.

Father's cheek muscles tightened with worry when he

leaned down to help her up. With one hand on her back, the other on her elbow, he gently guided her back to the chair and set her down like fine china.

Eleanor was swift to intervene, too. "Oh, Margie, you're ready for fun now that family is here, aren't you? But let's protect that noggin of yours. No more loose wires!" She let out a belly laugh dipped in a dose of kindness. My insides relaxed.

Mother's skin was still supple; the tone luminous, a warm hint of peach instead of the waxy color I remembered. White streaks of hair curled around her face, the only sign she had aged at all. Her hair was long now, and Eleanor put it in a French braid,, which gave her a natural, organic air. Her vacant green eyes remained youthful too, even without makeup. She could pass for a hippie, I decided.

Mother babbled, but the babbling was polka-dotted with words and phrases that made a little sense sometimes, like "curtains," and "sunny day," and "music to my ears."

When we said goodbye, Mother stared blankly into my face. I spoke as if I hadn't noticed it. "I'm coming back to see you tomorrow," I told her. "I love you." I walked to the other side of her chair and bent to kiss her cheek. "Scarlett wants to see you, too," and I heard her say, "Scarlett."

Father pressed his cheek against the side of her face. She turned her head shyly toward him, and he tenderly kissed her lips.

"Margie, it must be nice having Prince Charming here, isn't it honey?" Eleanor asked, fiddling with her hair, trying to catch the stragglers escaping from the braid. Then Eleanor followed us out the door.

"Margie's not well," Eleanor said slowly, "but I want you both to know, she is well, in her own way."

Father considered what she said. "We owe that to you,

Eleanor." He had more to say, but the words tumbled out awkwardly. "But," he struggled, "can we be certain she's safe for Zetty to be around?"

My head sprang up. "Dad! I'm fine. Tell him, Eleanor." as if I knew for a fact she would have my back.

And she did. "Zetty's right, Hank, sometimes it's hard to understand what your wife is trying to express, but I'll help Zetty."

"But if you're not around," he continued.

"Eleanor said she will teach me what to do, Dad," I told him with strength in my voice and then faced Eleanor. "I want to help take care of her the way you do," I told her. "I want to learn everything."

"We'll start tomorrow. With your father's permission, of course," she smiled.

Father crossed his arms over his chest. "I'm clearly outnumbered," he said. "I'll leave it to the two of you," he conceded.

"Okay then," Eleanor said. She leaned in and hugged me with such tender compassion, I could have fallen asleep right there in her arms. I remember thinking she had black power all right, and it was full of love.

WHEN WE STEPPED OUTSIDE, I SMELLED RAIN ON THE PAVE-ment, like moist dirt kicked up in the clammy air. It was musty, but pleasant just the same.

On the way home, Father turned on the windshield wipers and I listened to them squeak like a musical beat. I rolled down the window and propped my elbow on the edge, letting fat raindrops, swollen up from the humidity, splat against my arm.

"Zetty, I just have to say that if you ever take my keys and drive off like that again, well," he halted, "I don't know what. But it won't be good."

"I won't, Dad. I'll get my license. I'm going to need it so I can visit Mother and help take care of her."

"I'm proud of you, Zetty." He stretched his arms out straight from the wheel. "Hey, what do you think of me bringing in photos of our plane? I wonder if she'll remember."

"She might, but even if she doesn't, I think she'd like that."

All the puffed-up tension that had been swimming around us was finally gone. It was as if Eleanor had pulled the plug on it as soon as she walked in the room and let it sink. I could relax into the drive home.

"If I have kids someday, they won't have a grandma," I said, not sure where the thought came from. "They won't even know her."

"They'll know her," he said without a scrap of hesitation.

"No, I mean, know her the way she used to be."

"They'll know her," he said again. "They'll know her through you. You're so much like her, Zetty. You have no idea. That day you had her dress on—it threw me for a loop."

"I noticed," I said with only a little sarcasm.

He went on, "You looked so much like her when she was young." He inflated both cheeks and then released them, spitting a little. "I don't know why I couldn't just tell you that at the time."

I wasn't sure what to say; I almost wanted him to stop. "Well, I'm glad you told me now," I said. Another part of me wanted him to continue.

"You understand what I mean about having children someday?" He didn't let me answer. "Maybe you'll create stage plays with your children, teach them to dance, play piano, paint something, I don't know. But the fun you'll have together will show them who your mother was. In one way or another, the influence she's had on you will shine through when you're a mother. They'll know her, too."

It was the most Father had ever expressed to me. A sharp, yet painless tang of truth came through his words, and healed an unspoken hurt. "I'd like that," I told him.

The idea of staging plays with my own child was exhilarating, actually. I realized in that moment the chance to finish the cowgirl play remained a slow burning passion of mine.

Then Father said, "Thank you, Zetty."

"For what?" I asked shyly, stunned really.

"For growing up smarter than me."

WHEN WE GOT HOME, I CRAWLED INTO BED, CLUTCHED Tuffy's bandana, and talked to him as if he could hear me. "She didn't leave us, boy—Mother never left us," I said, and I knew it was the truth. "We left her," I said out loud. "All these years I had it backward."

The trees were bending from the wind again, and blowing ferociously. But I lay in my bed unafraid.

I wasn't afraid of the dark, or wind ghosts, or going crazy. I didn't feel angry at Mother, or Father, or God. I lay still only listening to my own beating heart and breathing, the ticking of the clock, and the wind bouncing across the window.

I was by myself, but I didn't feel alone anymore.

ALL IS NOT DARKNESS

I DEPOSITED MYSELF ON THE CRUSHED VELVET SEAT THE way I did for so many months, but this time the somersaults in my stomach came back. First, I had to apologize to Doc Sperling. Even though I rehearsed what I would say, the words still kicked and shoved each other all the way out of my mouth, "I'm sorry I lied to you."

Doc Sperling set a cup of tea on my table, and sat across from me. "I forgive you," she said.

"I hated lying to you, but it was the only way. I don't want you to think I enjoyed it but the truth is I have absolutely no regrets."

"I understand. It doesn't change the way I feel about you, Zetty." She swirled her tea bag around in the mug with the peace sign on it. "You know, you lie a lot less than you used to," she noted. We smiled and my stomach went back to normal.

"True," I said, feeling proud about that, at least. "But I'm not going to like it—ending therapy with you someday." I wiped the velvet nap back and forth on the arm of my chair making it turn different shades of lightness. "I'm telling you now, I can't take another ending." My face flushed from working hard to hold back from crying.

"You may not be ready yet, Zetty. But when you are, our ending can be different. Saying goodbye might be sad, but it doesn't have to be traumatic. And it won't just be an ending. It will also be a beginning. Trust me; only the beginning for you."

I studied her face, searching for what she meant. "But it will be an ending," I repeated.

"For this small, short chapter of your life, yes," she said, "but you'll have so many pages still to be written."

"It won't seem right not to tell you everything that happens."

"If you ever need me, and if I'm not a retired old lady by then," she smiled, "you can always come back."

"Good."

"And if I am retired, I have no doubt you'll find the right person to replace me."

I made a face, but resigned myself to what she said. "Okay."

"Maybe you'll carry me on your shoulder, if you'd like— the way you do Gabe. You know what we'll say whenever you need us. We all do that, you know—carry people with us that we need to hear." She leaned back a little. "Do you remember when I told you once it was an honor and a privilege to work with my patients, and that I received far more than I gave?"

"Yes, I wrote that down for the research paper I never wrote." We both laughed.

"Well, you've been that patient for me, all along, Zetty."

I couldn't speak, or respond. I felt pinned to the chair. The impact of her words moved through me in slow motion.

She continued, "No matter what happens, you have yourself to come back to now."

I listened without anxiety, and with all my attention. I took in what she said and believed it.

"I have my mother back because of you," I told her. "She's different, but she's still my mother."

"Isn't it nice that there's room for both," Doc Sperling said. "Who you remember, and who you have now. You don't have to lose one to have the other."

It's true, I thought, *she's right.*

Gratitude filled my heart, every crack and indentation; I knew there were no more wasted spaces. "How can I ever thank you enough?"

"You already have," she beamed.

When I left Doc Sperling's office that day, I was filled with light—if I were to paint it, I'd choose pale gold and lavender hues. It was the color of love, I think.

Gabe would say it was God. She would say it, and I would finally agree.

A TWINING OF DARKNESS AND LIGHT FELL ACROSS MOTHer's room. Her long braid, crisscrossed with streaks like pure snow, fell over one shoulder. Lying on the table next to her was a pile of papers bound together with a pink satin ribbon. A note was attached that said, "For Zetty. From your mother. Most written years ago. They're all meant for you. Love, Eleanor"

I lifted the stack carefully, realizing they were all hand written letters—the words of my mother, all meant for me. I counted eleven of them and placed them gently in my burlap hippie bag like they were sacred scrolls. There in my purse sat the evidence of our past. "This is an undreamed-of gift," I told her. We *were* still connected, I realized, even then.

I drew a chair in close to her bed and held up the silver crescent moon around my neck. "Do you remember this, Mother? Gabe and I shared it back and forth after you had to leave," I told her. "Gabe lets me wear it all the time now."

The words rang empty when I said it. I wanted nothing more than to see the necklace back around Gabe's neck where it belonged. Sometimes I envied Mother. She would never have to suffer the unspeakable grief of losing Gabe and Tuffy. I was grateful her condition at least spared her that.

I pulled our book out of my bag, being careful not to disturb Mother's letters, and set it carefully on my lap. Then I reached for Herbert and tucked him under her arm. His gray fur and bunny whiskers were worn, but he was soft as ever.

"It's time to finish our story about the adventures of Hitty, Mom. I can't wait to hear what happens next."

I opened to the page with the dog-eared corner and saw a yellowed-edged bookmark still lying in the crease of page number forty-four. I took in a lungful of air and then slowly respired the way I had instructed Sue Willy to during contractions. As usual, Mother appeared to be somewhere far away. Her eyes were centered on the wall away from me. I leaned in, inspecting her eyes, waved a hand energetically in front of her face, and whistled a little, just to see if I could get through. Clearly, my presence meant nothing to her.

And then I closed the book.

"Let me tell you another story," I said, and set *Hitty: Her First Hundred Years* aside. "This one's about a famous rootin' tootin' cowgirl and her little girl." I leaned forward to softly tuck away the escaped strands of hair dangling over her eye. It seems inane, even now, but I thought it might get in the way of her view.

"Once upon a time," I began in proper fairy tale fashion, "over a hundred years ago, the famous cowgirl and her daughter saved a town infected with stinking, evil-eyed outlaws. A bunch of scallywags. You know the kind." I never stopped hoping for some kind of reaction, but Mother continued to stare intently at nothing. Nevertheless, I felt a burst of cheer, pretending she understood my every word, riveted to the story we both loved so well.

"The cowgirl's daughter loved the red leather, carved cowgirl boots her mother gave her and wore them everywhere, even on stage. The mother danced, and sang, and performed, pretty as a queen, and taught her daughter everything she knew. Her daughter would tell you how much fun they had putting on shows for the whole town."

I felt myself fully reclaim the joy of our past, and embrace it.

"She was you, Mother. The famous cowgirl was you." I paused again, as I always did, waiting for some tiny glimmer of emotion to erase the vacant stare. "Not only that," I continued, "the famous cowgirl and her daughter became legends. Together, they could do anything. They were two of the strongest women who ever lived, Mother."

A wave of relief swept over me just then and I told her, "Nothing will separate us again. I promise." I relaxed against the back of my seat, knowing it was true.

Mother's love finally came back to me—different, changed, but it was there in the lines of her face, the curve of her lips, and at the tips of her fingers. "Thank you for giving me so much," I told her. Because I knew in nine short years she gave me everything I needed for a lifetime.

Mother had a persistent mental illness, and at the same time, held an extraordinary capacity to be a loving parent. And even though she never returned to the home we once had, the nostalgia, the yearning, and the grief for the lost places of my past no longer pulled at me. I had found my way back to a new and different home. To a new and different Mother. It wasn't bad, or good, or worse, or better. It was simply different. For me, at least, the bond and love we shared remained unbroken.

I went to the old clock radio I brought from home and dialed in the London Symphony. I re-positioned our book in my lap so the sunlight streamed across the pages. But when I rested one arm on the edge of her bed, ready to begin reading aloud page forty-four, something happened. Something about Mother changed. Her countenance transformed into softness; her eyes met mine, fully alert. It was as if her face had opened along with our story, and I could see the hidden parts of her former self, if only for a fleeting moment.

Out of nowhere, Mother swung her arm and flailed it wildly through the air, as if trying to swat at something.

I didn't move, or flinch, or do one thing. I watched calmly, and waited. But she didn't have the strength to keep it up and her hand dropped clumsily on top of my arm. I'll never know for sure, but when she reached down, grabbed hold of my hand, squeezed it tight, and didn't let go, I felt she was still there.

"This is where we left off," I told her.

She closed her eyes, and I began.

For More Information

National Alliance on Mental Illness (NAMI)

The stigma of mental illness was worse in the 1960's and 1970's but still persists today. Widespread prejudice and commonly held stereotypes require more education and a broadening of our perspectives. NAMI works to change the way the world sees mental health. It is the largest grassroots mental health organization dedicated to building better lives for the millions of Americans affected by mental illness. They provide information, support, education, advocacy, and referrals to people with mental illness and their families. To find your local NAMI office contact:

www.NAMI.org/The NAMI Helpline: 1-800-950-NAMI

The International Hearing Voices Network (Inter Voice)

This organization is working across the world to spread positive and hopeful messages about the experience of hearing voices. If you hear voices, know someone who does or want to find out more about this experience, contact:

www.intervoiceonline.org

Mothers Against Drunk Driving (MADD)

Every 51 minutes drunk driving ends a life. Every 2 minutes, someone is injured in a drunk driving crash. Each and every one of them is 100% preventable. Drunk driving is still the #1 cause of death on our roadways. MADD's mission is to end drunk driving, help fight drugged driving, support the victims of these violent crimes and prevent underage drinking. To get involved and be part of the solution contact your local MADD chapter:

www.madd.org/24-Hour Victim Help Line: 877-MADD-HELP

Acknowledgements

My gratitude reaches far and wide, first to those introduced to Zetty who championed her to the finish line and treated her like family: Maureen Thrash, Janice Carr, Rhoda Weber, my cousin—Corinne Marie, Kathryn Wilson, Susan Jorgensen, Tita Evans-Santini, Melissa Lind, Diana Griggs, Marilyn Lindsay, Nikki Ehrmantrout, Betsy Pownall, Judy Dippel, Sherrie Parsons Rosenberger, and Terri Eddy Wery. Thank you for boundless optimism and priceless friendship.

Weeks prior to the release of this novel, my cousin, Corinne, passed away. Cori's love and enthusiasm for *Zetty* was an inspration to me through all the years of writing it. It is with deep gratitude and love that I acknowledge her most of all.

For ongoing support and encouragement over many years, I also want to thank Jay Buckley, Jacqui Lichtenstein, Kurtis Mitchell, Ruth and Woody Wood, and all the staff at Direction Service Counseling Center.

To talented writers and friends who offered professional assistance along the way: free-lance writer, Cara Roberts Murez and author and journalist, Bob Welch.

Special thanks to the wonderful poet, Diana Griggs, for allowing me the honor of including her poems, "The House Remembers You", and "The Moon Necklace".

To literary agents, Susan Schulman, Annie Hwang and Michelle Brower for their generous gift of time offering feedback that influenced the subsequent revisions to this story.

To editor, Angela Egremont for providing the finishing

touch—truly a pleasure to work with. And to the publishing staff at Luminare Press, especially Patricia Marshall and Claire Flint who brought Zetty to life in such a beautiful way. My thanks to Kim Harper-Kennedy as well for her work on the manuscript. I am indebted to you all.

I am especially grateful to book editor, Elizabeth Lyon. Thank you for sharing your craft and insights, and of course, for keeping all the candles lit. This novel would still be sitting on the back shelf if I hadn't found you. Thank you for your kind and honest feedback; always constructive and true.

If you've never loved a dog, you may want to skip this paragraph. Sadie, my golden retriever, was an ever present companion during the years spent writing this novel. She was great inspiration for Tuffy and after she died, I felt her presence for months. Needless to say, Sadie's contributions to this story were numerous.

For a writer, there is nothing like the support of family. I am deeply grateful to my sister, Sherie, and brother-in-law, Paul. Thank you for your enthusiasm, ideas, and most of all for everything you do for our family.

Like the character in this novel, my own father built a home-built airplane. It took as many years to complete his airplane as it did for me to write this book. Both labors of love. Without the technical notes you corrected, Dad, poor Mr. McGee would have constructed a go-kart instead of an airplane. You believed in this book, and I thank you, as always, for ongoing inspiration. Your compass, like Hank's, always steers in the right way.

I earnestly and gratefully thank my mother who read the first half of this manuscript and insisted I finish it before she "croaked." Her enthusiasm and belief in this story spurred me on like no other, and gave me the impetus to complete it. My mother shines through parts of this story and on the book cover as well. Thank you, Mom, for allowing me to use your photo. It means the world to me.

Love and thanks to Katelyn, Kevin, and Eliza, because being a mother and "Nanni" has been one of life's most precious offerings. And, as always, thank you Katelyn for lending your creative eye and talent to all my projects.

Love to Bob—always true, who for so many years has taken on the thankless role of a writer's spouse. You are the one for me.

The last word belongs to my readers—thank you for creating space in your lives for this story. May you seize all the golden opportunities for joy that come your way, hold fast, and run with them.

—*Debra Whiting Alexander*

Reader's Discussion Guide

1. After Marjorie disappeared, who were the mother figures that stepped in for Zetty? Who do you believe Zetty's most significant support came from and why? Talk about mother figures you've had in your life.

2. Throughout the novel, Zetty's strength and resiliency are continually challenged. Which life events do you think impacted her development the most? Do you think personality and temperament are influenced more by nature, (biology and genetic predispositions) or nurture (environment and relationships)? Discuss this in relation to both Zetty and Marjorie's personalities and mental health challenges.

3. After Marjorie disappeared, why do you think it was difficult for Hank to be honest with Zetty about it? Do you agree that Zetty lost her father, too? If so, in what ways?

4. How did you feel about Hank as a father? How did you feel about Dennis as a father? Talk about your own father in comparison.

5. Did any of the female characters in this story resemble your mother? If so, who and why? Talk about childhood memories with your mom, or dad, and how they shaped your life.

6. Talk about the marriages in this story. What did you like or dislike about them?

7. What do you consider to be the most important or powerful psychological truth Zetty gained from Doc Sperling?

8. Talk about the stigma of mental illness. How is it different today than in the 1960's? Has this stigma been

present in your family? Do you see ways this has been harmful to people you love? If so, how?

9. Which character most closely represents your own spiritual life and beliefs, if any, and why?

10. *Don't ever turn your back on the ocean.* How is this symbolic to the story? What other symbolism in nature did you see throughout the novel?

11. Zetty and Gabe shared a lifelong bond and yet they were different in many ways. What, in your opinion, bonded them as friends? Talk about any friendships in your life that are similar to the friendships in this novel.

12. In your opinion, what are the qualities and experiences that help form lasting bonds between parents and their children? Talk about the presence or absence of these qualities between Zetty and Marjorie, Gabe and Scarlett, and Sue Willy and her mother.

Photo by Katelyn Kelley

About the Author

DEBRA WHITING ALEXANDER GREW UP ON THE beaches of San Diego, lived and worked in upstate New York, and finally settled in Oregon where she lives with her husband and two labs. Debra is a mother, "Nanni," writer, and mental health practitioner. She holds a Ph.D. in Psychology, is a licensed Marriage and Family Therapist, and the author of 16 non-fiction books including, *Children Changed by Trauma,* and *Loving Your Teenage Daughter (Whether She Likes It Or Not).* Her award-winning debut novel, *Zetty,* was inspired by her grandmother who died in a psychiatric hospital at the age of 41. Her next novel, *The Holding Tree,* is expected out next year.

To contact Debra please go to:

www.facebook.com/TheAuthorDebraWhitingAlexander
Part of a book group? Consider asking Debra to join you for a discussion of *Zetty.*